知識工場
Knowledge is everything！

知識工場
Knowledge is everything！

知識工場
Knowledge is everything！

Fast Learning! Natives Speak Like This.

用關鍵短句速成口說

懂得「挑句子背」，才能事半功倍！

張翔 / 著

It's a bargain.

I'm falling for you.

Yummy!

Fast Learning! Natives Speak Like This.

即學即用、多元話題說不完、互動不設限，

開口說不用等，關鍵 3 句就能溜英文！

Unit 01 從打招呼開始
Let's start by greeting each other.

1 關鍵 3 句，開口就能說！

聚焦於情境中最常使用，也最能展開對話的 3 個關鍵句；重點式學習，幫助讀者把最關鍵的句子學起來，學習輕鬆有效率。

主要關鍵句開口說

說出關鍵 3 句型，英文輕鬆脫口說　Track 001

Part 1 自我介紹是入門學問

① How do you do?
初次見面，請多指教。

② It's a pleasure to meet you.
很高興認識你。

③ How are you (doing)?
你好嗎？(過得如何？)

沒果仁邏輯 Americans　句型解析與用法說明

說明 ① How do you do 句型

此為初次見面的招呼語，在較正式的場合使用，類似中文的「久仰」。日常生活的口語英文比較不常使用此句，因為對美國人來說，這句話會讓人感到很拘謹。

說明 ② It's a pleasure to 句型

It's a pleasure to+動詞原形的句型表示「很開心做某件事情」。以例句It's a pleasure to meet you來說，meet有見面、認識的意思，整句話在初次與新朋友見面時使用，表達禮貌性的開頭招呼語。

說明 ③ How are you (doing) 句型

親友間見面最常使用的實用問候語。除了基本的禮貌問好之外，也同時帶有詢問近況的意味。

008

2 重點解析，理解度飆升！

根據每單元的 3 個關鍵句，介紹「沒果仁 (美國人) 邏輯」，提供句型解析或用法說明，完全參透 3 個關鍵句，要學就學得紮實。

沒果仁也愛的說法 Americans　對照「主看關鍵句」的類似說法

① Nice to meet you.
很高興認識你。

② Pleased to meet you.
很高興認識你。

③ How's life?
最近過得如何？

3 相通句替換，學習量翻倍！

除了 3 個關鍵句的用法之外，另外補充「沒果仁 (美國人) 也愛的說法」，提供其他與關鍵句意思相通的說法，學習量瞬間倍增。

這樣回答就對了 對應「主考嗶鍵句」的回答

① How do you do?
初次見面，請多指教。

② It's a pleasure to meet you, too. / Likewise.
我也很高興認識你。/ 我也是。

③ I am doing great. / Not too bad.
我過得很好。/ 我過得還不錯。

4 回應3句，對話巧妙答！

為讀者量身打造的「這樣回答就對了」，提供關鍵句的答覆法，確保讀者在實際情境中，能與人「你一言、我一語」地對談。

5 深入文化，拓展世界觀！

每單元的「世界觀小補充」，會介紹中外文化差異，深入理解外國人的思維與生活習慣，學英文會話不忘擴充世界觀。

世界觀小補充

美國人於見面時打招呼就像是歐洲人親臉頰一樣，非做不可。而招呼語也依熟識程度而有不同。How do you do? / It's a pleasure to meet you 於初次見面時使用，較為客套。在美國影集、電影當中，熟識的雙方見面也少不了招呼語，例如What's up?、How are you?等等，可見招呼語是基本禮儀。如同中文的「你好」，美國人使用問候句，通常並不是期望聽到對方的流水帳，而只是表達簡單的關心跟開啟話題而已，因此千萬不要以長篇大論的回答嚇跑對方。

6 相關實用句，超完整！

除了關鍵句之外，另外補充與每單元主題有關的「學校沒教的實用句」，完整介紹豐富又實用的情境例句，並隨句標示關鍵詞彙。

學校沒教的實用句

情境式主題句，學校沒有教，自己學起來！ Track 003

Part 1 自我

▶ Nice to meet you.
很高興認識你。

▶ I'd say the same. / Same here.
我也是

▶ My name is Mary Jane. What's yours?
我叫瑪莉珍，你呢？

▶ Could you repeat your first name / last name, please?
可不可以再說一次你的名字／姓氏？ repeat 重複；重說

7 模擬對話，確保應用力！

每單元最後的「關鍵一句模擬實境對話」，點出生活中絕對會遇上的4種狀況，模擬情境，進行對話練習。

關鍵一句模擬實境對話 Topic-related Conversations
以關鍵句破題的擬真實境對話 Track 004

Situation 1 正式場合初次見面
meeting someone in a formal situation

A How do you do?
您好，久仰。

B How do you do?
久仰了。

A Allow me to introduce myself. My name is John Walton, a senior engineer in ABC Co.
容我先自我介紹一下，我叫約翰·沃頓，ABC公司的資深工程師。

Part 1 自我

關鍵3句，許自己一個改變！

　　在過往的教學經驗中，遇到不少想精進自己英語能力的學生，抱著一本本的例句書背誦，但說起學習效率，這種方式就有待商確了。背誦例句的確是增加自己英語量的方法之一，但並非「即學即用」的保證。所以，我也遇到不少學生，在自己努力了半天後，跑來問我「老師，為什麼遇到外國人，我就是講不出英文呢？」

　　「學」與「用」並非完全相同的兩件事，學生們可能靠背誦「學」了很多，但遇到實際交談，需要「用」的情境，那些猛命記憶的元素卻用不上，這就可以看出問題在於「即使平常背了很多例句，但那些英文句沒有經過整理，而且偏向中規中矩的教室英文，所以不是一時間想不起來、用不上；就是好不容易用上，老外卻覺得你的英文很不生活化」。

　　我曾經遇過一位很優秀的學生，英文檢定考完全沒有問題，是許多人眼中優秀又努力的學習者。這樣的他，在出國打工度假回來後，和我聊到英文的問題。一開始，我並不覺得語言對他會產生問題，他這才向我提到「應用實力不足」的狀況。就像我上段提到的那樣，好不容易知道該如何回應，但講出來的英文卻過於中規中矩。舉個最簡單的例子，連打招呼的時候，都看得出差別。從學英文的經驗中，打招呼最常見的就是 How are you? 這句話，但老外在與朋友交流時，其實更常使用 Hey, what's up? 這句英文的意思其實很雷同，翻成中文有「嗨，你好嗎？」之意，但是有很多學習者，會誤解這句生活英語的用法，以為老外在詢問什麼狀況，回答時落落長答了一堆，才後知後覺地發現那只是打招呼的用語而已。

　　類似這樣的例子層出不窮，也就是為了這樣的學習者，我才規劃了本書「關鍵3句」的概念，在每一個主題之下，先提供讀者三句最實用也最好用的句子。在編寫時，也考量到「應用」的便利性，跳脫一板一眼的教室英語，編寫實際與老外面對面時用得上的便利句，希望藉由這樣的方式，讓學習者掌握生活中能運用的英語句庫。除此之外，為了那些想要擴充自己英文句量的學習者，我也希望能兼顧「量」這一面，所以在3個關鍵句之外，另外編寫其他相似說法、適合的回應、相關補充句以及會話。藉由這些練習，循序漸進地導入，會比不管三七二十一地背例句要來得有效率。

　　學英文，不僅僅是為了紙上的一筆分數，語言最重要的用途，還是在溝通。無法學以致用的話，就像空抱著一本本的英語字典般，有實力，卻始終無用武之地。這樣的情況，其實也會帶給學習者挫折感，變得愈來愈不敢開口，進入惡性循環的模式。想要打破這種情況，除了學習量以外，也必須從造成學習者開口的恐懼感著手，這也是我為什麼選擇以輕鬆的「關鍵3句」為主題的原因。

　　從投身教育界以來，發現學生各自有不同的問題，所以，我始終認為，教學必須隨著環境變化。條列式的背誦絕非唯一的學習方式，只要找到規律、整理出重點，就算是不擅長記憶的學生，也能有長足的進展，這也是我之所以無法放下教鞭的原因，有句話叫做「教學相長」，可以肯定的是，我確實從學生身上得到許多，也會持續投身教育，發展不同的面相，帶領學生走出屬於自己的「效率學習法」。

張翔

CONTENTS

Making Friends With

Foreigners Via 3 Patterns!

自我介紹是門學問

Unit 01 從打招呼開始

Let's start by greeting each other.

 主要關鍵句開口說

使出關鍵3句型，英文輕鬆開口說

Track 001

① **How do you do?**
初次見面，請多指教。

② **It's a pleasure to meet you.**
很高興認識你。

③ **How are you (doing)?**
你好嗎？(過得如何？)

沒果仁邏輯 Americans 句型解析與用法說明

說明
① **How do you do句型**

此為初次見面的招呼語，在較正式的場合使用，類似中文的「久仰」。日常生活的口語英文比較不常使用此句，因為對美國人來說，這句話會讓人感到很拘謹。

說明
② **It's a pleasure to句型**

「It's a pleasure to+原形動詞」的句型表示「很開心做某件事情」。以例句It's a pleasure to meet you來說，meet有見面、認識的意思，在初次與新朋友見面時使用，表達禮貌性的開頭招呼語。

說明
③ **How are you (doing)句型**

親友間見面最常使用的實用問候語。除了基本的禮貌問好之外，也同時帶有詢問近況的意味。

Part ① 自我介紹是門學問

Americans

沒果仁也愛的說法　　對照「主要關鍵句」的類似說法

① **Nice to meet you.**
很高興認識你。

② **Pleased to meet you.**
很高興認識你。

③ **How's life?**
最近過得如何？

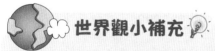

這樣回答就對了　　對應「主要關鍵句」的回答

① **How do you do?**
初次見面，請多指教。

② **It's a pleasure to meet you, too. / Likewise.**
我也很高興認識你。/ 我也是。

③ **I am doing great. / Not too bad.**
我過得很好。/ 我過得還不錯。

世界觀小補充

　　美國人於見面時打招呼就像是歐洲人親臉頰一樣，非做不可。而招呼語也依熟識程度而有不同。How do you do?、It's a pleasure to meet you於初次見面時使用，較為客套。在美國影集、電影當中，熟識的雙方見面也少不了招呼語，例如What's up?、How are you?等等，可見招呼語是基本禮儀。如同中文的「你好」，美國人使用問候句，通常並不是期望聽到對方的流水帳，只是用來表述簡單的關心跟開啟話題而已，因此千萬不要以長篇大論的回答嚇跑對方。

學校沒教的實用句

情境式主題句,學校沒有教,自己學起來!

Nice to meet you.
很高興認識你。

I'd say the same./Same here.
我也是。

My name is Mary Jane. What's yours?
我叫瑪莉珍,你呢?

Could you **repeat** your first name/last name, please?
可不可以再說一次你的名字 / 姓氏? **repeat 重複;重說**

Let me **introduce** myself first.
我先做個自我介紹。 **introduce 介紹;引薦**

How do you **spell** your name?
請問你的名字怎麼拼? **spell 用字母拼;拼作**

I am Sarah, with an h in the end.
我叫做莎拉,字尾以h作結。

I can't believe we have finally met! I've **heard** so much **about** you!
不敢相信我們終於見面了!久仰大名! **hear about 知道;得知**

Nice meeting you. I hope we'll see each other soon.
很高興見到你,希望我們不久後再見。

If only we could have met each other earlier! We **have** so much **in common**!
如果我們早點認識彼此就好了!我們的共通點還真多!
have ... in common 在…有共同之處

Have you met Ted? He is an old friend of mine from college.
你認識泰德嗎?他是我大學時代的老友。

Have we met? You look very **familiar**.
我們有見過面嗎?你看起來好面熟。 **familiar 熟悉的**

I just have **one of those faces**.
我只是有張大眾臉。 one of those faces 大眾臉

How's it/everything going?
最近還好嗎？

What brings you here today?
今天是什麼風把你吹來的？

How's life treating you?
日子過得如何？

What have you been **up to**?
你最近在忙什麼？ up to 忙於

Not much./Same old, same old.
沒什麼。/ 老樣子。

Could be **worse**.
還過得去。 worse 更壞的；更差的

Couldn't be better!
再好不過啦！

It's been such a while since the last time we met.
從上次見面到現在已經過了好久。

How's school?
學校生活如何啊？

I don't want to talk about it.
別提了。

Everything is going well. Thank you.
一切都很順利，謝謝。

How's work/the job?
你工作如何？

I've been **swamped**!
我最近忙翻了！ swamp 使忙得不可開交

關鍵一句模擬實境對話 *Topic-related Conversations*

以關鍵句破題的模擬實境對話

 Track 003

 Situation **1** 正式場合初次見面

meeting someone in a formal situation

A How do you do?
您好，久仰。

B How do you do?
久仰了。

A Allow me to introduce myself. My name is John Walton, a senior engineer in ABC Co.
容我自我介紹一下。我叫約翰・沃頓，ABC公司的資深工程師。

B I am Jenny Pierce from XYZ agency. I happen to know someone from your company!
我是XYZ公司的珍妮・皮爾斯，我恰巧認識你公司的一個人呢！

A What a small world!
世界真小！

 Situation **2** 結交新朋友

making new friends

A It's a pleasure to meet you here.
很高興在這裡認識你。

B Same here. We have so much to talk about.
我也覺得，我們有很多事好聊。

A Let me introduce you to my BFFs next time.
下次讓我把你介紹給我的姊妹淘吧。

B I'd love that. That's very sweet of you.
太好了，你人真好。

A We should all hang out together!
我們以後應該一起玩樂！

chatting with a friend

Ⓐ Hi, there. How's it going?
哈囉，最近如何？

Ⓑ I'm getting by. How about you?
還過得去，你呢？

Ⓐ I just fell off a cliff and got hit by a bike.
我剛從山崖摔下來，然後被腳踏車撞到。

Ⓑ What? Are you OK? Let me take you to the hospital.
什麼？你還好嗎？我帶你去醫院吧。

Ⓐ Just kidding!
開玩笑的啦！

Unit

01

從打招呼開始

Situation **4** 三人閒聊

a three-way chat

Ⓐ This is my sister, Rita. Rita, this is my close friend, Jane.
這是我妹妹，芮塔。芮塔，這是我的好友，珍。

Ⓑ Hi, nice to meet you. My brother has said a lot of nice things about you.
很高興認識你，我哥對你讚譽有加呢！

Ⓒ No way!
怎麼可能！

Ⓐ Yes way! You are one of the most talented people I've ever met.
有可能！你是我遇過最有才華的人之一。

Ⓒ Wow, I am so flattered.
哇，我真是受寵若驚。

Unit 02 致歉與感謝
Making apologies and showing appreciation

 主要關鍵句開口說

使出關鍵3句型，英文輕鬆開口說

 Track 00A

① **I am sorry. Please accept my apology.**
很抱歉，請接受我的道歉。

② **I didn't mean to make you mad.**
我不是故意要惹你生氣的。

③ **I appreciate it.**
謝謝。

 沒果仁邏輯 Americans 句型解析與用法說明

說明① **I am sorry句型**

「I am sorry for+名詞」表示對某件事情感到抱歉。例：I am sorry for the trouble I made the other day. 我對前幾天造成的麻煩感到抱歉。「I am sorry that+子句」的意思相同，但that後面接完整的句子。

說明② **I didn't mean to句型**

「某人+don't/doesn't mean to+原形動詞」表示某人並非故意做出後面的行為。使用此句型表示說話者並非有意，內心有歉意。

說明③ **I appreciate it句型**

I appreciate it.為單純表達感謝的句型，若想要詳細描述內容，可使用「I appreciate+名詞」。例：I appreciate your help. 感謝你的協助或「I appreciate that+子句」。例：I appreciate that you fed my cats. 感謝你幫我餵貓。

沒果仁也愛的說法

對照「主要關鍵句」的類似說法

① **I apologize.**
我很抱歉。

② **It's not my intention to hurt you.**
我沒有要傷害你的意思。

③ **I am really grateful.**
真的很感激。

這樣回答就對了

對應「主要關鍵句」的回答

① **Never mind.**
沒關係。

② **That's all right.**
沒事。

③ **Anytime.**
不客氣。

 世界觀小補充

　　「請、謝謝、對不起」大家都不陌生，從一進學校開始，我們就學著如何在正確的時機使用禮貌語，英語系國家也不例外。值得注意的是，一般學習者容易將Excuse me與I'm sorry的使用時機搞混。Excuse me是在引起聽話者的注意或在造成別人不便時使用。例如，想找路人問路，開場白就要用Excuse me，表達「不好意思」或「請問一下」，並不是在道歉；I'm sorry則是在錯誤發生後，說話者表示遺憾、道歉時使用。例：I'm sorry that I'm late. 抱歉，我遲到了。

學校沒教的實用句

情境式主題句，學校沒有教，自己學起來！

I'm truly sorry.
真的很抱歉。

Will you forgive me?
你會原諒我嗎？

I'm sorry to interrupt, but the bell is ringing.
抱歉打擾，電鈴響了。　interrupt 打斷

I did not intend to break your heart.
我不是故意要傷你的心。　intend 想要；打算

Sorry, my bad.
對不起，我錯了。

We apologize for all the inconvenience we caused.
我們為我們所造成的不便道歉。

If you'll excuse me, I have a meeting to attend.
我還有會議要參加，恕我先離席。

It's my fault. What can I do to fix this?
這是我的錯，我該怎麼彌補？　fix 修理；挽救；補償

Apology accepted.
我接受道歉。

Forget it!
算了！

Don't worry. It's no trouble at all.
沒關係，沒有問題的。

It doesn't matter at all.
真的沒關係。

Is there any way that I could make it up to you?
有沒有任何方法可以補償你？　make it up to sb. 對某人做出補償

I am so grateful for your assistance.
非常感謝你的協助。

I really appreciate your **generosity**, but I can't take it.
我真的很感謝你的慷慨，但我不能收下。　　generosity 寬宏大量；慷慨

I can't thank you enough.
實在太感謝你了。

I just don't know how to express my gratefulness.
我真的不知道要如何表達我的感激之情。

Much **obliged**!
非常感激！　　obliged 感激的

I'd like to say thank you to those who have supported me along the way.
我想要對一直以來支持我的人表達感謝。

Could you please express my **gratitude** to your parents?
可否請你將我的謝意轉達給你的父母？　　gratitude 感激之情；感謝

I'll never forget what you have done for me. Thanks a million.
我永遠不會忘記你為我做的事，萬分感謝。

That's very sweet of you to say so.
你這樣說真的很貼心。

The **pleasure** is all mine.
不用客氣，這是我的榮幸。　　pleasure 愉悅；歡樂；滿意

Don't mention it.
別謝了。

It's no big deal.
這只是小事。

It's nothing.
這沒什麼。

That's nothing to **speak of**.
沒什麼，不足掛齒。　　speak of 談到

Situation **1** 找位子
looking for a seat

Ⓐ Excuse me, this seat is taken.
不好意思，這位子有人了。

Ⓑ I am really sorry. I didn't notice.
真的很抱歉，我沒注意。

Ⓐ I think there's one available down the hall.
我記得沿著走廊下去還有一個空位。

Ⓑ Thanks a lot! I'll give it a shot.
非常感謝！我去看看。

Ⓐ You're welcome.
不客氣。

Situation **2** 食言而肥
unable to keep a promise

Ⓐ I can't go to the movie with you tonight. I'm terribly sorry.
我今晚不能跟你去看電影了，真的很抱歉。

Ⓑ You always make promises that you can't keep.
你老是食言而肥。

Ⓐ I never mean to! Something just came up!
我從來都不是有意的啊！就突然有事情。

Ⓑ Forget it. I'll go with someone else.
算了，我跟別人去。

Ⓐ Please don't be mad at me. We'll do it next time.
拜託不要生我的氣，我們下次再一起去吧。

家裡開趴
joining a house party

Ⓐ **Thank you for coming! Just make yourself at home.**
謝謝你來參加，別拘束，當自己家吧。

Ⓑ **Thanks. You have done a great job on your front porch!**
謝謝，你的前廊佈置得真棒！

Ⓐ **Thank you for noticing that. Here, try some of the hors d'oeuvres.**
謝謝你有注意到。來，嚐嚐這些開胃菜。

Ⓑ **Yummy. I'm in heaven.**
好吃，如同置身天堂呢！

Ⓐ **I'll take that as a compliment.**
我會把這話當作是讚美。

Unit
02
致歉與感謝

Situation 4 下班後的約會
a date after work

Ⓐ **I am sorry for being this late. I was stuck in traffic.**
抱歉遲到這麼久，我卡在車陣中。

Ⓑ **Don't worry. The table isn't ready anyway.**
沒什麼，反正桌子還沒準備好。

Ⓐ **This restaurant is always crowded during this time of the day.**
這家餐廳在這個時段總是座無虛席。

Ⓑ **That's why I ordered some drinks for us so that we won't get bored waiting.**
所以我先點了些飲料，免得等得很無聊。

Ⓐ **That's so thoughtful of you!**
你設想得真周到！

主要關鍵句開口說

使出關鍵3句型，英文輕鬆開口說

Track 007

① **Where are you from?**
你是哪裡人？

② **Where do you live?**
你住哪？

③ **Do you live in a house or an apartment?**
你住在獨棟房子還是公寓？

沒果仁邏輯 *Americans* 句型解析與用法說明

說明
① **Where are you from句型**

Where+be動詞+人名／代名詞+from，此句型是詢問對方從哪裡來(是哪裡人)。常用於談話的對象並非熟識者時。

說明
② **Where do you live句型**

Where+do/does+人名／代名詞+live為詢問對方居住地點的基本句。例句：Where does John live? 約翰住在哪裡？

說明
③ **Do you live in句型**

Do/does+人名／代名詞+live in的句型，可用於詢問對方是否居住在公寓或別墅，也可以詢問對方住在城市還是鄉下，或詢問是居住在A城市還是B城市等。例句：Do they live in New York or New Jersey? 他們住在紐約還是紐澤西？

沒果仁也愛的說法　對照「主要關鍵句」的類似說法

① **Where is your hometown?**
你老家在哪？

② **Do you live in the neighborhood?**
你住在這附近嗎？

③ **What kind of place do you live in?**
你住在什麼樣的地方？

這樣回答就對了　對應「主要關鍵句」的回答

① **I am from Taiwan.**
我來自台灣。

② **I live in a small town in the southern part of Taiwan.**
我住在台灣南部的一個小鎮。

③ **I live in an apartment.**
我住公寓。

 ## 世界觀小補充

　　美國是個文化大熔爐，來自世界各地不同的民族人種皆集結於此，因此，詢問對方從哪裡來或者老家在哪裡是很平常的問題。Where are you from?也是一開始認識新朋友的主要話題之一，因為跟你對話的新朋友很有可能跟你一樣是來自異國的外來客，趁早了解對方來歷也可以掌握對話的主題與方向，凸顯自己的世界觀喔！

What is your nationality?
請問你的國籍是？　　nationality 國籍

Which city do you live in?
你住在哪個城市？

Do you prefer living in a city or the countryside?
你比較喜歡住在市區還是鄉下？　　countryside 鄉間；農村

What is your address?
你的住址是？

What is the capital of your country?
你國家的首都是哪裡？

I come from Taiwan, a small island situated next to China.
我來自台灣，在中國大陸旁邊的一個小島。　　situated 位於…的

I was born in Hong Kong, but grew up in Vancouver.
我在香港出生，在溫哥華長大。

Have you ever been to Taiwan?
你有來過台灣嗎？

I live in a suburb close to Taipei.
我住在台北近郊。

Is there a bus stop close to the place you live?
你住的地方附近有公車站嗎？

There's a shuttle bus connecting the MRT station and the place I live.
我住的地方有接駁車可以到捷運站。　　shuttle bus 區間車

I commute to work by subway every day.
我每天搭地鐵去上班。

I prefer living in Taipei City because of its nightlife and shopping malls.
我喜歡住在台北市區是因為台北的夜生活跟購物中心。

I prefer living in the countryside, even if I have to spend an hour **commuting**.

即使我需要花一個小時通勤，我還是喜歡住在鄉下。　　commute 通勤

I am from **out of town**.

我是外地人。　　out of town 外地的

I live in downtown Taipei.

我住在台北市的鬧區。

Do you live with your family or alone?

你跟家人住還是一個人住？

Do you own or rent the house?

房子是你自己的還是用租的？

I live in a house with a garage.

我住在有車庫的房子。

I live in an apartment without any elevators.

我住的公寓裡沒有電梯。

I just had my house **renovated**.

我的房子剛裝修好。　　renovate 更新；修理

I live on the third floor.

我住在三樓。

I have been living here for ten years.

我在這裡住了十年。

She lives in a downtown apartment with **concierge** service.

她住在鬧區裡有管理員服務的高級公寓。　　concierge 門房

It is **obligatory** to mow the lawn in your front yard in the United States.

在美國，替前院除草是義務。　　obligatory 有義務的

I need to **pay a visit to** some of my neighbors for I just moved here.

我需要去拜訪一下鄰居，因為我才剛搬過來。　　pay a visit to 參觀；訪問

We live in the same neighborhood.

我們住在同一區。

以關鍵句破題的模擬實境對話

Track 009

Part 1 自我介紹是門學問

Situation 1 介紹家鄉位置
introducing your hometown

A Nice to meet you. Where are you from?
很高興認識你，你哪裡人？

B I am from Germany, and you?
我來自德國，你呢？

A I am from Taiwan. Have you ever heard of it?
我來自台灣，你聽過嗎？

B No, I've never heard of it. Where is it?
沒有耶，那在哪裡？

A It's an island in the Asia-Pacific.
台灣是位於亞洲太平洋上的一座島嶼。

Situation 2 文化交流
making cultural observations

A What is your nationality?
你的國籍是？

B My nationality is French.
我的國籍是法國。

A I have been to Paris once.
我去過一次巴黎。

B How did you like the city?
你覺得這城市如何？

A It is astonishingly beautiful, but the people are not friendly.
城市美得令人驚豔，不過人們不是挺友善。

Situation 3 城市 vs. 鄉下

city vs. countryside

A Do you prefer living in a city or the countryside?
你喜歡住在城市還是鄉下？

B I prefer the latter. I've always dreamt of living in a cottage by a lake.
我喜歡後者，我一直幻想能夠住在河邊的小屋。

A What about nightlife and convenience stores?
那夜生活跟便利商店呢？

B I'd rather drive an hour to do the shopping than put up with the noise.
我寧願開一個鐘頭的車去採買，也不想忍受噪音。

A I couldn't agree with you more.
我也深有同感。

Unit
03
住家環境描述

Situation 4 賴家王老五
boomerang kid looking for a place

A Do you still live with your parents?
你還跟父母親同住嗎？

B Yes, I do. What about it?
是啊，怎麼了嗎？

A Has it ever occurred to you that it's about time to live on your own?
你從來沒想過該是搬出來自立的時候了嗎？

B Well, you're right. Are there any vacant rooms in your apartment building currently?
也是啦，你那棟公寓現在有空房出租嗎？

A I have no idea, but I'll keep my eyes open for you.
不知道，不過我會幫你留意。

Unit 04 年齡、生日、星座
Your age, date of birth, and horoscope

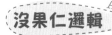 主要關鍵句開口說

使出關鍵3句型，英文輕鬆開口說 Track 010

① **How old are you?**
你幾歲？

② **When is your birthday?**
你哪天生日？

③ **What is your sign?**
你是什麼星座？

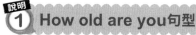 沒果仁邏輯 Americans 句型解析與用法說明

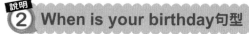

說明 ①　How old are you句型

「How+old+be動詞+人名／代名詞」是詢問對象幾歲的句型。例句：How old is your younger sister? 你妹妹幾歲？

說明 ②　When is your birthday句型

「When+be動詞+人名所有格／所有格代名詞+birthday」是用來詢問生日是什麼時候的問句。例句：When is uncle Sam's birthday? 山姆叔叔的生日是幾月幾號？

說明 ③　What is your sign句型

「What+be動詞+人名所有格／所有格代名詞+sign」用來詢問星座。直接講sign就可以簡單表達星座。例句：What is your boyfriend's sign? 你男友的星座是什麼？

① **What is your age?**
你幾歲？

② **What date is your birthday?**
你幾月幾號生日？

③ **What's your horoscope sign?**
你是什麼星座的？

這樣回答就對了 　對應「主要關鍵句」的回答

① **I am eighteen years old.**
我今年十八歲。

② **My birthday is Nov. 10.**
我的生日是11月10日。

③ **My sign is Scorpio.**
我是天蠍座的。

🌏💭 **世界觀小補充** 💡

　　星座可以說是各種場合增加談話內容的主要話題之一。不管是東方還是西方，大家對星座多少都有點了解。所以可以熟記12星座的英文，在與外國朋友聊天的時候，不僅增加可用字彙，同時也拓展了談話內容的豐富性喔！（各星座一覽表：Aries牡羊座，Taurus金牛座，Gemini雙子座，Cancer巨蟹座，Leo獅子座，Virgo處女座，Libra天秤座，Scorpio天蠍座，Sagittarius射手座，Capricorn摩羯座，Aquarius水瓶座，Pisces雙魚座）

Unit

04

年齡、生日、星座

學校沒教的實用句

情境式主題句，學校沒有教，自己學起來！

Do you **mind** telling me your age?
你介意告訴我你幾歲嗎？　　mind 介意

In which year were you born?
你幾年出生的？

I was born in the 80s.
我是80年代出生的。

I was born in summer.
我在夏天出生。

I was born on March 2, 1975.
我的出生日期是1975年3月2日。

I am seventeen going on eighteen.
我現在十七歲，即將邁入十八歲。

I am turning thirty next month.
我下個月就要滿三十歲了。

Her daughter is in her twenties.
她的女兒大概二十幾歲。

She looks much older than her age.
她看起來比實際年齡老許多。

Those twenty-**something** boys love to party.
那些二十幾歲的男孩喜歡狂歡。　　-something 年齡大約…；…左右

His student is an eight-year-old kid.
他的學生是個八歲大的孩子。

You can only obtain your **driver's license** when you turn eighteen.
你滿十八歲才可以考駕照。　　driver's license 駕駛執照

He was born in July. He is either a Cancer or a Leo.
他七月出生，有可能是巨蟹座或獅子座。

*I am five years younger/older than you.
我小 / 大你5歲。

*Are you an adult? Show me your **identity card**.
你成年了嗎？給我看看你的身分證。 | identity card 身分證 |

*You are not allowed to come in. You are only a **minor**.
你不能入場，你未成年。 | minor 未成年人 |

*I don't know what my sign is.
我不知道我的星座是什麼。

*I am a Gemini. What are you?
我是雙子座的，你呢？

*Do you believe in **horoscopes**?
你相信星座嗎？ | horoscope 占星術；星象 |

*I don't think my personality traits match my star sign.
我覺得我的個性跟星座不相符。

*My mom is a Libran and my dad is an Aquarian. They get along very well.
我媽是天秤座，我爸是水瓶座，他們兩個很合得來。

*What is your **animal sign**?
你的生肖是什麼？ | animal sign 生肖 |

*I believe in neither horoscopes nor animal signs.
我不相信什麼星座或生肖。

*The older generation are more familiar with Chinese animal signs.
老一輩的人比較熟悉中國生肖。

*I was born in the Year of the Dragon.
我是龍年出生的。

*There are twelve animal signs in the Chinese **zodiac**.
中國生肖當中有十二種動物。 | zodiac 黃道帶 |

*Many parents want their children to be born in the Year of the Dragon.
很多父母都希望他們的小孩在龍年出生。

Situation 1 最棒的讚美
the best compliment ever

A Would you mind telling me how old you are?
你介意告訴我你幾歲嗎？

B Not at all. I am thirty years old.
不介意，我三十歲。

A We are the same age! You don't look your age!
我們同年耶！你看起來不像這個年紀的人！

B What do you mean?
什麼意思？

A You look so much younger!
你看起來好年輕！

Situation 2 時光飛逝
time flies

A My son is celebrating his birthday this weekend.
我兒子這個週末要慶生。

B How old is he?
他幾歲啦？

A He is eighteen going on nineteen.
他現在十八，要十九歲了。

B My goodness! How time flies!
天啊！時間過得真快！

A Tell me about it!
就是說啊！

Situation 3 考駕照
getting driver's license

A I'll be able to get my driver's license by the age eighteen.
我十八歲就可以考駕照了。

B That'll be three years away.
那還要三年耶。

A That sounds like forever.
聽起來好久喔。

B What about me? I am two years younger than you.
拜託，那我呢？我還小你兩歲耶。

A Well, patience is a virtue.
嗯，耐心是種美德。

Situation 4 星座達人
master of the horoscope

A I guess you are a Leo.
我猜你是獅子座的。

B How do you know that?
你怎麼知道？

A You are very confident about yourself, and are straightforward with your opinions.
你對自己很有自信，而且勇於表達個人意見。

B Well, I guess I fit the personality traits of Leos.
嗯，我想我很符合獅子座的特色。

A Exactly!
的確如此！

Unit 05 身家背景調查
Background check

主要關鍵句開口說

使出關鍵3句型，英文輕鬆脫口說

Track 013

① **How many people are there in your family?**
你家一共有幾個人？

② **Are you single or married?**
你單身還是已婚？

③ **Do you have any kids?**
你有小孩嗎？

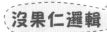
沒果仁邏輯 句型解析與用法說明

 說明
① **How many members are there句型**

「How+many+名詞+are there」的句型是在問某種情況／環境下有多少數量的句型。接在How many後面使用的是複數的可數名詞。

說明
② **single/married用法**

詢問對方的感情狀態，除了單身single、已婚married之外，還有很多發揮的空間。例如：Are you in a relationship? 你現在有交往的對象嗎？/Are you divorced? 你離婚了嗎？

 說明
③ **Do you have any kids句型**

any使用在否定以及疑問句中，表示「任何」之意。後接不可數或複數名詞。例如：Do you have any money? 你有錢嗎？（money為不可數名詞）；Do you have any mugs? 你有馬克杯嗎？（mug為可數名詞，用複數表達非指定的馬克杯）。

① **Do you come from a small or a big family?**
你來自小家庭還是大家庭？

② **What is your relationship status?**
你的感情狀態如何？

③ **Are you planning to have kids after getting married?**
婚後你有計劃要生小孩嗎？

Unit
05
身家背景調查

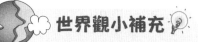

這樣回答就對了　　對應「主要關鍵句」的回答

① **There are four people in my family.**
我家共有四個人。

② **I am married.**
我已婚。

③ **Yes, I have two kids.**
有啊，我有兩個小孩。

世界觀小補充

　　對美國人來說，若被不熟的朋友問到較私人的問題，會覺得受到冒犯。所以當我們要開啟這類的話題之前，可要先三思喔。家庭人數及兄弟姐妹等基本訊息，屬於較安全的話題。若是問到感情狀況，建議等到彼此較為熟悉後再提。另外，美國人對於工作待遇的問題相當敏感，直接問薪資是相當不禮貌的。基本上有關身家問題的適切性，全球都差不多，若你心中的那把尺覺得這問題好像有點太過私密，建議還是少問少錯吧！

學校沒教的實用句

情境式主題句，學校沒有教，自己學起來！

There are four people in my family: my parents, my younger sister and I.
我們一家四口，包含我雙親、我妹妹跟我。

I was born in a big family in Taipei.
我出生在台北的一個大家庭裡。

How many brothers and sisters do you have?
你有幾個兄弟姐妹？

I am the oldest/youngest in my family.
我是家裡最年長 / 年輕的。

I am the only child.
我是獨子 / 獨生女。

I had a happy childhood.
我有一個快樂的童年。

I come from a small family, so I have few **relatives**.
我來自小家庭，所以我的親戚很少。 relative 親戚；親屬

I come from a **single-parent family** and was brought up by my mother.
我生於單親家庭，是我媽媽把我帶大的。 single-parent family 單親家庭

His parents were strict and paid a lot of attention to his academic performance.
他的雙親很嚴厲，而且很重視他的學業表現。

My father is **stern** while my mother is easygoing.
我爸很嚴格，而我媽很隨和。 stern 嚴格的

Like father, like son.
虎父無犬子。

What do your parents do?
你父母是做什麼的？

- My father is a well-known pediatrician and my mom is a **dedicated** nurse.

  我爸是知名的小兒科醫生，而我媽是個敬業的護士。　　dedicated 專注的；獻身的

- Unlike in the traditional marriage, it is my mom who **brings home the bacon**.

  不同於傳統家庭，我們家是我媽負責賺錢養家。　　bring home the bacon 養家糊口

- I get along pretty well with my family.

  我跟家人相處融洽。

- I **resemble** my father because of my round face and big eyes.

  我像我爸，因為我有圓臉跟大眼睛。　　resemble 像；類似

- I am the second child of three.

  我在家裡三個小孩中排行老二。

- All my siblings are good at music. It runs in the family.

  我的兄弟姐妹對音樂都很在行，那是家族遺傳。

- We usually have our **family reunion** on Christmas Day.

  我們家族通常在聖誕節聚會。　　family reunion 家庭聚會

- Ever since my grandparents passed away, our family members seldom see one another.

  自從我祖父母過世後，我們家族的成員就很少見到彼此了。

- Sean's brother was a juvenile delinquent, who set a bad example for him.

  西恩的哥哥是個問題少年，給他樹立了壞榜樣。

- I am a single mother.

  我是個單親媽媽。

- Who **looks after** your kids while you go to work?

  你去工作的時候，誰照顧你的小孩？　　look after 照顧；照看

- It is very difficult to support a family without a father.

  家裡缺少男主人的話，很難維持下去。

- Rosy thinks that family should **come first**.

  蘿西認為家庭應該排在第一順位。　　come first 首先要考慮到的

Unit
05

身家背景調查

Situation 1 人妻預備之路
preparing for the wedding

A Are you single?
你現在單身嗎？

B Yes, for now. I am going to get married at the end of this year.
目前是，我年底就要結婚了。

A Congratulations! You must be busy planning the wedding.
恭喜！你一定正忙著籌備婚禮。

B Yeah. I am lucky enough to have my sister as adviser!
對啊，我很幸運有我姊提供建議。

Situation 2 家庭聚餐苦與樂
all about family reunions

A How are you going to spend your Chinese New Year holidays?
你過年打算怎麼過？

B I have to spend two days in southern Taiwan for my family reunion.
我必須待在南部兩天，參加家庭聚會。

A I am so jealous! Family reunions sound warm and fun.
真羨慕你！家庭團聚聽起來既溫暖又開心。

B I wish we could switch places. I don't get along with my relatives!
我真希望能跟你交換，我跟我的親戚們處不來。

A You are such a big child!
你真是長不大的孩子耶！

Situation 3 八卦閒聊
making up rumors

A Amy comes from a single-parent family. She hasn't seen her mom since she was born.
愛咪是單親家庭的孩子，她出生後就再也沒看過她媽。

B It must be tough for both her and her father.
對她跟她爸來說，生活一定艱苦。

A Not quite. Rumor has it that her father is a famous politician.
也不盡然，謠傳她爸是個有名的政治家。

B So you're implying that she might be a love child.
所以你的意思是⋯她有可能是私生女囉？

A You are putting words into my mouth!
這可是你說的，我沒這個意思喔！

Situation 4 優秀家人壓力大
having an outstanding sibling

A What does your sister do?
你姊從事什麼行業？

B She is a surgeon in an overseas hospital, and her reputation is widespread.
她是海外某間醫院的外科醫生，她聲名遠播呢！

A Wow, it must be stressful living in her shadow.
哇，生活在她的光環下，壓力應該滿大的。

B And I always feel that I cannot live up to my parents' expectations.
而且我總是覺得自己沒辦法達到我爸媽對我的期望。

A Or maybe you just think too much.
但或許是你自己想太多了。

Unit 06 討論個性與外貌
Personality and appearance

主要關鍵句開口說

使出關鍵3句型，英文輕鬆開口說

Track 016

① **Are you an introvert or an extrovert?**
你個性內向還是外向呢？

② **How tall are you?**
你身高多高？

③ **Could you describe your boyfriend's appearance?**
可否描述一下你男友的長相？

沒果仁邏輯 *Americans*

句型解析與用法說明

說明 ① introvert/extrovert用法

introvert指「內向的人」，extrovert則為反義，表「外向的人」，兩者皆為名詞。使用方式請直接參考上面的關鍵句。

說明 ② How tall are you句型

「How tall+ be動詞+主詞」的句型用來詢問對方有多高，意即身高多少。如果主詞是第三人稱單數或是人名、單數名詞，則be動詞要用is，例如：How tall is her sister? 她妹妹多高？

說明 ③ Could you句型

使用could作為助動詞開頭，比使用can更有禮貌。若談話者是熟悉的對象，使用can即可；若是面對長輩或不熟的對象，建議使用could，聽起來較禮貌、謙卑，給對方的感覺會比較好。例：Could you pass me the salt, please? 可否請你將鹽遞給我？

沒果仁也愛的說法 ← 對照「主要關鍵句」的類似說法

① Are you an outgoing person or a quiet one?
你是活潑外向還是安靜的人？

② What is your height?
請問你的身高多少？

③ What does your boyfriend look like?
你男友長得怎樣？

這樣回答就對了 對應「主要關鍵句」的回答

① I am more of an extrovert.
我是比較外向的人。

② I am six feet tall.
我六呎高。

③ Sure! He has a long face and thick eyebrows.
當然可以！他的臉型偏長，而且是濃眉。

 世界觀小補充

　　美制度量衡單位與台灣使用的公制截然不同，例如長度的單位我們是以公分(centimeter)、公尺(meter)計算，而美國則是以英尺(foot)、英寸(inch)來度量；我們使用公克(gram)、公斤(kilogram)，他們則是講磅(pound)、盎司(ounce)。這會直接影響到日常談話的內容，如果你不知道怎麼換算，老美對於公制也不熟悉的情況下，話題就會不了了之。建議平常先將自己的身高體重等基本訊息，上網換算後記錄下來，往後與老外聊天時，就再也不怕無疾而終！

學校沒教的實用句

情境式主題句，學校沒有教，自己學起來！

John is an **introvert**. He keeps everything to himself.
約翰的個性內向，很多事情他都不會講出口。　　introvert 內向的人

My cousin is so outgoing to the point that my aunt is starting to worry about his school work.
我表哥外向到我阿姨都開始擔心這會不會影響到他的課業。

Duke is a man with **a short temper**.
杜克是個急性子。　　a short temper 急性子；脾氣暴躁

Jessica is patient and thoughtful.
潔西卡很有耐心又貼心。

People with Type A blood are considered to be slow and stubborn, but at the same time careful.
A型的人被認為是動作慢且頑固的，但同時也很細心。

I don't like to be around people who are self-centered and think of nothing but themselves.
我不喜歡跟自我中心、凡事只想到自己的人在一起。

I always use the horoscope and blood types as references to determine people's personality.
我總是以星座和血型作為判定他人性格的參考。

Miss Wang is not a straightforward person for she always beats about the bush.
王小姐不是個直來直往的人，她老喜歡拐彎抹角。

I think I am a bit impulsive because I sometimes don't think before I speak.
我覺得自己的個性有點衝動，因為我有時候沒經過思考就脫口而出。

He is **a man of his word**.
他是個守信用的男人。　　a man of his word 說話算話的人

She is a persistent woman, meaning she seldom **gives up on** things.
她是個堅持不懈的女人，也就是說，她不輕言放棄。　　give up on 放棄…

Part 1 自我介紹是門學問

She is five-feet-five-inches tall and weighs 130 pounds.
她身高五呎五吋，體重130磅。

My father has a square face, thin eyebrows and a pair of big eyes.
我爸有一個方臉、淡眉及一雙大眼。

Men like women with long and straight hair.
男人喜歡女人留直長髮。

He has a **stout** build and wears a Mohawk.
他身材粗壯且留著龐克頭。　　stout 結實的

Mary is tough on the outside but **vulnerable** on the inside.
瑪麗外表堅強，但內心脆弱。　　vulnerable 易受傷的

I want to wear one of those **braids** just like her!
我也想要跟她綁一樣的辮子！　　braid 髮辮

My sister is not satisfied with her single eyelids and decided to have a bit of **plastic surgery**.
我妹不滿意她的單眼皮，決定要去動整型手術。　　plastic surgery 整形手術

This little girl is so lovable, for she has rosy cheeks.
這小女生的臉頰紅潤，看起來真討喜。

My boss is bald, so he wears a **toupee** every day.
我老闆禿頭，所以他每天戴髮片。　　toupee 男士的假髮

She has a pair of long legs that attract everyone's attention every time she walks by.
她有一雙長腿，走到哪都會吸引路人的目光。

His girlfriend is a blue-eyed **brunette** with skinny limbs and big feet.
他女友有一雙藍眼及一頭褐髮，四肢乾瘦、有雙大腳。
brunette 深褐髮色的女子

My son is starting to have **zits** as he enters into his adolescence.
我兒子進入青春期後開始長痘痘。　　zit 青春痘；面皰

Is that a mole on your right arm?
你右手臂上的是一顆痣嗎？

Unit
06
討論個性與外貌

關鍵一句模擬實境對話
Topic-related Conversations

以關鍵句破題的模擬實境對話

Situation 1 談論老師們
commenting on your teachers

A What is the word that best describes your teacher?
用哪個詞來形容你的老師最貼切？

B I'd say "patient". She repeats the same subjects over and over again simply because a few students don't follow.
我覺得是「耐心」，她可以為了一些沒跟上的同學反覆講解一樣的主題。

A Mine is "stubborn".
我的則是「頑固」。

B Do explain!
快說為何！

A She always insists that we turn in our homework on time!
她老是堅持我們要準時交作業！

Situation 2 辦公室閒聊

a new guy in the office

A What do you think of Andrew, the new guy in the office?
你覺得辦公室新來的那個男生，安德魯怎樣？

B He is so my type! I like his smile.
他是我的菜！我喜歡他的笑容。

A In case you didn't notice, he smiles at every female colleague passing by.
也許你沒注意到，他對每個經過的女同事都會微笑。

B So what? He is just being polite!
那又怎樣？他只是很有禮貌而已嘛！

A You are hopeless...
你沒救了…

Part 1 自我介紹是門學問

Ⓐ **Please describe your ideal husband.**
請描述一下你理想的丈夫類型。

Ⓑ **He should be six-feet tall with average build and a handsome face.**
他要有六呎高、中等身材及一張俊俏的臉蛋。

Ⓐ **What about personality?**
那個性呢？

Ⓑ **He should be considerate, caring, loving and remember all our anniversaries!**
他應該要貼心、關心他人、有愛心，並且記得我們所有的週年紀念日！

Ⓐ **Good luck with you finding him in reality!**
祝你在現實生活中找到這樣的人！

Unit

06

討論個性與外貌

Situation 4 捉拿要犯
description of the fugitive

Ⓐ **Can you give the police a basic description of this fugitive?**
你是否能提供逃犯的基本特徵給警方？

Ⓑ **Yes, I'll try. He is approximately five-nine, 130 pounds and in his late thirties.**
好，我盡量。他大約180公分、60公斤左右、年近40歲。

Ⓐ **Are there any unique features on his face?**
他臉上有什麼特徵嗎？

Ⓑ **Yes. He has a scar on his left cheek.**
有，他左臉頰上有一條疤。

Ⓐ **Thanks for your information. We hope we can put this guy behind bars in no time.**
謝謝你提供的訊息，希望我們可以儘早將逃犯逮捕歸案。

Unit 07 談談宗教信仰
Religious beliefs

主要關鍵句開口說

使出關鍵3句型，英文輕鬆開口說　　　Track 019

① Do you belong to/practice/follow a religion?
你有信仰嗎？

② Do you believe in God?
你相信上帝嗎？

③ Are you superstitious?
你迷信嗎？

沒果仁邏輯　Americans

句型解析與用法說明

說明 ① Do you belong to/practice/follow a religion句型

religion表示宗教、信仰。belong to表示屬於、隸屬；practice表示實踐；follow在此處表示追隨信奉。「Do/Does+人名／代名詞+上述動詞+religion」即為詢問某人是否有信仰。

說明 ② Do you believe in句型

believe in後面接名詞，表示對某種信念、意識型態表達相信的態度。believe in 這個片語所表達的相信，比單純只用believe還要強烈。例如：Do you believe in love? 你相信愛情嗎？/Did he believe in your story? 他相信你的故事嗎？

說明 ③ Are you superstitious句型

「Is/Are+人名／代名詞+superstitious」即在詢問對方是否迷信。不管對方信仰哪個宗教，都能使用這個句型來詢問。

沒果仁也愛的說法 *Americans*

對照「主要關鍵句」的類似說法

① What is your religion?
你的宗教信仰是什麼？

② What is your opinion about God?
你對上帝有什麼看法？

③ Are you a zealous person when it comes to religion?
談及宗教時，你會很狂熱嗎？

這樣回答就對了

對應「主要關鍵句」的回答

① Yes, I am a Christian.
有，我是基督徒。

② No. I am an atheist.
不相信，我是無神論者。

③ Yes, I am.
是的，我很迷信。

世界觀小補充

　　歐美國家的社會觀念較為開放，多能包容各種不同的文化類型，各式宗教亦蓬勃發展。透過不同文化的融合，天主教／基督教已不再是歐美人士的主要信仰，甚至有愈來愈多年輕人趨向無神論的另類信仰。而多元化社會如美國，有來自世界各國的移民，也帶來各國不同的文化習俗，宗教便是其中一環。與老外聊聊彼此的宗教信仰，或許也是增加談話的豐富性及延續話題的好方法。但不建議初次見面就觸及此話題，在國際禮儀上，宗教議題還是較為敏感。

學校沒教的實用句

情境式主題句，學校沒有教，自己學起來！

*There are a lot of **Buddhists** here in Taiwan.
台灣有很多佛教徒。　Buddhist 佛教徒

*Local people **worship** in temples on a regular basis.
當地人固定在廟宇祭祀。　worship 崇拜；信奉

*Buddhists and Taoists are two major religious populations in Taiwan.
佛教徒跟道教徒為台灣兩大宗教人口。

*Using **incense** while praying for a blessing is part of the rituals in Buddhism.
祭拜時焚香是佛教的儀式之一。　incense 香；焚香時的煙

*He is very **pious**, for he never misses any church service.
他很虔誠，因為他從來不缺席教堂的禮拜。　pious 虔誠的

*There are a lot of ceremonies for worshiping in temples.
在廟裡祭拜時有很多儀式。

*Most of the vegetarians in Taiwan are for religious reason.
在台灣，吃素的原因大多跟宗教有關。

*Do you believe in **reincarnation**?
你相信輪迴轉世嗎？　reincarnation 輪迴說

*My friend says prayers before meals.
我的朋友在用餐前都會禱告。

*My family **goes to church** and sings gospel every Sunday morning.
我家人每週日上午都會去教堂唱福音。　go to church 上教堂

*I'm going to be **baptized** next month.
我下個月要受洗。　baptize 行浸禮

*Have you ever seen any religious ceremonies?
你有看過任何宗教儀式嗎？

*Can you distinguish between Catholicism and Christianity?

Part 1 自我介紹是門學問

你能夠區分天主教和基督教嗎？

It seems that there are several taboos in the Islamic world.
在回教世界中，似乎有一些禁忌不能犯。

Superstition can be seen in various cultures.
迷信在不同文化中都能見到。

*We call July of the **lunar** calendar "ghost month".*
我們稱農曆七月為鬼月。　　lunar 陰曆的

People in Taiwan don't play in water during the ghost month of the lunar calendar.
台灣人在農曆鬼月的時候不會去玩水。

Fortune telling is considered superstitious.
算命被視為迷信。

Jason's parents brought him to have his face and palm read.
傑森的雙親帶他去看面相及手相。

*A **prophet** is someone who can foresee your future.*
預言家就是可以預見你未來的人。　　prophet 先知；預言者

Chinese think the number 4 means bad luck, which is how Americans think about the number 13.
中國人認為數字4不吉祥，就像美國人認為數字13不吉祥一樣。

It is thought to be bad luck not to clean debts with others before Chinese New Year.
不趕在農曆過年前償還積欠的債務(欠債欠過年)被認為會帶來壞運氣。

Chinese people believe that face-reading can tell a lot about a person's life.
中國人認為面相術可以看出一個人的未來。

Feng shui is an important part of traditional Chinese culture.
風水在中國傳統文化中是很重要的一項。

*There are a lot of **dos and don'ts** when it comes to superstition.*
提到迷信，總是有很多該做及不該做的注意事項。　　dos and don'ts 規則；準則

Unit
07

談談宗教信仰

以關鍵句破題的模擬實境對話

Track 021

Situation 1 拜拜
worshiping the spirits

A It is the fifteenth day of the lunar calendar.
今天是農曆十五號。

B No wonder I saw my boss preparing fruit, snacks and flowers early this morning.
難怪我今天早上看到我老闆準備了水果、零食及花卉。

A My colleagues always buy abundant offerings before worshiping.
我同事總是買很多拜拜的供品。

B I am sorry, but I can't join you.
很抱歉，不過我無法參與。

A Right! You are a Christian.
對喔！你是基督徒。

Situation 2 教會禮拜
Sunday service

A The best part of Sunday service is singing the gospel.
禮拜天的教會禮拜最棒的部分就是唱福音。

B What about the sermons?
那布道呢？

A It depends. Sometimes the preachers are eloquent, sometimes not.
看情況，有時候傳道者口若懸河，有時候則不。

B That only shows one thing - you are not pious enough.
這證明一件事，你不夠虔誠。

A True. I still have a long way to go.
是啦，我的學習之路還很長。

A Do you believe in God?
你相信上帝嗎？

B Yes. As a matter of fact, I am Catholic.
我信，事實上，我是天主教徒。

A Do you attend Mass or any other religious activities?
你有參加彌撒或其他宗教活動嗎？

B I live in a remote area, so I attend Mass only once in a while.
我住的地方比較偏遠，所以我偶爾才參加一次彌撒。

A Maybe you are not that religious.
或許你比較沒那麼虔誠。

Unit
07

談談宗教信仰

Situation 4 讀手相新手
palm reading

A Your palm tells me you will live a long life.
你的手相告訴我你會長壽。

B That's not difficult to tell because my life-line is long and deep.
這不難知道，因為我的生命線又長又深。

A I can't see your heart line! You will never be in a relationship.
我看不到你的感情線耶！你永遠不會有戀情。

B As a matter of fact, I am seeing someone now.
事實上，我正在跟某人穩定交往。

A Ok, I'll give you a refund.
好吧，我退錢給你。

主要關鍵句開口說

使出關鍵3句型，英文輕鬆開口說

Track 022

① **Which school do you go to?**
你上哪一間學校？

② **Do you live on campus or off campus?**
你住校還是住外面？

③ **What is your major?**
你主修哪一科？

沒果仁邏輯 Americans

句型解析與用法說明

說明
① **Which school do you go to句型**

「Which+地點／場合+do/does+人名／代名詞+go+to」用以詢問對方去哪一個地點或場合。例：Which gym does your brother go to? 你哥哥是去哪一間健身房啊？

說明
② **Do you live on campus or off campus句型**

「Do/does+人名／代名詞+live+介系詞+地點」是用於詢問對方住在哪裡的句型。campus指校園，on campus就是在校園中，off campus就表示住在校園以外的地方，即外宿之意。

說明
③ **What is your major句型**

此句型專門用於詢問對方的主修科系為何，特別是指大學生及專科院校的學生。major指主修科系，副修科系則為minor。

沒果仁也愛的說法

對照「主要關鍵句」的類似說法

1. **Which school do you attend?**
   你就讀哪所學校？

2. **Do you live in a dormitory?**
   你住學校宿舍嗎？

3. **Which department do you study in?**
   你是哪個系所的？

這樣回答就對了

對應「主要關鍵句」的回答

1. **I go to New York University.**
   我就讀紐約大學。

2. **I live off campus.**
   我住學校外面。

3. **I study in the School of Law.**
   我唸法律系的。

世界觀小補充

　　學校生活向來充滿話題性及樂趣。除了輕鬆的生活化主題之外，也可先大致了解各國不盡相同的學制，以免雞同鴨講。美國沒有國中與高中的區分，從小學一年級(first grade)一直到十二年級(twelfth grade)等同台灣的國小、國中、高中。所以當你聽到美國人說自己是tenth grade時，對照來看，他就是台灣的高一生。英國的教育制度則不同，5-16歲學齡的學生強制受國民教育。16歲離校前通過中學教育入學考試，畢業後可直接就業或繼續上大學深造。

學校沒教的實用句

情境式主題句，學校沒有教，自己學起來！

▌ What grade are you in?
你讀幾年級？

▌ I am sending my girl to a **kindergarten** this summer.
我今年夏天準備要送我女兒上幼稚園。　　kindergarten 幼稚園

▌ It is her first day at school, and she is not comfortable being around so many strangers.
今天是她第一天入學，身邊都是陌生人讓她感到不自在。

▌ We have a **transfer student** in the class today.
今天我們班上來了一位轉學生。　　transfer student 轉學生

▌ My son is good at every subject except for math.
我兒子除了數學以外的科目都很棒。

▌ Elementary school teachers often **call the roll** before class begins.
國小老師常常在上課前點名。　　call the roll 點名

▌ I have been bad at English since day one.
我從一開始英文就很差。

▌ The teacher announced that the final exam begins a week from today.
老師宣布期末考在一週後開始。

▌ William is studying hard for the college entrance examination.
威廉正在為大學入學考試苦讀中。

▌ Time's up. Put down your pens and hand in your papers.
時間到了。把筆放下、考卷交上來。

▌ Tom scored a hundred on this chemistry exam by cheating.
湯姆藉著作弊在化學考試上獲得滿分。

▌ I pulled an **all-nighter** last night for my social report.
我昨晚為了我的社會報告挑燈夜戰。　　all-nighter 通宵的工作

I'd like to apply for several post-graduate programs, and I am wondering if you could write a recommendation letter for me.

我想要申請研究所，不知道您可否幫我寫推薦信？

The gym is situated right next to our student center where there are professional equipment and an indoor swimming pool.

健身房在學生中心的旁邊，有著專業的設備以及室內游泳池。

My favorite subject is PE because I like sports.

我最喜歡的科目是體育課，因為我愛運動。

I major in sociology and **minor in** education.

我主修社會學，副修教育。　　minor in 副修

I have a **double major** in accounting and journalism.

我雙主修會計學跟新聞學。　　double major 雙主修

Chloe is **working her way through** college, meaning that she does not have any financial support from her family.

克蘿伊大學半工半讀，也就是說她沒有家中的經濟支持。

work one's way through 半工半讀

Will you take any second foreign languages when you enter your **sophomore** year?

你升大二會選修第二外語嗎？　　sophomore 大學、高中的二年級學生

To complete her master's degree, my niece is working on her dissertation arduously.

為了拿到碩士學位，我姪女努力撰寫她的碩士論文。

Dylan skipped so many courses that he flunked out of school at the end of the semester.

狄倫翹太多課，所以在學期末被退學。

Our mid-term is going to be an open-book exam.

我們的期中考將會是開卷式考試。

I feel like **auditing** this class before I decide whether or not to take it.

我想在決定修這堂課之前先旁聽。　　audit 旁聽

How many **credits** did Dad take in college to be able to graduate?

爸在大學的時候總共要修多少學分才能畢業啊？　　credit 學分

以關鍵句破題的模擬實境對話

Track 02A

Situation **1** 翹課事不過二
don't skip a class twice

🅐 **Do you think the Chinese teacher will take attendance tomorrow?**
你覺得國文老師明天會點名嗎？

🅑 **I can't say for sure.**
不知道耶。

🅐 **I want to skip the class but don't want to get caught.**
我想翹課，但又不想被抓包。

🅑 **Haven't you learned your lesson?**
你還沒記取教訓啊！

🅐 **Alright. I'll attend the class.**
好啦，我會去上課的。

Situation **2** 上學如同中樂透
enrollment through drawing lots

🅐 **It is so hard to get into a private elementary school these days.**
這年頭要上私立小學還真難。

🅑 **Why is that?**
為何？

🅐 **Enrollment is not guaranteed even if you are financially capable.**
即使你經濟富裕，也不一定能就學。

🅑 **How come?**
為什麼？

🅐 **You have to draw lots to see if you are allowed to enroll!**
能不能入學還得看有沒有抽到籤呢！

3 校園八卦
somebody's got flunked out

A Have you heard that Daniel was kicked out of school last semester?
你有聽説丹尼爾上學期被退學了嗎？

B No! Do tell!
沒有！快説怎麼回事！

A He skipped a lot of courses, cheated during the finals and didn't turn in any assigned reports.
他翹了很多堂課、考試作弊又連一份報告都沒交。

B That explains it.
那也難怪了。

A No wonder nobody feels sorry for him.
怪不得沒有人覺得他可憐。

Unit
08
校園生活雜談

4 運動非人人愛
not everyone's the sporting kind

A PE is a mandatory class in university.
體育課在大學是必修。

B I am totally okay with that arrangement. I do well in all kinds of sports.
我覺得這樣安排很好，我運動方面很強。

A I am bad at sports! I wish I could avoid taking the class.
我很差啊！真希望可以避開這堂課。

B You can run, but you can't hide!
逃得了一時，躲不了一世！

A I'll just try and do my best, I guess.
那我只好盡力而為了。

Unit 09 興趣及專長
Hobbies and specialties

 主要關鍵句開口說

使出關鍵3句型，英文輕鬆開口說

Track 025

① **What's your hobby?**
你的興趣是什麼？

② **What do you specialize in?**
你的專長是什麼？

③ **What's your favorite pastime?**
你最喜歡的休閒活動是什麼？

沒果仁邏輯 Americans 句型解析與用法說明

說明 ① What's your hobby句型

hobby表示嗜好、業餘興趣，「what+is/are+人名／代名詞所有格+hobby」就是問對方從事的業餘嗜好是什麼。

說明 ② What do you specialize in句型

specialize in這個片語意指專精在某領域上，in後面接名詞，表示專精的領域、項目等。What+do/does+人名／代名詞+specialize+in是詢問對方專精的領域。例：What does your professor specialize in? 你教授專精的領域是什麼？

說明 ③ What's your favorite pastime句型

pastime意指消遣、娛樂，特別指用來消磨閒暇時間的活動。例：Baseball has been a national pastime for years. 棒球長久以來都是全國性的消遣活動。

沒果仁也愛的說法 Americans

對照「主要關鍵句」的類似說法

① **What's your interest?**
你的興趣是什麼？

② **What's your specialty?**
你的專長是什麼？

③ **What do you do in your free time?**
平常閒暇時，你都做些什麼？

對應「主要關鍵句」的回答

① **One of my hobbies is playing piano.**
我其中一個興趣是彈鋼琴。

② **I specialize in on-line games.**
我的專長是玩線上遊戲。

③ **My favorite pastime is writing my blog.**
我最喜歡的休閒活動是寫網誌。

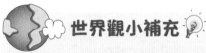

世界觀小補充

　　在社交場合詢問談話者的嗜好或閒暇興趣是相當輕鬆的話題。如果你想要避免一直討論氣候，可以多學學如何詢問對方興趣的對話，說不定能因而交到興趣相合的好友！談論興趣時最常見到的兩個英文單字：hobby及pastime，很容易被混淆，造成文義上的誤解。hobby是指嗜好、業餘愛好；pastime則指閒暇時的消遣活動，兩者的使用是有區別的。hobby特別指工作之餘會花時間投入的愛好，而pastime則傾向為了消磨時間所進行的活動。

學校沒教的實用句

情境式主題句，學校沒有教，自己學起來！

Track 026

My best friend and I share the same **hobbies**.
我好友跟我的嗜好相同。 hobby 業餘愛好；嗜好

Our hobbies include oil painting, sketching and pottery.
我們的嗜好包括油畫、素描及陶藝。

Who do you spend your **free time** with?
你閒暇時間都跟誰過？ free time 空閒時間

How long have you had your hobby?
你有這個嗜好多久了？

Judy has had the hobby of knitting ever since her daughter left home for college five years ago.
自從女兒五年前為了上大學而離家後，茱蒂開始有編織這個嗜好。

Can you think of any hobbies which are popular with both children and adults?
你可否想出哪些嗜好是小朋友跟大人都喜歡的？

Are there any activities that you used to do but don't do anymore?
有沒有哪些活動是你以前會做，但現在再也不做的？

I spend most of my free time working out at the gym.
我閒暇時都在健身房健身。

Do people's **leisure** time activities change as they get older?
人喜愛的休閒活動會因年紀漸長而改變嗎？ leisure 閒暇

I think running is one of the cheapest hobbies.
我覺得跑步是最便宜的嗜好之一。

Biking around the island has become one of the major **pastimes** for Taiwanese lately.
騎腳踏車環島近來成為台灣人主要的休閒活動之一。 pastime 消遣；娛樂

Do you like **gossiping** in your free time?
你空閒時喜歡聊八卦嗎？ gossip 傳播流言蜚語

Which hobbies cost nothing at all to do?
哪些嗜好完全不用花錢？

Are there any hobbies you would like to try?
有哪些嗜好你會想要試試看？

One of my favorite pastimes is watching theatrical performances.
我最喜歡的休閒活動之一就是看劇場表演。

In his pastime, John likes to fish.
約翰喜歡在閒暇之餘去釣魚。

I do home improvement mostly on weekends.
我主要在週末進行居家修繕。

Tommy tried to get to know the girl by asking her about her hobbies.
湯米試著以詢問對方興趣的方式來了解這個女孩。

I am good at linguistics and specialize in it.
我擅長語言學，並專精於此。

My dad has a great **appreciation** for wine tasting.
我爸在品酒這個領域很有鑑賞力。　　appreciation 欣賞；鑑賞

Our professor is an expert in economics.
我們的教授是經濟學專家。

Jody has a great reputation in the fashion industry.
裘蒂在時裝界負有盛名。

I am **proficient** in seven different languages.
我精通七國語言。　　proficient 精通的；熟練的

My uncle is mastering in English.
我的舅舅精通英文。

My grandfather is very influential in the publishing industry.
我爺爺在出版界很有影響力。

My mom is capable of taking care of her kids and working efficiently at the same time.
我媽很有能力，能兼顧小孩與工作。

關鍵一句模擬實境對話 Topic-related Conversations

以關鍵句破題的模擬實境對話

Situation 1 擁有多元強項
a man with multiple strengths

A The new guy in my department specializes in Internet security.
我們部門的新人專精於網路安全。

B Sounds professional. I thought that's your specialty.
聽起來好專業，我以為那是你的專長。

A Well, that's one of my specialties.
嗯，那的確是我其中一項專長。

B So you're saying you're better than him?
所以你的意思是，你比他強囉？

A I'm just saying I have multiple strengths.
我只是在說我的強項很多。

Situation 2 語言專才
language proficiency

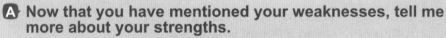

A Now that you have mentioned your weaknesses, tell me more about your strengths.
既然你剛剛提到自己的弱點，現在說說你的長處吧。

B I am mastering in different languages. My proficiency in English and Spanish can hold up to any test.
我精通多種語言，我英文和西班牙文的程度都經得起考驗。

A How did you manage to pull it off?
你是如何辦到的？

B I listen to English and Spanish songs on the radio every day.
我每天都利用廣播聽英文和西文的歌曲。

免錢的嗜好
a hobby that costs nothing

A Can you think of any hobbies that don't cost anything?
你能想到完全不用花錢的嗜好嗎？

B How about hiking?
登山怎麼樣？

A I thought so too in the beginning, but then I realized the expenditure of the gear is shockingly high.
我一開始也這樣想，但是後來發現購買裝備的花費高得驚人。

B Well, then, what about spacing out?
那發呆呢？

A That's not a hobby at all!
那根本稱不上是嗜好，好嗎？

Unit
09

興趣及專長

Situation 4 美味的閒暇活動
free time activities

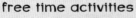

A I like to read science fiction in my free time. What about you?
我閒暇時喜歡閱讀科幻小說，你呢？

B I have been into baking lately.
我最近喜歡上烘焙。

A Good for you. Is there any chance I can try some of your baking?
真好，我有機會品嚐到你的作品嗎？

B Sure! When will you have free time?
當然有！你什麼時候有空？

A Anytime!
隨時都有空！

 主要關鍵句開口說

使出關鍵3句型，英文輕鬆開口說 Track 028

① **What ambition do you have regarding your career?**
對於職涯，你有什麼樣的抱負？

② **What do you want to be when you grow up?**
你長大後想要成為什麼樣的人？

③ **Are you an ambitious person?**
你是個有野心的人嗎？

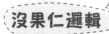 沒果仁邏輯 _Americans_ 句型解析與用法說明

 What ambition do you have句型

「What+名詞+do/does+人名／代名詞+動詞」的句型，可套用不同的動詞做變化。例：What colors do you like? 你喜歡什麼顏色？/What languages does he speak? 他說什麼語言？

 What do you want to be when you grow up句型

What+do/does+人名／代名詞+want+to+be詢問某人想要成為什麼，be也可用become代替，回答時要在be/become後面加名詞。例：I want to be a ballerina. 我想要成為一名芭蕾舞者。

 Are you an ambitious person句型

ambitious是ambition的形容詞，詢問他人是否有野心可用Are you an ambitious person? 也可用Is/Are+人名／代名詞+ambitious? 這個句型。

① **Do you long to get ahead in your career?**
你渴望在職場上領先他人嗎？

② **Where do you see yourself in ten years?**
你十年後會在哪裡呢？

③ **Are you strongly motivated?**
你深受激勵嗎？

這樣回答就對了　對應「主要關鍵句」的回答

① **I want to open up a firm and practice law in the near future.**
我希望能在不久的將來開一間事務所，從事法律業務。

② **I want to be a nurse when I grow up.**
我長大後想要當護士。

③ **Yes, I believe so.**
是的，我認為我是。

 世界觀小補充

　　東方人從小被灌輸的觀念就是：偉大的志向等同於成為醫生 (doctor)、律師(lawyer)、法官(judge)等，其他職業不足掛齒。歐美文化對於多元發展則抱持較為開放的心態及觀念，雄心壯志並不一定發揮在職場上，只要能在生活上為了達成目標而努力，這種積極的生活態度就是一種抱負。這個主題也是個很好發揮的話題，面對較為熟識的朋友就可以問問貼近個人想法的問題，交心之餘也可以體驗不同文化間的火花！

Unit
10
抱負及未來志向

學校沒教的實用句

情境式主題句，學校沒有教，自己學起來！

Nick is trying so hard to **get ahead** in his career that he doesn't have time to get into a serious relationship.

尼克太致力於在職場上拔得頭籌，以至於沒時間認真談感情。

> get ahead 領先；進步

How would you define **ambition**?

你會如何定義「抱負」？

> ambition 雄心；抱負

I think ambition is a powerful desire that drives you to be successful and achieve your goals.

我認為抱負是一種驅使你想要成功與達成目標的強大欲望。

Do you consider yourself to be an ambitious person?

你認為自己是一個很有抱負的人嗎？

What if I don't have any ambition?

如果我沒什麼雄心壯志呢？

His ambition was to win a gold medal at the Olympics.

他的志向是贏得奧運金牌。

Do you think that ambition can be taught or do you think we are born with it?

你覺得有抱負是可以後天培養的，還是與生俱來的特質？

Does ambition always bring success?

有抱負絕對可以帶來成功嗎？

What are the positive results of being ambitious?

有雄心壯志會帶來哪些正面的影響？

What kind of sacrifices would you make to have your dreams **come true**?

為了實現夢想，你會做什麼樣的犧牲呢？

> come true 實現

What do you think is the difference between an ambition and a dream of doing something?

你覺得志向跟夢想的差別在哪裡？

Part 1 自我介紹是門學問

Darrel is very ambitious when it comes to eating.
戴洛在吃這方面相當有雄心壯志。

I picture myself as a doctor fifteen years from now and feel greatly motivated.
我想像十五年後的自己會成為一位醫生，也因此充滿幹勁。

Why are some people determined to succeed at any cost, yet others seem to lack any drive whatsoever?
為什麼有些人不擇手段、堅持要成功，而有些人則是無論如何都喪志？

What do you think causes a person to be ambitious – family, genes, or the culture in which he/she is raised?
你認為什麼驅使一個人有抱負？家庭因素、基因還是一個人成長的文化背景？

She was so career-driven that she doesn't allow any interruption from work.
工作至上的原則導致她無法接受工作以外的干擾。

Do you think someone can lose his or her ambition?
你覺得一個人有可能喪失自己的志向嗎？

Do you think younger people are more ambitious than older people?
你覺得年輕人會比年長者還要有抱負嗎？

Sally wants to be a productive writer when she finishes her bachelor degree.
莎莉拿到大學文憑後，想要成為一位多產的作家。

My long-term goal is to run my own business, which is to open up a small café.
我的遠程目標是經營自己的事業，也就是開一間小咖啡店。

I've already planned out my short-term goal, and I am going to carry that out at my own pace.
我已經記劃好我的近程目標，而且會依自己的步調來實現它。

The company screened out applicants motivated only by money.
這間公司將只看重金錢的應徵者刷掉。

I want to be a **freelancer** because working 9 to 5 doesn't suit me.
我想要成為自由作家，因為朝九晚五的工作不適合我。　　freelancer 自由作家

以關鍵句破題的模擬實境對話 Track 030

Situation **1** 含著金湯匙出生又怎樣？
can social status impact?

🅐 Do you think one's social status as a child, whether rich or poor, affects his/her ability to succeed later in life?
你覺得一個小孩的背景，有錢或貧困，是否會影響他(她)在未來成功的能力？

🅑 I'd say there's no definite answer.
我覺得很難說。

🅐 What makes you think that?
你為什麼這麼覺得？

🅑 Throughout history, we've seen poor kids become millionaires and rich ones go bankrupt.
綜觀古今，有許多窮小孩成為百萬富翁，有錢小孩卻破產的例子。

🅐 Makes a lot of sense.
有道理。

Situation **2** 長大的志向
future ambitions

🅐 Our teacher wanted us to write an essay on "What do you want to be when you grow up?"
我們老師要我們寫一篇主題是「你長大後想做什麼」的文章。

🅑 How did you do?
你寫得如何？

🅐 The teacher gave me an A+!
老師給我A+的成績！

🅑 Wow! What did you write?
哇！你寫了些什麼呢？

🅐 I wrote that I want to be an English teacher just like ours.
我寫說我想要當一位跟我們英文老師一樣的老師。

3 爸媽的冀望
parents' expectations

A My parents hope that I can be a civil servant after I graduate from college.
我父母希望我大學畢業後去當公務員。

B I've heard it's hard to be one since you have to pass the notoriously difficult exam first.
我聽說要當公務員很難，因為你得先通過相當有難度的考試。

A The bottom line is that I don't see myself as a civil servant.
重點是我不覺得我適合當公務員。

B What do you see yourself then?
那你覺得你適合做什麼？

A I want to be a contemporary dancer!
我想要當現代舞的舞者！

Unit

10

抱負及未來志向

Situation 4 人各有志
different people, different aspirations

A Will you attend the company lecture on "How to get a promotion in a year"?
你會參加公司有關「如何在一年內獲得升遷」的座談會嗎？

B No, I think I'll pass.
不，我想我不去了。

A Why? I think it's a great opportunity to learn something and get motivated.
為何？我覺得這是很好的學習機會，同時還能被激勵。

B I am not as ambitious as you are.
我不像你這麼有雄心壯志。

A Alright, just suit yourself.
好吧，隨便你。

Part 2

處理日常生活雜務

Unit 11 到銀行辦事
In the bank

主要關鍵句開口說

使出關鍵3句型，英文輕鬆開口說

Track 031

① **I would like to open a bank account.**
我想要開立一個銀行帳戶。

② **I'd like to deposit some money.**
我想要存錢。

③ **I need to withdraw some money.**
我需要領錢。

沒果仁邏輯 ·····Americans

句型解析與用法說明

說明① I would like to open a bank account句型

would like to為禮貌性用法，表達想要進行、辦理的事情。通常不論是電話上要求、商店裡購物、餐廳點菜，只要是表達自己想要的東西或想法，都可以用I would like to開頭。

說明② I'd like to deposit some money句型

此句型同I would like to，只是將I would以I'd表示。此為委婉用法，會比直接講I want更婉轉有禮。

說明③ I need to withdraw some money句型

人名／代名詞+need+to+do something表示某人需要做某件事情。例：I need to go to the restroom. 我需要去盥洗室。

處理日常生活雜務

沒果仁也愛的說法 Americans

對照「主要關鍵句」的類似說法

① **What kind of account can I open here?**
我可以在這裡開哪種帳戶？

② **I'd like to make some deposits.**
我想要辦理存錢。

③ **I want to make some withdrawals.**
我想辦理提款的業務。

 這樣回答就對了

對應「主要關鍵句」的回答

① **What kind of account do you want, a checking or a savings account?**

您想要開哪一種戶頭，支票存款還是儲蓄存款？

② **How much are you depositing?**
您要存多少金額呢？

③ **How much would you like to take out?**
您想要提領多少金額呢？

世界觀小補充

　　在現行的經濟與交易制度之下，人們與銀行的往來已經變成不可或缺的日常行程之一，無論是要查詢帳戶餘額(balance)，還是要轉帳(transfer)，或者是要提款(withdraw)，都必須透過銀行等金融機構。全球的銀行體系大致上相同，在國外，不管你是當地人還是外國人，都免不了會需要用到銀行的服務。把基本的銀行用語、片語記下來，就不會進了銀行大門卻什麼事都沒辦成了！

學校沒教的實用句

情境式主題句，學校沒有教，自己學起來！

I am heading to a local bank to open a **checking account**.
我正要去本地銀行開支票存款戶頭。　checking account 支票存款戶頭

The teller asked the man if he wanted to set up a **savings account**.
櫃員詢問男子他是否想要開戶。　savings account 儲蓄存款戶頭

The account comes with a bank card so you can withdraw your money at any time.
這個帳戶會附一張提款卡，你可以隨時用這張卡提領現金。

My husband and I want to buy a house, so we decide to apply for a mortgage.
我先生跟我想要買房子，所以我們決定去申請貸款。

Please take the number ticket first and fill out a **deposit slip**.
請先領取號碼牌，並填寫存款單。　deposit slip 存款單

Can I open an account if I am a foreign student of ABC school without a social security number?
我是ABC學校的外籍學生，而且我沒有社會安全碼，請問我可以開戶嗎？

I would like to **transfer** some money.
我想要轉帳。　transfer 轉帳

You have to hand in a written **remittance** slip to the teller to transfer your money.
你必須要將寫好的匯款單交給行員去轉帳。　remittance 匯款

I would like to open a checking or savings account that requires no minimum balance and with which I can use ATM cards.
我想要開一個不需要最低存額、而且有自動櫃員機提款卡的支票帳戶或儲蓄存款帳戶。

What's your **interest rate** for your checking accounts?
你們的支票存款利率是多少？　interest rate 利率

A savings account has a slightly higher interest rate.
儲蓄存款帳戶的利息高一些。

Part **2** 處理日常生活雜務

I have never gotten a **bank statement** for the fees that I owe.
我從來沒有收到有關我欠繳費用的銀行通知。　　bank statement 銀行結單

I want to **deposit** it into my checking account.
我想要將錢存入我的支票存款帳戶。　　deposit 把(錢)儲存

You need to deposit at least $50 into both accounts.
你需要存至少50元到這兩個帳戶裡。

I will be depositing $300 today.
我今天會存300元。

How do I order checks?
我要怎麼申請支票？

Give it about a week, and you should get your checks in the mail.
大約等一週，你就會收到含支票的郵件。

I wrote a check for $100, and it **bounced**.
我開了一張100元的支票，但跳票了。　　bounce (支票)被拒付而退還給開票人

Do you have enough money in your account?
你帳戶裡有足夠的錢嗎？

I want it transferred into my checking account.
我想要把這筆錢轉到我的支存戶頭裡。

Could you sign the back of the check, please?
可否請你在支票背面簽名？

Slide your card into the machine, type your PIN in, click on whichever option you want, and you're done.
將你的卡片插入機器、輸入密碼，再點選你要的服務就可以了。

You need to keep a minimum balance in your account, at least $100.
你的帳戶需要維持最少100元的最低存款額。

If you don't meet that requirement, you will be charged $25.
如果你沒有符合規定，就會被收取25元的費用。

Situation 1 房屋貸款
applying for a mortgage

A We'd like to apply for a mortgage.
我們想要申請貸款。

B How much would you like to borrow?
你們希望的貸款額度是多少呢？

A Well, we are interested in a property which costs $180,000, but we have a down payment of only $50,000.
這個嘛，我們對於一間要價180,000元的房子很感興趣，但我們只有50,000元的頭期款。

B So you need a $130,000 loan. Do you have an account with this bank?
所以你們需要貸款130,000元，請問你們在本行有帳戶嗎？

A No, neither of us does.
我們都沒有。

Situation 2 留學生開戶
foreign students opening up a bank account

A I just opened an account at this local bank.
我剛剛在這間本地銀行開戶了。

B Is the application complicated for foreign students?
對外籍學生來說，申請帳戶會不會很麻煩？

A Not at all! Just bring your passport, your residence permit and fill out some forms.
一點都不會！只要準備好你的護照，居留相關證件，填寫表格就行了。

B Doesn't sound that difficult.
聽起來不難。

credit card anomaly

A There were charges on my credit card that I never made.
我的信用卡上有我不曾消費過的扣款記錄。

B Do you have a statement for your credit card?
請問你有帶資料來嗎？

A I do.
有的。

B Which charges are you talking about?
你說的是哪幾筆呢？

A They are the last four charges. Please freeze this card before you look into it.
最後四筆，在你們查明之前，請先暫停扣款。

Situation 4 **取消支票**
canceling a check

A I would like to cancel a check.
我想要取消一張支票。

B Is there a problem?
請問有什麼問題嗎？

A I wrote out the check for too much. It was supposed to be for $100, but I put $150 instead.
我金額寫太多了，應該只有100元，我卻寫成150元。

B I'll cancel that check for you.
我會幫你取消。

A I really appreciate your help.
非常感謝你的幫忙。

出外靠租房
Renting an apartment

主要關鍵句開口說

使出關鍵３句型，英文輕鬆脫口說

Track 034

① Are there any apartments for rent?
有沒有公寓要出租？

② What kind of apartment would you like to rent?
你想要租什麼樣的公寓？

③ When can I see the apartment?
我什麼時候可以看看公寓？

沒果仁邏輯 Americans

句型解析與用法說明

說明
① Are there any apartments for rent句型

「Is/are+there+any+名詞」是用來詢問某種狀態、事物有或沒有的問句。
例：Is there some water in this bottle? 這水瓶裡有沒有水？

說明
② What kind of apartment would you like to rent句型

「What+kind+of+名詞」用來詢問類型，後面接疑問句。例：What kind of exercise do you usually do? 你平常都做什麼樣的運動？/What kind of girls does John like? 約翰喜歡什麼類型的女生？

說明
③ When can I see the apartment句型

When+助動詞+人名／代名詞+原形動詞，目的是要問什麼時候可以進行某件事情。使用When是詢問大範圍的時間，諸如季節、年份、時間、時段等，例：（問）When will we meet next time? 我們下次何時見面？/（答）Maybe in winter. 大概是在冬季的時候。

① **Do you know how I could find an apartment for rent?**
你知道我該如何找到要出租的公寓嗎?

② **What are your criteria for renting an apartment?**
你在租公寓方面有哪些條件?

③ **When can you show me around the apartment?**
你什麼時候可以帶我參觀一下公寓?

 這樣回答就對了　對應「主要關鍵句」的回答

① **I am afraid there is none at the moment.**
不好意思,目前沒有。

② **I want to rent an apartment with two bedrooms.**
我想要租有兩房的公寓。

③ **Anytime. I would suggest you go in the daytime.**
隨時都可以,但我建議白天來看。

🌏💭 世界觀小補充

　　無論是出國唸書或短期遊玩,「住」都是相當重要的一環。不僅是住的地區(neighborhood)很重要,要怎麼樣與房東(landlord/landlady)打交道也是一門學問。租屋該注意的事項不外乎是確認自己的需求跟房東所提供的是否吻合,租屋前一定要實地參觀過再做決定。另外租金(rent)、押金(deposit)、水電費(utilities)等都必須要在簽下租約(lease)之前跟房東確認。了解正確的說法,才能避免吃悶虧!

Unit

12

出外靠租房

學校沒教的實用句

情境式主題句，學校沒有教，自己學起來！

I'd rather rent a **studio** than stay in the dormitory on campus.
我寧願租套房也不要住學校宿舍。 studio 套房

As an **overseas** student, it took me quite some time to find accommodations.
身為一位海外學生，找住處花了我不少時間。 overseas 海外的；國外的

They moved down from upstairs because the **rent** was cheaper.
因為房租較便宜，所以他們從樓上搬下來。 rent 租金

I decided to move out of my parents' place and start living on my own.
我決定從父母家裡搬出來自己住。

I searched in the newspaper classified ads for apartments for rent and found a place not too far from work.
我在報紙的分類廣告尋找有關出租公寓的訊息，找到一間離公司不遠的公寓。

The monthly rent for a two-bedroom apartment would be $800.
含兩間臥室的公寓每月租金是八百元。

There is no air conditioner and **heater** in the bedroom.
臥室裡面沒有冷氣跟暖氣。 heater 暖氣機

The **landlord** showed me around the apartment.
房東帶我參觀公寓。 landlord 房東

The studio meets my requirements, so I signed the rental agreement.
這間套房符合我的需求，所以我簽了租約。

You'll have to pay a deposit, which you might get back when you move out, given that the apartment stays in the same condition as when you moved in.
你必須要先付押金，當你搬走時可以取回，前提是公寓的狀態與你剛搬入時一樣。

Would you rather rent a place just for yourself or with friends?
你寧願自己一個人租房子，還是跟朋友一起住？

People often look for cheap apartments or **condominiums** to rent when going off to college.

上大學的時候，很多人會找便宜的公寓或套房來租。　　condominium 公寓大樓

The apartment has three bedrooms and one bathroom.

這間公寓內有三間臥室和一間浴室。

My landlord renovated the whole apartment right before I moved in.

就在我搬進來之前，我房東才替公寓做了一次大整修。

The rent is $650 a month, and electricity, water and gas are not **included**.

一個月的租金是650元，水電及瓦斯沒有包含在內。　　included 被包括的

The apartment **complex** I am about to rent doesn't allow any pets.

我要租的這間公寓大樓禁止住戶養寵物。　　complex 綜合設施

My condo looks empty because it's not **furnished**.

因為沒有附設傢俱，我的公寓看起來很空。　　furnish 給(房間)配置傢俱

The **tenant** signed a one-year lease with the landlord.

這個房客與房東簽了為期一年的租約。　　tenant 房客；承租人

Should I contact my landlord if the washing machine **breaks down**?

如果洗衣機壞了，我是不是應該聯絡房東？　　break down 故障

The house is centrally heated and double-glazed.

這棟房子有中央空調，而且有雙層玻璃窗。

The rent is NT$100,000, but I believe the owner would be willing to accept an offer.

租金是新台幣十萬元，但我相信屋主願意接受講價。

All the furniture comes with the apartment. The kitchen is quite large, with a gas stove and a big fridge.

公寓有附傢俱。廚房滿大的，有一個瓦斯爐跟大冰箱。

The neighborhood is very popular with young people. There are lots of bars, restaurants, parks and shops.

這一區頗受年輕人歡迎，附近有很多酒吧、餐廳、公園跟商店。

Rent should be paid every month through **wire transfer**.

房租每個月以電匯的方式繳納。　　wire transfer 電匯

Unit

12

出外靠租房

Situation 1 電話詢問空房
inquiring about vacancies over the phone

A I'm calling about the apartment you advertised.
我看到你的公寓出租廣告，想詢問細節。

B Yes. When do you need it?
是，你什麼時候需要呢？

A Sometime around next week. What can you tell me about this apartment?
大概下個星期，你可以先介紹一下這間公寓嗎？

B Well, it's a two-bedroom apartment, well furnished. Gas and water are included.
這間公寓有兩間臥房，附全套傢俱，瓦斯和水費都包含在租金中。

A Thanks! May I come over to take a look?
謝謝你！我可以過去看看嗎？

Situation 2 租屋找仲介
hunting for apartments through an agent

A How many rooms do you want?
你們想要找幾房的房子？

B Two bedrooms and one drawing room.
兩間臥房以及一間畫室。

A Do you have any floor preference?
你們有偏好住哪一層樓嗎？

B I prefer an apartment on the first floor.
我喜歡住在公寓的一樓。

A OK. I will show you a good apartment according to your requirements. Let's go.
沒問題，我帶你們看一間符合你們需求的公寓，走吧！

3 東西壞了找房東
complaining about broken facilities

A The water heater is not working properly.
熱水器沒辦法正常運作。

B I'll contact the plumber to have a look.
我會連絡水電工去看看。

A Could you please ask him to check on the air conditioner as well?
可不可以也請他看看冷氣呢？

B What about it?
冷氣怎麼了？

A It has been making a lot of noise recently.
最近常發出噪音。

Unit

12

出外靠租房

4 賀成交
making a deal

A The rent is reasonable and the location is ideal. I'll take it.
房租很合理，地點也很理想，我要租這間。

B Great! Let's sign the contract now. Do you have your ID with you?
太棒了！那就現在簽約吧，你有帶身分證嗎？

A Here you go. Let's take a few minutes to go over the lease, shall we?
在這裡。我們花個幾分鐘，瀏覽一遍合約，可以吧？

B Absolutely. And be sure to sign it.
當然沒問題，記得要簽名。

A Ok, will do.
好，會的。

主要關鍵句開口說

使出關鍵3句型，英文輕鬆開口說

Track 037

① **What's your favorite food?**
你最喜歡的食物是什麼？

② **Do you know how to cook?**
你會做菜嗎？

③ **I am on a diet.**
我正在節食。

沒果仁邏輯 Americans

句型解析與用法說明

說明① What's your favorite food句型

「What's+所有格+favorite+名詞」用於詢問某人最喜歡的東西為何。例：What's Mom's favorite casserole? 媽媽最喜歡的砂鍋是哪一個？/What's Jimmy's favorite NBA team? 吉米最喜歡的NBA球隊是哪一支？

說明② Do you know how to cook句型

「Do/does+人名 / 代名詞+know+how+to+原形動詞」是詢問某人是否知道如何做某事的問句。例：Does Joan know how to drive? 瓊知道怎麼開車嗎？/Do you know how to use a smartphone? 你知道如何使用智慧型手機嗎？

說明③ I am on a diet句型

人名 / 代名詞+is/are+on+a+diet，表示某人正在節食。on a diet這個片語有節制飲食之意，目的就是減重。

① **What kind of food do you like the most?**
你最喜歡什麼類型的食物？

② **Can you cook?**
你會做菜嗎？

③ **I am trying to lose weight.**
我在減肥。

這樣回答就對了　對應「主要關鍵句」的回答

① **My favorite food is Italian.**
我最喜歡義大利菜。

② **Of course I do!**
當然會啦！

③ **Try to stay away from junk food.**
請遠離垃圾食物。

 世界觀小補充

　　吃到好吃的東西就說Yum!，表示「真好吃！」難吃則說Yuck!或It's yucky. 民以食為天，各國都一樣。一天有相當比重的時間都花在飲食上，所以飲食成為文化中很重要的一部分，同時也是聊天的主要話題。如果歐洲人在中式料理的臭豆腐跟皮蛋上大做文章，無法理解這些奇臭無比又沒有賣相的料理為何受歡迎，那我們也可以了解一下為什麼歐洲的發霉起司還有臭掉的魚罐頭可以被拿來當做前菜。類似這樣的話題不僅能增加世界觀，同時也相當有趣。

Unit
13
烹飪家常料理

學校沒教的實用句

情境式主題句，學校沒有教，自己學起來！

Track 038

I have been cooking over ten years and can cook traditional Chinese food very well.
我煮菜的經驗超過十年，而且我擅長烹煮傳統中式料理。

There is a growing number of **vegetarians** around the world.
全球吃素的人口有逐漸增長的趨勢。　vegetarian 素食者

Rice is the **staple** food of more than half the world's population.
全球人口當中，有超過半數的人以白米為主食。　staple 主要的

Many youngsters love eating **junk food**.
很多年輕人喜歡吃垃圾食物。　junk food 垃圾食物

It is not good for your health to **skip** breakfast.
不吃早餐對身體不好。　skip 略過

Do you like food from other countries?
你喜歡來自其他國家的料理嗎？

It is not our **custom** to eat desserts after dinner.
我們沒有晚餐後吃甜點的習慣。　custom 習俗

It is quite **ordinary** for most Europeans to drink wine during meals.
對大多數歐洲人來說，吃飯配紅酒是很平常的事。　ordinary 通常的；平常的

I am so hungry that I could eat a horse.
我餓到可以吃下一匹馬。（意思是我餓壞了！）

My sister is **allergic** to seafood.
我妹妹對海鮮過敏。　allergic 過敏的

There are generally three to four courses in Western-style **cuisine**.
西餐通常包含三到四道菜餚。　cuisine 菜餚

First, there's an appetizer, then a salad, a soup of the day, a main course and a dessert to wrap it up.
首先有開胃菜，再來是沙拉、本日湯品、主餐，最後以甜點作結。

Margaret has been so obsessed with losing weight that she is now struggling with an eating disorder.

瑪格麗特太執著於減重，導致她現在患了飲食失調症。

In order to make this dish, you need to slice the onions, smash some garlic, cut the carrots in chunks and blanch the beef.

要做出這道菜，你必須先將洋蔥切絲、剁碎大蒜，將胡蘿蔔切塊，然後將牛肉以沸水燙過。

At home, my father is the main chef, whereas my mom the **sous chef**.

在家裡，我爸爸是主廚，我媽反而是副主廚。　　sous chef 副主廚

One of my birthday wishes is to eat at one of the Michelin-star restaurants in town.

我的生日願望之一就是可以在城裡的米其林餐廳用餐。

My brother likes to call for pizza delivery every weekend and asks for the same toppings every single time.

我哥哥每個週末都喜歡叫外送披薩，而且每次都點一樣的配料。

Let's go eat a spicy hotpot! It's on me!

我們一起去吃麻辣鍋吧！我請客！

Do you know that both Chinese and Italians make dumplings and that the ingredients and flavors differ greatly?

你知道中國人跟義大利人都會做餃子，但是使用的食材跟口味非常不一樣嗎？

Are you going to bring homemade cooking to a potluck lunch next week?

下週的百樂餐聚會，你會帶自家做的料理去嗎？(potluck是一種由參加者各自準備菜餚，並帶到指定地點的聚會。)

When I travel to a foreign country, I always eat at local diners or food stands because I think it's the best way to know the culture of a country.

當我到異地旅遊，我總是會嚐嚐當地的餐館或小吃攤，因為我認為這是認識當地文化最好的方式。

In some countries, animal organs are considered **delicacies**.

在某些國家，動物的內臟被視為佳餚。　　delicacy 美味；佳餚

Situation 1 美味關鍵
the key process

A Why is this dish tasteless?
這道菜怎麼淡而無味？

B I think the problem may be that you didn't marinate the pork.
我想問題出在你沒有先將豬肉滷過。

A Was that necessary?
這是必要的嗎？

B Yes. Through this process, you let the meat soak up the sauce, and it will unleash the entire flavor of the dish.
當然，經由這道手續，豬肉會吸收醬汁，而後將味道釋放於菜餚中。

A Alright, lesson learned.
好吧，學了一課。

 Situation 2 不可信的廚藝
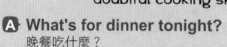 doubtful cooking skills

A What's for dinner tonight?
晚餐吃什麼？

B Whatever meal that you plan on making.
你打算煮什麼，我就吃什麼。

A Do you trust my cooking skills?
你信得過我的烹飪技術？

B I'm so done for the day. I'll eat whatever is put in front of me.
我今天超累，放在我眼前的我都吃得下去。

A In that case, let's order takeout.
這樣的話，我們叫外送好了。

Part ②

處理日常生活雜務

Situation 3 烹飪門外漢
joining a cooking class

A Do you want to join a cooking class with me?
你要不要跟我一起去上烹飪課？

B What do they teach?
他們會教些什麼？

A Well, just some basic stuff like how to cut and prepare ingredients, season them, and know the differences among frying, deep frying, steaming, grilling and so on.
這個嘛，就一些基礎的東西，像是如何切菜跟準備食材、調味，和分辨煎、炸、蒸、烤等料理方式。

B It's all Greek to me!
有聽沒有懂！

A Then you should definitely go with me!
那你更應該要跟我一起去啦！

Situation 4 烹飪課堂上
in the cooking class

A You are here today to learn basic cooking skills.
你們今天是要來學習基礎的烹飪技巧。

B Excuse me. What if I don't know how to peel or slice ingredients? Is this the place to be?
請問，如果我不會削皮或切食材，來這邊適合嗎？

A You've come to the right place.
你來這就對了。

B What if I also want to learn how to cook some French cuisine?
如果我還想要學法式料理呢？

A No rush. One step at a time.
別急，一步步來吧。

Unit 14 開心歡度節慶
Happy holidays

 主要關鍵句開口說

使出關鍵3句型，英文輕鬆脫口說

 Track 040

① **What holidays do you celebrate?**
你們會慶祝哪些節日？

② **What is the biggest holiday of the year in your country?**
你們國家一年之中最盛大的節日是什麼？

③ **Do you have a favorite holiday? What is it?**
你有最喜歡的節日嗎？是什麼節日？

沒果仁邏輯 Americans 句型解析與用法說明

 ① What holidays do you celebrate句型

「What+名詞+do/does+人名／代名詞+動詞」為基本句型，詢問某人對於某件事的做法或看法。例：What colors do you like? 你喜歡什麼顏色？／What language does he speak? 他會說什麼語言？

 ② What is the biggest holiday of the year in your country句型

What+is+the+形容詞最高級+名詞，詢問某物之最。例：What is the most expensive dish in this restaurant? 這間餐廳最貴的一道菜為何？

 ③ Do you have a favorite holiday句型

以Do或Does開頭的助動詞為Yes/no疑問句，即單純問對方是或不是。例：Do you go to work by bus? 你搭公車上班嗎？

沒果仁也愛的說法　▷ 對照「主要關鍵句」的類似說法

① **What are the major holidays in your country?**
你們國家的主要節慶有哪些？

② **Name one holiday that's emphasized in your country.**
說一個你們國家很看重的節日。

③ **What's your favorite holiday?**
你最喜歡的節日為何？

 對應「主要關鍵句」的回答

① **We celebrate Chinese New Year and Dragon Boat Festival.**
我們會慶祝中國新年和端午節。

② **It should be Chinese New Year.**
應該就是中國新年了。

③ **Yes. My favorite one is Valentine's Day.**
有啊，我最喜歡的是情人節。

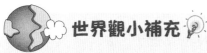 **世界觀小補充**

　　雖然很多節慶都全球化了，但各國間因為傳統、文化、宗教等因素，仍然保有各自的節慶。了解來自不同國家的節慶不僅可以增廣見聞，若有機會到該國遊歷，遇到特殊的節慶也不會大驚小怪。例如歐洲國家，在特定節慶前，糕餅店會推出一種叫「國王派」的甜品，這糕餅的由來與宗教節慶有關，是在慶祝耶穌誕生的主顯節時享用。除了品嚐，派餅裡還暗藏玄機。糕餅師傅會塞入陶製小瓷偶(fève)，吃到這個幸運物的人，就是當天的國王或皇后，意味這一整年都會很幸運！

學校沒教的實用句

情境式主題句，學校沒有教，自己學起來！

It's traditional in America to eat turkey on Thanksgiving Day, which usually falls on the last Thursday in November.

在十一月的最後一個星期四，感恩節當天吃火雞是美國的一項傳統。

Halloween is a holiday when adults dressed in costume attend parties and children knock on doors, yelling "Trick or treat!"

萬聖節是個大人變裝參加派對，而小孩敲門大喊「給糖不然就搗蛋」的節日。

Santa Claus and Christmas trees always come to mind when we talk about Christmas.

當我們提到聖誕節，就會想到聖誕老公公跟聖誕樹。

There are some traditions when celebrating Christmas. For example, decorating Christmas trees, unwrapping Christmas presents, kissing under the mistletoe and so many more.

慶祝聖誕節時總有一些傳統，像是佈置聖誕樹、拆聖誕禮物、在槲寄生下親吻等等。

Is there any special food connected with holidays in your country?

在你們國家，有什麼特殊的食物是和節慶有關的嗎？

Eating rice dumplings on Dragon Boat Festival is a Chinese custom passed down for centuries.

端午節吃粽子是流傳了好幾個世紀的中國習俗。

How do you usually **celebrate** Chinese New Year?

你通常怎麼慶祝中國新年？　　celebrate 慶祝

People get together and have family reunion dinner on Chinese New Year's Eve.

中國人在除夕夜的時候都會團聚，一起吃年夜飯。

On the day before Chinese New Year, parents give children red envelopes with money inside.

中國新年的前一天，父母親會發裝有壓歲錢的紅包給小孩。

Dining out on Valentine's Day is such a rip-off that I refuse to conform.

在情人節外出吃飯簡直就是被敲竹槓，因此我拒絕盲從。

Part ② 處理日常生活雜務

Are holidays approved by the government in your country, or are they based on traditions?

節慶在你們國家是經由政府允許，還是依據傳統而訂？

I couldn't care less about some holidays. I think they are way too commercialized.

我對於某些節慶真的再無感不過，我覺得它們都被操作得太商業化了。

I have mixed feelings about Chinese New Year. I like the festive atmosphere but don't like the weight I put on.

我對新年的感覺很複雜，我喜歡節慶的氣氛，但不喜歡變胖的結果。

We now celebrate some holidays that have come from other countries, such as Valentine's Day, Halloween, Christmas and so on.

我們現在會慶祝一些外來的節慶，例如西洋情人節、萬聖節、聖誕節等。

Does Mother's Day fall on the second Sunday of May in your country as well?

你們國家的母親節也是在五月的第二個禮拜天嗎？

I love singing Christmas songs and saying greetings to people during Christmas holidays.

我愛在聖誕佳節唱聖誕歌曲，並向人們傳遞祝福。

There's no school and work on most of the **national holidays** in Taiwan.

台灣大部分的國定假日都放假。　　national holiday 國定假日

Don't you think that the New Year countdown should be considered a world holiday now that people from around the world celebrate in similar fashion?

你不覺得新年倒數應該要成為一個全球共同的節慶嗎？畢竟世界各地的人都以類似的方式在慶祝。

I would rather stay indoors than be stuck in traffic during holidays.

假日期間，我寧願待在室內也不想塞在車陣中。

According to a recent survey, one of the least desired gifts on Mother's Day is cake.

根據一項最近的調查，媽媽們在母親節最不希望收到的禮物之一就是蛋糕。

Easter, one of the religious holidays, is to celebrate the resurrection of the Lord, Jesus Christ.

宗教節日之一的復活節，是為了要紀念耶穌復活的那一天。

Situation 1 不想一人過節
spending holidays with family

A How will you celebrate this coming Chinese New Year?
你打算怎麼過即將來臨的新年？

B I'm flying back to the States.
我要飛回美國。

A Why is that?
為什麼？

B Most of my relatives are there, so it would be lonely to stay here all by myself.
我大部分的親戚都在那邊，所以我一個人待在這邊會很寂寞。

A That's very true.
這倒是。

Situation 2 單身情人節
spending Valentine's Day alone

A What's your plan today?
你今天有什麼計畫？

B Am I supposed to have one?
我應該要有嗎？

A Well, just asking. It's Valentine's Day!
只是隨便問問，今天是情人節啊！

B Whatever. I am so going straight home after work. I can't bear seeing all the love birds on the street.
隨便啦，我今天下班後鐵定要直接回家，我受不了看到街上成對的閃光。

A Poor you. Here, hope my homemade chocolate can cheer you up.
可憐蟲，來，希望我親手做的巧克力能讓你開心點。

Situation 3 月餅節流變
food on Mid-Autumn Festival

Ⓐ Is there any special food you eat on Mid-Autumn Festival?
你中秋節會吃什麼特別的食物嗎？

Ⓑ Traditionally, we eat moon cake, which is a kind of Chinese pastry.
傳統上，我們會吃一種叫做月餅的中式甜點。

Ⓐ Does the younger generation follow the tradition?
年輕一輩的也照著傳統嗎？

Ⓑ No. Having a BBQ on Mid-Autumn Festival has become a trend.
沒有，中秋節烤肉已經變成年輕一代的主流趨勢。

Ⓐ Sounds like fun!
聽起來很有趣！

Unit
14

開心歡度節慶

 Situation 4 萬聖節變裝
costume ideas for Halloween

Ⓐ I am going to dress up as Spider-Man on Halloween. And you?
我萬聖節要裝扮成蜘蛛人，你呢？

Ⓑ I still haven't decided.
還沒決定。

Ⓐ It's only three days away. You have to come up with something.
只剩三天了，你得要想出些什麼才行。

Ⓑ Help me! I haven't got the slightest idea.
快幫幫我！我一點主意都沒有。

Ⓐ Since you are below-average height, I think dressing up as a Hobbit shouldn't take too much effort.
既然你身高偏矮，我想你裝扮成哈比人應該不會太費力。

Unit 15 參加派對
Attending parties

 主要關鍵句開口說

使出關鍵3句型，英文輕鬆開口說

 Track 043

① **I will dress up for the party tonight.**
我將為今晚的派對盛裝打扮。

② **Who is invited to the party?**
有誰受邀參加派對呢？

③ **Should I bring anything to the party?**
我該帶些什麼去參加派對嗎？

 沒果仁邏輯 Americans

句型解析與用法說明

 說明① **I will dress up for the party tonight句型**

dress up for=為了某個場合盛裝打扮。例：She dressed up for the blind date. 她為了這次相親盛裝打扮。

說明② **Who is invited to the party句型**

be invited to=受邀至某場合，例：Debby was invited to an international conference last week. 黛比上週受邀參加一場國際會議。

 說明③ **Should I bring anything to the party句型**

bring something/anything to=帶某樣東西去某地方，Should I 用來詢問他人的建議。例：Should I bring my boyfriend to your wedding reception? 我該不該帶我男友去參加你的婚禮呢？

① I will dress nicely for the party tonight.

我將為今晚的派對特別打扮。

② Who else is going to the party?

還有誰會去派對？

③ What should I bring to the party?

我該帶什麼去派對呢？

這樣回答就對了 　對應「主要關鍵句」的回答

① Me, too. I'm so excited!

我也是，真是太令人興奮了！

② I have no idea. The only guest I know is you.

不清楚，我認識的賓客就只有你了。

③ No. The hostess said in particular that all guests should come empty-handed.

不用，女主人特別說客人要兩手空空地去。

 世界觀小補充

　　歐美人很愛舉辦各種主題的派對，從好萊塢電影的劇情中便可略知一二。派對不僅是年輕人或學生的活動，社會人士也透過派對與他人進行交流、認識新朋友。有慶祝喜獲新生兒(baby shower)、新居落成或喬遷(house warming)、升遷(promotion)、生日等等的派對，也有正式的酒會、雞尾酒宴會(cocktail party)等。除非活動前有特別指定服裝(dress code)，一般而言，美國人都會盛裝打扮。若有機會參加，千萬不要穿著居家服就前去了。

學校沒教的實用句

情境式主題句，學校沒有教，自己學起來！

Part 2

處理日常生活雜務

Who is going to throw a **birthday party** for Rita?
誰要幫芮塔辦慶生派對？　　birthday party 生日會

I am not going to send out any **invitations** for the party this time.
這次派對我不會發任何邀請函。　　invitation 請帖

R.S.V.P. at the end of an invitation stands for "Please reply" in English.
邀請函最後的R.S.V.P.在英文裡代表「請回覆」的意思。

Tom is thinking about a simple BBQ party at his backyard to celebrate his promotion.
湯姆想要在他家後院辦一個簡單的BBQ派對，來慶祝他的升遷。

John partied hard in his college years and now he seldom goes to parties.
約翰在大學時期玩得很瘋，現在他很少參加派對了。

Are you going to invite a DJ to this party or haven't you thought about it yet?
你這次派對有打算邀請DJ嗎？還是你根本還沒想過這件事？

You have to invite Jason. He's always the life of the party, and he keeps things exciting.
你一定要邀請傑森，他是派對的開心果，能炒熱氣氛。

I'd like to invite you to my **house warming** party this weekend.
我想邀請你來參加我這週末舉辦的新居落成派對。　　house warming 慶祝喬遷聚會

I'd love to go, but I already have another appointment on that day. Terribly sorry!
我很想去，但是我那天已經有約了，真的很抱歉！

We're having Ted's birthday party this Saturday at 8:00 at my house.
本週六八點開始，我們會在我家舉辦泰德的生日趴。

Please make yourself at home.
請別拘束，就當自己家吧。

Track 044

Are you a party starter, goer or pooper?
你是一個派對主辦人、參加者還是砸派對的人？

I am not attending if it's a "BYOB" party. (BYOB=Bring your own bottle)
如果這是一個「請自備飲料」的派對，我就不去了。

The dress code for the party is polka dot. Try to think outside the box, guys!
這次派對的服裝主題是「點點風」。各位，請盡情發揮創意吧！

Throwing a potluck party isn't as simple as I expected. As an organizer, you have to plan ahead and assign dishes to the guests.
舉辦一個百樂趴並沒有想像中容易。身為主辦人，你必須事先規劃好，分派每位客人該準備的料理。

Sarah even made a **to-do list** for the party she is going to hold this month.
莎拉甚至還為這個月要舉辦的派對列待辦清單。　　to-do list 執行表

You could create a beverage stand with a variety of drinks where guests can help themselves.
你可以設置一個飲料檯，上面放有各種飲料讓賓客自助飲用。

Julie considered making a big barrel of fruit punch the night before the party.
茱麗考慮要在派對前一晚製作一大桶水果酒。

I want to show off my new house and also get a chance to meet my new neighbors by throwing a house warming party.
我想要辦個新居落成派對，秀一下我的新住所，也可藉機認識新鄰居。

As the host of Mary's baby shower, I am carefully selecting the guests and making name tags for all of them.
身為瑪麗的準媽媽派對主辦人，我很小心地挑選賓客名單，並為每一位客人製作名牌。

I am going to a bridal shower, but I still have no idea what kind of gift I should buy for the bride.
我準備去參加準新娘派對，但是我還沒想到要買什麼禮物給準新娘。

What do you say we plan a surprise party for Mom's coming birthday?
我們來為媽媽即將到來的生日規劃驚喜派對吧？

Part ② 處理日常生活雜務

Situation 1 音樂美食趴
attending a party

🅐 **Are you going to the party on Saturday?**
你會參加週六的派對嗎？

🅑 **I am still thinking about it. Are you?**
我還在考慮，你呢？

🅐 **Yeah, I heard it's going to be a lot of fun. This party is going to have a DJ, food, and drinks.**
我會去，聽說會很好玩。這次的派對有DJ，也會提供食物跟飲料。

🅑 **Really? That does sound like fun. What time does it start?**
真的假的？聽起來的確很好玩，幾點開始？

🅐 **It starts at 8:00, and I really think you should go.**
八點開始，我真的覺得你一定要去。

Situation 2 邀請來同樂
inviting friends to a party

🅐 **Listen, I'm going to have a party this Saturday. Would you like to come?**
聽著，我週六要辦一場派對，你想來嗎？

🅑 **Oh, I'd love to go. Who's going?**
喔！我當然要去，有誰會去啊？

🅐 **A number of people haven't told me yet. But, Peter and Mark are going to help out with the cooking.**
有些人還沒回覆我，不過彼得跟馬克會幫忙料理食物。

🅑 **Hey, I'll help, too!**
嘿，我也要幫忙！

🅐 **Would you? That would be great!**
你也要來嗎？那太好了！

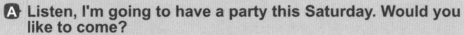

Situation 3 出席確認
confirming guests

A It's Dan. I just received the invitation to your party.
我是丹，我剛剛收到你的派對邀請函。

B Can you make it?
你能來嗎？

A Well, let's see. It's next Saturday night, right? Should I bring anything?
我看看，下星期六晚上對吧？我要帶什麼東西去嗎？

B Just yourself.
人來就好。

A Fantastic! I'll be there.
太好了！我會到。

Situation 4 規劃派對
planning a party

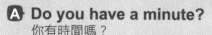

A Do you have a minute?
你有時間嗎？

B Sure, what's it about?
當然，什麼事？

A It's about Kathy's bridal shower. I had made a guest list, and I think we should go over it and see if everything's in order.
是關於凱西的準新娘派對。我擬了一張賓客清單，我想我們應該看一遍，確定事情都已安排妥當。

B I'd love to, but what could possibly go wrong?
我很樂意，不過，會有什麼不妥的安排嗎？

A Anything could happen!
任何事情都有可能發生！

Part
2

處理日常生活雜務

 主要關鍵句開口說

使出關鍵3句型，英文輕鬆開口說

 Track 046

① **Do you have a driver's license?**
你有駕照嗎？

② **Do you drive a manual or an automatic car?**
你是開手排車還是自排車？

③ **John got into a car accident last night.**
約翰昨晚發生車禍。

沒果仁邏輯 Americans 句型解析與用法說明

說明
① **Do you have a driver's license句型**

「Do/does+人名／代名詞+have+名詞」為詢問某人有沒有某物的問句。
例：Does your sister have any sense of humor? 你妹有沒有一點幽默感
啊？/Do they have enough food? 他們有足夠的食物嗎？

說明
② **Do you drive a manual or an automatic car句型**

Do/does+人名／代名詞+drive+名詞，詢問對方駕駛哪一類的交通工具，
大多是在問車子。(註：manual car手動排檔車／automatic car自動排檔車)
例：Does your boyfriend drive a Mercedes? 你男友開賓士車嗎？

說明
③ **John got into a car accident last night句型**

「人名／代名詞+get(依時態變化)+into+某件事情」表示某人跟後面的事情
扯上關係。例：Albert got into a street fight last night. 艾伯特昨晚被捲入街
頭惡鬥。

① **Do you know how to drive a car?**
你會開車嗎？

② **Is your car a stick shift or automatic?**
你的車是手排還自排？

③ **John hit a car that stopped in front of him.**
約翰撞到停在他前方的車子。

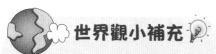

這樣回答就對了　對應「主要關鍵句」的回答

① **Yes, I do. I've had one since I turned eighteen.**
我有，我從滿十八歲那年就有駕照了。

② **I drive an automatic.**
我開自排車。

③ **Is he alright and what about the people in the other car?**
他還好吧？另外一車的人也還好吧？

🌍💭 **世界觀小補充** 💡

　　在美國，年滿16歲就可以報考路考，比台灣法定的18歲還要年輕。美國路考的項目跟台灣也有所不同，我們所謂的倒車入庫在美國來說就不需要成為必備的考試項目，因為美國幅員廣大，住家通常為獨棟建築，有自己的車庫，停車只需要直角轉入車庫。而路邊停車(parallel parking)倒是跟我們一樣列為考試項目。其他的轉彎(make a turn)、變換車道(switch lanes)、打方向燈(signal)等基礎路考也都相去不遠。

Part 2

處理日常生活雜務

My friend bought an SUV the other day and invited us for a road trip around Taiwan.

我朋友買了台修旅車，並邀請我們環島。

Buckle up and let's **hit the road**.

繫好安全帶，準備上路。　　hit the road 上路；出發

If there are no traffic lights, I never stop at a zebra crossing even if there are people waiting to cross.

如果沒有交通號誌，即使有行人等過馬路，我也絕不停在斑馬線後方。

Running through a red light may cost you a fortune if you get caught.

如果你闖紅燈被逮到，罰鍰可是很重的。

Driving under the **influence** is not allowed here in Taiwan.

在台灣，酒駕是被禁止的。　　influence 影響；作用

You will run the risk of having your driver's license **revoked**.

你會冒著被吊銷駕照的風險。　　revoke 撤銷；廢除

People in Japan drive on the left side of the road whereas people in Taiwan do the opposite.

在日本，大家開車都靠左側的路上，在台灣則是相反的。

You were driving on the wrong side of the road.

你開錯邊了。

Have you heard that there's no **speed limit** on highways in Germany?

你知道德國的高速公路沒有速限嗎？　　speed limit 速度限制

Is this a **rental** car?

這是租賃的車嗎？　　rental 收取租金的

You were driving too fast.

你剛才開得太快了。

She went over the speed limit and was **pulled over** by the police.

她的車速超過速限，被警察攔了下來。　　pull over 把…開到路邊

You're driving the wrong way on a **one-way** street.

你在單行道上逆向開車。　　one-way 單行道的

You were traveling too close to the car in front of you.

你開的離前車太近。

You cut off another car.

你超了其他車。

Ken's car broke down and he was **stranded** on the side of the road.

肯的車子壞了，所以只好先擱在路邊。　　stranded 擱淺的

Duncan's **personality** changes every time he is behind the wheel.

鄧肯只要一握到方向盤，就變了個人。　　personality 人格；個性

Do you know how to change a tire on your car?

你知道怎麼換車子的輪胎嗎？

Amy **slammed** on the brakes before she almost ran over a dog.

愛咪在差點碾過一隻狗之前緊急踩下煞車。　　slam 猛推

There are special devices on the market that can detect the location of speed cameras.

現在市面上有特殊的儀器可以偵測出測速照相機的位置。

A truck **flipped over** on the highway and caused a traffic jam.

一輛卡車在高速公路翻覆，造成交通堵塞。　　flip over 翻轉

I had a **flat tire** and couldn't start my engine. I needed to have my car towed.

我輪胎爆胎，而且無法發動車子，我需要找人來拖吊。　　flat tire 爆胎

Step on it! Don't you feel annoyed that the car behind you is **tailgating**?

快加速！你不覺得後面那台車貼那麼緊很煩嗎？　　tailgate 緊跟著前車行駛

This man in a coma was the victim of a **hit-and-run**.

這位昏迷的男人是那場肇事逃逸車禍的受害人。　　hit-and-run 肇事逃逸

Your license expired three months ago.

你的駕照已經逾期三個月了。

Unit
16
行車安全與意外

Part ② 處理日常生活雜務

Situation **1** 酒駕付出代價
zero tolerance for drinking and driving

Ⓐ **Can I see your driver's license, please?**
我可以看看你的駕照嗎？

Ⓑ **Here you go, officer. May I ask why you pulled me over?**
警官，請看，我可否請問你為何攔下我嗎？

Ⓐ **Have you been drinking tonight, Mr. Davidson?**
你今晚是不是有喝酒，戴維遜先生？

Ⓑ **I had one or two drinks. I'm okay to drive, though. I know my limit.**
是有喝一兩杯，但我還可以開車，我知道自己的酒量。

Ⓐ **I'm afraid that we have zero tolerance for drinking and driving.**
很抱歉，酒後駕車是被禁止的。

Situation **2** 路考
the road test

Ⓐ **Good morning. Let's see how you start your vehicle.**
早安，我們來看看你如何發動車子。

Ⓑ **Okay, I'm done.**
好了。

Ⓐ **Good job. Now, tell me how you leave the curb.**
相當好。現在，告訴我你要怎麼開出車道。

Ⓑ **First, I need to turn my head and look back for passing cars. Also, I need to signal before entering traffic.**
首先，我必須轉頭確認有無往來車輛，開出車道前，還必須打方向燈。

Ⓐ **Very nice! It's a good start.**
非常好！這是個很好的開始。

₃爆胎這樣做
dealing with a flat tire

A Oh, boy, I think we have a flat tire.
哇，我覺得輪胎好像爆了。

B What should we do? Do you think we can make it to the nearest exit?
我們該怎麼辦？你覺得我們有辦法撐到最近的匝道出口嗎？

A I think we need to pull over on the shoulder.
我覺得我們得要停靠在路肩了。

B And what next?
那接下來呢？

A Then we call the towing service.
接下來就連絡拖車服務囉。

Unit
16
行車安全與意外

₄養車花費大
the expenditure on a car

A It's time again for my car's regular tune-up.
又到了我保養車子的時間了。

B I just had mine. I have to say that having a car is like raising a kid.
我才剛保養過我的，我必須要說，養車跟養小孩一樣。

A I couldn't agree with you more.
非常認同。

B In order to cut down on car maintenance expenses, I do some basic car maintenance myself.
為了要節省車子的保養費，我會自己做一些基本的保養。

A Same here. I buy engine oil from retailers and change my oil and filter on my own.
我也是，我會跟零售商購買機油和燃料過濾器，自行更換。

主要關鍵句開口說

使出關鍵３句型，英文輕鬆開口說

Track 049

① **How's the weather today?**
今天天氣如何？

② **It looks like it's going to rain.**
看起來快要下雨了。

③ **What kind of weather do you like?**
你喜歡什麼樣的天氣？

沒果仁邏輯 Americans 句型解析與用法說明

說明① **How's the weather today句型**

How is the weather是詢問當下天氣狀況的基本問句；「How was the weather+過去時間」則在詢問過去某個時間點的天氣狀況。

說明② **It looks like it's going to rain句型**

It looks like it's going to+天氣狀況的動詞，表示說話者經由天色等因素判斷天氣將有什麼變化，因為除了專業氣象分析師，一般人談起天氣皆屬臆測，因此常會以It looks like(看起來像是)開頭。例：It looks like it's going to clear up. 看起來天氣要放晴了。

說明③ **What kind of weather do you like句型**

「What+kind+of+名詞」表示詢問者想了解種類，後面接疑問子句。例：What kind of exercise do you usually do? 你平常都做什麼樣的運動？／What kind of girls does John like? 約翰喜歡什麼類型的女生？

106

沒果仁也愛的說法

對照「主要關鍵句」的類似說法

① **How is it today?**
今天天氣如何？

② **It is cloudy.**
天色烏雲密佈。

③ **What's your favorite weather?**
你最喜歡的天氣為何？

 這樣回答就對了

對應「主要關鍵句」的回答

① **It's cloudy today.**
今天是陰天。

② **No surprise. It's the rainy season.**
不驚訝，現在是雨季。

③ **I like it when it's warm and sunny.**
我喜歡溫暖又晴朗的天氣。

世界觀小補充

　　無論是在歐美或世界各地，天氣一直是最好用的破冰話題。不熟識的人剛見面，沒什麼共通點可以聊，就拿天氣來做文章。就像有名的戲劇大師Oscar Wilde(王爾德)所說："Conversation about the weather is the last refuge of the unimaginative."(天氣相關的對話是缺乏話題者的最後一個避難所)，可見天氣的話題有多重要。不涉及個人隱私，不論男女老少都可以問，所以熟記幾句常用的天氣對話句，對於日常會話將大有幫助！

學校沒教的實用句

情境式主題句，學校沒有教，自己學起來！

Beautiful day, isn't it?
今天天氣很棒，對吧？

Can you believe all of this rain we've been having?
這陣子下不停的雨是不是令人難以置信？

It sure would be nice to be in Hawaii right about now.
此刻若可以在夏威夷，就太棒了。

I hear they're calling for **thunderstorms** all weekend.
我聽他們說整個週末都會有暴風雨。 　thunderstorm 大雷雨

We couldn't ask for a nicer day, could we?
這天氣真是再好也不過了，對吧？

Lovely day!
好棒的天氣！ 　lovely 美好的；令人愉快的

It's **turned out** nice again.
天氣又轉好了。 　turn out 結果成為

Terrible weather, isn't it?
這天氣真糟，對吧？

I hear it'll **clear up** later.
我聽說天氣晚點就會轉晴。 　clear up 放晴

I cannot imagine life without air-conditioning in summer in Taiwan.
我無法想像在台灣夏天沒有冷氣的日子。

What's the average low temperature in Taiwan?/It's approximately ten degrees Celsius.
台灣最低溫平均幾度？/ 大概是攝氏10度。

We have not had any rain for several weeks.
我們這裡已經好幾個星期沒下雨了。

I didn't expect any thunderstorm this afternoon and didn't bring an umbrella when I went out.

我沒料到今天下午會有暴雨，所以出門沒有帶傘。

It was **pouring** rain and Jessie was soaking wet.

因為這場傾盆大雨，潔西全身都溼透了。　　pour 傾注；倒；灌

Isn't it a beautiful day for a walk?

今天真是個適合散步的好天氣！

What's the **weather forecast** for the rest of the week?

這整週的天氣預報為何？　　weather forecast 氣象預報

They're saying we will have blue skies for the rest of the week.

他們說本週剩下的幾天會是大晴天。

It's going to rain by the looks of it.

這天色看起來像是要下雨了。

We're in for **frost** tonight.

今天晚上的溫度會冷到結霜喔。　　frost 霜

They're **expecting** snow in the north.

他們預期北邊會下雪。　　expect 預期⋯可能發生

I hear that showers are coming our way.

我聽說不久後就會下陣雨。

The sun's trying to **come out**.

太陽嘗試著探出頭。　　come out 露出；出現

It finally decided to rain!

終於天降甘霖啦！

What strange weather we're having!

最近的天氣真的很奇怪！

Cold and gloomy weather makes me depressed.

又冷又陰暗的天氣讓我感到沮喪。

I heard **a cold front** is approaching soon.

我聽說會有冷鋒接近。　　a cold front 冷鋒面

Situation **1** 一起去海邊
good beach weather

A It would be nice to go to the beach sometime this weekend.
這週末找時間去海邊應該很好。

B What's the weather going to be like? I may want to go, too.
天氣如何？我可能也想去走走。

A The weather this weekend is supposed to be warm.
這週末的天氣應該很溫暖。

B Will it be good beach weather?
會是個好的沙灘日嗎？

A I think it will be.
我覺得會喔！

Situation **2** 颱風快消失吧
a severe typhoon on the way

A The weatherman on tonight's news said a powerful typhoon will lash Taiwan soon.
晚間新聞的氣象播報員說即將會有強大的颱風侵襲台灣。

B I am looking forward to a day off.
我好期待颱風假。

A You should be worrying about heavy rain, flooding, and possible landslides!
你應該要擔心豪雨、淹水跟可能發生的土石流吧！

B You're right. Let's hope it changes its course then.
你說的對，那希望它轉向。

A I hope it vanishes into thin air.
我希望它徹底消失。

3 惡性循環
a vicious circle

A Don't you think it's getting hotter in summer here in Taiwan?

你不覺得台灣的夏天愈來愈熱嗎？

B I wonder if it's because of global warming.

我在想是不是因為全球暖化的關係。

A Most definitely. Global warming has caused gradual increase in the average temperature of the Earth's atmosphere.

八九不離十，全球暖化已經造成地球大氣層的平均氣溫升高了。

B Even if I were willing to save energy and create less pollution, I couldn't survive without air conditioning.

即便我很想要節約能源跟減少污染，但不開冷氣的話，我根本撐不下去。

A It's a vicious circle.

這是惡性循環。

Unit

17

變化多端的天氣

4 會咬人的風
freezing wind outside

A It's freezing cold out there.

外面冷得刺骨。

B I think it's minus five degrees Celsius.

我覺得這是零下五度的天氣。

A Are you sure you're going for a run right now?

你確定要在這種天氣出去跑步？

B I'll put my hi-tech windbreaker on.

我會穿上我的高科技防風外套。

A Be careful! The wind in this season bites!

小心點！這季節的寒風可是會咬人的！

18 到酒吧放鬆心情
Buying booze in a bar

 主要關鍵句開口說

使出關鍵3句型，英文輕鬆開口說

 Track 052

① How about going for a drink after work?
下班後去喝一杯如何？

② When is Happy Hour at XYZ bar?
XYZ酒吧的暢飲時間是幾點？

③ Hi, there, what can I get you today?
嗨，今天要點什麼飲料？

沒果仁邏輯 Americans 句型解析與用法說明

 說明
① How about句型

當說話者提出建議、邀約活動，想詢問意見時可用How about開頭，後面直接加上提議內容，可以用現在分詞(V-ing)或名詞。

說明
② When句型

When為詢問時間的疑問詞。跟What time相比，When可問時間、星期、月份、季節、年份等。舉例：When will you be coming home? 你什麼時候回家？/I'll be home at 20:00. 我晚上八點到家，或I'll be coming home this winter. 我今年冬天會回家。

 說明
③ What can I get you句型

在餐飲店點餐時，店員常使用的句型之一。get在這裡表示提供／準備之意。當餐廳服務生提出這問題時，可直接敘述要點的內容。

Part **②** 處理日常生活雜務

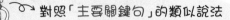

① Let's go get a drink.
去喝一杯吧。

② Are there any discounts on the drinks from 4 to 7 p.m.?
飲料下午四點到七點有沒有折扣？

③ Can I take your orders?
可以幫你們點了嗎？

這樣回答就對了　對應「主要關鍵句」的回答

① Sure, let's go.
當然好，走吧。

② No idea. We can ask around.
不清楚，我們可以問問。

③ I'd like a beer and a whisky on the rocks, please.
我要一杯啤酒跟一杯威士忌加冰塊。

 世界觀小補充

　　歐美人士也有下班後小酌的文化。在美國，很多餐廳、酒吧為了拉攏客人增加生意，推出了特定時段的酒精飲品半價促銷活動Happy Hour(暢飲時間)。在早期，這個特殊的促銷時段通常在週五下午接近下班時間到晚餐前，讓上班族開始「暖身」進入週末的歡樂氣息。不過，愈來愈多餐飲業者為了刺激消費，已經將Happy Hour推廣得淋漓盡致，從飲品衍伸到特定餐點。總之，往後若有機會到美國遊玩，看到標示著Happy Hour的招牌，不妨趁機撿便宜！

Part ② 處理日常生活雜務

🖊 What a day! **What do you say** we go out for a drink?

好累的一天！我們去喝一杯如何？　　what do you say 你覺得…怎樣？

🖊 **Awesome!** I could use a drink!

太棒了！我需要喝一杯。　　awesome 很好的

🖊 I'd like a cocktail/a beer/a Scotch.

我要一杯雞尾酒 / 啤酒 / 蘇格蘭威士忌。

🖊 What kinds of wine do you have?

你們這邊有什麼種類的紅酒？

🖊 **Cheers!** Here's to us!

敬我們！　　cheers 大家乾杯！

🖊 I spent too much money on wining and dining this month.

我這個月花太多錢在吃喝上面了。

🖊 He was short and fat, with a large **beer belly**.

他又矮又胖，還有著大大的啤酒肚。　　beer belly 啤酒肚

🖊 All the beers are **on the house** tonight.

今晚所有啤酒都由本店招待。　　on the house 店家招待

🖊 We have stout, ale, draft, bitter, and light beers.

我們有黑麥啤酒、麥芽啤酒、生啤酒、苦啤酒跟淡啤酒。

🖊 Let's go hit the club that opened last week.

我們去上禮拜開幕的那間夜店吧。

🖊 It's ladies' night tonight, meaning free **entry** for ladies.

今晚是淑女之夜，所有女性可免費入場。　　entry 入場

🖊 I feel a bit **tipsy**.

我有點微醺了。　　tipsy 微醉的

🖊 What I need now is nothing but a drink.

我現在最需要的就是一杯酒。

📝 "**Bartender**, a glass of Chardonnay, please."

「酒保，請給我一杯白葡萄酒。」　bartender 酒保

📝 I want some beer. Make it a **pitcher**.

我想要喝啤酒，來個一壺好了。　pitcher 水壺

📝 Let's make sure who's going to be the **designated driver** before we go to the bar tonight.

今天晚上我們去酒吧前，先確定誰要負責開車吧！　designated driver 指定司機

📝 Drink with **discretion**. I hope you know your limit.

謹慎飲酒，希望你清楚自己的酒量。　discretion 謹慎

📝 John was drunk with only a shot of tequila and a **chaser**.

約翰只喝了一小杯龍舌蘭跟一杯淡酒精就醉了。　chaser 飲烈酒後喝的飲料

📝 I don't drink. Do you offer any kind of non-alcoholic **beverages**?

我不喝酒，你們有提供不含酒精的飲料嗎？　beverage 飲料

📝 It's free entry for anyone wearing a mini-skirt tonight.

任何穿迷你裙的人今晚入場一律免費。

📝 That guy over there is seriously **wasted**.

那邊的那傢伙已經醉得不成樣了。　wasted 喝醉的

📝 You'll get drunk easily if you mix drinks.

如果你混酒喝，很容易就醉了。

📝 The **wine list** is on the second page of your menu.

酒單在菜單的第二頁。　wine list 酒類一覽表

📝 All the drinks are half price during **happy hour**.

所有的飲料在暢飲時間內都半價。　happy hour 快樂時光(酒類促銷時段)

📝 Would you like to order anything off the **appetizer** menu?

你想要在開胃菜單裡點些什麼嗎？　appetizer 開胃菜

📝 People who are under age 18 are not allowed to hang out at bars.

未滿十八歲的人不能進酒吧。

Part ② 處理日常生活雜務

Situation 1 光顧新酒吧
hitting the bar

🅐 Good evening, Sir. What would you like to drink today?
先生晚安，今天想要喝點什麼？

🅑 Do you have any Belgian beers?
你們有賣比利時啤酒嗎？

🅐 You have come to the right place! We happen to have a great selection.
你來對地方了！我們正好有些上選。

🅑 Then I'll have a Stella Artois.
那給我來瓶時代啤酒吧。

🅐 Sure. Coming right up!
好的，馬上來！

Situation 2 催酒
drinking to elevate the mood

🅐 Bottoms up!
乾杯！

🅑 Dude, slow down! It's not water you're drinking.
老兄，喝慢點！你又不是在喝白開水。

🅐 I had a bad day. I need this.
我今天過的不順，我需要這樣喝。

🅑 Alright then. Here's to a better tomorrow!
好吧，那就敬明天會更好！

🅐 That's the spirit!
沒錯，就是要這樣！

Situation 3 在酒吧約會
dating in a bar
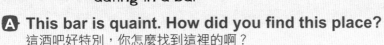

A This bar is quaint. How did you find this place?
這酒吧好特別，你怎麼找到這裡的啊？

B I saw the ads on Facebook and thought we might as well check it out ourselves.
我在臉書看到廣告，想說乾脆我們一起來看看。

A (Flipping through the menu) And the price is fairly reasonable.
(翻菜單的同時)而且價錢也相當合理。

B Let me buy you a drink first while you decide on the appetizers.
那我先幫你點杯飲料，你就慢慢決定開胃菜要點什麼吧。

A You're the sweetest!
你最好了！

Situation 4 酒吧一隅的窘境
making a scene in a bar

A OK, I think you've had enough.
好了，我覺得你該停止了。

B What? No!!! It's still happy hour. Let's carry on!
什麼？不行！現在還是暢飲時間，繼續喝吧！

A Listen to yourself! You're stone drunk! It's midnight.
看看你！你醉了吧！都已經半夜了。

B Seriously?! I'm not feeling well...
真的嗎？我不太舒服…

A Let's get you a cab.
我幫你叫台計程車吧。

Unit 19 換髮型換心情
Getting a new hairstyle

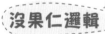

主要關鍵句開口說

使出關鍵3句型，英文輕鬆開口說

Track 055

① **Did you get a haircut?**
你剪頭髮了嗎？

② **How would you like your hair cut?**
你想要剪什麼樣的髮型？

③ **What do you want to do with your hair?**
你想要怎麼用你的頭髮？

沒果仁邏輯 ·····Americans 句型解析與用法說明

① Did you get a haircut句型

「Do/did+人名 / 代名詞+get+受詞(名詞)」用來詢問某人是否得到或拿到某樣東西。例：Did you get your transcripts? 你拿到成績單了嗎？剪頭髮get a haircut是特別值得一記的生活片語。

② How would you like your hair cut句型

「Would+人名 / 代名詞+like+to+動詞」表示某人想做某事的意圖，使用How開頭則用來詢問某人想要用什麼方式達成某樣事情。例：How would you like your steak cooked? 你的牛排想要幾分熟？

③ What do you want to do with your hair句型

「What+do/does+人名 / 代名詞+want+to+動詞」為詢問他人想做什麼事情時用的句型。例：What does he want to eat on his birthday? 他生日的時候想要吃什麼？

沒果仁也愛的說法

對照「主要關鍵句」的類似說法

① **Did you have your hair cut?**
你把頭髮剪了嗎？

② **What kind of hairstyle do you want?**
你想要什麼樣的髮型？

③ **What can I do for you today?**
今天可以幫您做什麼呢？

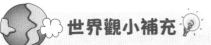

這樣回答就對了

對應「主要關鍵句」的回答

① **Yes. You noticed!**
是啊！你注意到了。

② **I only want a trim.**
我只想簡單地修剪一下。

③ **I want to perm and color my hair.**
我想要燙髮跟染髮。

🌏 世界觀小補充 💡

　　美國的美容院跟台灣的差不多，通常需要透過電話預約。在非面對面的電話預約中，會簡單地提到日期及需要的服務項目，等到約定當日抵達現場，才會進一步跟設計師細談想要的髮型。另外，美國也有很多複合式的美容店，同時提供美髮與美甲的服務，所以透過下頁的實用句一併了解足部跟手部的美甲單字，可以大致了解服務項目，以免不小心選到自己不想要的服務。

學校沒教的實用句

情境式主題句，學校沒有教，自己學起來！

I made a reservation at the **hair salon** I usually go to.
我在常去的那家美容院預約了時間。 `hair salon 美容院`

Do you have a regular hairdresser, or should we **assign** one for you?
你有指定的美髮師嗎？還是我們幫你選定一個？ `assign 指派`

I have had my hair long and **curly** for the past five years and feel like a change now.
我留長捲髮已經五年了，現在想要改變。 `curly 捲髮的`

Melody cut her hair short because she can't stand the summer heat.
美樂蒂因為無法忍受夏天的酷熱而把頭髮剪短。

Do you think I would look okay with **bangs**?
你覺得我留瀏海適合嗎？ `bang 前瀏海`

What kind of female hair style is most **trendy** this year?
哪一種女性髮型今年最流行？ `trendy 時髦的；流行的`

We discussed the **hairstyles** with the hairstylists first, and then we had our hair shampooed.
我們先跟設計師討論髮型，然後才去洗了頭髮。 `hairstyle 髮型`

The hairstylist will usually wash my hair, towel dry it, and comb my hair out before starting to cut my hair.
設計師通常會先幫我洗頭、用毛巾擦乾、梳理整齊後才開始剪頭髮。

One of the best things about going to a hair salon is that we can have our heads massaged and enjoy the newest treatments on the market.
去美容院最棒的事情之一就是可以享受頭皮按摩跟市面上最新的美髮產品。

The salons in my neighborhood also offer other services, from massages and pedicures to manicures and nail art.
我家附近的美容院也提供其他服務，從按摩、足部護理一直到美甲護理、美甲藝術都有。

Do you want your nails done?
你想要做指甲嗎？

What color of **nail polish** would you like?

你想要擦什麼顏色的指甲油？　　nail polish 指甲油

Are you in for a hair cut or a **perm**?

你想要剪還是燙頭髮？　　perm 燙髮

Do you want to color your hair today?

你今天想要染頭髮嗎？

Making an appointment is generally recommended, but not required because they take people on a first-come, first-serve basis.

基本上，建議你先打電話預約，但並非必要，因為他們採取先來先服務的機制。

I usually ask my hairdresser to cut a little off the top and sides, and trim off any split ends.

我通常會要求我的理髮師修剪我的髮尾，並修掉分岔。

Jerry only wanted a trim, so he went down to a barber shop near his place.

傑瑞只想要修剪一下頭髮，所以他去家裡附近的理髮院。

Can you cut about two inches off the length?

你可否剪掉大約兩吋的長度？

I want one inch off the top and the sides shaped.

我想要剪掉一吋上面的頭髮，並將側邊頭髮剪出個型。

Can you layer my hair?

可否幫我頭髮打層次？

I would like a **straight** perm today.

我今天想要離子燙。　　straight 平直的

Can you color my hair to brown?

可否幫我把頭髮染成咖啡色？

Can you **thin out** my hair a little bit?

可否幫我把頭髮打薄一點？　　thin out 變稀薄

In addition to paying at the front desk, Claire always tips her hairdresser because she is always satisfied with her new look.

除了去櫃檯結帳，克萊兒總會給設計師小費，因為她對新造型總是很滿意。

Unit

19

換髮型換心情

關鍵一句模擬實境對話
Topic-related Conversations

以關鍵句破題的模擬實境對話

Track 057

Situation 1 急需剪髮
asking for a haircut

A I need to get my haircut. Do you have any openings today?
我需要剪髮，你們還有空出來的時間嗎？

B Do you have a regular hairstylist?
你有指定的設計師嗎？

A No. Any hairdresser will do.
沒有，任何一個都可以。

B If that's the case, you can come anytime you want.
若是這樣的話，你隨時可以過來。

A Great, I'll come right over.
太好了，我這就過去。

Situation 2 新造型
getting a new look

A I like your new look!
我喜歡你的新造型！

B Is it that obvious? I just had my hair cut.
這麼明顯嗎？我才剛剛剪了頭髮。

A You look good in short hair.
你剪短髮很適合。

B Are you sure I'm not looking weird?
你確定看起來不會很怪嗎？

A Take it easy. You look fabulous!
放輕鬆，你看起來很棒！

Situation 3 救星出手
rescuing a bad haircut

A I'm in desperate need of your help.
我急需你的幫忙。

B Wow. You do look like it.
哇，你看起來的確很需要。

A I got this very bad haircut while traveling. Look at these excessive layers!
我出國玩的時候剪壞了頭髮，你看看這些過度的層次！

B I'll curl your ends toward your face to add volume. You'll look great.
我會將髮尾朝臉部內捲，增加厚度，你看起來會很美的。

A You're my savior!
你真是我的救星！

Unit 19
換髮型換心情

Situation 4 美容院服務
in the hair salon

A Morning. What would you like to do with your hair today?
早安，你今天想要怎麼用你的頭髮？

B I'd like to have it trimmed and a straight perm.
我想要稍微修剪，然後離子燙。

A Got it. So how much do you want to cut off your hair?
知道了，你想要剪多少？

B Just within an inch would be enough.
一吋以內就夠了。

A OK. Let me get you a glass of water first.
好的，我先幫你倒一杯水。

Unit 20 護膚美容保養
Treat yourself to a facial

主要關鍵句開口說

使出關鍵3句型，英文輕鬆開口說

Track 058

① **I have a facial once a month.**
我一個月做一次臉。

② **Have you ever had a massage?**
你有給人按摩過嗎？

③ **What kind of service do you have here?**
你們這邊提供哪些服務？

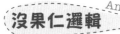沒果仁邏輯 句型解析與用法說明

說明① **once a month用法**

表達頻率的用語。once一次、twice兩次、three times三次、four times四次以此類推。頻率once a day/week/month/season，分別表示一天一次、一週一次、一個月一次以及一季一次。

說明② **Have you ever句型**

此為現在完成式，用以詢問某人是否曾經有過後述的經驗。例：Have you ever been to Japan? 你曾經去過日本嗎？

說明③ **What kind of句型**

What kind of+名詞，詢問的重點在哪一類，後面接完整疑問句。例：What kind of food do you like? 你喜歡吃什麼樣的食物？/What kind of music is your mother interested in? 你媽對什麼樣的音樂感興趣？

Americans

沒果仁也愛的說法　　對照「主要關鍵句」的類似說法

① **I go to a beauty parlor every month.**
我每個月去一次美容院。

② **Have you tried a massage before?**
你以前有試過按摩嗎？

③ **What kind of treatment do you have here?**
你們這邊有什麼療程？

這樣回答就對了　對應「主要關鍵句」的回答

① **Does it cost much?**
做臉會很貴嗎？

② **No, I've never had one.**
不，我從沒給人按過。

③ **We have massage, facials, aromatherapy and sauna.**
我們這邊提供按摩、做臉、芳香療法跟桑拿(蒸汽浴)的服務。

🌐 世界觀小補充 💡

　　美容業隨著時代演變，項目跟內容五花八門。在美國，按摩跟一些精油療法對美國人來說算是舶來品。早期所謂的美容院療程，也就是當地俗稱的facial，大多侷限在臉部的清潔保養。日後因為美容業發展趨於規模化，歐美都加上法規的限制。美容院也逐漸搭配了健康療養概念，納入精油等芳香療法，有spa等新增項目。時代演變至今，還有將微整形也納入的護膚保養，因此衍生出更多與美容相關的用詞。

Part ② 處理日常生活雜務

Do I have to make a reservation **in advance**?
我需要先預約嗎？　　in advance 預先

I try to go for a massage and a **facial** once a month.
我試著每個月做一次按摩跟臉部保養。　　facial 臉部美容

We have traditional Thai massage, oil massage, body scrub, and facial massage with aromatic oil.
我們這裡提供傳統的泰式按摩、精油按摩、身體磨砂(去角質)、使用芳香精油的臉部按摩等服務。

What kind of service are you interested in?
你對什麼樣的服務感興趣呢？

Do you do **body wrapping** here?
你們有提供身體裹敷嗎？　　body wrap 身體裹敷(一種身體美容療程)

We offer a Thai body herbal wrap, tomato-and-honey body wrap, detox body wrap, and seaweed body wrap.
我們提供泰式草本裹敷、蕃茄跟蜂蜜裹敷、排毒身體裹敷以及海藻身體裹敷。

What does a body package include?
請問身體套組包含什麼內容？

It includes a body scrub, body massage, herbal sauna and body wrap.
有包含身體磨砂(去角質)、全身按摩、草本沐浴以及身體裹敷。

A nice massage can **relieve** stiffness and help improve your blood flow.
好的按摩可以減輕僵硬，並促進血液循環。　　relieve 緩和；減輕

Oil massage is a kind of aroma therapy. The aromatic oil can help you relax, and it reduces stress.
精油按摩是一種芳香療法，芳香精油可以幫助你放鬆，並減緩壓力。

The herbal sauna helps open your pores and thus release toxins. The body scrub improves blood circulation and removes dead cells.
草本沐浴能打開你的毛孔，進而排出毒素。身體磨砂促進血液循環並去除角質。

The body wrap warms up your body and boosts the **release** of body toxins.

身體裹敷溫熱你的身體，並加速身體毒素的釋放。 release 釋放

Body and facial massage help rid you of your muscle tension. You will feel totally relaxed.

身體與臉部按摩能去除肌肉緊繃的狀態，你將會感到通體舒暢。

First, you'll have to take a shower and put on the clothes we prepared for you. Remember to take off your watch and jewelry.

首先，你需要淋浴並穿上我們為你準備的衣服，記得要脫手錶跟珠寶。

Be careful not to eat a heavy meal before the session.

切記不要在療程之前吃大餐。

護膚美容保養

You should drink a glass of water before the sauna and another glass of water after the service.

你應該要在桑拿(蒸汽浴)之前喝一杯水，結束之後再喝一杯。

Wait about one hour before taking a shower. This is to let your body absorb the effects of the treatment.

要等一個鐘頭之後再洗澡，這是為了要讓身體吸收療程的效果。

The price will be 15% off if you pay for the annual package.

如果您購買一年份的服務，我們將替您打85折。

I can guarantee you a 5% discount if you pay in cash.

如果您付現，我可以給您5%的折扣。

The beautician used some herbal mask on her face to purify her **pores**.

美容師在她臉上使用草本面膜來淨化她的毛細孔。 pore 毛孔

The session will begin in three minutes. Please relax and feel free to give us some feedback.

療程將在三分鐘後開始，請放鬆，歡迎隨時向我們反應。

The **masseuse** will start to massage your head and then go all the way down to your toes.

按摩師將會開始按摩你的頭部，並一路按到腳指頭。 masseuse 女按摩師

I like having aromatherapy because it makes my skin glow.

我喜歡芳香療法，因為它會讓我的皮膚發亮。

關鍵一句模擬實境對話 *Topic-related Conversations*

以關鍵句破題的模擬實境對話

 Track 060

Situation **1** 抓住青春的尾巴
asking about facial treatment

A My facial skin is becoming loose. Can you suggest some treatment for it?
我的臉部皮膚有點鬆垮，可不可以建議我一些療程？

B Sure! We do have some facial treatments that will tighten your skin.
當然沒問題！我們的確有一些臉部的療程可以緊緻您的肌膚。

A Are these treatments safe?
這些療程安全嗎？

B Don't worry. We only use certified and tested products.
別擔心，我們只使用檢驗合格並經過認證的產品。

A Great. When can I start?
太棒了，我什麼時候可以開始？

Situation **2** 耳根子軟的客人
buying a treatment package

A What does this promotional package include?
這個促銷的組合包含什麼？

B It includes body scrub, essence oil massage, manicure and pedicure.
包含身體磨砂、精油按摩、手部跟足部護理。

A It does sound like a bargain.
聽起來蠻划算的。

B Yes, it does! And the promotion will end this week.
沒錯！而且促銷活動只到這禮拜喔。

A Make sure I get one, please!
我要買一份！

Part **2** 處理日常生活雜務

Situation 3 做臉時間
facial appointment

A Welcome to ABC Beauty Parlor. How can I help you?
歡迎來到ABC美容院，有什麼可以幫您服務的？

B My name is Vicky Chang. I made a reservation the other day.
我叫做張薇琪，我前幾天有打電話預約。

A Oh, yes. You are having a facial today.
喔是的，您今天要做臉。

B How long does it normally take?
通常要做多久？

A It takes about an hour.
大約一個鐘頭。

Situation 4 按摩服務
massage therapy

A Hello, Madame. Have you ever tried Thai therapy before?
夫人您好，您有試過泰式療法嗎？

B No. It's my first time.
沒有，這是我初次嘗試。

A Before we begin, there's something you need to know in advance.
在我們開始之前，有件事先要告訴您。

B Ok, I'm listening.
好的，我在聽。

A If you feel pain or any uncomfortableness, please feel free to let me know.
如果您感到疼痛或有任何不適，請不用客氣，隨時讓我知道。

Part 3

小資族的職場
生活甘苦談

主要關鍵句開口說

使出關鍵3句型，英文輕鬆開口說

Track 061

① **I am looking for a job.**
我正在找工作。

② **Do you know if there are any job openings?**
你知道有任何職缺嗎？

③ **How's the job hunting going?**
工作找得怎麼樣呢？

沒果仁邏輯 Americans 句型解析與用法說明

① **I am looking for a job句型**

look for＝尋找。找工作通常會是一段時間持續進行的動作，所以動詞用現在進行式來表示。

② **Do you know if there are any job openings句型**

Do/Does+人／代名詞+know+if+子句＝詢問某人對於後述的狀況了不了解。例：Does Mom know that you are not coming home for dinner? 媽媽知不知道你晚上不回家吃飯？

③ **How's the job hunting going句型**

How+be動詞+人／事+going用來詢問、關心某人或某事的狀況如何。例：How is John doing? 約翰最近還好嗎？/How are the marketing campaigns going? 行銷活動辦得如何？

沒果仁也愛的說法　Americans

對照「主要關鍵句」的類似說法

① **I'm trying to find a job.**
我正試著找工作。

② **Do you know if the company is hiring?**
你知不知道那間公司有沒有在徵人？

③ **Have you landed a good job yet?**
你找到好工作了嗎？

這樣回答就對了

對應「主要關鍵句」的回答

① **I am not trying to scare you, but the unemployment rate has reached the highest point these days.**

我不想嚇你，不過這陣子的失業率才創了新高。

② **Not that I am aware of.**
就我所知是沒有。

③ **I've just posted my resume online.**
我才剛在網站上登錄了我的履歷。

世界觀小補充

　　各國就業前的求職過程大同小異，找尋工作的管道也差不多。而找工作最重要的工具之一——個人履歷，要多花心思撰寫。著名的求職網站如Beyond.com，資訊量豐富，如果你想尋找一份新工作，想綜合評估某個職位，該網站會提供全面的資訊。由於美國人很重視求職者的實際能力，建議可在履歷表中多著墨求學時期的活躍程度，包含是否積極參與團體活動、領導特質或實際的企業實習經驗等，會比單純描述身家背景與教育過程的自傳來得吸引人。

學校沒教的實用句

情境式主題句，學校沒有教，自己學起來！

Part ③ 小資族的職場生活甘苦談

Finding the **ideal** job often takes a lot of research and patience.
找到理想工作之前，會花不少時間尋找，要有耐心。　　ideal 理想的；完美的

Diana just graduated this summer, and she eagerly asked her family and friends to tell her who might work for companies that are presently hiring.
黛安娜這個夏天剛畢業，她積極地詢問家人和朋友所在的公司是否有在徵人。

Looking in the local newspaper under the classified ads to see if there are any job postings is considered old-fashioned nowadays.
在地方報紙刊登的分類廣告找職缺現今已被視為老派的作法了。

Attending job fairs held at colleges or conventions might provide leads to job openings.
參加學校所辦的校園博覽會可能取得應徵職缺的機會。

I've sent out about thirty resumes and gone to four interviews so far this month.
我這個月目前已經送出三十份履歷，並去了四家公司面試。

How long have you been **looking for** a new job?
你找新工作找多久了？　　look for 尋找

I am a fresh graduate and I am worried that I won't be **qualified** for many opportunities.
我是社會新鮮人，真擔心自己不符合很多機會的標準。　　qualified 合格的

I think I am qualified for all the requirements of the **job description** posted on this website.
我認為這網站所列的應徵條件我都符合。　　job description 工作說明

Sam is looking for a job in the **IT** industry.
山姆在找跟資訊產業有關的工作。　　IT=information technology 資訊科技

The government has set up a job hunting unit for assisting the **unemployed** to get a job.
政府成立了求職小組來協助失業者找工作。　　unemployed 失業的

I have connections with a guy who works for a computer company, and

he might be able to pull a few strings and line you up with an interview.
我認識一個在電腦公司上班的人，他或許能夠幫忙牽線，幫你安排面試。

Are there many good job **vacancies** in your company?
你公司有沒有好的職缺呢？　　vacancy 空缺

Do you often check the jobs ads in newspapers or on the Internet?
你通常是透過報紙還是網路找職缺？

It is getting harder for fresh graduates to locate a job because of the dwindling opportunities in the job market.
對於社會新鮮人來說，要找到工作愈來愈難，因為就業市場一直萎縮。

My sister has sent dozens of resumes to different companies and is now anticipating getting some replies.
我妹已經寄出十幾份履歷表給不同公司，現在正在等候回音。

Some companies require a certain amount of experience and others are willing to train.
有些公司要求一定的相關經驗，而有些則願意訓練新人。

Jamie has been looking for a job for over a month on his own, and now he is turning his head towards some recruiting agencies.
傑米已自行找了一個多月的工作，現在他轉向一些徵才機構尋求協助。

I've always wanted to **apply for** a job as a publicist.
我一直都想應徵公關人員這個職位。　　apply for 申請

"Hello, I'm answering the advertisement for a sales assistant that was in the China Post. Could you please tell me who I should speak to about it?"
你好，我打來詢問有關在中國郵報上刊登業務助理一職的廣告。請問我應該要找哪位洽詢？

The moving company is advertising for several truck drivers.
搬家公司現正招募數名卡車司機。

In order to get ahead in job hunting, I need to go over my resume several times and make sure there are no typos and errors.
為了成功求職，我必須檢查履歷表很多次，確定沒有拼錯字或其他錯誤。

Any fresh graduate is welcome to apply for this **position**.
我們歡迎所有應屆畢業生來應徵這個職位。　　position 職位

Situation 1 求職ING
job hunting

A So how's the job hunt going?
工作找得如何？

B I have gone to five interviews so far.
我已經去面試過五次了。

A Wow! You're on a roll! Any word from that consulting job for the cosmetics company?
哇！你很有進度啊！上次那個化妝品公司的顧問職缺回覆你了嗎？

B Not yet. They said they'd get back to me, but I haven't heard from them.
還沒耶，他們說會通知我，但到現在都還沒有任何消息。

A Well, make sure you follow up. It shows initiative.
總之記得主動詢問，展現你的積極態度。

Situation 2 非走不可
looking for a better job

A Do you know if there are any job openings?
你知道有任何職缺嗎？

B No, Why? Did you leave your last job?
不清楚，為什麼問這個？你離職了？

A Yes. My boss treated me badly, and I didn't like my chances for advancing in the company.
嗯，我老闆對我很不好，而且我不看好在那邊升遷的機會。

B That's too bad.
太糟了。

A Please keep your eyes open for me.
麻煩請幫我多注意了。

Situation **3** 電話詢問職缺
asking for job vacancy information

A Hi, my name is Joe Smith. I've learnt there's a vacancy for a sales executive in your company.
您好，我叫做喬·史密斯。我得知貴公司有一個業務主管的職缺。

B That's right. We are looking for an experienced salesperson.
是的，我們在找有經驗的業務人員。

A Sounds good. I have got four years of sales experience.
聽起來很棒，我有四年的業務經驗。

B Great! What sort of products have you sold?
太好了！你之前販售什麼樣的商品？

A I've sold computers.
我賣電腦的。

Situation **4** 來電約面試
calling to set up an interview

A Hello. Is that Mr. Mark Anderson?
您好，請問是馬克·安德森先生嗎？

B Yes. May I ask who's calling?
是的，請問你是？

A I am calling from ABC Corp. You've applied for a job with us. We received your resume.
我這裡是ABC公司。您有來應徵本公司的職缺，我們收到你的履歷。

B Oh yes! I am interested in your vacancy for a computer programmer.
對！我對貴公司電腦工程師的職缺有興趣。

A Can you come in for an interview?
您可以來見個面談一談嗎？

Unit 22 面試決勝負
Job interview

Part ③ 小資族的職場生活甘苦談

主要關鍵句開口說

使出關鍵３句型，英文輕鬆脫口說

Track 06A

① **I am here for my interview.**
我是來這裡面試的。

② **Can you tell us about yourself?**
你能自我介紹一下嗎？

③ **How much do you know about our company?**
你對我們公司了解多少？

沒果仁邏輯

Americans
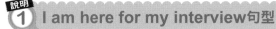
句型解析與用法說明

說明① **I am here for my interview句型**

人名／代名詞+be動詞+here+for+某活動／事件＝某人是為了某活動／事件來此。例：Will is here for free beers. 威爾是為了免費啤酒來的。

說明② **Can you tell us about yourself句型**

Can+人名／代名詞+tell+受詞+about+人／事／物＝詢問某人是否能夠對另一對象說明某事件。例：Can this Gypsy woman tell me about my future? 這個吉普賽女郎可以預知我的未來嗎？

說明③ **How much do you know about our company句型**

How+much+do/does+人名／代名詞+know+about+人／事／物＝詢問某人對於某事了解的程度。使用How much代表之後所接的人／事／物是一種不可數的「概念」。例：How much do you know about Claire's extramarital affairs? 你對克蕾兒外遇的事情知道多少？

① **I have an appointment for an interview today.**
我今天有預約面試。

② **Can you introduce yourself?**
你能不能自我介紹？

③ **Do you know what our company does?**
你知道我們公司是做什麼的嗎？

這樣回答就對了 對應「主要關鍵句」的回答

① **Take a seat. The interviewer will be here shortly.**
請稍坐一會兒，面試官馬上就會來了。

② **I have a master's degree in computer science.**
我是資訊工程碩士。

③ **Your company has been in the leading position in the industrial design industry.**
貴公司一直都引領工業設計業界的潮流。

世界觀小補充

　　無論是東方文化，還是西方文化，建立良好的第一印象很重要，因此儀容要依場合調整。由於各國的文化國情不同，在面試不同國家的企業時，要注意的細節以及強調的個人優勢也有所差異。例如到日商公司應徵時，請針對自己的履歷、儀表檢視，並強調自己嚴謹、負責任的個性；若是美商，除了英文履歷上要多加著墨實際經驗之外，面試時若能落落大方、言之有物，則有加分的效果。

學校沒教的實用句

情境式主題句，學校沒有教，自己學起來！

To prepare for a job interview, the most important thing to do is to make sure you know the company and what **services** or products it provides.
準備面試最重要的一環，就是要確定你了解這家公司的主要業務，以及公司在販售的商品。
`service 服務`

Focus on being relaxed. Don't forget to smile, shake hands and be genuinely interested in what their company is about.
注意要放鬆心情，別忘了微笑、握手並真誠地對他們的公司感興趣。

Showing calmness and modesty during a job interview helps you make a great impression.
面試時展現出鎮定及謙遜的態度可以幫你的第一印象加分。

Dressing up as a professional for any job interview demonstrates that you take the job seriously.
在面試時穿著正式服裝能展現出你認真看待這份工作的態度。

Are you most interested in a good, steady job with benefits or one that will allow you to quickly advance?
你對於穩定、福利佳的工作最有興趣，還是一份可以讓你迅速升遷的工作？

I really appreciate the opportunity to **interview** for this position.
我對於能夠面試這份工作感到相當感激。
`interview 面試`

Do you feel that you are exceptionally **good at** anything in particular?
你覺得你在哪方面特別有優勢？
`good at 精於；擅長`

I think I have a pretty good understanding of the job. I believe that I can handle it **with ease**, and I hope to have the opportunity to work for you.
我認為我對這份工作有相當程度的了解，相信我可以輕鬆勝任，希望能有機會為您工作。
`with ease 容易地；從容地`

Can you tell me something about yourself?
你可否談談你自己？

What do you **know about** our organization?
你對於我們的組織有什麼樣的認知？
`know about 知道關於…的情形`

I have a bachelor's degree in English Literature, and I am hoping to find a job in which I could make the full use of the language.

我有英國文學的學士文憑，希望做一份能發揮我文學專才的工作。

What can you do for us that someone else can't?

有哪些事情是別人做不到，唯獨你能替我們辦到的？

I am proficient in three different languages, and I have nothing but enthusiasm to do the job well.

我精通三國語言，而且我對於把工作做好有著強烈的熱誠。

Though I may be a fresh graduate with no work experience, I am passionate about learning new things.

雖然我是沒有任何工作經驗的社會新鮮人，但我對於學習新事物充滿熱情。

Your resume suggests that you may be over-qualified or too experienced for this position. What's your opinion?

你履歷上的經驗非常豐富，來應徵這份工作有點大材小用，你覺得呢？

I am confident in my managerial **potential** because I am a good listener and can always put myself in others' shoes.

我對於我的管理潛力很有信心，因為我很善於傾聽，總是能將心比心。

potential 潛力

I have over ten years of experience in this field, and I think you will like what my references have to say about me.

我在這領域有超過十年的經驗，而且我認為你會喜歡我的推薦人對我所下的評語。

My long-range goal is to achieve an executive position and to lead a team of my own.

我的長期目標是做到管理階級，並能夠領導屬於我自己的團隊。

May I ask you how much this position pays per year?

可否請問這職位的年薪是多少？

Do you have any **practical** experience in teaching?

你在教書這方面有任何實務經驗嗎？　　practical 實際的

Thanks for your interest in this job. We'll be **getting back to** you.

謝謝你對這份工作有興趣，我們會再與你聯絡。　　get back to 再與…電話聯絡

Situation **1** 面試問題
interview questions

A Good morning. Thank you for the interview.
早安，謝謝安排面試。

B No problem. Now, do you prefer working with others or flying solo?
不會。那麼，請問你偏好團隊合作還是單打獨鬥？

A Actually, I enjoy both.
其實兩種我都喜歡。

B Would you be able to relocate?
你能接受外派嗎？

A I am open to relocating.
我對外派抱持接受的態度。

Situation **2** 面試前的閒聊
a little chat before the interview

A Good morning. I am here for my interview.
早安，我是來面試的。

B Hello, nice to meet you. Did you have any trouble finding the place?
很高興認識你，這邊會不會很難找？

A No problem.
沒問題的。

B How did you get here?
你怎麼來的呢？

A I go everywhere with public transportation. I'm used to commuting.
我出門都搭乘大眾運輸工具，很習慣通勤。

Part **3** 小資族的職場生活甘苦談

Situation 3 反問面試官
asking the interviewer questions

A May I ask you how much this position pays per year?
可否請問這個職位的年薪是多少？

B This job pays sixty-five thousand dollars per year.
這份工作的年薪是六萬五千美元。

A What kind of benefits does this job have?
這份工作有提供什麼福利嗎？

B This job provides full medical, dental, and disability.
這份工作提供完整的醫療和勞工保險。

A Thanks for the details.
謝謝提供詳盡資訊。

Situation 4 面試改期
rescheduling an interview

A Hello, may I speak to Mr. Cheng?
你好，請問鄭先生在嗎？

B Yes, this is he.
我就是。

A I am calling from Market Corp. You have an interview scheduled with us for the 5th.
這裡是市場公司，你跟我們約在五號面試。

B Yes, I know. I will be there as required.
我知道，我會依照指定時間抵達。

A Well, I am sorry, but we need to shift it to the 6th. You see, the person who is supposed to interview you will be out of town.
很抱歉，我必須跟你改到六號，因為你的面試官那天剛好出差。

主要關鍵句開口說

使出關鍵３句型，英文輕鬆開口說

Track 067

① **It's my first day at work.**
今天是我第一天上班。

② **Welcome aboard!**
歡迎加入！

③ **Let me show you around the office.**
我來帶你參觀一下公司。

沒果仁邏輯
Americans

句型解析與用法說明

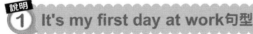

說明 ① It's my first day at work句型

It's+所有格+first+day+地點＝某人在人生新階段的第一天。通常指的是求學、工作等的新階段。例：It's Todd's first day at school and he is very nervous. 今天是陶德第一天上學，他非常緊張。

說明 ② Welcome aboard句型

aboard本意指的是「在船／飛機／火車上」，Welcome aboard表示歡迎搭乘本船次／航班／車次等。在新成員加入公司組織時使用，引申有「歡迎加入我們」的意思。

說明 ③ Let用法

Let(使役動詞)+人名／受格+原形動詞，注意後方的動詞一定要使用原形。例：Let us finish this together! 讓我們一起來完成這事吧！

沒果仁也愛的說法

Americans

對照「主要關鍵句」的類似說法

① **Hello, I am new here.**
嗨，我是新來的。

② **Pleased that you are here.**
很高興你能來。

③ **I'll give you a tour of our facility.**
我帶你看一下公司的設施。

這樣回答就對了

對應「主要關鍵句」的回答

① **Looking forward to working with you.**
很期待與你共事。

② **Thanks! It's an honor to be here.**
謝謝！能來這裡是我的榮幸。

③ **I really appreciate it!**
真的很感謝！

世界觀小補充

　　新進員工的職前訓練，不但可幫助新進員工熟悉公司運作及明瞭其工作的職責，更可使員工產生一種被重視和被尊重的感覺，因而能改變員工的思維以及工作習慣。職前訓練常用orientation一詞，有認識方位之意，即協助新進人員認清自己所在之位置及工作。新進人員職前訓練(Orientation Training, O.T.)被視為是教導(indoctrination)或指導訓練(induction training)，通常由人力資源部門介紹各種職位所承辦的業務、福利政策和運作程序。

Track 068

Part **3** 小資族的職場生活甘苦談

Let me take you to your cubicle and then you can get familiar with the environment.
讓我帶你去你的位子，然後我再帶你熟悉環境。

A senior colleague gave me a tour of our office so that I would know my way around here.
資深同事帶我參觀了辦公室，好讓我了解這裡的環境。

Although the first day of work really is more about listening, you can and should ask questions when necessary.
雖然第一天上班主要是在聽人介紹，不過你可以、也應該要在必要的時機發問。

Try to get to the office fifteen minutes earlier than you're supposed to on your first day of work.
第一天上班，建議你比公司規定的上班時間再早到十五分鐘。

Don't get too stressed out on your first day and remember to relax so that you can optimize your productivity.
第一天上班不用太過緊張，記得要放鬆心情以將自己的產能最大化。

First impressions matter, so please wear a smile on your face every time you meet new people in the office.
第一印象相當重要，所以在辦公室看到新面孔時請面帶微笑。

No need to try too hard to **impress** people.
沒有必要為了要讓人印象深刻而過於做作。　　impress 給…極深的印象

First of all, you'll need to report to the **Human Resources** Department.
首先，你要向人資部門報到。　　human resources 人力資源

Your **supervisor** is the one with grey hair who is now sitting in his corner office.
你的主管是那位坐在大辦公室的灰髮男子。　　supervisor 監督人

Do I need to **clock in** and out?
我上下班需不需要打卡？　　clock in 打卡上班

Do I need to stay in the office all day or do I get to go out and about?

我需要一整天待在辦公室，還是要常常出去跑？

Use your lunch hours to get together with your co-workers.
利用你的午休時間與同事相處。　　lunch hour 午餐時間

Don't complain about your boss, your office mates, any other co-workers, or your previous job.
不要抱怨你的老闆、你的辦公同仁、任何同事或你之前的工作。

Keep a positive attitude and an open mind. Your life has changed, and it will take time getting used to.
保持樂觀的態度及開闊的心胸。你的生活改變了，需要花點時間去適應。

Continue to arrive at work early and don't rush out the door at the end of the day.
保持上班準時，並且不要在第一時間趕著下班。　　rush out 衝出

Figure out who has the authority to give you work to do and who is just trying to have you do their work.
想清楚誰有權限交派工作給你，而誰是想利用你幫忙做他的工作。

You should also pay attention to the clothing and appearance on the first day of work.
第一天上班你也應該要注意服裝儀容。　　pay attention to 注意；關心

I notice that the fax machine and the copier are in the next room, aren't they?
我注意到傳真機跟印表機在隔壁房間，對吧？

Don't hesitate to come to me if you encounter any questions.
如果你遇到任何問題，不要遲疑，馬上來問我。　　hesitate 躊躇；猶豫

The best thing anyone can do in the first few days of a new job is listen and observe.
一位新進員工到職的前幾天，最重要的事情是傾聽與觀察。　　observe 觀察

It is highly suggested that you put your cell phone on silent to show you are 100% attentive.
強烈建議你把手機關靜音，表示你對工作的專注程度百分百。

Try to mingle with your peer group by being friendly and approachable.
試著表現出友善跟平易近人的態度，以融入公司的同儕。　　peer 同輩；同事

Unit **23** 新進菜鳥訓練

關鍵一句模擬實境對話
Topic-related Conversations

以關鍵句破題的模擬實境對話

Track 069

Situation 1 辦公室文具申請
ordering office supplies

A Excuse me. I was wondering how to order office supplies.
不好意思，我想知道該如何申請文具。

B We have a requisition form on the company website. What type of supplies do you need?
公司網站有線上的申請表格，你需要什麼樣的文具？

A I need paper, ink cartridges, and paper clips.
我需要紙、墨水匣以及迴紋針。

B How quickly will you need your supplies?
你多快需要這些東西？

A I need all of my supplies right away.
我馬上就要了。

Situation 2 新人報到的寒喧
first day at work

A Good morning, Mr. Lake.
雷克先生，早。

B Good morning, Ms. Green. Welcome to your first day in our company. Joanna will introduce you to the team.
格林小姐，早，歡迎加入本公司。喬安娜將會向團隊介紹你。

A Thank you very much, Mr. Lake.
謝謝你，雷克先生。

B Glad to have you on our team.
很高興本團隊多了你一員生力軍。

Ⓐ Hi, I'll be assisting you with your training assignment.
你好，我會協助你進行訓練工作。

Ⓑ Hi, nice to meet you. So where should we start?
很高興認識你，我們該從哪裡開始呢？

Ⓐ Well, you've got to learn about our practices. We have rules for everything in this company, you know.
你要先了解我們的執業方式。公司裡的每個環節都有規矩的，知道嗎？

Ⓑ Oh. That's interesting.
喔，挺有趣的。

Ⓐ Don't worry. I am just talking about the rules for handling customers. We like to make sure that our customers are happy here.
別擔心，我是在說我們對於處理客戶都有一套規矩，我們希望能確保客戶的滿意度。

Unit

23

新進菜鳥訓練

Ⓐ Could you show me the accounting department?
可否請你告訴我會計部怎麼走？

Ⓑ Sure. Are you new here?
當然，你是新來的嗎？

Ⓐ I've just joined as the payroll clerk. I need to meet the CFO.
我才剛加入擔任發放薪資的人員，我需要拜見財務長。

Ⓑ Well, it's good that I ran into you here. I am the CFO.
那我在這邊遇到你還真好，我就是財務長。

Ⓐ Really? Nice to meet you, Sir.
真的？很高興見到您，長官。

主要關鍵句開口說

使出關鍵3句型，英文輕鬆開口說

Track 070

① Hello, this is Susan Chang calling.

你好，我是張蘇珊。

② Thank you for calling ABC Corp. Carol speaking. How can I help you?

感謝您來電ABC公司，我是凱倫。請問您需要什麼協助呢？

③ May I speak with Mr. Wang, please?

請找王先生。

沒果仁邏輯 Americans 句型解析與用法說明

說明① this is _____ calling句型

說明是誰來電要用This is開頭，而非I am或 My name is。因為通電話時只聞其聲不見其人，所以用I am表明來電者不恰當。

說明② _____ speaking句型

人名+speaking的作用在向電話另一端的聽話者告知現在講電話的人是誰。例：Nathan speaking. 我是奈森。

說明③ May I speak with Mr. Wang, please句型

若受話者並非要找的對象，或聽不出來對方是否為要找的對象，又或者想禮貌性地開場時，可使用此句型指名欲通話的對象。回答時可用This is he/she. What's it about? 我就是，有什麼事嗎？

沒果仁也愛的說法

對照「主要關鍵句」的類似說法

① **Hello, it's Susan Chang.**
嗨，我是張蘇珊。

② **You've reached ABC Corp. How may I be of help to you?**
這裡是ABC公司，能幫您什麼樣的忙呢？

③ **Would Mr. Wang be available?**
王先生方便講電話嗎？

這樣回答就對了

對應「主要關鍵句」的回答

① **Could you please repeat that?**
能不能請你再說一次？

② **May I speak to anyone from the accounting department?**
可否幫我轉會計部？

③ **I'll put you through. Please hold.**
我幫您轉接，請稍等。

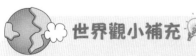

世界觀小補充

　　美國的電話禮儀是用This is開頭。因為通電話時只聞其聲不見其人，所以不使用I am...的句型。此外，辦公室的電話禮儀又更正式，除了來電者要表明身分外，來電目的、受話者等訊息也要表達清楚。例：Hello, this is Ronald Spencer from WWW travel agency. May I speak with Mr. Watson, please? I am returning his previous phone call. (您好，我是WWW旅行社的雷諾・史賓瑟，我找華森先生。我要回覆他上一通電話。)

May I speak with Olivia Morgan, please?
麻煩找奧莉薇雅·摩根。

Please hold, and I'll **put you through** to his/her office.
請稍等，我為您轉接。 put...through 為…接通電話

I'm afraid he's **stepped out**. Would you like to leave a message?
很不巧，他剛剛離開辦公室，您要不要留言呢？ step out 暫時外出

Actually, this call is rather urgent. We spoke on the phone yesterday. Did he leave any information with you for me?
事實上，這通電話頗緊急。我們昨天已經通過電話了，他有沒有留下任何訊息給你呢？

All of our operators are busy at this time. Please hold for the next available person.
所有的接線生都在忙線中，請稍候，我們將盡快為您服務。

I've written down your message and your name. Would you mind spelling your last name for me?
我將您的訊息及姓名都記下了，能否麻煩您再拼一次您的姓氏？

I'm sorry, Lisa's not here at the moment. Can I ask who's calling?
很抱歉，麗莎現在不在，請問您哪裡？

The signal is breaking up. Can you **call** me **back** later?
訊號不穩定，你能否晚點再回電給我？ call back 回電

Can you please hold for a minute? I have another call.
可不可以請你稍等一下？我有插撥。

I'll make sure she gets the **message**.
我會確保她有收到留言。 message 口信；訊息

Can you tell him his wife called, please?
能否請你告訴他，他老婆來電呢？

That's okay. I'll call back later.

Part 3 小資族的職場生活甘苦談

沒關係，我晚點再撥。

It's James from Yoyo Inc. When do you expect her back in the office?
我是優優公司的詹姆士，她大概什麼時候會回辦公室呢？

Could you ask him to call his mom when he gets in?
可不可以請他進公司的時候，打電話給他母親？

Do you have a pen **handy**? I don't think he has my number.
你現在方便抄嗎？我想他應該沒有我的電話號碼。　handy 手邊的；近便的

My number is 222-3456, **extension** 12.
我的電話是222-3456，分機12。　extension 電話分機

Sorry, wrong number.
抱歉，我打錯了。

Unit
24
電話基本用語

Hello. You've reached 222-6789. Please leave a detailed message after the beep. Thank you.
您好，這裡是222-6789的電話，請在嗶聲後留下詳細的留言，謝謝。

Hi, this is Miranda. I'm sorry I'm not available to take your call at this time. Leave me a message, and I'll get back to you as soon as possible.
嗨，我是米蘭達。很抱歉我現在無法接聽您的電話。請留言，我將盡快回電。

Well, I guess I'd better **get going**. Talk to you soon.
嗯，我想我得先掛電話了，我們再聊。　get going 出發

Thanks for calling. Bye for now.
謝謝來電，先這樣。

I have to let you go now.
我得掛電話了。（禮貌的講法，意思是不佔用對方時間，好讓對方掛電話去做別的事。）

I have another call **coming through**. I'd better run.
我有插撥，得先掛了。　come through 接通

Hello, Mr. Lin, I've got Michelle Watson on the phone for you. Are you going to take this?
哈囉，林先生，線上是蜜雪兒‧華生要找你，你現在方便接嗎？

Situation **1** 基本辦公室電話對應
basic phone conversation

A Hello, you've reached ABC Corp. How can I help?
您好，這裡是ABC公司，請問有什麼事？

B Yes, can I speak to Rosa Wilson, please?
是，請找蘿莎‧威爾森。

A Who's calling, please?
請問您哪裡找？

B It's Richard Davies here.
我是李察‧戴維斯。

A Certainly. Please hold, and I'll put you through.
好的。請稍等，我幫您轉接。

Situation **2** 留言
leaving a message

A Hello, ABC Company.
您好，這裡是ABC公司。

B Hi, this is Janet from AT&T. May I speak with Alex, please?
你好，我是AT&T的珍妮特，請問亞力士在嗎？

A He's in a meeting right now. Would you like to leave a message?
他現在正在開會，您要留言嗎？

B Yes. Can you have Alex call me back when he is available?
好，請亞力士有空的時候回我個電話。

A Certainly. I'll make sure he gets the message.
好的，我會替您轉達。

Part **3** 小資族的職場生活甘苦談

Situation 3 打錯電話
wrong number

A Hi, this is Mason. May I talk to Patricia?
哈囉，我是梅森，請問派翠西亞在嗎？

B There's no one here by that name.
這裡沒有這個人。

A Um, is this 2555-9999?
喔，請問這裡電話是2555-9999嗎？

B No. You dialed the wrong number.
不是，你打錯電話了。

A Sorry about that.
不好意思。

Situation 4 收訊不良
bad reception

A Hello, hello, still there? Can you hear me?
哈囉，哈囉，還在嗎？聽的到嗎？

B Um, I'm sorry. There seems to be some problem with our connection.
很抱歉，我覺得線路有點問題。

A Do you want me to call you back later?
要不要我晚點再打來？

B No, it's fine. Could you repeat what you just said?
不用，沒關係，可不可以請你再重覆一次剛剛講的事情？

A Ok. Here it comes.
好，聽好了。

主要關鍵句開口說

使出關鍵3句型，英文輕鬆脫口說

Track 073

① **We're here today to discuss the marketing campaign.**
我們今天開會的目的是要討論行銷活動。

② **First, let's go over the report from the last meeting.**
首先，我們先來瀏覽一下上次的會議紀錄。

③ **Shall we get down to business?**
是否就進入正題了呢？

沒果仁邏輯 ~Americans~ 句型解析與用法說明

說明
① **We're here today to discuss the marketing campaign句型**

人名／代名詞＋be動詞＋here＋to＋動詞＝某人於此時此地要進行某件事情，此句型常見於群聚集會時，發表演説者説明集合目的時使用。

說明
② **First, let's go over the report from the last meeting句型**

go over表示從頭瀏覽到尾。Let's go over something表示一起瀏覽某文件、書籍等。例：Let's go over the outline of our final report. 我們一起從頭看一遍期末報告的大綱吧。

說明
③ **Shall we get down to business句型**

shall開頭的問句為禮貌的提議問句，表示詢問在場者是否一同執行問句所提到的動作。例：Shall we dance? 我們來跳舞吧？／Shall we move on to the next page? 我們是否可以進行到下一頁了呢？

沒果仁也愛的說法 對照「主要關鍵句」的類似說法

① **I called this meeting to discuss the marketing campaign.**
我召開本次的會議是為了討論行銷活動。

② **Here are the minutes from our last meeting.**
這是上次的會議紀錄。

③ **I'd like to move on to today's topic.**
我想要進入今天會議的主題了。

這樣回答就對了 對應「主要關鍵句」的回答

① **Let me summarize the main points of the last meeting.**
讓我概述一下上次會議的重點。

② **Excuse me, but I haven't received a copy of the report yet.**
不好意思,但是我還沒有拿到紀錄的影本。

③ **Yes, please.**
好的,麻煩你了。

🌍 世界觀小補充 💡

　　商務會議的成員通常有主席(chairperson)、紀錄(person in charge of the minute)、司儀(emcee)、出席人員(members in attendance)。若為公司內部的例行性會議,就不需要那麼正式的編制。主管可擔任會議的主持人,紀錄由員工擔任。會議一開始通常會檢視前一次的會議紀錄(go over the minute)與執行狀況等,接著進入正題並依議程進行(introduce agenda),討論各項細節(discuss items),最後總結並結束會議(close the meeting)。

Part 3

小資族的職場生活甘苦談

▮ We're pleased to welcome the new vice president to say a few words before we get started.
在會議開始前，我們很榮幸邀請到新任副總裁來說幾句話。

▮ Who will be the **chair** of the meeting?
誰要當這次會議的主席？ chair 會議的主席

▮ I **skimmed over** the document before the meeting.
我已經在開會前瀏覽過這份文件了。 skim over 瀏覽；略讀

▮ By the end of this meeting, I'd like to have a **tangible** conclusion.
會議結束前，我希望能有具體的結論。 tangible 明確的；實際的

▮ I'm afraid Dr. Lee can't be with us today. She is doing research overseas at this time.
李博士目前在海外做研究，她今天恐怕沒辦法參與了。

▮ Sandra, can you tell us how the charity project is progressing?
珊卓，可否請你告訴我們慈善計畫目前進行到哪個階段？

▮ So, if there is nothing else we need to discuss, let's move on to today's agenda.
如果沒有其他需要討論的，我們就直接進行今天的議程。

▮ I suggest we each give a little background on the suggestions we discussed last week.
我建議大家將上週討論的建議事項做一點背景介紹。

▮ We don't have all day, so could you please **cut to the chase**?
我們的時間不多，所以請講重點。 cut to the chase 切入正題

▮ There are three items on the **agenda**.
今日議程有三件事項要討論。 agenda 議程；待議事項

▮ Let's **brainstorm** about some solutions.
我們一起腦力激盪出解決方案吧。 brainstorm 腦力激盪；集思廣益

▮ Elsa has agreed to take the **minutes**.

伊萊莎同意當會議紀錄。　　minutes 會議紀錄

*Joseph has kindly agreed to give us a report on this matter.
約瑟夫同意要針對這個議題為大家做簡報。

*We will hear a short report on each point first, followed by a discussion round the table.
針對每件要項，我們會先聽簡報，然後才是與會的討論。

*We'll have to keep each item to ten minutes. Otherwise we'll never get through.
每件事項的報告請控制在十分鐘之內，不然我們會討論不完。

*I don't **see eye to eye with** Sherry on this matter.
針對這個議題，我跟雪莉的意見不合。　　see eye to eye with... 與…看法一致

*I think we can **leave** this point **aside** for now.
我想我們可以先將這點擱著，晚點再討論。　　leave aside 不考慮

*We may need to vote on item 5, if we can't get a unanimous decision.
如果我們沒有辦法達成一致的決定，我們就必須針對議案5投票表決。

*Let's **come back** to this point at the end.
我們最後再回來討論這一點。　　come back 回來

*Before we close, let me just **summarize** the main points.
結束前，讓我將要點做個總整理。　　summarize 總結

*It looks as though we've covered the main items. Is there any other business?
看起來我們每一點都討論到了，還有什麼其他事項要處理嗎？

*Can we **fix** the date for the next meeting, please?
可不可以敲定下次的會議時間呢？　　fix 確定；決定

*The next meeting will be on Wednesday, the third of June in this same room.
下次會議就在這個地點，時間是六月三號，星期三。

*Thank you all for **attending**.
感謝各位參與會議。　　attend 出席；參加

關鍵一句模擬實境對話 *Topic-related Conversations*

以關鍵句破題的模擬實境對話

 Track 075

Situation 1 確認會議的時間和主題
meeting time and topic confirmation

Ⓐ We're having a meeting tomorrow. Can you make it?
我們明天要開會，你有辦法參加嗎？

Ⓑ When is it taking place?
幾點開始？

Ⓐ We're planning on 10 o'clock. Is that OK?
我們預計從上午十點開始，可以嗎？

Ⓑ Yes, that'll be fine.
可以，時間沒問題。

Ⓐ We're going to go over last quarter's sales figures.
我們將討論上一季的銷售額。

Situation 2 會議前的回顧
reviewing the last meeting

Ⓐ I assume that everyone has a copy of the agenda of today's meeting?
我想每個人都有拿到今天會議的議程吧？

Ⓑ Sorry, chairman, but I think there are some latecomers.
抱歉，主席，我想有些人還沒到。

Ⓐ In that case, I'd like to ask you to skim over the minutes of the previous meeting first.
既然這樣，我想請你們先瀏覽上次的會議紀錄。

Ⓑ Could we quickly go over the conclusion of the last meeting just to keep in the loop?
請問能否快速地講一遍上次會議的結論，好進入狀況？

Ⓐ Sure, let's do that.
當然可以，就這麼辦。

Part **③** 小資族的職場生活甘苦談

Situation 3 會議當中介紹成員
introducing members of the meeting

A I'd like you to join me in welcoming Robert Dickenson, our northeast area sales vice president.
我想請各位跟我一同歡迎羅伯‧狄克森，我們東北區的業務副總裁。

B Thank you. I'm looking forward to today's meeting.
謝謝大家，我很期待今天的會議。

A I'd also like to introduce Jessica Quinn, who recently joined our team.
我也想藉此機會，介紹最近加入我們團隊的潔西卡‧昆恩。

B May I also introduce my assistant, Bob Thompson.
同時我也介紹一下我的助理，包柏‧湯普森。

A Well, since everyone is here, we should get started.
既然人都到齊了，我們就開始開會吧。

Situation 4 會議紀錄
taking the minutes

A Before we go into details, I'd like to ask Danny to lead point 1. Will someone take the notes?
進入詳細的報告之前，我想要請丹尼主持第一點，誰願意幫忙做紀錄？

B I'll do it.
我來。

A Be sure to record all the results and conclusions.
記得將所有的結果跟結論都記錄下來。

B Shall I email the notes to all the attendees later?
會議紀錄之後要寄發給所有與會的人員嗎？

A Not before I check them.
在給我檢查之後才寄。

Unit 26 洽談出貨事宜
Shipping goods

 主要關鍵句開口說

使出關鍵3句型，英文輕鬆開口說 Track 076

① I need to get an estimate before deciding to place an order.

我要先拿到估價單，才會決定是否下單。

② This price is way beyond my budget.

這價錢超出我預算太多了。

③ Do you ship door-to-door?

你們有幫忙送貨到府嗎？

 沒果仁邏輯 Americans 句型解析與用法說明

說明① **place an order用法**

place an order=下訂單，大型生意跟小量購買都適用此片語。例：I need to place an order for a carton of mangos. 我想要下單買一箱芒果。

說明② **way beyond用法**

way beyond=遠超出，後面接名詞。例：The movie was way beyond my expectations. 這部電影遠超出我的預期。

說明③ **door-to-door用法**

door-to-door在國際貨運業來說，就是從廠房門口運出，直到客戶指定地點的配送服務，甚至包含了出口的手續在內。例：The company provides door-to-door shipping service. 這家公司提供送貨到府的貨運服務。

① **I need to know the quoted price before I make the purchase.**
我需要知道報價才能下訂。

② **The price is above my limit.**
價格超出我的限度。

③ **Can you deliver to the designated address?**
你可以運送到指定地點嗎？

Unit
26

洽談出貨事宜

這樣回答就對了 對應「主要關鍵句」的回答

① **You'll have it by the end of this week.**
這禮拜會給你(估價單)。

② **It's the best I can offer.**
這是我能給的最低價了。

③ **Yes, all shipments are door-to-door.**
是，我們所有的運送都送貨到府的。

🌍💭 **世界觀小補充** 💡

　　跟外國客戶洽談生意，需要夾雜專業行話，所以要多花心思熟
悉。例如下訂單(place the order)、付款條件(payment term)、付款方
式(payment method)等，國際貿易(International Trade)甚至是大學主
修的專門學問。從初期尋找交易對象，信用調查發出招徠函、目錄、
價目表(price list, P/L)、詢價、報價、確認簽約到訂單確認，每個環節
都有專門用語喔！

學校沒教的實用句

情境式主題句，學校沒有教，自己學起來！

I'd like to **place an order** for a number of your standard bookshelves.
我想要下訂單購買你們的標準型書櫃。　place an order 下訂單

How many are you interested in ordering for **purchase**?
你想要下訂多少量呢？　purchase 買；購買

I need to know the quantity before **quoting** you a more precise price.
在提供報價給你之前，我需要知道確切的下訂量。　quote 報價；開價

The price is not what I expected. Is there any way that you could **lower** it?
這價錢跟我預期的有出入，你可以再降價嗎？　lower 降下

Where are your products **manufactured**?
你們的商品是在哪裡生產的？　manufacture 製造

Most of our products are manufactured abroad, but a number are also produced here in the United States.
我們大部分的產品在國外製造，但其中一部分在美國生產。

Do you have many available in the **warehouse**?
你倉庫裡的現貨還有很多嗎？　warehouse 倉庫

We keep a large supply **in stock**.
我們存有大量現貨。　in stock 有庫存；有現貨

What does the **estimate** include?
這個報價包含哪些項目？　estimate 估價；估計

Estimates include merchandise, packaging and shipping, duty if required, any taxes and insurance.
這個報價包含商品單價、包裝、運送費，若有稅金也會記載，還有保險費用。

Delivery dates depend on your location, but we can usually deliver within fourteen business days.
送達日期端看你的所在地而定，但我們通常在十四個工作天內會完成運送。

I'm concerned about the delays we're experiencing with some of our

Part 3 小資族的職場生活甘苦談

suppliers.

我對於最近供應商交貨的延期感到擔憂。 `supplier 供應商`

*What type of logistical structure do you have?

你們的物流配送方式為何？

*What type of **distribution** services do you provide?

你們提供什麼型態的配送服務？ `distribution 分配；分發`

*We distribute to both wholesale and **retail** outlets.

我們的配送從批發端到零售端都有。 `retail 零售的`

*The bill of lading lists the merchandise shipped. It's included with every shipment or delivery.

海運提單列出了運送的商品清單，每次運送都一定會附上。

*Sometimes, larger packages are delayed because of a bottleneck at the distribution point.

大型包裹的運送有時會延遲是因為發貨點遇到狀況。

*We often work with delivery services such as UPS, FedEx or DHL for our most urgent shipping.

我們的急件通常會跟UPS、FedEx或DHL這類型的快遞公司配合。

*What are the **terms** of your payment?

你們的付款條件為何？ `term 條件；條款`

*The payment terms are 90-day net.

付款條件是貨到九十天付清。

*Our attorney is still going through the terms and **conditions**.

我們的法務正在審核合約條款。 `condition 條件`

*We both see eye to eye on this agreement.

我們雙方對於這份合約的看法相同。

*Deal! Let's **sign a contract**.

一言為定！簽約吧。 `sign a contract 簽合約`

*It's a two-year contract. We need to be extra careful before signing it.

這是個為期兩年的合約，我們簽約之前一定要格外謹慎。

Unit

26

洽談出貨事宜

以關鍵句破題的模擬實境對話

 Situation **1** 訂購文具
ordering stationery

A I need to order some more supplies. I need three dozen of ballpoint pens, as well as six black markers.
我還需要訂購文具。我要三打原子筆，六支黑色麥克筆。

B Did you want six dozen black markers or six?
你是要六打還是六支？

A Oh, it was six each.
喔，六支。

B Would you like this order delivered, or will you pick it up?
商品需要配送嗎？還是自取呢？

A Please deliver it to our headquarters and send it COD.
麻煩送到我們總公司，貨到付款。

 Situation **2** 訂單殺價
asking for a discount

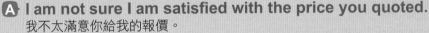

A I am not sure I am satisfied with the price you quoted.
我不太滿意你給我的報價。

B It's not the first time we have done business together. You know that's the best I can offer.
我們又不是第一次合作，你知道我已經給你很多優惠了。

A What do you say if we increase the purchase quantity to thirty thousand pieces?
如果我們將訂單量增加到三萬件呢？

B I will get back to you with a new price tomorrow.
我明天會重新擬一份報價單給你。

A That's what I'm talking about!
這才像話！

Part **3** 小資族的職場生活甘苦談

Situation 3 email訂購
email order

A I am attracted to some of the items in your catalogue.
我對你們型錄上的一些產品有興趣。

B Do you need any samples before purchasing?
購買前您需要看樣品嗎?

A It's not necessary. How do I place the order?
不需要,我要怎麼下訂呢?

B You can email to the service account printed on the cover of the catalogue. We will handle the order as soon as the email is received.
您可以寄Email到型錄封面所標示的地址,我們會在收到信後立即處理訂單。

A Ok, that sounds convenient.
了解,聽起來滿便利的。

Unit

26

洽談出貨事宜

Situation 4 付款條件
payment terms

A We'd like to order three cartons of watermelons and please have them delivered tomorrow.
我們想要訂購三箱西瓜,請於明天出貨。

B We only accept half the total payment as a deposit and the balance is paid off within fifteen days.
我們只接受先預付一半的訂金,而且尾款要在十五天內付清。

A Can the payment terms be more flexible?
付款條件能再有彈性一些嗎?

B Sorry. It's agricultural produce we are dealing with here.
抱歉,我們經營的是農產品的生意。

A Alright, I understand.
好吧,我了解。

Unit 27 問問薪資及福利制度
About salary and welfare

主要關鍵句開口說

使出關鍵3句型，英文輕鬆開口說

Track 079

① **What kind of benefits does the company offer?**
公司提供什麼樣的福利？

② **Do I get any bonus?**
我會得到分紅嗎？

③ **The company covers labor and health insurance.**
公司提供勞健保。

沒果仁邏輯 Americans 句型解析與用法說明

說明
① **What kind of benefits does the company offer句型**

What kind of+名詞+do/does之子句，可用來詢問後方子句具體的種類為何。例：What kind of service does the company provide? 這間公司提供什麼類型的服務？

說明
② **Do I get any bonus句型**

bonus=分紅、比預期還要好或多的獲利。Do/does+人名／代名詞+get+any+bonus就是詢問會不會有分紅。例：This extra three-day holidays is a bonus for us. 這多出來的三天假期真是額外的收穫。

說明
③ **The company covers labor and health insurance句型**

描述保險涵蓋的範圍時，會用cover這個動詞。保險就像是一把無形的保護傘，將我們覆蓋在裡面，使用cover這個動詞極具意象。例：medical coverage 醫療險給付。

168

沒果仁也愛的說法　Americans

對照「主要關鍵句」的類似說法

① **Are the benefits at your new job any good?**
你新公司的福利好嗎？

② **Is there any year-end bonus?**
有年終獎金嗎？

③ **Labor and health insurance are included in the benefit plan.**
勞健保包含在福利制度中。

 這樣回答就對了

對應「主要關鍵句」的回答

① **We cover health and labor insurance.**
我們提供勞健保。

② **It depends on the increase of company's profits.**
這要視公司的獲利成長情況而定。

③ **Is there any other medical insurance included?**
還有包含其他的醫療保險嗎？

世界觀小補充

　　美國企業的福利制度和台灣不同，例如：福利多元且彈性、福利也延伸到直系血親、休假比起本土企業來的多、員工教育訓練完善及有機會申請輪調海外等。還有些特殊的福利制度諸如牙醫保險，是我們比較陌生的。很難想像牙齒也要納入保險。在美國，看牙齒是相當花錢的一項醫療行為。是否曾經覺得很多去美國唸書的朋友，有機會回台灣都要看牙醫很奇怪呢？千萬不要這麼覺得，因為他們飛回來一趟的機票錢，都比在當地看牙還經濟實惠！

學校沒教的實用句

情境式主題句，學校沒有教，自己學起來！

I will **take a day off** tomorrow.
我明天要請一天假。　　take a day off 請假休息一天

June is taking her **maternity** leave now and won't be back in the office until next month.
瓊恩現在正在請產假，下個月才會回公司。　　maternity 產婦的；孕婦的

Our company offers free, **unlimited** training courses to all the full-time employees.
公司提供所有正職員工免費的訓練課程，不限次數。　　unlimited 無限量的

I think we have a health and **dental** plan.
我記得我們有提供健保以及牙醫保險。　　dental 牙科的

I think my company is offering a good **benefits** package.
我認為我公司的福利制度很好。　　benefit 利益；津貼

I've heard from some of the small-business owners that they cannot afford to offer benefits to employees.
我耳聞一些小企業的雇主說他們無法負擔員工福利。

The law in Taiwan requires employers to provide employees with certain benefits, such as labor and health insurance.
台灣法律規定雇主要提供員工基本福利，例如勞保及健保。

Joey is a salesman who gets a **minimum wage** plus some commission.
喬伊是個領基本薪資外加佣金的業務員。　　minimum wage 基本薪資

We provide paid vacations for full-time employees who have been in the company over five years.
對於年資超過五年的正職員工，公司提供有薪假給他們。

Most employers in the US provide paid holidays for New Year's, Memorial Day, Independence Day, Labor Day, Thanksgiving Day and Christmas Day.
美國很多企業主會提供員工新年、陣亡將士紀念日、獨立紀念日、勞動節、感恩節以及聖誕節的有薪假。

The consultant suggests the owner offer the right benefits in order to help his business jump-start its growth.

顧問建議這名雇主提供適當的福利，以協助生意快速成長。

Company benefits are often a significant portion of the employee's compensation package.

公司的福利通常是員工待遇裡很重要的一環。

When considering an offer, the candidate should examine the benefits offered by the prospective employer.

在考慮是否要接下工作時，應徵者應該要檢視未來雇主所提出的福利。

My boss promised a raise after I achieve a 10% sales growth.

我的老闆答應在我達成十個百分比的業績成長後替我加薪。

Health insurance is an important benefit; it is less expensive through the employer at group rates than when taking it out on one's own.

健保是個很重要的福利，公司團體加保的費率會比單一人加保來得實惠。

Should the employee become ill or have an accident, his or her medical treatment is adequately covered.

若有員工生病或發生意外，他 / 她的部分醫療費用將由保險負擔。

Many US employers now help cover the expense of childcare facilities in their communities.

許多美國的雇主現在都會協助支付社區內兒童保育設施的費用。

Another important benefit our company offers is **flextime**, which allows the employees to vary their working hours, within limits, each day.

我們公司另外一項重要的福利就是提供彈性工作時間，讓員工可以在一定的限度內，調整自己每天的工作時段。　flextime 彈性工作時間

Employees with flextime **tend to** be happier at work.

享有彈性工時的員工上班時的心情會比較愉悅。　tend to 傾向；易於

My cousin's company is offering pension plans that guarantee a fixed monthly sum to retirees.

我表哥的公司提供退休金，保證退休員工每月有定額的退休金可領。

There is the stock ownership plan in my company, which permits the employees to buy shares of the company's stock at subsidized prices.

我們公司有員工持股的福利制度，讓員工以補助價認購公司的股票。

關鍵一句模擬實境對話 *Topic-related Conversations*

以關鍵句破題的模擬實境對話

 Track 081

Situation 1 臨時請假
calling in sick

A Where is Alice? I haven't seen her all morning.
愛麗絲呢？一整個早上都沒看到她。

B She is taking a day off today.
她今天請一天假。

A What happened to her? Is everything alright?
怎麼了？都還好吧？

B She called in sick.
她臨時打來請病假。

A Oh, I see.
喔，我知道了。

Situation 2 詢問福利
inquiry about company benefits

A 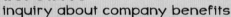Before ending this interview, are there any questions you might want to ask?
面試結束前，你有沒有任何問題想問我們？

B I am quite concerned about the company's benefits.
我對於公司的福利滿關心的。

A 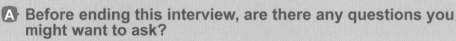Our company covers basic insurance, such as labor and health insurance.
我們公司提供基本的保險，例如勞保及健保。

B How many days of annual leave will I have?
我會有幾天的年假？

A You will have a one-week annual leave after your probation period.
試用期過後，你一年會有七天的年假。

Situation 3 薪資機密
the salary is top secret

A What's your starting salary?
你的起薪是多少？

B That is rather personal. I'd like to keep it to myself.
這個問題很私人，我不想告訴別人。

A Come on, I am your mom. I have the right to know!
拜託，我是你媽耶，我有權利知道！

B Let's just say that I get the minimum wage plus commission and year-end bonus.
反正就是基本薪資加佣金，再加上年終啦。

A Sounds promising!
聽起來大有可為喔！

Situation 4 辦公室硬體福利
recreation facilities

A Where do you normally work out?
你通常在哪裡健身？

B I usually work out at my office if I arrive early.
如果提早進公司，我通常會在公司運動。

A At your office? Or near your office?
你是指在公司裡，還是公司附近啊？

B We have a state-of-the-art gym on the top floor of my company.
我們公司頂樓有一個頂級的健身房。

A Wow, I envy you!
哇，真羨慕你！

Unit 28 人事異動
Staff reassignment

主要關鍵句開口說

使出關鍵3句型，英文輕鬆開口說

Track 082

① **I got a promotion last week.**
我上禮拜升官了。

② **Dan got laid off because of the downsizing.**
因為縮編，丹被解雇了。

③ **I don't know how to ask for a raise.**
我不知道該怎麼要求加薪。

沒果仁邏輯 Americans

 句型解析與用法說明

說明① **I got a promotion last week句型**

get a promotion＝在職場上受到提拔、升官。例：Amy is hoping that she will get a promotion after the project is finished. 愛咪希望在專案結束後有升遷的機會。

說明② **Dan got laid off because of the downsizing句型**

get laid off＝被解雇；downsizing＝企業縮編。例：After getting laid off, Laurence went to the bar and got himself drunk. 被解雇之後，羅倫斯去酒吧把自己灌醉。/The company is planning to downsize next year. 這間公司計劃在明年進行人員的縮編。

說明③ **I don't know how to ask for a raise句型**

ask for＋某事物＝要求、索取某樣東西或事情。例：A foreigner is asking for help. 一位老外正向人要求幫忙。

沒果仁也愛的說法 (Americans)

對照「主要關鍵句」的類似說法

① **I was promoted last week.**
我上禮拜升官了。

② **Dan was let go because of the downsizing.**
因為縮編,丹被解雇了。

③ **I have no clue as to how to negotiate a raise.**
我不知道該怎麼談加薪。

這樣回答就對了

對應「主要關鍵句」的回答

① **This is great news!**
這真是好消息!

② **That's too bad.**
太糟糕了。

③ **You need to plan ahead what you are going to address.**
你必須事先計劃要說的內容。

世界觀小補充

　　美國企業主很注重數字,認為具體的數據是會說話的 (Statistics talk)。當員工想要求加薪或希望能在組織內有升遷的機會時,除了得拿捏好時機外,在溝通前也必須擬好自己的論述重點,譬如在過去幾年為公司帶來多少的業績成長(sales increase)、因為辦理某專案而提升部門間的綜效(synergy)、或是自己的特殊專長和經驗加速了業務達成等,將自己的籌碼具體化,並有條理地與主管溝通才是上策。

Unit
28

人事異動

I want to move up the **corporate** ladder.

我想要在公司沿職務位階晉升。　　corporate 公司的

A high position means more responsibility. Are you sure you're ready for that?

職位愈高，責任愈重，你確定你準備好了嗎？

I hope I will be able to **cope with** all the new responsibilities.

我希望自己能處理之後所要面臨的新責任。　　cope with 處理；解決

Sometimes being **promoted** doesn't guarantee you a raise.

有時候升官不代表加薪。　　promote 晉升

Being a supervisor means building a good team where members work well with each other.

擔任主管意味著要建立好的團隊，讓成員們能良好地與彼此共事。

Before bringing up the subject of a raise to your boss, it is best to consider if the department is currently functioning well.

在跟主管談加薪前，最好先考量你的部門現階段是否運作良好。

As an employee, you sometimes need to ask yourself whether you are worth the price the company pays.

身為員工，你有時該想想自己是否無愧於公司支付給你的薪水。

Rosa didn't succeed in asking for a raise because she didn't request a meeting with her manager and caught him off guard.

蘿莎要求加薪未果，因為她沒有事先跟經理安排面談，反而冒失地去找他。

Due to the organizational restructuring, I have to let go some of the senior employees.

由於組織重整，我必須要請一些資深的員工離開公司。

Layoffs are extremely tough because they can happen to loyal and productive employees who have done nothing wrong.

資遣很難，因為有些忠誠、有產能又沒做錯事的員工也會受到衝擊。

My boss needed to tighten the budget since the business had slowed due to the recession.

因為經濟蕭條導致生意成長緩慢，所以老闆需要縮減開支。

How long has it been since your last **pay increase**?

你上次加薪是多久以前的事？　pay increase 加薪

Steven is now jobless because his former company was forced to liquidate the business.

史蒂芬前一個公司被迫結束營業，所以他目前失業。

Our company is facing a financial crisis, so you have no grounds to ask for a raise.

我們公司面臨財務危機，所以你沒有要求加薪的理由。

The factory workers are going on a **strike** because of the overdue wages.

因為工廠積欠的薪水，所以工人們準備罷工。　strike 罷工

May I apply to be **transferred** to another department?

我可否要求轉調其他部門？　transfer 調任；調動

This is my old business card. I just got transferred to another department.

這是我之前的名片，我才剛轉調至新部門。

You might need to make an appointment with your supervisor and discuss it with him.

你可能需要先跟主管約個時間討論。

Tara might lose her job because she failed to achieve the sales goal this month.

泰拉沒能達到這個月的業績，所以可能被辭退。

Make sure you get your severance pay if you are let go.

若遭解雇，請確保你有拿到資遣費。

His company is going bankrupt and is being forced to **shut down**.

他的公司即將破產，而且要被迫關閉。　shut down 關閉；停工

I hate to have to say this, but you are fired!

我很不想這麼說，但是，你被解雇了！

Situation 1 要求升官
asking for a promotion

A I have been working in this company for over a decade. I think it's about time to ask for a promotion.
我在這間公司已經服務超過十年了，也該是時候要求升遷了。

B Do you think you've got what it takes to be a supervisor?
你覺得你有資格擔任一位主管嗎？

A Sure. Who has better experience than I have?
當然啦。有誰比我還有經驗呢？

B I suggest that you outline your point and be rational.
我建議你先立個大綱，並且要合情合理。

A Thanks for your suggestions. I will.
謝謝你的建議，我會的。

Situation 2 通報好消息
spreading good news

A I have really good news today.
我今天有個大好消息。

B What is your good news?
是什麼呢？

A I got a promotion today. You are looking at the new supervisor of the marketing department.
我今天升官了，你正在跟未來的行銷部主管講話呢！

B Wow, this is great news! I am so glad for you.
哇，真是個好消息！真為你開心。

A I will probably start my new job a week from Monday.
下週一開始，我可能就要忙新業務了。

Situation 3 加薪失敗
failing to get a raise

A Boss, got a minute?
老闆，有空嗎？

B What is it?
什麼事？

A It's about my salary. You see, I got so tied up by the house mortgage lately and...
是關於我的薪水，我最近被房貸壓得喘不過氣，所以…

B I know what you're getting at, but it's not appropriate to bring up a subject like this.
我知道你要講什麼，但是突然提這種要求並不妥當。

A Alright, I was just trying my luck.
好吧，只是想說說看。

Situation 4 進行解雇
letting people go

A Boss, you wanted to see me?
老闆，你找我嗎？

B Yes. It seems to me that you've been coming late recently.
是的，你最近似乎一直遲到。

A Um...guilty as charged.
嗯…我錯了。

B Punctuality is what the company values most. I am afraid I have to let you go.
準時是公司最看重的，很遺憾，我必須要請你離開公司。

A What? Don't I deserve a second chance?
什麼？不能再給我一次機會嗎？

 主要關鍵句開口說

使出關鍵3句型，英文輕鬆開口說

 Track 085

① **I want to quit my job.**
我想要辭職了。

② **My colleague is going to retire this week.**
我的同事這禮拜準備要退休。

③ **I don't know how to write a resignation letter.**
我不知道該怎麼寫辭呈。

 沒果仁邏輯 句型解析與用法說明

Americans

說明
① **to quit my job用法**

quit one's job＝辭職。例：I heard Jerome just quit his job。我聽說傑若姆辭職了。

說明
② **My colleague is going to retire this week句型**

retire＝退休。人名／代名詞+be+going+to+retire表示未來即將要退休。例：My dad is turning 65 this year and is going to retire soon after. 我爸爸今年就要65歲，之後馬上要準備退休了。

說明
③ **I don't know how to句型**

人名／代名詞+don't+know+how+to+動作／執行某事件，意即某人不知道該怎麼做或完成某件事情。例：She doesn't know how to cook. 她不會下廚。

沒果仁也愛的說法　Americans

對照「主要關鍵句」的類似說法

① **I am considering a career change.**
我在考慮轉換跑道。

② **My colleague is preparing for his retirement.**
我同事準備要退休了。

③ **Can you show me how to write a resignation letter?**
可否教我怎麼撰寫辭呈？

這樣回答就對了　對應「主要關鍵句」的回答

① **How come?**
為什麼？

② **Who will be taking over his work after he retires?**
他退休後誰來接他的工作呢？

③ **You can find several references online.**
你可以在網路上找到範本。

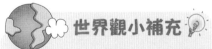 世界觀小補充

　　和台灣相對穩定的就業生態相比，在美國換工作是很平常的事，企業間人才的流動也時常發生。想要提出辭呈時，基本的禮貌及話術是必備的，必須事先做好準備。記得要先找主管當面提出這件事，口頭告知，之後再提出書面辭呈。整個過程若能以平和且理性的語言傳達，對自己未來在職場上的風評才會有正面的幫助。

學校沒教的實用句

情境式主題句，學校沒有教，自己學起來！

I can't stand my boss anymore, so I quit.
我再也無法忍受我老闆，所以辭職了。 〔quit 辭職〕

I have been getting a bit sick and tired of my job recently.
我最近對我的工作逐漸心生厭倦。 〔sick and tired of 厭惡；厭倦〕

I don't get along well with my coworkers and feel like leaving this job.
我跟我的同事處不來，所以想要離職。 〔get along well 和睦相處〕

David finds that he is not cut out for being a salesperson and wants a career change.
大衛發現自己不適合當業務，所以想要轉換跑道。 〔cut out for 適合從事…工作〕

A new opportunity is being offered and I want to further my career.
有一個新的機會，而我也想藉此更精進我的職涯。 〔further 促進；助長〕

You need to give a resignation letter to your current employer.
你需要向現在的雇主提出辭呈。 〔resignation 辭職〕

There's another better offer, and I am thinking about taking it.
有一個更好的職缺，而我也滿想要接受。

I am really grateful for working under you since you've been a natural leader and I have learnt a lot from you.
能在你底下工作，我心懷感激，因為你是一位稱職的主管，我也跟你學到了很多。

I no longer have any passion toward this job anymore.
我對這份工作已經毫無熱忱了。 〔passion 熱情〕

Kim is not sure whether she could put up with this unbelievable workload anymore.
金不確定自己是否能繼續忍受這難以置信的工作量。 〔workload 工作量〕

Most companies would ask for a two-week notice before the resigning employees step down from their positions.
很多公司會要求員工提前兩週告知離職一事。 〔step down 辭職〕

You'll need at least a month to pass down your duties before you leave

this job.

在你離職之前，需要至少一個月的時間來交接你的工作。

I have a wonderful opportunity to work at a different company. I am putting in my two-week notice.

別家公司提供了一個很棒的工作機會給我，我現在要提早兩週遞辭呈。

I enjoyed my time here, but I shouldn't pass this opportunity up.

我很喜歡待在這邊的時光，但我不想要錯失這個大好機會。

He **retired** at the age of 68.

他在68歲的時候退休。 retire 退休

She **vacated** the position when she got pregnant.

她懷孕的時候就離職了。 vacate 辭職

My supervisor is not yet mentally ready for going into retirement.

我的主管在心態上還沒有準備好要退休。

The financial consultant **topped out** at age forty because he was burned out.

那名財務顧問在四十歲就停止晉升，因為他已經身心俱疲。 top out 不再上升

That publicist **resigned** over a financial scandal.

那位公關因為一樁金融弊案而辭職。 resign 辭職

My mom left her position with the New York Times.

我媽離開了紐約時報的工作。

The coworkers have planned a **farewell party** for Damian, who is going to retire very soon.

同事為了即將要退休的戴米安籌辦一場歡送會。 farewell party 歡送會

I am very willing to help train a **replacement** during the transition.

我很樂意協助交接工作給接任者。 replacement 代替者

You can always reach me on my cell phone if there are any questions.

如果有任何問題，隨時都可以打我手機找我。

I am at a point where I want to find other challenges. I hope you can understand.

我到了一個想要尋求其他挑戰的關頭，希望你可以諒解。

關鍵一句模擬實境對話 Topic-related Conversations
以關鍵句破題的模擬實境對話

Situation 1 茶水間聊離職
wanting to leave your job

Ⓐ Hey, just between you and me. I've had it with this job and want to leave ASAP.
跟你講一件事，不要跟別人說，我已經受夠這份工作，想馬上離開。

Ⓑ Hold your horses. It's standard to give a two-week notice.
先別急，一般來說都要提前兩週告知。

Ⓐ I know. But do you know how to write a resignation letter?
我知道，但你知道怎麼寫辭呈嗎？

Ⓑ I am an expert of writing letters.
我是寫信專家。

Ⓐ Great! Let me get a pen and my notebook.
太好了！我去拿一支筆跟筆記本。

Situation 2 與主管談離職
bringing up reasons for quitting a job

Ⓐ Alex, I received an offer from a different company. This is a great opportunity for me, so I accepted it.
亞力士，我接到其他公司的邀約，我覺得是相當好的機會，所以我接受了。

Ⓑ I see. Is there anything wrong with your current job?
我了解，你現在的工作有什麼問題嗎？

Ⓐ My decision has nothing to do with my duties here. I really enjoyed working with you.
我的決定跟現在的工作情況無關，我真的很喜歡與你共事。

Ⓑ Then why do you have to leave?
那麼你為什麼要離開呢？

Ⓐ I think I need a change.
我想我需要一點改變。

離職及交接
leaving and handing over a job

A I got your resignation letter. You didn't state a specific date for leaving.
我收到你的辭呈了，你沒有提到確切的離職時間。

B I think I can work for another month and wait for a replacement to take over.
我想我可以再待一個月，等接任者接手。

A OK, it makes sense.
嗯，這樣很合理。

B And if you want, I can train the new employee.
如果需要的話，我可以協助新員工了解我的工作領域。

A Yes, that would be necessary.
是，這是需要的。

退休同仁道別
a retirement party

A Henry has been like a father to me, and he is going to retire soon.
亨利一直像爸爸一樣照顧我，而如今他即將要退休了。

B What do you say we hold a farewell party for him?
我們幫他辦一場歡送會怎麼樣？

A That's an awesome idea!
這主意太棒了！

B What do you want this party to be like?
你想要辦什麼樣的派對？

A Let's just keep it warm and simple.
辦得溫馨、簡單就好。

Part 4

血汗人生必要的
休閒娛樂

Unit
30

購物去－百貨公司篇
Shopping: In the department store

Part
4
血汗人生必要的休閒娛樂

 主要關鍵句開口說

使出關鍵３句型，英文輕鬆開口說 Track 088

① **QQ Mall is having a big sale this weekend. Do you want to go?**

QQ百貨這週末有特惠，你想去嗎？

② **Are you looking for something in particular?**
有特別在找什麼樣的商品嗎？

③ **Just browsing.**
只是逛逛。

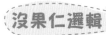 沒果仁邏輯 Americans 句型解析與用法說明

 說明① **have a big sale用法**

have a big sale＝舉辦大打折，任何有在舉辦大型促銷方案的銷售場合皆可使用此句型。例：The bookstore in my neighborhood had a big sale last month. 我家附近的書店上個月有大型特惠。

 說明② **look for something in particular句型**

look for=尋找；in particular=特定地。例：She is looking for her lost puppy. 她的小狗不見了，她正在找牠。/She likes to see movies, horror movies in particular. 她喜歡看電影，特別是恐怖片。

 說明③ **Just browsing句型**

I am just browsing的簡化版本。browse＝不經意地瀏覽，逛街時使用此句型表示沒有特定要買什麼，只是隨意逛逛而已。

① **Are you having a sale right now?**
你們現在有打折嗎？

② **Can I help you find something or are you just looking?**
需要我幫你找什麼嗎？還是你只想先看看？

③ **I am just looking.**
我只是看看而已。

這樣回答就對了

對應「主要關鍵句」的回答

① **Sure. I'll go with you.**
好啊，我跟你去。

② **I am looking for the latest running shoes.**
我在找最新的跑步鞋。

③ **Ok. If you need me, just shout!**
好的，如果有什麼需要，就喊一聲吧！

🌏 **世界觀小補充**

　　美國幅員廣大，百貨公司或者暢貨中心的規模相對大很多。百貨公司與暢貨中心的所在位置與形態不同。通常百貨公司在市區，例如紐約鬧區的Saks Fifth Avenue, Macy's, Bloomingdale, Barneys及Bergdorf Goodman等，中價位到高檔的商品琳瑯滿目；暢貨中心因為大多販售過季商品或庫存品，有些會提供相當低的折數，流行度不如百貨精品，所以不適宜設在寸土寸金的鬧區裡，通常都設在近郊。

Part 4 血汗人生必要的休閒娛樂

That's a **rip-off**!
這是敲竹槓嘛！　rip-off 剝削；詐騙

Do you have these shoes in size seven?
你這雙鞋有七號的嗎？

If you can't find them on the rack, they may be **out of stock**.
如果你在架上找不到的話，那可能就是沒貨了。　out of stock 無庫存；無現貨

Do you think it's possible to get a **discount**?
有沒有可能打折呢？　discount 折扣

Let me check in the **stockroom** first, and I'll be right back.
讓我確認一下庫存，馬上回來。　stockroom 倉庫

If there's a flaw in this vacuum machine, can I **return** it?
如果吸塵器有瑕疵，我可以退貨嗎？　return 退回

If a problem with it comes up, you can show it to us and we'll give you a **refund**.
如果產品有問題，你可以先拿來給我們看，之後我們會退款給你。　refund 退款

Would you like to use the **fitting room** to try it on?
你想要去試衣間試穿嗎？　fitting room 試衣間

I think I'll take it! It's a **bargain**.
我想我會買這個，真的很划算！　bargain 特價商品；便宜貨

How would you like to pay?
您要如何付款呢？

Do you take credit cards?
你們收信用卡嗎？

I'm almost maxed out on my credit card, so I think I'll pay with a **check**.
我的信用卡快超支了，我會用支票付款。　check 支票

There's a discount of 30% on this **blouse**.

這件襯衫打七折。　　　blouse 短衫

This jumper goes well with my trousers.
這件針織上衣跟我的褲子很搭。　　　jumper 針織上衣

Have you got this in another color?
你這件還有別的顏色嗎？

Shall I gift-wrap it?
請問要幫您包裝嗎？　　　gift-wrap 用包裝紙包裝

You don't happen to have any change, do you?
您沒有零錢，對吧？　　　change 零錢；找零

That's NT$2,000 altogether.
總共是新台幣兩千元。　　　altogether 全部；合計

Are you a price-conscious shopper?
你是個買東西很注意價位的人嗎？　　　price-conscious 留意價格的

The department's annual sale is coming up, and we're expecting a crowd of excited female consumers in the cosmetics section.
百貨公司的週年慶快要到了，我們可以預期到化妝品區將會有一群興奮的女性消費者聚集。　　　annual sale 週年慶

We have a good range of jogging shoes from all the major brands.
我們有各大品牌的全系列慢跑鞋。

Don't throw the receipt away too quickly, in case that there's something wrong with the purchase.
收據不要太早丟掉，以防你買的東西有問題想要換。　　　receipt 收據

I don't take the elevator while shopping in a department store because waiting in line is a waste of time.
我去百貨公司逛街時不搭電梯，因為我覺得排隊很浪費時間。

If you don't know your way around a huge department store, ask directions at the information desk on the first floor.
如果你搞不清楚大型百貨公司內的方位，可以到一樓的服務台詢問。

Part 4 血汗人生必要的休閒娛樂

Situation 1 被敲竹槓
what a rip-off!

Ⓐ How much did you pay for it?
這東西花了你多少錢？

Ⓑ 200 bucks.
兩百塊。

Ⓐ 200 bucks for a piece of junk like that? That's a rip-off!
用兩百塊買一個垃圾？真是被坑了！

Ⓑ What do you mean?
你什麼意思？

Ⓐ It's not worth it.
這東西根本不值這個價錢。

Situation 2 購物諮詢
in a shop

Ⓐ Pardon me. Could you help me?
不好意思，可以幫我個忙嗎？

Ⓑ Of course. How can I help you?
當然，請問您需要什麼？

Ⓐ I am looking for a sweater.
我想找一件毛衣。

Ⓑ What size do you wear?
您穿什麼尺寸？

Ⓐ Medium, I think.
好像是M號。

3 想買圍巾
looking for a scarf

A Hi, are you being helped?
您好，請問有人招呼您嗎？

B No, I'm not. I'm interested in some scarves.
沒有，我想看看圍巾。

A Let's see. What do you think of this one here? It's made of silk.
我看看，這件您覺得如何？這是絲製的。

B It looks nice, but I'm looking for something for the winter.
看起來不錯，但我想找適合冬天的圍巾。

A Maybe you would like a heavy wool scarf. Let me show you some.
也許您會比較喜歡厚重的羊毛圍巾，我挑幾款給您看看。

4 人擠人煩死人
can't stand the crowd

A Let's do some window shopping at the mall this weekend.
週末我們去百貨公司逛逛吧！

B I'll pass. I can't stand lining up for the elevator.
我不去，我受不了排隊等電梯。

A We can take the escalator, silly!
我們可以搭手扶梯啊，傻瓜！

B Still, it's such a waste of time.
我還是覺得很浪費時間。

A I'll go myself then.
那我自己去了。

Unit
30

購物去 — 百貨公司篇

主要關鍵句開口說

使出關鍵3句型，英文輕鬆開口說

Track 091

① **I am going grocery shopping.**
我要去採買了。

② **Do you go to big supermarkets or small grocery stores?**
你是去大型超市還是小型雜貨店？

③ **We are running out of rice.**
我們的米快吃完了。

沒果仁邏輯 ~~Americans~~ 句型解析與用法說明

說明
① **go grocery shopping句型**

go grocery shopping＝買菜、採買生活物資。使用不同時態表達去採買的時間。例：I go grocery shopping once a week. 我每個禮拜去買菜一次 // I went grocery shopping the other day. 我前幾天去買菜了。

說明
② **big supermarkets or small grocery stores用法**

supermarket＝超級市場，規模較大且商品多元。grocery store＝雜貨店，位於住家附近，規模較小，但具便利性的店面。

說明
③ **We are running out of rice句型**

片語run out of＝用盡、欠缺。使用現在進行式表示「快要用盡」之意。例：We are running out of gas. 我們快沒汽油了。

沒果仁也愛的說法

對照「主要關鍵句」的類似說法

1 **I need to do some shopping.**
我需要做些採買。

2 **Where do you usually go grocery shopping?**
你通常都去哪邊採買？

3 **I am short of rice.**
我現在缺米。

這樣回答就對了

對應「主要關鍵句」的回答

1 **Get some frozen food for me.**
幫我買些冷凍食品。

2 **I shop mostly at big supermarkets.**
基本上，我都在大型超市買。

3 **Be sure to put it on your shopping list.**
記得把這一項放入你的購物清單。

🌐 世界觀小補充 💡

　　美國幅員廣大，通常要進行大量的採買都得要舟車勞頓一番，因此，一般家庭會固定於週末開車前往大型超市，一次性地採買大量生活物資。也因為這樣的消費型態，所以大型超市或量販店的販售規格，大部分都量大又低價，利用以量制價的概念經營。而雜貨店在美國提供的則是鄰近的便利性，有點類似台灣的便利商店(convenience stores)。如果家裡臨時缺生活雜貨，當然就得仰賴鄰近的雜貨店來解套了，因為提供的是便利性，所以價格無彈性。

Part 4 血汗人生必要的休閒娛樂

Can you stop by the **grocery store** on your way home?

你回家的時候可以順道去一下雜貨店嗎？　grocery store 雜貨店

We're out of soy sauce. Can you run to the nearest grocery store and get some for me?

我們沒醬油了，你可不可以跑一趟最近的雜貨店，幫我買一瓶？

We have already **run out of** eggs. So, get a carton of eggs also.

我們的雞蛋早就用完了，順便買一盒回來吧。　run out of 用完；耗盡

Mom wanted me to buy enough groceries for the whole week. Besides meat, some fish and vegetables, we can buy whatever else we want for snacks and breakfast.

媽要我幫忙買一整個禮拜用的食品雜貨。除了肉、魚跟蔬菜之外，我們可以買其他我們想要的零食跟早餐。

Please get two **loaves** of bread and a box of vanilla ice cream.

請買兩條麵包跟一盒香草冰淇淋。　loaf (一條或一塊)麵包

I am used to bringing my own **reusable** bags while doing grocery shopping.

我去採買的時候習慣自己帶環保袋。　reusable 可多次使用的

You can find milk, dairy and yogurt in the **dairy** section.

在奶製品區你可以找到牛奶、乳製品跟優格。　dairy 牛奶製的

Do you have more flour in the back? I see the **shelf** is empty.

你們倉庫裡面還有麵粉嗎？我看貨架上都是空的。　shelf 架子；貨架

Can you tell me where the **produce** section is?

可不可以告訴我生鮮食品區在哪裡？　produce 農產品

Pasta is in **aisle** 5. Just go straight down and you'll see it.

義大利麵在第五條走道，繼續直走你就會看到了。　aisle 走道

Let's go to the **express** checkout. We are only buying five items.

我們去快速結帳櫃檯吧，我們才買五樣東西。　express 快的

Do you need a coin to get a **shopping cart**?
你需要零錢去拿購物推車嗎？　　shopping cart 購物手推車

Where can I find some **detergent**?
哪邊可以找到清潔劑？　　detergent 洗潔劑

Really sorry, but our **canned** tuna is out of stock for now.
很抱歉，我們的鮪魚罐頭目前缺貨。　　canned 罐頭裝的

That will be $100 dollars. How would you like to pay?
一共是100元，請問您要怎麼付款？

Do you need any **plastic** bags? They cost one cent each.
你需要塑膠袋嗎？一個一分錢。　　plastic 塑膠的

Wait for me in the **checkout** line! I forgot to get some bags of chips.
在結帳隊伍那邊等我！我忘了買洋芋片。　　checkout 付款台

If you find any problems with anything you've bought, you have 14 days from today to return them or exchange them for something else.
商品有十四天的鑑賞期，如果產品有任何問題，您可以拿來退貨或換貨。

You can have a **full refund** if you keep your receipt.
如果您有保留收據，就可以全額退款。　　full refund 全額退款

Don't buy any wine on sale before you try some free samples.
不要買特價的紅酒，除非你有試喝過。

Look at my shopping list! I guess by the time I get to the cashier, I will probably have a full shopping cart.
看我的購物清單！我猜我去結帳時，我的購物車應該會全滿。

Many foods are advertised at membership prices. Without a card, you'll pay a higher price.
很多食物都以會員價在做廣告，沒有會員卡的話，就要付比較多錢。

Son, place that **divider** after our items so that the lady behind us can start placing her groceries down, too.
兒子，把分隔棒放在我們買的商品後面，這樣排在我們後面的女士就也能把東西放在輸送帶上了。　　divider 分隔物

關鍵一句模擬實境對話
以關鍵句破題的模擬實境對話 Track 093

 Situation 1 幫忙採買物資
lending a helping hand

A I am only half way through my assignment and cannot go to the supermarket.
我功課才做了一半，沒辦法去超市買東西。

B I can do that for you. What do you need?
我可以幫你跑一趟，你要買什麼？

A Some toilet paper, deodorant, fruits and meat.
衛生紙、芳香劑、水果跟肉。

B I need more details.
我需要商品的詳細資訊。

A Here's my shopping list.
這是我的購物清單。

 Situation 2 為週末大菜做準備
doing grocery shopping for the weekend

A I will make a roast chicken on Sunday. Let's go grocery shopping first.
我週日要做烤雞，我們先去買菜吧。

B What ingredients do you need?
你需要什麼樣的材料？

A I need to buy a whole chicken, some onions, apples, a stick of butter and some fresh herbs.
我需要全雞、一些洋蔥、蘋果、一條牛油跟新鮮香草。

B What's for dessert?
那甜點呢？

A Let's buy some pastries there.
我們就直接在那裡買些糕點吧。

Situation 3 詢問東西哪裡買
asking where to find groceries

A Excuse me, where can I find some ketchup?
請問，蕃茄醬在哪裡？

B It's in the condiments section in aisle 2.
在醬料區，第二走道那邊。

A And do you have any chewing gum?
你們有賣口香糖嗎？

B You will find it at the checkout counter.
你在結帳櫃檯就可以看到。

A Great, that's convenient.
太好了，真方便。

Unit
31

購物去—超級市場篇

Situation 4 排隊等結帳
lining up at a checkout counter

A You can go ahead of me. You're just buying a few things.
你先吧，你買的東西比較少。

B Wow, that's very nice of you.
哇，你人真好。

A No problem. Besides, my husband is getting some steak at the deli.
沒什麼，而且我先生正在生鮮區買牛排。

B Oh, that's a bit far. It might take a few minutes given that it's the weekend.
喔，那有點遠。而且又是週末，可能要等好幾分鐘。

A Exactly! So, please go ahead.
沒錯！所以別客氣，你先請吧。

Unit 32 互揪看電影
Let's go to the movies

 主要關鍵句開口說

使出關鍵３句型，英文輕鬆開口說

 Track 094

① **How about going to a movie theater on Saturday night?**
禮拜六晚上去看部電影怎麼樣？

② **What is your all-time favorite movie?**
你最喜歡的電影是哪一部？

③ **Do you usually watch movies at home or at a movie theater?**
你通常會在家看電影，還是去電影院？

沒果仁邏輯 ~~Americans~~

句型解析與用法說明

說明①　How about句型

How about+V-ing＝提議一同進行某事的問句。例：How about going to the beach this afternoon? 今天下午一起去海邊怎麼樣？

說明②　What is your all-time favorite句型

all-time favorite＝一直以來的喜好。例：Chinese food is my all-time favorite food. 中國菜是我一直以來最喜歡的料理。

說明③　Do you usually句型

Do/Does+人名／代名詞+usually+原形動詞＝詢問某人是否經常進行後述動作。例：Do you usually go out on weekends? 你週末經常出門嗎？

① **What do you say we go to the cinema on Saturday night?**
週六晚上去看電影，你覺得如何？

② **What is the movie that you like the best?**
哪部電影是你最愛看的？

③ **Where do you prefer watching movies?**
你喜歡在哪裡看電影？

Unit

32

互揪看電影

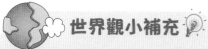 對應「主要關鍵句」的回答

① **Excellent idea!**
好主意！

② **My all-time favorite movie is** *Gone With The Wind*.
一直以來，我最喜愛的電影是《亂世佳人》。

③ **I prefer going to a movie theater.**
我偏好去電影院。

世界觀小補充

　　美國電影業舉世聞名，眾所皆知的好萊塢(Hollywood)，也因六大重量級電影公司皆設立在此，成為全世界對於美國電影認知的代名詞。此六大電影公司包含：哥倫比亞電影公司(Columbia Pictures)、華納兄弟影片(Warner Bros)、華特迪士尼影業(Walt Disney Pictures)、環球影業(Universal Studios)、二十世紀福斯影片公司(20th Century Fox)以及派拉蒙影視公司(Paramount Pictures Corporation)。

學校沒教的實用句

情境式主題句，學校沒有教，自己學起來！

Do you know that *Spiderman III* will be **coming out** in theaters this weekend?

你知道《蜘蛛人3》這週末要上映嗎？　　come out 出版；發表

My sister goes to see movies on a regular basis.

我妹經常去看電影。

What is your favorite **genre** of movie?

你最喜歡的電影類型是哪種？　　genre 文藝作品之類型

My favorite genres are action and **horror movies**.

我最喜歡的類型是動作片和恐怖片。　　horror movie 恐怖片

I'm glad that they didn't have any love scenes. Sometimes a love scene destroys a good movie.

我很開心這部片沒有感情戲，有時候，感情戲會毀了一部好電影。

This movie is the best **comedy** of the year.

這部電影是今年度最佳喜劇。　　comedy 喜劇

I couldn't stop laughing throughout the entire movie.

這部電影讓我從頭笑到尾。

Let's definitely go see this Oscar-winning film.

我們一定要去看這部奧斯卡得獎影片。

Every time my boyfriend asks me to see a sci-fi movie with him, I make up excuses to turn him down.

每次我男友要我陪他去看科幻電影，我都會找藉口拒絕他。

My brother is going to see a chick flick because he is going on a date tomorrow night.

我哥要去看年輕女孩兒的電影，因為他明晚要約會。

I will definitely see that movie again when it comes out on DVD.

這片子出DVD的時候，我一定還要再看一遍。

Don't forget to **switch off** your cell phone before the movie begins.

電影開始前，別忘了要將手機關機。　　switch off 關上

I like to watch movies at home because I like to eat los of chips and popcorn while watching.

我喜歡在家看電影，因為我喜歡邊看邊吃很多的洋芋片跟爆米花。

It's too bad that this hit movie is R-rated because I can't take my kids to see it.

這部強檔片被歸在限制級實在很可惜，我不能帶我的孩子一起去看。

That motion picture is said to be breaking **box office** records this year.

那部院線片據說將會打破今年的票房紀錄。　　box office 售票室：收入

What do you think about all the **special effects** in that 3D movie we just saw?

你覺得我們剛剛看的3D電影的特效如何？　　special effects 特殊效果

Name three movies that you like to watch over and over again.

舉出三個你會一直反覆看的電影。

I felt really annoyed by the guy sitting next to me who couldn't stop talking during the movie.

坐我隔壁的傢伙整場電影講話講不停，真是煩死人了。

The movie didn't have many **cheesy** or stupid scenes.

這部電影沒有太多俗氣或白癡的鏡頭。　　cheesy 下等的

I regret reading the **review** of the movie I am about to see.

我後悔讀了我即將要去看的電影的影評。　　review 評論

I don't like Scarlett Johansson. I think she is **overrated**.

我不喜歡史嘉蕾·喬韓森，我覺得她的評價高得莫名。　　overrate 對…評價過高

The Transformers series immediately became blockbusters once they hit the theaters.

《變型金剛》系列一上映，就馬上成為票房冠軍。

I think *The Godfather* is one of the greatest films ever made.

我覺得《教父》是電影史上最棒的電影之一。

It's so hilarious to see several celebrities appearing as guest stars in that TV show.

這個電視節目裡有些明星客串的鏡頭實在很好笑。

Unit 32 互揪看電影

關鍵一句模擬實境對話 *Topic-related Conversations*

以關鍵句破題的模擬實境對話

Track 096

Situation 1 週末電影院人潮
a less-crowded movie

A I'm going to the movies with a friend this weekend. How about you?
我這個週末要跟朋友去看電影，你呢？

B I'm not sure yet.
還不確定。

A Well, do you want to go to the cinema with us?
那你想要跟我們一起去看電影嗎？

B Tempting, but I don't like the crowds.
滿想的，但我不喜歡人擠人的感覺。

A Don't worry. We'll go to the least crowded one.
別擔心，我們會去最不擠的那間戲院。

Situation 2 好電影值得一看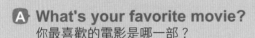
my favorite movie

A What's your favorite movie?
你最喜歡的電影是哪一部？

B That would be *The Sound of Music*.
應該是《真善美》。

A Oh, why is that?
喔，為什麼？

B All the actresses and actors sing beautifully and the dialogue is touching.
裡面演員的歌聲優美，對白又感人。

A I should go see it as well.
我也應該看看。

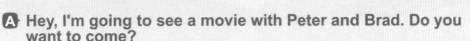

3 邀約一同看電影
movie invitation

A Hey, I'm going to see a movie with Peter and Brad. Do you want to come?
嘿，我要跟彼得還有布萊德去看電影，你要來嗎？

B When are you guys going?
你們什麼時候要去？

A We're going to see the eight o'clock showing.
我們要看八點那場。

B That would be great. Where are you guys meeting?
太好了，你們約在哪碰面？

A We're meeting at the theater at seven thirty.
我們七點半要在戲院集合。

Unit
32

互揪看電影

4 喜愛的電影大不同
my favorite movie genre

A What kind of movies do you like?
你喜歡哪一種類的電影？

B I like documentary films.
我喜歡紀錄片。

A Wow, you're deep. I like comedies because I don't want to use my brain while watching movies.
哇，你好有深度。我喜歡喜劇，因為我看電影的時候不想用大腦。

B I was just kidding. I like romance films.
開玩笑的，我喜歡愛情電影。

A Oh, same here. Let's go see one!
喔，我也是，那我們找一部去看吧！

Unit 33 來看場球賽
Let's go to a ball game

 主要關鍵句開口說

使出關鍵3句型，英文輕鬆開口說

 Track 091

① **Basketball is a popular game here in Taiwan.**
籃球比賽在台灣很受歡迎。

② **Who's your favorite soccer player?**
你最喜歡的足球員是誰？

③ **Have you ever watched games at a baseball field?**
你有到棒球場看過比賽嗎？

沒果仁邏輯 —Americans 句型解析與用法說明

 說明
① **Basketball is a popular game句型**

popular＝受歡迎的； game＝比賽。例：Table tennis is a popular game in China. 乒乓球在中國大陸很受歡迎。

 說明
② **Who's your favorite句型**

Who+is+人名／所有格+favorite＝詢問誰是某人的最愛。例：Who is your mother's favorite impressionist painter? 你媽媽最喜歡的印象派畫家是誰？

 說明
③ **Have you ever句型**

Have/Has+人名／代名詞+ever＝詢問某人是否曾經做過某事。例：Have you ever heard of Tanzania? 你有聽過坦尚尼亞這個國家嗎？

沒果仁也愛的說法 Americans

對照「主要關鍵句」的類似說法

① **There are many people who are into basketball in Taiwan.**
台灣有很多人喜歡籃球。

② **Which soccer player are you interested in following?**
有哪個足球員是你有興趣關注的？

③ **Have you ever been to Yankee Stadium?**
你去過洋基體育場嗎？

 這樣回答就對了

對應「主要關鍵句」的回答

① **I am a big fan of it myself!**
我自己也是個球迷！

② **Definitely Beckham!**
鐵定是貝克漢啊！

③ **No. I hope I will have a chance in the future.**
沒耶，希望以後有機會去。

 世界觀小補充

　　美國的NBA職業籃球賽季跟MLB職棒大聯盟相信連外國人都耳熟能詳，更別說是本國人了。NBA正式賽季於每年11月的第一個星期二開始，分為例行賽和季後賽。將各州球隊分為東、西區競爭，來自不同區域的人支持自家的隊伍，讓比賽的氣氛更加火熱。MLB例行賽於4月初展開。每支球隊在球季中要打162場比賽，棒球是美國最早開始發展的職業運動，從粉絲的狂熱中，也可窺知美國人瘋棒球的程度呢！

Part 4

血汗人生必要的休閒娛樂

My boyfriend always gets too **carried away** during the NBA season.

我男友在NBA賽季時，總是變得魂不守舍。　　carry away 吸引住

I am so excited by the **slam dunk** contest coming up this weekend!

我對這週末要舉辦的灌籃大賽感到非常興奮。　　slam dunk 灌籃；扣籃

Michael Jordan is a **legendary** NBA player.

麥可・喬丹是美國職籃的傳奇人物。　　legendary 傳奇的

His three-pointer **shot** in the last second changed the whole outcome of the game.

他最後一秒的三分線射籃改寫了比賽的結果。　　shot 投籃

What a game!

真是精采的比賽！

Watching games makes me want to shoot some **hoops**.

看著比賽讓我也想打籃球了。　　hoop 籃；籃框

It was clearly a **blocking** foul!

這明顯是個阻擋犯規。　　blocking 阻礙；阻擋

The athlete finished the game with a **layup** shot.

這名球員上籃得分，結束了這場比賽。　　layup 上籃

Americans are crazy about Major League Baseball.

美國人很瘋迷職棒大聯盟。

If you ever have a chance to go to America, you have to see a ball game at a **stadium**.

如果你有機會去美國，一定要去球場看場球賽。　　stadium 球場

Baseball is so much fun. I like to **slide** into the bases.

棒球好有趣，我喜歡滑壘。　　slide 滑壘

Many people in Taiwan are baseball **fanatics**.

台灣有很多人都是棒球狂熱份子。　　fanatic 狂熱者

For a baseball beginner like me, it will take me quite a while to learn the rules and vocabulary.

對於一個棒球新手來說，我需要花很多時間學習規則跟棒球術語。

There are usually nine **innings** in a baseball game.

一場棒球比賽通常有九局。　　inning (棒球)局

The pitcher on the mound is the ace of the team.

投手丘上那位投手是隊上的王牌。

He **struck out**!

他遭到三振出局！　　strike out 三振出局

He hit a **home run** and ended the game!

他擊出一支全壘打，比賽結束！　　home run 全壘打

Who do you think will win the World Cup?

你覺得誰會贏得世界盃冠軍？

Some fans think of soccer games as a matter of **life and death**.

有些球迷覺得足球比賽的結果就如同生死大事般重要。

life and death 生死攸關的

Who is your favorite World Cup player?

誰是你最喜歡的世界盃球員？

What country are you **following** in the World Cup?

你支持哪一支世界盃隊伍？　　follow 密切注意

Let's go to a sports bar and watch the World Cup **final**.

我們去運動酒吧看世界盃決賽吧！　　final 決賽

Some people are more interested in the **gambling** rather than the game itself.

和比賽相比，有些人對比賽的賭盤更有興趣。　　gambling 賭博

I don't want to miss out on the game the German **goalkeeper** is playing in tonight.

我不想要錯過今晚德國門將會出賽的這場球賽。　　goalkeeper 守門員

How many goals has he **scored** so far?

他目前已經射門得分多少球了？　　score 得分

Situation 1 網球界重要賽事
the Grand Slam

Ⓐ Do you watch The Wimbledon Championships?
你有看溫布頓杯嗎？

Ⓑ Yes. I like tennis very much, and I watch the games on TV.
有，我很喜歡網球，會看電視轉播。

Ⓐ Me, too. I never miss a single game.
我也是，我不會錯過任何一場比賽。

Ⓑ Which tennis player is your favorite?
你最喜歡哪個網球球員？

Ⓐ That would be Maria Sharapova.
莎拉波娃。

Situation 2 現場看球賽
going to a live baseball game

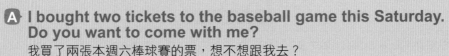

Ⓐ I bought two tickets to the baseball game this Saturday. Do you want to come with me?
我買了兩張本週六棒球賽的票，想不想跟我去？

Ⓑ Sure. Where are the seats?
當然，座位在哪裡？

Ⓐ Two infield-reserved tickets behind the home plate.
本壘板後方的內野保留票。

Ⓑ Wow! That must have cost you a fortune.
哇！應該花不少錢吧。

Ⓐ Never mind.
沒關係的。

Situation 3 看球賽何必去酒吧
watching World Cup at home

A I bet all the sports bars downtown will be packed tonight.
我跟你賭今天晚上市區的運動酒吧一定爆滿。

B Is it because of the World Cup final?
是因為世界盃總決賽嗎？

A Duh.
不然哩。

B Why don't we just watch it at home?
我們何不乾脆在家裡看轉播？

A That's what I was going to say.
我正準備這麼說。

Situation 4 看球賽要有洋芋片
watching the NBA with potato chips

A Did you get some chips at the supermarket?
你去超市有買洋芋片嗎？

B No. What for?
沒有，為什麼需要？

A What? How could you not prepare some chips at home when it's the NBA playoffs?
什麼？現在是美國NBA季後賽耶，怎麼能不準備幾包洋芋片在家啊？

B Who the heck knows what that is!
誰會知道那是什麼東西啊！

A Argh... It is the post-season tournament, and it is very important.
呃…這是美國職籃整季終了的決賽啦，非常重要！

Unit 34 全民瘋路跑
Marathon and jogging

 主要關鍵句開口說

使出關鍵3句型，英文輕鬆開口說

Track 100

① **Let's go for a run!**
我們去跑步吧！

② **Have you ever run a marathon?**
你有參加過馬拉松嗎？

③ **Are there any running guides for a beginner like me?**
有沒有給像我這種初學者的跑步指南？

沒果仁邏輯 ~~Americans~~ 句型解析與用法說明

 說明 ① **Let's go for a run句型**

Let's+原形動詞＝提議一同進行某件事。例：Let's order some takeout. 我們叫些外賣吧！

 說明 ② **run a marathon用法**

run a marathon=參加馬拉松賽事。marathon也可做延伸運用，舉凡任何賽事、活動需耗費比一般多的時間或耐力，都可以用此單字表達。舉例：a dance marathon (舞蹈馬拉松賽，比賽時間可能很長或者接續多天進行)、a sales marathon (特賣會馬拉松，延續很長時間)。

 說明 ③ **Are there any句型**

Is/Are+there+any用以詢問某樣東西／某種狀態是否存在。例：Are there any other planets in the universe? 宇宙間有沒有其他星球？

① **How about going out for a run?**
去跑個步如何？

② **What kind of running events have you been to?**
你參加過什麼樣的跑步比賽？

③ **Are there any beginner's running programs I could take?**
有沒有專為跑步初學者開設的課程？

Unit
34
全民瘋路跑

這樣回答就對了　　對應「主要關鍵句」的回答

① **I'd rather stay at home.**
我寧願待在家裡。

② **No. But I am training for the one in the end of this year.**
沒有，不過我正在為年底的馬拉松訓練中。

③ **Yes, there are countless online guides to choose from.**
有的，網路上有很多的指南可挑選。

 世界觀小補充

　　馬拉松傳自歐洲，在美國發揚光大。很多國際性的賽事場地皆在此舉辦，許多具備經驗的跑者都會想一嚐波士頓馬拉松賽的洗禮。雖說台灣近幾年與路跑相關的賽事與發展盛況空前，不過美國起步更早，有關跑步的資訊也更加完善，因此喜歡路跑的人也可以多利用國外的路跑網路資訊，從新手上路的訓練、5K/10K/半馬/全馬的教戰手冊一直到營養補充、運動後保健等等，五花八門的訊息不怕你挑戰搜尋。

I go to an elementary school across from my house and jog a few **laps** around the playground every night.

我每天晚上都在我家對面的小學操場慢跑幾圈。　lap 一圈

I go **jogging** in the morning when the air is still fresh.

我趁早上空氣還新鮮的時候慢跑。　jogging 慢跑

Some people find jogging stressful, but I see it as a way to relieve some of my stress.

有些人覺得慢跑壓力很大，但我覺得這是一個可以紓壓的管道。

It feels so good after jogging for half an hour.

慢跑了半個小時後，讓人感覺舒暢。

I usually jog on a **treadmill** because it's convenient.

跑步機很方便，所以我通常都用它練跑。　treadmill 跑步機

Running on a treadmill is the last **resort** for me, and I only do it if it's raining.

如果一直下雨，我才會使出在跑步機上跑步的最後一招。　resort 憑藉的手段

I like taking **aerobic** classes instead of running outside.

和在室外跑步相比，我比較喜歡有氧課程。　aerobic 增氧健身運動的

I decided to start jogging one day and **fell for** it right away.

我有天決定開始跑步，後來就愛上了這項運動。　fall for 對⋯傾心

I find it hard to **catch my breath** when running.

跑步的時候，我感覺自己快喘不過氣了。　catch one's breath 喘氣

Running has become a **trendy** exercise in Taiwan in the past few years.

近幾年，跑步在台灣成為一項主流的運動。　trendy 流行的

I am training for my first half **marathon** this winter.

我在為今年冬天的半程馬拉松做訓練。　marathon 馬拉松賽跑

I think most people can run as long as they **set their minds to** it.

我覺得只要有心，每個人都可以跑步。　set one's minds to 有心想⋯

Some people think they are not capable of running because they don't have the habit of working out on a regular basis.

有些人因為沒有固定運動的習慣，所以會覺得自己無法跑步。

My parents keep stressing their belief that running might hurt your knees.

我父母親一直強調跑步傷膝蓋的觀念。

There are hundreds of running events held each year in Taiwan.

每年有幾百場的跑步賽事在台灣舉辦。

Don't try too hard in your first race, or you might end up getting disappointed.

初次參加賽事的時候別太勉強，否則你會以失望收場。

Don't overtrain yourself, or you might experience unexpected **injuries**.

不要訓練過度，否則會導致意想不到的運動傷害。 ⬗injury 傷害

I always buy a new pair of running shoes when I wear the old pair out.

我總是等舊的鞋子穿壞了，才買新的跑步鞋。

Learn correct form before you even hit the **pavement**.

上路開跑之前，請先學習正確的姿勢。 ⬗pavement 人行道

You need to keep a steady **pace** in order to endure a longer run.

你需要維持一定的速度，才能跑的久。 ⬗pace 步速

I try to exhale and inhale with a fixed tempo so that I don't pant like a dog.

我試著以穩定的節奏吸吐氣，才不至於喘得跟隻狗一樣。

I invest a big sum of money in all kinds of running **gear**.

我花了很多錢在各種跑步配件上。 ⬗gear 工具；設備

I find that the only two important gear I need are shoes and shirts.

我發覺兩件最重要的跑步配件是鞋子跟上衣。

My friend likes to run in groups, whereas I like to jog alone.

我朋友喜歡成群結隊地跑，但我喜歡獨自跑步。

關鍵一句模擬實境對話

以關鍵句破題的模擬實境對話

Situation 1 慢跑來減肥
jogging to lose weight

A There are more and more people running in the park.
有愈來愈多人在公園跑步。

B I know. I just don't understand what makes them start?
是啊，但我不懂是什麼讓他們開始想跑的？

A Losing weight may be among the top three reasons.
減肥應該是排行榜前三名。

B Speaking of which, I think I need to lose some myself.
說到減肥，我覺得我也應該要減一些。

A What do you say we join the crowd in the park as well?
那我們也加入公園的群眾，你覺得如何？

Situation 2 健身何必化妝
why wear makeup?

A Come on, just put on your shoes and let's get going.
快點穿上鞋子，我們該出發了。

B Wait, I need to powder my nose first.
等等，我要先補個妝。

A Are you insane? We're out for a run, not a beauty contest!
你瘋了嗎？我們是出去跑步，又不是參加選美！

B I can't stand going out without makeup.
我不能忍受素顏出門啦！

A Suit yourself. Wait till you see that big zit on your face.
隨便你，等著看你臉上長出痘痘吧。

3 慢跑小撇步
tips for jogging

A You've been running for so many years. Can you give me some tips on running?
你已經跑步好幾年了，可否告訴我一些撇步呢？

B First of all, you need to get a pair of high-impact running shoes.
首先，你要去買一雙能吸收高衝擊的跑步鞋。

A Got it. Anything else?
了解，還有呢？

B Never skip warm-ups.
千萬不可省略暖身運動。

A Thanks for the tips.
謝謝你和我分享這些撇步。

Unit
34
全民瘋路跑

4 跑步還是戶外好
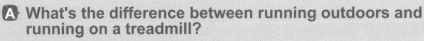
running outdoors vs running indoors

A What's the difference between running outdoors and running on a treadmill?
在室外跑步跟用室內跑步機跑有什麼差別？

B For starters, you can't enjoy the fresh air by running indoors.
首先，你在室內跑是呼吸不到新鮮空氣的。

A Makes sense.
有道理。

B Also, your body will adapt to all kinds of terrain if you run outdoors.
而且，如果在戶外跑，你的身體就能適應各種地形。

A Sounds like you are for running outdoors.
聽起來你是贊成到戶外跑步的人。

Unit 35 全民瘋泳渡
Swimming

 主要關鍵句開口說

使出關鍵3句型，英文輕鬆開口說

① **Do you know how to swim?**
你會游泳嗎？

② **What style of swimming do you specialize in?**
你游泳專精哪一式？

③ **How often do you swim?**
你都多久游一次泳？

 Americans 句型解析與用法說明

沒果仁邏輯

 ① **Do you know how to句型**

Do/does+人名／代名詞+know+how+to＝詢問某人是否知道如何進行某件事情。例：Does Jocelyn know how to use a washing machine? 喬塞琳知道如何使用洗衣機嗎？

② **What style of＋名詞＋do you specialize in句型**

What+style+of+N+do/does+人名／代名詞+specialize+in＝詢問某人擅長的運動形式是哪一種。例：What style of dances does your partner specialize in? 你的夥伴擅長哪一種類型的舞蹈？

③ **How often do you句型**

How often是用來詢問頻率的句型，主要在問對方間隔多久進行某件事情。例：How often does he stop by for a visit? 他多久來拜訪一次？

沒果仁也愛的說法

Americans

對照「主要關鍵句」的類似說法

1 **Can you swim?**
你會游泳嗎？

2 **What style of swimming are you familiar with?**
你熟悉哪種游法？

3 **Do you go swimming often?**
你常常去游泳嗎？

這樣回答就對了

對應「主要關鍵句」的回答

1 **No, I know nothing about swimming.**
不，我是個旱鴨子。

2 **I specialize in the butterfly stroke.**
我特別擅長蝶式。

3 **I swim twice a week.**
我一個禮拜游兩次。

🌐 世界觀小補充

　　美國在游泳這項運動上也是世界翹楚。麥可·弗雷德·菲爾普斯二世(Michael Fred Phelps II)是美國游泳運動員，男子個人混合泳、蝶泳三項世界紀錄的保持者。他在2004年的雅典奧運上一人拿下游泳項目上的六枚金牌，成為得到金牌數最多的運動員。泳式種類的英文有自由式freestyle、蛙式breaststroke、仰式backstroke、蝶式butterfly stroke。中文的蛙式跟仰式在英文中是以胸部(breast)還是背部(back)在水裡來區分，小心不要因為單字看起來相似而搞混了！

Part 4

血汗人生必要的休閒娛樂

I'm not a good swimmer. The only style I know is the **dog paddle**.
我不擅長游泳，我唯一會的是狗爬式。　　dog paddle 狗爬式游泳

I can't hold my breath long enough to be an effective **swimmer**.
我沒辦法憋氣太久，所以無法成為優秀的游泳健將。　　swimmer 游泳者

I can **hold my breath** for a minute and a half.
我可以憋氣一分半鐘。　　hold one's breath 暫時屏住呼吸

My kids are taking swimming lessons at a local swimming pool during summer vacation.
我孩子暑假的時候去本地的游泳池上游泳課。

The instructor taught us how to not be afraid of the water by learning how to put our face under the water and holding our breath for a few seconds.
教練教我們把臉放在水裡，憋氣幾秒鐘，用這樣的方式來教我們不要害怕水。

Learning how to float on your back is one of the basic skills acquired in the first few swimming lessons.
學習如何利用自己的背部漂浮是在前幾堂游泳課程中必學的基本技巧。

I learned how to do some of the basic strokes, including freestyle, breaststroke, backstroke and butterfly this summer.
我今年夏天學了幾個基本的泳式，包含自由式、蛙式、仰式以及蝶式。

Younger students are allowed to **dive** off the side of the pool or from the diving board.
年輕的學員可以從泳池旁邊跳水，或選擇從跳板跳水。　　dive 跳水

I'm on the swimming team.
我是游泳隊的一員。

I made the **varsity** swimming team.
我進了大學的游泳校隊。　　varsity 大學代表隊

Where is a good place to go swimming near here?
這附近有什麼地方適合游泳？

I like **freestyle** swimming, but I'm better at the butterfly.

我喜歡游自由式,但我擅長的是蝶式。　freestyle 自由式的

I'm pretty quick at the **backstroke**.

我的仰式游得滿快的。　backstroke 仰泳

Some people go to the beach not to swim but to **sunbathe**.

有些人去海邊不是為了游泳,而是為了享受日光浴。　sunbathe 沐日光浴

I've been swimming ever since I was six years old.

我六歲就開始游泳了。

I swim four times a week.

我一個星期游四次泳。

I believe swimming is very healthy, especially for the **joints**.

我認為游泳有益健康,尤其是對關節很好。　joint 關節

I've done my ten laps for the day.

我已經游完今天的十圈了。

Swimming can increase your **cardiovascular** performance as well as your muscle strength.

游泳可以強化你的心肺功能與肌耐力。　cardiovascular 心血管的

Are there any **lifeguards** at your community swimming pool?

你家社區的游泳池有沒有救生員?　lifeguard 救生員

If you are a beginner, please stay in the **shallow** end and practice.

如果你是初學者,請待在淺水區練習。　shallow 淺的

Be sure to put on some **sunscreen** if you don't want to get burned.

如果你不想被曬傷的話,記得擦防曬乳。　sunscreen 防曬乳

Get your **goggles** and swimming suit ready. Let's go for a swim!

把你的蛙鏡跟泳衣準備好,我們去游泳吧!　goggle 護目鏡

Let's go to the beach. I want to show off my new bathing suit.

我們去海灘吧,我想要秀一下我的新泳衣。

Danny fell asleep under the sun with only trunks on and got a **sunburn**.

丹尼只穿了泳褲在太陽底下睡著,結果就被曬傷了。　sunburn 曬傷

關鍵一句模擬實境對話 *Topic-related Conversations*

以關鍵句破題的模擬實境對話

 Track 105

Situation 1 游泳機
a swim station

A Is there a swimming pool in this hotel?
這家飯店有游泳池嗎？

B We don't have a full-sized swimming pool, but we do have individual swim stations.
我們沒有游泳池，但我們有供個人使用的游泳機。

A What exactly does that mean?
那是什麼東西啊？

B Well, it is like a treadmill, except instead of running, you swim.
它就像跑步機一樣，只是你用它來游泳，而不是跑步。

A That sounds really cool.
聽起來很酷耶。

Situation 2 不想曬太黑
putting on sunscreen

A Have you got dressed yet? Don't forget your goggles.
你換好衣服了沒？別忘了帶蛙鏡。

B I am almost ready. Have you applied some suntan lotion?
我快好了，你有塗助曬乳嗎？

A I don't want to get too tanned this summer, so I put on some sunblock lotion.
我今年夏天不想要曬太黑，所以我擦了防曬乳。

B Can I have some of that as well?
我可以也借用一點嗎？

A Sure. Here you go.
當然，拿去。

3 專業級的練習
hard-core swim training

A How often do you guys go swimming?
你們多久去游一次泳？

B We set a goal of swimming five times a week.
我們立下一週要游五次泳的目標。

A Wow. And how long do you swim each time?
哇，那你們一次都游多長？

B I don't really keep track, but we swim 50 laps, which equals 2,500 meters every time.
我沒有特別記錄，不過我們每次大概都游50趟，相當於2,500公尺。

A My goodness; that's hard-core!
天啊，那太專業了！

Unit
35
全民瘋泳渡

Situation 4 自由式教學
asking for a freestyle demonstration

A What style of swimming are you most familiar with?
你最熟悉哪一種游泳姿勢？

B Freestyle.
自由式。

A Oh, can you show me how to swim this stroke correctly?
喔，那你可否教我如何正確游自由式？

B I suggest you surf the internet first. There are a lot of how-to clips you can start right away on your own.
建議你先上網找資料。網路上有很多教學影片，你回家馬上就能自學了。

A Sure, I will. But will you still demonstrate it for me in the water?
我回去當然會找，但你還是能在水裡示範給我看吧？

主要關鍵句開口說

使出關鍵3句型，英文輕鬆開口說

Track 106

① **Can you ride a bike?**
你會騎腳踏車嗎？

② **Do you own a bike or do you use a rental bike?**
你自己有腳踏車還是用租的？

③ **I love riding on the bike path along the river.**
我喜愛在沿著河畔的腳踏車道騎行。

沒果仁邏輯 Americans

句型解析與用法說明

① Can you ride a bike句型

Can為表示可否、能夠的助動詞，通常在詢問對方能力時使用。例：Can he play guitar? 他會不會彈吉他？

② Do you own a bike or do you use a rental bike句型

own＝擁有、rental bike＝出租腳踏車。or＝或者，是連接詞，連接兩個子句，在問句當中使用，結果不是子句一就是子句二。例：Do you prefer going to bed late or staying up all night?/I can't live without rest. I'd rather go to bed late. 問：你偏好晚睡還是熬夜？/ 答：沒休息我沒辦法活，我選擇晚睡。

③ I love riding句型

love+V-ing＝一直以來喜愛做的事情。例：Lance loves painting the house. 蘭斯一直以來都很喜歡粉刷房子。

Americans

沒果仁也愛的說法　對照「主要關鍵句」的類似說法

① **Do you know how to ride a bike?**
你知道怎麼騎單車嗎？

② **Do you have a bike of your own?**
你有自己的腳踏車嗎？

③ **I enjoy riding along the coastline.**
我喜歡沿著海岸線騎車。

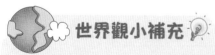

這樣回答就對了　對應「主要關鍵句」的回答

① **Yes, I can.**
我會騎車。

② **I always rely on the bike rental service in Taipei.**
我都仰賴台北市的腳踏車租賃服務。

③ **Take me with you next time, please.**
拜託下次帶我一起去吧！

世界觀小補充

　　歐洲很早就把腳踏車當作除了代步工具之外的健身器具，另外還為單車規劃了專用道、賽事活動等。環法自由車賽 (Le Tour de France)早在20世紀初就已經開始，現在已經聞名世界。歐洲城鎮的單車租賃服務模式也是台北Ubike參考的指標之一。雖然一開始歐洲城鎮的單車租賃不如現今自動化，不過卻相當普及，一方面也是因為城鎮的腹地不大，環境適宜自行車穿梭。觀光客到歐洲若想要在各城鎮遊歷，也可以考慮使用單車觀光的方式探索。

Part 4

血汗人生必要的休閒娛樂

I think riding a bike is more eco-friendly than taking any other type of transportation.

我覺得騎腳踏車比其他任何交通工具都要來得環保。

I learned how to **ride a bike** when I was seven.

我七歲的時候就學會騎腳踏車。　　ride a bike 騎腳踏車

The key to learning to ride is that you should not be afraid to **fall off**.

學會騎車的關鍵就是你必須不害怕摔倒。　　fall off 落下

Cycling around Taiwan has been one of the hottest pastimes for the past several years.

騎車環島在近幾年成為台灣最熱門的休閒活動之一。　　cycling 騎腳踏車兜風

Several bike trails along the riverside circling Taipei are well-established and attract many bikers to visit during weekends.

有幾條沿著河邊的環台北自行車道建造得相當完善，吸引很多自行車騎士在週末期間造訪。

Cyclists **pedaled** at their own pace and shared their experiences after the ride.

騎士按自己的步調踩踏前進，並在騎完之後分享經驗。　　pedal 踩踏板

I've decided to start mountain biking to get **in shape**.

為了雕塑身形，我決定開始騎越野自行車。　　in shape 處於良好的健康狀況

I took my bike into a cycling shop to get a **tune up**.

我把腳踏車拿去自行車行檢查。　　tune up 調整

My bike was in pretty bad shape, so I wasn't sure if it would serve my needs.

我的腳踏車狀態相當差，所以我不確定是否能符合我的需求。

The mechanic at the shop adjusted my brakes, oiled the chain, fixed my flat tire, and adjusted the spokes in my wheels.

自行車行的技術人員調整了我的剎車、幫鍊條上油、修好洩氣的輪胎，並調整好車輪的輪輻。

I'm thinking about getting a lighter bike, but my current bike will have to do for now.

我有考慮要買一台輕一點的腳踏車,但我現在這台暫時也還堪用。

I need a new bike helmet to protect my head in case I fall off the bike.

我需要一頂新的安全帽來保護我的頭部,以免我從腳踏車上摔下來。

In order to train myself for the triathlon, I have set a four-week cycling program of over 200 km per week.

為了要訓練鐵人三項的競賽,我制定了四週計畫,每週要騎超過200公里的自行車。

Make sure your **brakes** are functioning normally.

一定要確定你的煞車運作正常。　　brake 煞車

Have you ever ridden racing bikes, mountain bikes, BMX bikes or other recreational bikes?

你是否騎過比賽用腳踏車、越野腳踏車、小輪賽車或其他休閒用腳踏車呢?

Cyclists should always wear **protective** gear.

騎士上路應該要全程配戴保護配件。　　protective 防護的

There are more and more people cycling to work thanks to the public rental bikes all around Taipei.

由於台北公共腳踏車的租賃愈來愈普及,有愈來愈多人騎腳踏車上班。

For your own safety, when riding a bike in the dark, be sure to dress in a bright-colored outfit.

安全起見,在天黑後騎腳踏車時,一定要穿著亮色系的衣服。

This bike has 12 **gears**.

這台腳踏車有12段變速。　　gear 排檔

One of my dreams is to participate in the Tour de France, one of the most prestigious cycling events in the world.

我的夢想之一就是要參加環法賽,全世界最著名的自行車賽之一。

I went on a cycling tour this summer and rode 900 kilometers in total.

我這個夏天參加了自行車之旅,一共完成了900公里的距離。

I always bring a **portable** air pump when riding outdoors.

我外出騎乘的時候都會帶著可攜式幫浦。　　portable 便於攜帶的

Unit

36

全民瘋單車

Situation 1 腳踏車諮詢
looking for a bike

A What kind of bike are you looking for?
你在找什麼樣的腳踏車？

B I'm really not sure.
我不太確定。

A We carry road bikes, mountain bikes, beach cruisers, and racing bikes.
我們有公路車、越野車、沙灘自行車以及比賽用自行車。

B I'll be riding mainly to work, but I want something versatile enough for anything.
我主要是騎去上班，但希望它的功能盡量多一點。

A I would either go for a road bike or a mountain bike.
要是我的話，會選擇公路車或越野車。

Situation 2 放手一搏
give it a try

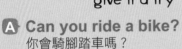

A Can you ride a bike?
你會騎腳踏車嗎？

B I can't and don't think I will ever learn.
我不會，而且也不覺得我學得成。

A Everyone can learn! Let me teach you.
每個人都學得會！讓我來教你。

B I am afraid of getting hurt, and I have poor balance.
我很怕受傷，而且我平衡感很差。

A How do you know the results if you never try?
如果你不試，怎麼會知道結果呢？

Part 4 血汗人生必要的休閒娛樂

228

Situation **3** 代步工具
various purposes of a bike

A Can you tell me a little bit about the difference among the various bikes?

可不可以請你告訴我這些腳踏車的差別呢？

B The mountain bikes are very sturdy for off-road cycling. Beach cruisers have just one speed, so you won't be shifting any gears.

越野車在非一般道路上使用也很穩健。沙灘自行車只有一個定速，所以不用換檔。

A I just want a simple tool for transportation.

我只想要一個簡單的代步工具而已。

B Just go for a utility bike, then. The gears are simple without many complicated functions.

那就挑選萬用的工具腳踏車吧。檔速很單純，沒有太多複雜的功能。

Situation **4** 環台旅行
cycling around Taiwan

A What's your plan for the five-day national holiday?

五天的國定假日你有什麼計畫？

B My best buddy and I are going to cycle around Taiwan, along the sea coast.

我跟我最好的朋友要一起沿著海岸線環島台灣。

A Wow, you are so adventurous. Have you ever done that before?

哇，你好有冒險精神，你以前環島過嗎？

B No. I am a first-timer.

沒有，我第一次參加。

A Oh, you'd better start to plan the entire route.

喔，那你最好開始規劃全程路線了。

主要關鍵句開口說

使出關鍵3句型，英文輕鬆開口說

Track 109

① **Have you ever been camping?**
你有露過營嗎？

② **I don't know how to pitch a tent.**
我不會搭帳篷。

③ **Let's build a campfire!**
我們來升營火吧！

沒果仁邏輯 *Americans* 句型解析與用法說明

說明① Have you ever been camping句型

Have/has+人名／代名詞+ever+過去分詞表示詢問某人是否有過某種經驗。
例：Has your mom ever cooked chicken soup? 你媽媽有煮過雞湯嗎？

說明② I don't know how to句型

人名／代名詞+don't/doesn't+know+how+to＝某人不知道如何處理某件事
情。例：Margaret doesn't know how to drive. 瑪格麗特不會開車。

說明③ Let's build a campfire句型

Let's+動詞原形＝提議一同進行某件事情。例：Let's clean the house. 我們
來打掃房子吧。

沒果仁也愛的說法

對照「主要關鍵句」的類似說法

1 **Have you ever been on a camping holiday?**
你曾經在放假時去露營嗎？

2 **I can't pitch a tent.**
我不會搭帳篷。

3 **Let's start a campfire!**
一起來升火吧！

Unit
37

登山露營好健康

這樣回答就對了

對應「主要關鍵句」的回答

1 **Yes, I have.**
是的，我有露營過。

2 **Let me show you how.**
讓我來示範給你看。

3 **Let me catch my breath first.**
先讓我喘口氣再說。

世界觀小補充

　　美國腹地廣大，有時候從A地開車到B地，可能要花好幾天的時間才會到達，所以公路旅行(road trip)這樣的活動在美國很流行。年輕人常常約朋友一同開著車到各州遊歷，開累了就找個臨時的下榻旅舍。除了這種旅行方式之外，露營也因為地大物博、景致變化多端而顯得更為有趣。美國很多地方都設有露營區，規劃一區讓開露營拖車(trailer car)的人可以停放，享受露營的樂趣。在美國公路上看到大型的露營拖車也是稀鬆平常的事情。

Before going camping, I went to the sporting goods store to get some new gear.

去露營之前，我跑了一趟運動用品店，買了新的配件跟用具。

I chose to camp at a **campsite**.

我選擇在露營區露營。　　campsite 露營地

What are the advantages and disadvantages of **camping out**?

在野外露營有什麼優缺點？　　camp out 搭帳篷露營

It's better to arrive at the site before dark. I don't want to **pitch a tent** in the dark.

最好在天黑前抵達露營區，我不想要摸黑搭帳篷。　　pitch a tent 搭帳篷

My friend randomly picked a site for the tent and ended up spending a painful night with roots and stones digging into his back.

我朋友隨便找了個地方搭帳篷，結果整個晚上慘遭樹枝跟石頭戳背。

Modern tents are very light and very easy to pitch.

現代化的帳篷很輕，也很容易搭建。

I bought a new sleeping bag, one that was waterproof for the camping trip.

我買了一個具有防水功能的新睡袋，露營時可以使用。

My dad just finished lighting a **campfire** right before it started to rain.

我爸才剛把火升好，結果就開始下雨了。　　campfire 營火

I will only go camping with you if you have a camping trailer. I can't stand sleeping in a tent.

除非你有露營車，我才跟你去露營，實在無法忍受睡在帳篷裡。

I've got a Swiss knife, gas and a **stove** ready, so let's cook!

我有瑞士刀、瓦斯以及爐子，來下廚吧！　　stove 火爐

Are there shower **facilities** at this campsite?

這個露營區有淋浴設備嗎？　　facility 設施；設備

The least interesting thing during a camping trip is **taking down** the tent.

露營之旅最無趣的就是拆帳篷的時候了。　　take down 拆掉

The campsite **overlooks** the whole lake.

露營區俯瞰整個湖區。　　overlook 眺望；俯瞰

The view around the site was **breathtaking**!

營區附近的景緻真是美不勝收。　　breathtaking 驚人的

I usually reserve a campsite at a campground in the **canyon**.

我通常會在峽谷的露營地預約一個露營區。　　canyon 峽谷

Some campsites are non-reservable and are available on a first-come, first-served basis.

有些露營區不接受預約，而是以「先到先服務」的機制營運。

We always look for a campsite that has a lot of shade from the sun, is near a water source, has a good fire pit, and has a good spot to pitch a tent.

找營區的時候，我們總是注重要有很多遮陽處、靠近水源、有好的火坑，而且是個好搭帳篷的地點。

What do you say we unload our gear from the car, set up our tent, and start a fire to prepare dinner?

你覺得我們先從車上卸下裝備、搭帳篷，然後升火準備晚餐如何？

Building a fire isn't difficult if you have the right tinder and wood to get it going.

要升火並不困難，如果你有適合的火種跟助燃的木頭就很容易。

I like to roast marshmallows after **setting up** the campfire.

升好營火後，我喜歡烤棉花糖。　　set up 豎立；建造

Besides bringing all the camping gear, a **first aid kit** shouldn't be ignored.

除了攜帶全套的露營配備之外，急救箱也別忘了帶。　　first aid kit 急救藥箱

After dinner, we sometimes sit around the fire and tell stories or sing songs.

用過晚餐後，我們有時會圍著營火坐一圈，說故事跟唱歌。

以關鍵句破題的模擬實境對話

 Track 111

Situation 1 手機＝手電筒

using a smartphone as a flashlight

A Two sleeping bags, a gas stove, and some canned food.
兩個睡袋、一個瓦斯爐、還有一些罐頭食品。

B Check, check, check.
打勾、打勾、打勾。

A Ah, you must have forgotten the flashlight.
啊，你一定忘了要帶手電筒。

B That wouldn't be necessary. We all have smartphones, don't we?
不需要，我們都有智慧型手機，不是嗎？

A Oh, you mean using the flashlight app as a substitute?
喔，你是說用手電筒應用程式來取代嗎？

Situation 2 你到底會什麼？

a useless guy

A Go and pitch the tent.
去搭帳篷。

B I don't know how.
我不會。

A Then, go and set up a campfire.
那去生火。

B Um, you'll have to show me how.
喔，那你必須示範給我看。

A What exactly can you do?
你到底會做什麼？

A Do you want to go camping next month?
你下個月想不想去露營？

B Are we going to sleep in a real tent?
我們要睡在真的帳篷裡嗎？

A Duh. Where else are we going to sleep?
不然呢？還有哪裡可以睡？

B I thought there would be some trailers so that we could sleep indoors.
我以為會有露營車，我們就可以睡在室內了。

A Well, my kind of camping involves staying in the woods and sleeping in the open air.
嗯，我所謂的露營是要待在森林裡，睡在大自然中的。

Unit
37

登山露營好健康

Situation 4 沒有輕便旅行這回事
traveling light is not an option

A Do we need to buy a tent and some sleeping bags?
我們需不需要買帳篷跟睡袋？

B I think we can rent everything at the campsite we are going to.
營區那裡應該都有得租。

A Great. So we can travel light this time.
太棒了，那我們這次可以享受輕便旅行了。

B There's no such thing as traveling light. I am bringing lots of food and drinks.
沒有輕便旅行這回事，我要帶很多食物跟飲料。

A Brilliant idea!
好主意！

 主要關鍵句開口說

使出關鍵３句型，英文輕鬆開口說 Track 112

① **What kind of music do you like?**
你喜歡什麼類型的音樂？

② **Can you play a musical instrument?**
你會演奏樂器嗎？

③ **Do you prefer oldies or new hits?**
你喜歡老歌還是新曲？

沒果仁邏輯 Americans 句型解析與用法說明

 說明 ① **What kind of句型**

What+kind+of+名詞＝哪種類型，後面加上主要問句。例：What kind of drinks can I get you? 要我幫你拿哪種飲料呢？

 說明 ② **Can you play a musical instrument句型**

can＝詢問能力、徵求許可或要求幫忙的助動詞。例：Can I come in? 我可以進來嗎？/Can you please pass the salt? 可以請你把鹽遞過來嗎？

 說明 ③ **Do you prefer句型**

prefer＝偏好，後面接名詞或動名詞。例：Do you prefer staying indoors or going out on weekends? 你週末喜歡待在室內還是外出？

Part 4 血汗人生必要的休閒娛樂

沒果仁也愛的說法

對照「主要關鍵句」的類似說法

① **What musical genres do you like?**
你喜歡什麼種類的音樂？

② **Do you know how to play a musical instrument?**
你知道怎麼彈奏樂器嗎？

③ **Do you like listening to oldies or new hits?**
你喜歡聽老歌還是新曲？

這樣回答就對了

對應「主要關鍵句」的回答

① **I like classical music best.**
我最喜歡古典音樂。

② **Yes, I can. I've been playing piano since I was six.**
我會，我六歲就開始彈鋼琴，一直到現在。

③ **I like both, actually.**
其實我兩種都喜歡。

世界觀小補充

　　美國的音樂史相當豐富且錯綜複雜，不同種類的音樂型態崛起跟當時的歷史事件或不同族群所碰撞出的火花有密切的關係。例如越戰時期的反戰歌曲就是由歷史事件所引發的特定音樂風格。不同年代也會因為演奏的樂器或者外來文化的影響而產生不同的音樂風格，像是早期的British Invasion，就是英國搖滾流行音樂「入侵」美國的時期，披頭四(The Beatles)風靡全球是最明顯的代表例子。

Part 4 血汗人生必要的休閒娛樂

I think music is **indispensable** and the spice of life.
我認為音樂是生活中不可或缺的調味品。　indispensable 必需的

I enjoy listening to Broadway **musicals**.
我喜歡聽百老匯的音樂劇。　musical 歌舞劇

My mom was invited to a classical concert performed in a **concert hall**.
我媽受邀參加在音樂廳表演的古典音樂會。　concert hall 音樂廳

Did you hear the new song by Coldplay on the **radio** yesterday?
你昨天有聽到廣播放的酷玩樂團的新歌嗎？　radio 收音機

I will most definitely buy the CD when the new album is **released**.
這新專輯的光碟一出，我一定會去買。　release 發行；發表

I can't work without music, which means I listen to music practically everyday.
我工作的時候不能沒有音樂，也就是說，我基本上是天天聽音樂。

He is the most old-fashioned guy I've ever met! He still listens to music on a cassette player!
他真的是我見過最老派的人了！他現在還在用卡帶播放器聽音樂。

I am trying to make up my own music by playing the **ukulele**.
我嘗試用烏克麗麗來創作音樂。　ukulele 烏克麗麗琴

Someone told me that the ukulele is one of the simplest musical instruments to learn.
有人跟我說烏克麗麗是最容易易學的樂器之一。

I download most of the music online and listen to it on my iPod.
我的音樂幾乎都是線上下載，再存到iPod上面聽。

There are more and more live concerts being held in the Taipei Arena these days.
台北小巨蛋近期舉辦的演唱會愈來愈多。

My brother's favorite type of music is heavy metal, and he is also a member of an amateur band.

我哥最喜歡的音樂類型是重金屬，他同時也是業餘樂團的成員。

There are now several smart phone apps, which provide diversified music services.

現在有一些智慧型手機的應用程式提供多元化的音樂服務。

The Billboard charts are the major indication of the popularity of songs and albums in the United States.

告示牌排行榜是美國音樂或專輯受歡迎程度的主要指標。

I have a long workout playlist in my phone that I cannot do without!

我手機裡有一長串的健身專用音樂是我萬萬不能缺少的！

EDM (electronic dance music) is so popular and is often heard in **nightclubs**.

電音舞曲很受歡迎，在夜店常常會聽到。　nightclub 夜總會

I am watching Elton John's live performance on YouTube. His voice is amazing!

我在YouTube上看艾爾頓·強的現場演唱會，他聲音超迷人！

Have you ever tried singing in a karaoke bar?

你有在卡拉OK唱歌的經驗嗎？

Can you memorize the **lyrics** of all the songs you like?

你可以記得所有你喜愛歌曲的歌詞嗎？　lyric 歌詞

I like jazz music in general, be it ragtime, blues, big band swing, bebop and so many other types.

幾乎所有種類的爵士樂我都喜歡，不論是拉格泰姆、藍調、大樂團、咆勃爵士樂或其他種類，我都喜愛。

When I hear the music from the '80s, I always feel like dancing to the beat.

當我聽到80年代(1980-1989)的音樂時，我總是會想要跟著節奏起舞。

My brother misses the **old-school** hip-hop of his college years.

我哥懷念他大學時期的老式嘻哈音樂。　old-school 老派的

Situation **1** 音樂配美食
appetite-enhancing music

A What kind of music do you think we should play during the dinner party this Saturday?
這週六的晚餐聚會，你覺得我們應該播放什麼樣的音樂啊？

B I am thinking about something upbeat and mellow.
我覺得輕快溫和的音樂比較好。

A I happen to have several CDs of jazz music.
我剛好有一些爵士音樂的CD。

B What types of jazz?
什麼種類的爵士樂？

A Mostly female vocal jazz and bossa nova.
大部分是女伶演唱的爵士跟巴薩諾瓦。

 Situation **2** 支持正版
say no to piracy

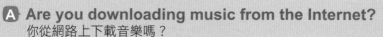

A Are you downloading music from the Internet?
你從網路上下載音樂嗎？

B Yeah, I have a huge collection of pop music in my computer.
對啊，我電腦裡有一整套的流行音樂。

A I thought it was illegal.
這樣是違法的耶。

B Well, who would know? Everybody is doing it.
誰會知道？每個人都這麼做。

A I'd rather spend extra money buying the originals to show my respect to the composers and singers.
我寧願多花點錢買正版，表達我對作曲者跟演唱者的尊重。

Part **4** 血汗人生必要的休閒娛樂

Situation 3 舒心禪樂
Zen music

A Why do you call the file "Zen music"?
你為什麼把這個檔案夾取名「禪樂」？

B Oh, this file contains all the music I play when I do Yoga.
喔，這裡面存了所有我做瑜珈時候要聽的音樂。

A Can I listen to some songs?
我可以聽幾首嗎？

B Go ahead. You can download them if you want.
請自便，如果你想要的話，也可以下載啊。

A That's very generous of you!
你真大方！

Unit

38

隨時隨地好音樂

Situation 4 年度頒獎大典
the Grammy's

A Are you going to watch the Grammy Awards tonight?
你今天晚上要看葛萊美頒獎典禮嗎？

B Oh, I totally forgot! I'm going to cancel my dinner date.
喔，我完全忘記了！我要取消晚餐約會。

A Wow, you take the Grammy's seriously.
哇，你真看重這場頒獎典禮。

B Absolutely. My favorite singer, Lady Gaga, will be performing at the Grammy's.
當然，我最愛的歌手女神卡卡將會在典禮上表演。

A We must not miss out on that!
那我們可不能錯過囉！

Unit 39 健身房體能訓練
Let's go to the gym!

 主要關鍵句開口說

使出關鍵3句型，英文輕鬆開口說

 Track 115

① **Where do you work out?**
你都在哪裡健身？

② **I joined ABC Health Club a couple of months ago.**
我幾個月前加入了ABC健身俱樂部。

③ **I've been working out a lot lately.**
我最近經常去健身。

Americans 沒果仁邏輯 句型解析與用法說明

說明 ① **Where do you work out句型**

where＝何處；work out為動詞片語，表示健身、運動之意。例：Where are you going? 你現在要去哪？/I am heading to the gym to work out. 我要去健身房健身。

說明 ② **I joined ABC Health Club a couple of months ago句型**

join a club＝加入某俱樂部成為會員。例：Thomas joined a book club in his community college. 湯瑪士加入了社區大學的讀書會。

說明 ③ **I've been working out a lot lately句型**

have/has+been+V-ing+lately是完成進行式的句型，所要表達的意思是「從過去一直到現在，且未來也都會持續進行」的事情。例：Joyce has been doing research on chimpanzees lately. 喬伊絲最近一直都在做與黑猩猩有關的研究。

沒果仁也愛的說法

對照「主要關鍵句」的類似說法

① **Are you a member of a gym?**
你是健身房的會員嗎？

② **I work out at ABC Gym.**
我在ABC健身房運動。

③ **I've been exercising for the past few weeks.**
我過去幾個禮拜以來都在運動。

這樣回答就對了

對應「主要關鍵句」的回答

① **I work out at QQQ Gym.**
我在QQQ健身房健身。

② **How much does a gym membership cost?**
健身房的會員費怎麼算？

③ **No wonder you look fit.**
難怪你的身材看起來很健美。

世界觀小補充

　　美國人運動健身行之有年，台灣很多大型的國際連鎖健身房幾乎都是從美國「進口」的。網路上針對有關健身的資料琳瑯滿目，舉凡基礎的有氧舞蹈(aerobics)、肌耐力訓練(muscular endurance)、重訓(weight training)等一直到最新的核心肌群(core conditioning)、新式有氧訓練(cardiovascular training)等都有。如果對健身有興趣，想要掌握最新資訊，除了上健身房直接請教練指導之外，也可以搜尋健身的關鍵單字，遊走網際網路！

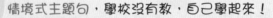

Part 4

血汗人生必要的休閒娛樂

I go to a health club two or three times a week to stay in shape and stay fit.

我一個禮拜去健身房兩到三次以保持身形跟維持健康的體態。

I ran several miles on a treadmill and did some **stretching** on a yoga mat.

我在跑步機跑了幾哩，接著在瑜珈墊上做伸展操。　stretch 延伸；拉長

Alvin lifts weights and discusses nutrition with his personal trainer at the gym.

亞文在健身房舉重，並與他的健身教練討論營養的話題。

My brother trains on machines and then relaxes in the Jacuzzi for a few minutes to alleviate his muscle pain.

我弟使用機器鍛鍊自己，再去按摩浴池泡幾分鐘，以減緩肌肉酸痛的現象。

I love doing aerobics to improve my cardiovascular **fitness**.

我喜歡上有氧課程來增強我的心肺功能。　fitness 健康

Exercise also lets me **burn off** stress from work.

運動也能舒緩工作帶給我的壓力。　burn off 燒掉(某物)

I will take a day off from exercising, because my **muscles** need rest.

我會找一天休息不去運動，因為肌肉也需要休息。　muscle 肌肉

My gym pal and I are a little bit too obsessed with workouts, for we hit the gym almost every single day.

我的健身房夥伴跟我有點太沉迷於健身，我們幾乎每天都去健身房報到。

They say it's much more **effective** if you work out over an hour.

他們說健身超過一個鐘頭比較有效果。　effective 有效的

I need to work on my biceps and triceps. What kind of exercise do you recommend?

我需要加強我的二頭肌跟三頭肌，你建議我做什麼樣的運動？

When you **bench press**, how many reps and sets do you do?

當你做臥推舉的時候，你都做幾下？共做幾組？　bench press 臥推

Do you do low reps with heavy weights, or many reps with light weights?
你都用很重的訓練用具做少量訓練，還是減輕重量但增加訓練次數？

I started lifting weights about two years ago.
我兩年前開始練舉重。　lift weights 舉重

I can bench press 220 pounds.
我的臥推舉最多可以增加到約220磅的重量。　pound 磅

I squat 400 pounds and curl 90 pounds.
我深蹲可承受400磅，二頭舉啞鈴可到90磅。　squat 深蹲

I'm trying to gain bulk, so I'm doing low reps with heavy weights.
我想要練肌肉，所以我用強力的重量搭配少量訓練。　bulk 巨大；大塊

I'm trying to get ripped, so I'm doing a lot of repetitions.
我想要練出肌肉線條，所以我做很多次的訓練。

Besides cardio workouts, I do lunges and squats, and I lift free weights every other day.
除了心臟功能的訓練，我每隔一天還會做弓箭步、深蹲及舉重。

I do jumping jacks, run in place, and jump rope on the balcony.
我會在家裡的陽台做交互蹲跳、原地跑步和跳繩等運動。
jumping jack 交互蹲跳

Before I do my calisthenics, I stretch. And every morning, I do sit-ups, push-ups, and pull-ups.
我做體操前會先做伸展操，每天早上，我會做仰臥起坐、伏地挺身以及引體向上。

I've just had the best workout at the gym!
我剛剛在健身房的運動，是我到目前為止最順利的一次！

I must be doing something wrong. My muscles are aching already.
我應該是什麼動作做錯了，我的肌肉已經開始隱隱作痛了。　ache 疼痛

Have you thought about getting a personal trainer?
你有想過要找個私人教練嗎？　trainer 訓練員

I'm calling it a day. I'm off to the locker room.
今天就到此為止吧，我要去更衣室了。　locker room 更衣室

Unit

39

健身房體能訓練

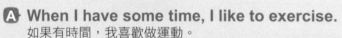

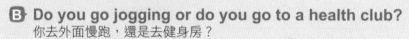

Topic-related Conversations

以關鍵句破題的模擬實境對話

Track 117

Situation 1 健身興趣

exercising at a health club

A When I have some time, I like to exercise.
如果有時間，我喜歡做運動。

B Do you go jogging or do you go to a health club?
你去外面慢跑，還是去健身房？

A I joined Happy Gym a couple of months ago.
我幾個月前加入了快樂健身房。

B How do you exercise?
你都做什麼運動？

A I usually spend 30 minutes on the bicycle for the cardio, and then I lift weights for about 45 minutes.
我通常花半小時在腳踏車上做有氧運動然後舉重約四十五分鐘。

Situation 2 有規劃的重訓

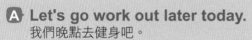

weight training exercise

A Let's go work out later today.
我們晚點去健身吧。

B Sure. What time do you want to go?
當然好，你幾點要去？

A How about at 3:30?
三點半如何？

B That sounds good. We can work on legs and forearms.
聽起來很棒，我們來鍛鍊腿和手臂的肌肉吧。

A I just played basketball earlier, so my legs are a little sore. Let's work out on arms and the stomach today.
我剛剛去打籃球，腳有點酸，我們今天還是鍛鍊手臂跟肚子吧。

Part 4 血汗人生必要的休閒娛樂

Situation 3 久久不見你變了
somebody is bulking up

Ⓐ Wow, You got big.
哇，你變的好大隻。

Ⓑ Yeah, I've been working out a lot.
對啊，我最近很常健身。

Ⓐ How long have you been lifting weights?
你舉重舉多久啦？

Ⓑ For a year and a half.
一年半。

Ⓐ Yeah. Last time I saw you, it was like two years ago.
對喔，上次見到你大概是兩年前了。

Situation 4 新的訓練課程
TRX training

Ⓐ Have you seen anyone doing the latest training program at the gym?
你有看到健身房誰在做最新的訓練課程嗎？

Ⓑ No. What's the program like?
沒有，那是什麼課程？

Ⓐ I think it's called TRX, and I saw people working out with some sort of flexible rubber tubing attached to a machine.
好像叫TRX，我看到有人使用一條從機器拉出來的彈力繩做訓練。

Ⓑ Sounds very up-to-date.
聽起來好先進。

Ⓐ Let's join the program next time!
我們下次也去參加吧！

Part 5

連假就是要
出國找樂子

Unit 40 機場出入境
In the airport lobby

 主要關鍵句開口說

使出關鍵３句型，英文輕鬆脫口說 ▶Track 118

① **Where's the check-in counter for American Airlines?**
請問美國航空的櫃台在哪裡？

② **Here are my passport and my e-ticket.**
這是我的護照跟電子機票。

③ **I'd like an aisle seat, please.**
我想要坐靠走道的位子。

沒果仁邏輯   句型解析與用法說明

說明
① **Where's the check-in counter for American Airlines句型**

where＝何處；check in＝辦理登記作業，表示確認並查核人已經抵達。
例：Where are you going? 你現在要去哪？/I am checking in the hotel. 我正在飯店辦理入住手續。

說明
② **Here are my passport and my e-ticket句型**

Here+is/are+名詞＝告知受話者所要求的物件已經在手邊。例：Here's the sandwich you ordered. 你剛剛點的三明治來了。

說明
③ **I'd like an aisle seat, please句型**

人名／代名詞+would+like為禮貌用語，表示希望／想要某樣東西或進行某件事情。例：The student would like to hand in the test. 這位學生想要繳交試卷。

① **I am flying with AA. Where do I check in?**
我搭乘美國航空，請問我應該要到哪邊登記劃位？

② **(May I have your passport and ticket, please?) Here you go.**
（麻煩出示您的護照跟機票。）在這裡。

③ **I prefer an aisle seat.**
我喜歡坐在走道旁邊。

這樣回答就對了　對應「主要關鍵句」的回答

① **Go straight. You'll see a sign marked G5, and there it is.**
往前直走，你會看到一個寫著G5的標誌，就在那邊。

② **Are you checking any bags?**
你有要拖運行李嗎？

③ **Noted.**
知道了。

世界觀小補充

　　國際機場是人種多樣化程度最高的場所之一，因此使用英文就成了普遍的現象。從一開始辦理登記劃位的櫃台，一直到登機，都有機會聽到英文對話。在機場最需要注意的就是登機時間以及確認登機門號，一旦錯過劃位登機時間，不僅機票落空，之後的行程都會延宕，相當得不償失。所以一定要牢記機場會用到的基礎字彙，這樣的話，就能確保旅程有個順利的開始囉！

Unit
40
機場出入境

學校沒教的實用句

情境式主題句，學校沒有教，自己學起來！

Most people nowadays book their **airline tickets** online.

現在很多人都會上網買機票。 `airline ticket 機票`

Where are you flying today?

您今天要飛往哪裡呢？

I am placing you in 25A. The gate number is D3. It is on the bottom of the ticket. They will start **boarding** twenty minutes before the departure time.

您的位子在25A，登機門是D3，資料都註明在票的最下方。起飛前二十分鐘開始登機。 `board 登機；上飛機`

If you're on an international flight, I believe you have to check-in three hours before your flight.

如果你是搭乘國際航班，我認為你應該要在起飛前三個小時辦理報到登記。

Even though you bought your ticket online, you will need a boarding pass to get on the plane.

即使是在網路上購票，還是得有登機證才能登機。

You'll have to go through security before arriving at your gate. I hope you don't have any metal in your pockets!

前往登機門之前，你必須先通過安檢。希望你口袋裡面沒有放什麼金屬物喔！

There has been a **gate** change.

登機門有異動。 `gate 登機門`

United Airlines **flight** 880 to Miami is now boarding.

美國聯航前往邁阿密的880班機現正進行登機。 `flight 班次`

Please have your **boarding pass** and identification ready for boarding.

請將您的登機證以及證件準備好，以便登機。 `boarding pass 登機證`

We would like to invite our first- and **business-class** passengers to board first.

我們先邀請頭等艙以及商務艙的旅客登機。 `business class 商務艙`

We are now inviting passengers with small children and any passengers

Part 5 連假就是要出國找樂子

requiring special assistance to begin boarding.

我們現在邀請攜帶小孩的旅客，以及需要特別協助的旅客開始登機。

We would now like to invite all **passengers** to board.

我們現在邀請所有旅客進行登機。　　passenger 乘客；旅客

This is the final boarding call for United Airlines flight 880 to Miami.

這是美國聯航880班機前往邁阿密的最後登機廣播。

Passenger John Smith, please proceed to the United Airlines desk at Gate 12.

乘客約翰‧史密斯先生，聽到廣播後，請您前往美國聯航12號登機門的櫃檯處。

Unit
40

機場出入境

I would check that bag in. It is too big to bring with you.

要是我的話，會託運那袋子。就隨身行李來說，這太大了。

This airline allows two **carry-on** bags per passenger.

這家航空公司允許一位乘客攜帶兩件登機袋。　　carry-on 可隨身攜帶的

We got to the airport really early, so I decided to try to get on an earlier flight as a stand-by passenger.

我們太早抵達機場，所以我試著登記早班航空的候補機位。

What time do we **take off**?

我們的班機幾點起飛？　　take off (飛機)起飛

What time are we going to board?

我們幾點要登機？

Is there a shuttle bus that goes between **terminals**?

航廈之間有沒有接駁公車？　　terminal 航廈；航空站

With airfare being as expensive as it is, it is smart to just take your bag as a carry-on.

飛機票價如此昂貴，隨身行李直接登機會比較聰明一點。

Please lay your bags flat on the conveyor belt, and use the bins for small objects.

請將你的袋子平放在運輸帶上，並將小型物品置於籃中。

Be sure to take coins and keys out of your pocket, so that the alarm won't **go off**.

記得要將零錢跟鑰匙拿出口袋，警報器才不會響。　　go off 響起

關鍵一句模擬實境對話

以關鍵句破題的模擬實境對話

Situation 1 早班航班
an early flight

A Can you drive me to the airport? I'm heading off to Japan for business tomorrow morning.
可否載我去機場？我明天早上要去日本出差。

B Sure. What time is your flight?
當然，你飛機幾點？

A The plane takes off at 8:00 a.m. I'd like to get to the airport by 6:00.
飛機是早上八點的。我想我要早上六點到。

B Yeah, arriving 2 hours early is considered standard for international flights.
對，提早兩個鐘頭是國際航班標準的規定。

A So, we'll have to wake up really early tomorrow morning!
所以明天我們得要起個大早了！

Situation 2 辦理劃位登記
at the check-in counter

A Good afternoon. Where are you flying to today?
午安，您今天飛往哪裡呢？

B Los Angeles.
洛杉磯。

A Your passport, please. Are you checking any bags?
請出示護照，您要託運行李嗎？

B Yes, I am checking one bag.
要，我要託運一件行李。

A OK, please place your bag on the scale.
好的，請將您的袋子放在秤上。

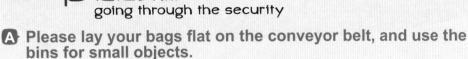

Situation 3 通過安檢
going through the security

A Please lay your bags flat on the conveyor belt, and use the bins for small objects.
請將您的袋子平放在運輸袋上，並將小型物品放在籃子裡。

B Do I need to take off my shoes, too?
鞋子也需要脫掉嗎？

A Yes, you do. And make sure you take out everything in your pockets.
是的，並請確認您口袋裡的東西都拿出來了。

B Ok. I am done.
好，我好了。

A Okay, come on through.
好的，請過去吧。

Unit

40

機場出入境

Situation 4 入境
at the arrival customs point

A Here it is. (Handing his passport to Customs officer)
都在這了。（將護照相關資料交給海關）

B Where are you coming from?
您從哪裡來？

A I'm coming from Seoul, South Korea.
我從南韓首爾過來。

B What is the purpose of your visit?
您這次旅行的目的是？

A I'm here on business.
我來出差的。

Unit 41 機上之旅
On the plane

 主要關鍵句開口說

使出關鍵3句型，英文輕鬆睜口說

 Track 121

① **I am traveling first class/economy class.**
我搭乘頭等艙 / 經濟艙。

② **Could you tell me where 12D is?**
可以告訴我座位12D在哪裡嗎？

③ **Could I get something to drink, please?**
請問我可以點些飲料嗎？

沒果仁邏輯 ~~Americans~~ 句型解析與用法說明

說明① I am traveling first class/economy class句型

在飛機上搭乘某艙種的表達方式，也可以說I am flying+某艙等。first class＝頭等艙、business class＝商務艙、economy class/tourist class＝經濟艙。

說明② Could you tell me where 12D is句型

使用could開頭的問句表示禮貌，尋求對方的協助。例：Could you kindly help me unpack my bag? 可不可以麻煩你幫我打開袋子？

說明③ Could I get something to drink, please句型

使用could開頭的問句表示禮貌。句尾加上please又再次更禮貌的表示「請」，有時候也可將please放在句中。例：Could somebody please answer the phone? 請問誰可以去幫忙接個電話嗎？

256

沒果仁也愛的說法

對照「主要關鍵句」的類似說法

1 **I am flying first class/economy class.**
我搭乘頭等艙 / 經濟艙。

2 **Could you tell me where I can find my seat?**
可否告訴我如何找到我的座位？

3 **Could you please get me a Coke, please?**
可否給我一杯可樂呢？

這樣回答就對了

對應「主要關鍵句」的回答

1 **Have a nice flight!**
祝你旅途愉快！

2 **It's the third row, on your right hand side.**
在您右手邊的第三排。

3 **Sure. What would you like to drink?**
沒問題，請問您想要喝點什麼？

 **世界觀小補充**

在飛機上，遇到不會中文的機組人員的機率很高，對方會詢問的問題很單純，因為空服員提供的服務就那幾樣(例：Please fasten your seat belt and put your seat in an upright position. 請繫好您的安全帶，並將椅背豎直。/What would you like to drink? Tea or coffee? 您要喝什麼？茶或咖啡？/Which would you like for dinner, beef, chicken or fish? 您晚餐想吃牛肉、雞肉還是魚呢？)，這些對話並不困難，可別因為害怕開口而吃了悶虧喔！

Could you help me put this bag in the **overhead** compartment?

可否幫我將這袋子放進上方的行李艙中？　　overhead 在頭上的

We'll have a **layover** in Denver, and then we will continue to Los Angeles.

我們在丹佛會短暫地停留一下，然後就會繼續飛往洛杉磯。　　layover 臨時滯留

When you travel from Paris to Taipei, you will probably have **jet lag**.

當你從巴黎旅行到台北，你可能會有時差須調整。　　jet lag 時差

I always watch the **safety instructions** at the start of the flight.

每次飛機起飛前，我都會看安全指南。　　safety instruction 安全介紹

I get motion sickness easily. Any turbulence will get me sick as a dog.

我容易有動暈症，任何一點亂流都能讓我變得跟條病狗一樣。

Once the pilot announces that we've reached our cruising altitude, you can get up to go to the bathroom.

一旦機師廣播說我們到達巡航高度時，你就可以起身去廁所了。

I get a little nervous when there is turbulence. I'm always convinced that the plane is going down!

飛機一遇到亂流我就會開始緊張，總覺得飛機要掉下去了！

Grab the **barf bag**. He's going to puke!

快點拿嘔吐袋來，他要吐了！　　barf bag 嘔吐袋

Most people like Jet Blue because there is free in-flight entertainment.

很多人喜歡捷藍廉價航空，因為他們提供免費的娛樂節目看。

Hopefully, they will have some good in-flight entertainment, and I will be too distracted to get sick.

希望他們在機上有提供有趣的娛樂節目，這樣就能分散我的注意力，而不會覺得不舒服了。

Could I get another **blanket**, please? I'm a little cold.

可以再多給我一條毯子嗎？我有點冷。　　blanket 毛毯

Could I have a pillow and a **headset**?

可以給我一個枕頭跟一副耳機嗎？　　headset 雙耳式耳機

Could I have some water/coffee/tea?

可以給我一點水 / 咖啡 / 茶嗎？

Could you also lend me a pen to fill out this **immigration form**?

可否也借我一支筆，讓我填寫入境表格？　　immigration form 入境表格

Do you know when we will be **landing**?

你知道飛機什麼時候會降落嗎？　　land 降落

I requested a vegetarian meal. Can you check to confirm?

我有要求要素食餐點，可否幫我確認一下？

Will they be showing an **in-flight** movie?

他們會播放機上電影嗎？　　in-flight 飛行過程中的

I just had a hard landing and almost had a nervous breakdown!

我剛剛才經歷一場嚇人的降落，我差點要精神崩潰了！

It's the exit row, the second row past the first-class **cabin**. You're in Seats A and B, which are on the right side of the plane behind the lavatory.

這在緊急出口那一排，也就是過了頭等艙後的第二排。你們的位子是A跟B，在飛機右邊、廁所的後面。　　cabin 客艙

Please direct your attention to the flight attendants throughout the first-class and economy-class cabins for a few safety announcements.

請將您的注意力轉向在頭等艙以及經濟艙的空服員，有關幾項安全須知的報告。

Please fasten your seatbelt. You insert the buckle into the latch and adjust the belt so it fits low and firmly.

請繫好您的安全帶。請將扣環扣入座位的插梢，並調整綁帶使其穩固。

Please push the call button if you need anything.

若您需要任何服務，請按服務鈴。

Please make sure to switch off any **electronic** devices during take-off and landing.

飛機起飛及降落時，請確保您的電子儀器關機。　　electronic 電子的

Track 123

Situation 1 機上餐點
in-flight meal

Ⓐ Would you like chicken or pasta?
您想吃雞肉還是義大利麵？

Ⓑ I'll have the chicken.
我要雞肉。

Ⓐ Anything to drink?
喝點什麼呢？

Ⓑ What kind of soft drinks do you have?
你們有什麼樣的飲料？不含酒精的。

Ⓐ Coke, Diet Coke, Sprite, and Juice.
可樂、建怡、雪碧跟果汁。

Situation 2 還有供餐嗎？
asking for meal service

Ⓐ Excuse me, how long will it take to reach Seattle?
請問，到西雅圖大概要多久？

Ⓑ It's a long journey. We still have five hours before landing.
這路程滿長的，降落前還有五個小時的飛行時間。

Ⓐ Will there be any more meals before we land?
降落前還會提供餐點嗎？

Ⓑ Yes, another meal will be served in two hours, but I can get you a small snack now, if you like.
有的，兩個小時後會提供另外一餐。需要的話，我現在可以拿點小點心給您。

Ⓐ Yes, that would be great.
這樣就太好了。

Part 5 連假就是要出國找樂子

Situation 3 填寫入境表格
immigration form

A Here's an arrival card for immigration, Ma'am.
女士，這是入境的填寫卡。

B Thanks. Could you lend me a pen, please?
謝謝，可否借我一支筆呢？

A Another cabin crew member will be bringing pens around in a moment.
另外一位機組人員等一下將會拿筆給您。

B Great. I need to fill out this immigration form before we land.
太好了，我必須在降落前填好這表格。

A Sure. Someone will bring you a pen shortly.
沒問題，馬上就會有人拿筆給您了。

Situation 4 與空服員的對話
in-flight instructions

A Can I ask you some questions about the in-flight instructions?
可不可以問你有關飛機內的介紹？

B I would be happy to help you clarify anything you need help with.
我很樂意為您解答。

A Could you help me find out where my nearest exit is?
可否告訴我，離我位子最近的緊急逃生口在哪裡？

B There is a card in your seat pocket that shows you where. Yours is two rows in front of you.
您座位前方的口袋中有一張卡片有標明。在您座位前兩排就有一個。

A Thanks for your explanation.
謝謝你的說明。

Unit 42 下榻飯店
In the hotel

 主要關鍵句開口說

使出關鍵3句型，英文輕鬆開口說 Track 124

① **Hi, my name is Steinfield, and I have a reservation for tonight.**

你好，我姓史丹斐，我今天晚上有預約訂房。

② **I'd like a room for two people for three nights, please.**

我需要一間兩人房，待三個晚上。

③ **How much is the charge per night?**

房價一個晚上是多少呢？

 沒果仁邏輯 Americans 句型解析與用法說明

 說明① **I have a reservation for句型**

have a reservation for＝預約訂位。例：I have a reservation for three people at Bistro Provence. 我在普羅旺斯小館訂了三人的位子。

說明② **I'd like句型**

人名／代名詞+would+like為禮貌用語，表示希望／想要某樣東西或進行某樣事情。主詞為代名詞時可使用縮寫。例：She would like＝she'd like。

 說明③ **How much句型**

How much句型在詢問不可數名詞主詞的數量時使用；詢問對象若為可數名詞，則使用How many。例：How much time have you got? 你還有多少時間？(時間為不可數名詞)

① **Hi, my name is Steinfield. I booked a room for tonight.**
你好，我姓史丹斐，我之前有訂了今天晚上的房間。

② **I need a double room for three nights.**
我需要一張雙人床的房間，共三個晚上。

③ **How much does a room cost?**
一間房間怎麼計費？

這樣回答就對了　對應「主要關鍵句」的回答

① **Let me check. Yes. A twin room for one night.**
我幫您查一下，有的，一間兩人單人床房型，待一個晚上。

② **Do you have a reservation?**
請問您有先訂房嗎？

③ **The rate I can give you is USD90 with tax.**
含稅價我可以給你90美元。

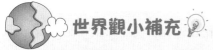 世界觀小補充

　　國外住宿需要注意的禮節之一，就是小費。如何給以及什麼時機給都是一門學問。例如在較有規模的飯店裡，幫忙提行李至房間的行李小弟(a hotel porter)是需要給小費的。所以在櫃檯辦理登記入住，提供房間鑰匙後，也會禮貌性地詢問客人是否需要協助提行李。有些客人想省下小費，就會婉轉拒絕。另外，若待在同一間房超過一晚，第二天會有清潔人員進房提供客房清理的服務(housekeeping service)。因此出門前，別忘了將給清潔工的小費放在床頭櫃。

✎ Do you take credit cards?
你們收信用卡嗎？

✎ I'd like to **make a reservation** for next week.
我想要預訂下週的房間。　　make a reservation 預約；預訂

✎ How long will you be staying?
您要停留多久呢？

✎ I'd appreciate it if you could give me a room with a view of the lake.
如果你可以幫忙安排能俯瞰湖景的房間，那就太感謝了！

✎ Do I pay now or when I check out?
我是現在付款還是等退房的時候再付呢？

✎ The **elevator** is just around the corner. Do you need any help with your bags?
電梯就在轉角處，您需要協助拿行李嗎？　　elevator 電梯

✎ Is there anything else we can do to help you **enjoy** your stay?
還有什麼需要服務的地方，可以讓您待得更開心？　　enjoy 享受

✎ Can you give me a **wake-up call** at 7:00?
你明早七點可否給我一個晨喚電話？　　wake-up call 電話叫醒服務

✎ You can use the clock radio in the room, or you can program the telephone in your room to ring at 7:00.
您可以使用房間裡的廣播鬧鐘，也可以設定房間電話在七點整時自動響。

✎ We recommend that you make a reservation, though. It's still considered **peak season** then.
我們還是建議您先預訂房位，現在這期間還算是旺季。　　peak season 旺季

✎ There are only a few vacancies left.
現在只剩下幾間空房而已了。

✎ Do you have any rooms with two double beds? We're a family of four.
你們有兩張雙人床的房型嗎？我們一家四口同行。

We do require a fifty dollar credit card **deposit** to hold the room.
我們有規定要先用信用卡扣款50元付押金來預訂房位。 `deposit 押金`

Cable television is included, but the movie channel is extra.
有線電視包含在房間費用內，但電影頻道要額外付費。

The **dining room** is open from 4 p.m. until 10 p.m.
餐廳營業時間為下午四點到晚上十點。 `dining room 餐廳`

I'd like to order **room service**, please.
我想要叫客房服務，謝謝。 `room service 客房服務`

Can I leave the room key at the counter when I go out?
在我外出時可以把房間鑰匙留在櫃檯嗎？

Does this hotel have a **shuttle bus** to the airport?
這間旅館有沒有接駁車到機場？ `shuttle bus 接駁車`

I'd like to check out, please.
我要退房，謝謝。

Do you do **group bookings**?
你們接受團體訂房嗎？ `group booking 團體預約`

I will be needing the room until the 1st of September.
我將會下榻於此房間至九月一號。

I'm in 408, and my **hairdryer** doesn't seem to be working.
我是408號房的房客，我的吹風機不能用。 `hairdryer 吹風機`

Do the rooms come **equipped with** irons?
房間裡有熨斗可使用嗎？ `equip with 給…配備`

How much should I tip a hotel **porter**?
我該給行李小弟多少小費？ `porter 搬運工`

Enjoy your stay, and please do not hesitate to contact me at any time if you ever need any assistance.
祝您居住愉快，若需要任何服務，請不用客氣，隨時都可聯絡我。

以關鍵句破題的模擬實境對話

Situation 1 辦理入住
checking in

A Hi, I am Connery. I have a reservation for tonight.
嗨，我是康納力，我有預訂今天晚上的房間。

B Good afternoon, sir. Yes, a single room for two nights.
先生，午安，是的，一間單人房，待兩個晚上。

A That is correct.
正確。

B Your room number is 1511, on the 15th floor. Here is your key card.
您的房號是1511，在15樓。這是您的房卡。

A Thanks a lot!
感謝！

Situation 2 現場訂房
asking for vacancies

A I'd like to have a room for four people for three nights.
我想要一間四人房，住三個晚上。

B Do you have a reservation?
您有預訂嗎？

A No, I don't.
沒有。

B That would be $200 including continental breakfast.
這樣總共是兩百元，有包含歐陸早餐。

A Can I pay with a credit card?
我可以刷卡嗎？

Situation β 總統套房
the presidential suite

A How much is the charge per night?
一個晚上多少錢呢？

B For the presidential suite, the rate I can give you is $3,000, tax included.
若是總統套房，我可以給您含稅價3000元。

A The rate is not my major concern. I want to make sure the room has a view overlooking the lake.
價錢不是我主要考量。我想要確定這房間可以俯瞰湖面的風景。

B That I can assure you!
這點我可以跟您保證。

A Fine, I'll take it.
很好，那我要了！

Situation 4 房型確認
making a reservation

A I would like to make a hotel reservation.
我想要預約訂房。

B What day will you be arriving, and how long will you be staying?
請問您哪一天抵達，打算停留多久呢？

A I will be arriving on May 14 and will be needing the room for three nights.
我五月十四日抵達，需要住三個晚上。

B Would you like a smoking or non-smoking room?
您想要吸煙還是非吸煙的房型？

A A non-smoking room, please.
麻煩給我非吸煙房。

主要關鍵句開口說

使出關鍵3句型，英文輕鬆開口說

Track 127

① **Where can I find a bus stop?**
我在哪裡可以找到公車站牌？(公車站牌在何處？)

② **Would you like a round-trip ticket or a one-way ticket?**
您要來回票還是單程票？

③ **Do you know where I can get a taxi?**
你知道我要在哪裡招計程車嗎？

沒果仁邏輯 ⸱⸱⸱ Americans

句型解析與用法說明

說明① Where can I find a bus stop句型

where＝詢問何處的WH開頭問句。Where+can+人+find+something＝某人可以在哪裡找到某物。例：Where can I find the nearest McDonald's? 在哪裡可以找到最近的麥當勞呢？(最近的麥當勞在何處？)

說明② Would you like a round-trip ticket or a one-way ticket句型

對話中經常使用的禮貌詢問語，would like＝詢問對方或表達自己想要…。例：Would you like something to drink? 你想要喝點什麼嗎？/I would like to speak with the person in charge. 我想要和負責人談談。

說明③ Do you know where I can get a taxi句型

Do/does+人+know+子句＝詢問某人是否知情，探聽消息。例：Do you know when the latest iPhone would release? 你知道最新的iPhone何時會上市嗎？

 Americans

沒果仁也愛的說法

> 對照「主要關鍵句」的類似說法

1 **Where can I catch a bus?**
我要在哪邊搭公車？

2 **One way or return ticket?**
單程還是來回票？

3 **Could you organize a taxi for me for this evening, please?**
可否幫我安排今天傍晚的計程車？

 這樣回答就對了

> 對應「主要關鍵句」的回答

1 **Go straight ahead and you'll see the bus stop.**
往前直走，你就可以看到公車站牌了。

2 **A round-trip ticket, please.**
請給我來回票。

3 **You can catch one anywhere on the street.**
你可以沿路隨意招計程車。

 世界觀小補充

　　去美國旅遊，建議租車。若在大城市觀光倒可以依賴大眾運輸工具。美國很多大城可搭乘捷運，若捷運到不了，公車或長程巴士也是另一種選擇。若不想購買儲值卡，只要自備零錢，投入公車上的投幣箱即可，相當方便。另外也要花點時間認識外國銅板(美元硬幣 a penny=1 cent 一分錢=$0.01；a nickel=5 cents 五分錢=$0.05；a dime=10 cents 十分錢 / 一角=$0.10；a quarter=25 cents 二十五分錢/二角五分=$0.25；half dollor=50 cents 五十分/五角=$0.50)，免得多投了錢！

您要搭乘？(交通工具)

學校沒教的實用句

情境式主題句，學校沒有教，自己學起來！

There are many buses to the hotel where I am staying.
我住的飯店有很多公車會到。

How long does it take to **get to** Central Station from my hotel?
從我飯店到中央車站大概要花多久時間？　　get to 抵達；把⋯送到

I just arrived and need help getting **transportation** to my hotel.
我剛剛才到，需要能夠帶我去飯店的交通方式。　　transportation 運輸工具

This bus goes **all the way** to the Lille Museum, right?
這公車一路會到里爾博物館，對嗎？　　all the way 整個途中

There is one thing that one must do when traveling by bus and that is, keep change handy with you.
有一件事情是使用公車代步的人需要注意的，那就是隨時將零錢準備好。

There are shuttles, taxis, and buses that go **all over** the city.
這城市有接駁車、計程車跟公車穿梭往來。　　all over 到處；各處

Does this bus stop at the National Museum?
這公車在國立博物館有設停靠站嗎？

Excuse me, where can I get a bus for Market Street?
請問要往市場街去的公車在哪邊等？

Where is the **ticket office**?
請問售票處在哪裡？　　ticket office 售票處

I **hitchhiked** my way across the United States last year.
我去年用路邊搭便車的方式穿越美國本土。　　hitchhike 搭便車旅行

The car **rental** agencies are next to the information counter as you exit.
租車公司在服務台旁邊，你出去的時候就會看到。　　rental 出租；租賃的

I want to be able to get around easily, so I'm looking into buying a cheap train **pass** or tickets to make travel in Europe a little easier.
我想要到處遊走，所以在找便宜的火車通行套票，這樣可以讓在歐洲的旅程輕鬆些。　　pass 通行證；憑證

I bought a kind of pass that allowed me to **get on** and off the train at any stop during my trip last year.

我去年買了一種通行票，讓我可以在不同的火車站上下車。　get on 上車

My friend who went to Europe two months ago suggests looking online for Internet specials on train passes.

兩個月前去歐洲的朋友建議我上網找特殊優惠的火車套票。

You can find the car number and the **seat number** on the ticket.

你可以在票上找到車廂編號以及座位號碼。　seat number 座位號碼

Can I check my **luggage** instead of carrying it on the train?

我可以託運我的行李，而不自己拿上火車嗎？　luggage 行李

Let's wait at the **platform**. I think our train will be arriving in 10 minutes.

我們去月台等吧，我想我們的火車十分鐘內就要到了。　platform 月台

Get your bag ready, because we will be **getting off** the train at the next stop.

準備好行囊，因為我們下一站就要下車了。　get off 下車

How much is the typical taxi **fare** to downtown New York?

去紐約市中心的標準計程車價位是多少？　fare 車資

I'm really in a hurry, so can you take the quickest **route**, please?

我趕時間，可以麻煩你走最快抵達的路線嗎？　route 路線

Keep the change.

不用找錢了。

Just take this card and walk through the **turnstile**. Put your card in this slot and then retrieve it as you pass through.

只要拿著這張卡走過十字轉門，將你的卡片放入孔中，通過後記得將票卡從另一頭取走。　turnstile 十字轉門

Take a look at this **subway** map showing all of the lines. That's the station we want.

看看這張顯示所有線路的地鐵圖，這是我們要去的那站。　subway 地下鐵

Take the brown line to Grand Park **Station** and then change to the red line to get to City Hall Station.

你要搭棕色線到宏園站，再換紅線到市政府站。　station 車站

Part 5

連假就是要出國找樂子

Situation **1 詢問公車資訊**
asking for bus info

A Where can I find a bus stop near my hotel?
在我住的飯店附近有公車站嗎？

B There's one right across the street.
對面就有一個。

A Which bus should I take to get to Central Park?
我要搭哪一班車才會到中央公園？

B You can catch the 12. It comes every eight minutes.
你可以搭乘12路，每隔八分鐘就有一班。

A Thanks a lot!
感謝！

Situation **2 購買來回火車票**
buying train tickets

A Would you like a round-trip ticket or a one-way ticket?
您要購買來回車票還是單程車票？

B I am coming back soon, so I want a round-trip ticket.
我很快就會回來，所以我要買來回票。

A When are you leaving and when will you be returning?
你什麼時候要出發？回程是什麼時候呢？

B I am leaving tomorrow, Thursday. Please give me a return ticket for Friday.
我明天週四離開，回程麻煩給我週五的票。

A Sure. Right away.
好的，馬上好。

Situation 3 飯店叫車服務
booking a taxi

A Do you know where I can get a taxi?
請問我要在哪裡招計程車呢？

B I can book one for you if you want.
如果您需要，我可以幫您電話預約。

A That would save me a lot of trouble.
那會省下我很多麻煩。

B When will you need to be picked up?
您需要計程車幾點來接？

A Around 7 p.m. I need to go out for a business dinner.
晚間七點左右。我需要外出參加商務晚會。

Situation 4 下錯車站
getting off at the wrong stop

A Is this our bus stop?
我們在這站下嗎？

B I think it is. Let's get off.
好像是耶，快下車。

A Dude, where are we at?
老兄，我們現在是在哪啊？

B I have no idea.
我不知道。

A I think you made us get off early.
我覺得你剛剛讓我們提早下車了。

Unit 44 東南西北霧煞煞(迷路)
Asking for directions

 主要關鍵句開口說

使出關鍵3句型，英文輕鬆脫口說

 Track 130

① **Could you tell me how to get to Central Park?**
可否請你告訴我該怎麼去中央公園嗎？

② **I am looking for the Holiday Inn.**
我在找假日飯店。

③ **Let's ask for directions then.**
我們還是來問路好了。

沒果仁邏輯 ⸺ Americans  句型解析與用法說明

 說明① **Could you tell me how to句型**

could開頭的問句帶有禮貌的請求的意涵，通常用在不熟的談話對象。例：
Could you tell me where to line up? 可否請你告訴我要在哪裡排隊？

說明② **I am looking for the Holiday Inn句型**

look for＝尋找，為動詞片語，尋找人或物時都可以使用這個片語。例：
Jonathan was looking for his long-lost friend through Facebook. 強納森透過臉書找尋他失聯已久的朋友。

 說明③ **Let's ask for directions句型**

ask for＝詢問，為動詞片語。direction＝方向；ask for directions就是問路。例：Men in general don't like to ask for directions. 男人通常都不喜歡問路。

① **Can you give me the directions to Central Park?**
你可以告訴我往中央公園的方向嗎？

② **I don't know where the Holiday Inn is.**
我不知道假日飯店在哪裡。

③ **Let's get someone to give us directions.**
我們向別人問路吧。

這樣回答就對了　對應「主要關鍵句」的回答

① **Turn right at the next block, and you'll see it right away.**
在下個路口右轉，你馬上就會看到了。

② **There's one right across the street.**
對面就有一間。

③ **Let's do that!**
就這麼辦吧！

🌍💭 世界觀小補充 💡

　　出國遊歷，迷路或找不到路是家常便飯，跟當地人互動問路是最好的方法。當然，除了要特別注意自身安全，最好可以結伴問路，也不要在暗巷或人煙稀少的地方顯示自己迷路或者茫然的樣子，免得招來不必要的麻煩。如果到了英語系國家，使用英文問路時最好先禮貌性地用Excuse me做為開場白。畢竟太冒失地攔截路人多少會嚇到人。如果手上有地圖，問起路來也會比較方便。對方若講太快，至少也可以按圖索驥，得到大概的方位。

Unit
44
東南西北霧煞煞（迷路）

275

Part **5** 連假就是要出國找樂子

Can you tell me how to get to the city **library**?
可否告訴我要如何去市立圖書館？　　library 圖書館

I am new in town. Can you tell me where the **City Hall** is?
我剛搬來到這一區，請問市政廳在哪裡呢？　　city hall 市政廳

Excuse me. Is there a grocery store around here?
請問，這附近有雜貨店嗎？　　excuse me 請問；請原諒

Excuse me. I'm afraid I can't find a bank. Do you know where one is?
不好意思，我似乎找不到銀行，你知道哪裡有嗎？

Go straight ahead on this street until the third traffic light. Take a left there, and continue on until you come to a bus stop.
這條街往前直走，到第三個紅綠燈左轉，繼續走，直到你看到一個公車站。

Do you know what the name of the street is?
你知道那條街的街名是什麼嗎？

Go straight ahead on this street to the second **traffic light**.
這條街直走，到第二個紅綠燈那邊。　　traffic light 紅綠燈

Walk straight on 8th Avenue for about 100 yards, and past a supermarket until you come to another traffic light. Take a left and continue on for another 200 yards. You'll see the bank on the right.
在第八大道上直走約100碼，經過一間超市後，你會遇到另一個紅綠燈。在這裡左轉，繼續走個200碼，你就會看到銀行在你的右手邊。

I think I might be lost. I need to ask for **directions**.
我擔心會迷路，我需要問個路。　　direction 方向；方位

Could you give me directions to the nearest **post office**?
可不可以指引一下最近的郵局方向在哪裡？　　post office 郵局

You'll see the restaurant you're looking for on your left hand side, after 200 yards or so.
你將會看到你要找的餐廳在你的左手邊，大概離這200碼左右的距離。

Where is the historic site mentioned in this **brochure**?

這張傳單上面提到的歷史遺跡在哪裡？　　brochure 小冊子

How do I get to the museum from here?

我要怎麼從這裡到達博物館呢？

Which way is the museum?

博物館要往哪個方向走呢？

The museum is right opposite Central Park.

博物館就在中央公園的對面。

What's the best way to get to the **neighboring** town?

要到鄰近的城鎮，最佳方式為何？　　neighboring 鄰近的

Hi, I am looking for a café named Deja vu. Have you ever heard of it?

嗨，我在找一間咖啡廳，叫做似曾相識，你有聽過這間店嗎？

I think it's just a few **blocks** away.

我記得只隔幾條街吧。　　block 街區

Try going straight down the road for a couple of minutes and ask any **passerby** there.

試著沿路往下直走幾分鐘，然後再問附近的路人吧。　　passerby 行人

I am not sure. You might need to ask someone else.

我不是很清楚，你可能需要再去問問別人。

It's a bit complicated. I might as well take you there myself.

有點複雜，乾脆我帶你去好了。

It's a 20-minute **drive**.

大概是二十分鐘的車程。　　drive (開車)車程

It'll take you about fifteen minutes to get there **on foot**.

你步行大概要花十五分鐘左右才會到。　　on foot 步行

Could you show me the way?

可不可以請你指引方向？

Thank you very much for taking the time to explain this to me!

很感謝您花那麼多時間解釋給我聽！

以關鍵句破題的模擬實境對話

Situation 1 路邊問路
asking for directions

A Could you tell me how to get to the nearest post office?
可否請你告訴我，最近的郵局要怎麼去？

B Go straight for a couple of minutes and turn left to a small alley.
往下直走約幾分鐘後，左轉到一條小巷子。

A OK. Sounds easy so far.
好，目前聽起來算容易。

B You'll have to walk for at least five minutes until you see a small statue right next to the post office.
你還必須再走至少五分鐘，之後會看到郵局旁邊的小雕像。

Situation 2 旅遊書介紹餐廳
looking for a famous restaurant

A I am looking for this famous restaurant printed in this guidebook.
我在找這本旅遊書介紹的有名餐廳。

B I am not familiar with this restaurant. Let me see the address first.
我不太熟悉這家餐廳，先讓我看看地址。

A Isn't this restaurant famous in town?
這間餐廳在這裡不有名嗎？

B Maybe the book isn't up-to-date. It doesn't seem far.
說不定這本書的內容沒有更新，看來似乎離這裡不遠。

A If that's the case, I'll go try my luck then.
如果是這樣的話，那我去碰碰運氣吧。

Situation β **堅持不問路**

insisting on NOT asking for directions

Ⓐ We are so lost! Let's ask for directions.
我們完全迷路了！來問路吧。

Ⓑ Hold on! I think I can figure it out myself.
等等！我覺得我能找到路。

Ⓐ What's up with you? We've been circling around for the past forty-five minutes.
你到底是要怎樣？我們都已經在這裡繞圈繞了四十五分鐘了耶。

Ⓑ I am on it! Everything is under control.
我在處理啊！每件事都在我的控制當中。

Ⓐ Whatever...
隨便啦。

Situation 4 **同樣不熟悉**

we both are new here

Ⓐ Can you tell me where the closest police station is?
請問，最近的警局在哪裡？

Ⓑ You're asking the wrong person. I am new here, too.
你問錯人了，我對這一區也很不熟。

Ⓐ Oh, are you a tourist as well?
喔，你也是觀光客嗎？

Ⓑ No. I just moved into town very recently.
不，我是最近才搬到這裡的。

Ⓐ That's OK. I'll ask someone else.
沒關係，那我問別人吧。

Unit 45 道地美味佳餚
In the restaurant

 主要關鍵句開口說

使出關鍵3句型，英文輕鬆開口說

 Track 133

① **Do you have a reservation?**
請問您有訂位嗎？

② **Are you ready to order?**
請問可以點餐了嗎？

③ **What are today's specials?**
今日特餐有什麼？

沒果仁邏輯 ^{Americans} 句型解析與用法說明

 說明
① **Do you have a reservation句型**

reservation＝預約、訂位；have a reservation for＝訂了幾個人的位子。
例：Samuel has a reservation for two tomorrow night.(預約兩人)

 說明
② **Are you ready to order句型**

be動詞+ready+to+動詞原形＝準備好進行某件事。例：Are you ready to go? 你準備好要走了嗎？

 說明
③ **What are today's specials句型**

Today's special專指餐飲店的本日特餐或促銷菜餚。尋問本日特餐是什麼的時候就用what開頭的wh句型來問。

沒果仁也愛的說法 Americans

對照「主要關鍵句」的類似說法

① **Have you got a reservation?**
請問您有訂位嗎？

② **Can I take your order?**
我可以幫您點餐了嗎？

③ **What do you recommend?**
你有什麼推薦的菜色嗎？

Unit

45

道地美味佳餚

這樣回答就對了

對應「主要關鍵句」的回答

① **Yes, I made a reservation the other day for tonight.**
有，我之前已經訂了今天晚上的位子。

② **I'm still trying to decide.**
我還沒決定好。

③ **One is poached salmon and the other is grilled shark.**
水煮鮭魚，另一個是碳烤鯊魚。

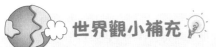

世界觀小補充

　　歐美餐點大體上分成開胃菜、沙拉、湯、主食、甜點，更為複雜的還有搭配餐前酒的小點跟甜點搭配的酒，料理也講求一道道上菜，所以正統的西式料理需要的用餐時間頗長。另外，在飲料的部分，除了有搭配不同料理的紅白酒或烈酒之外，餐廳通常不會附白開水。如果到歐美國家，點餐時點到水，服務生會送上礦泉水(mineral water)或氣泡水(sparkling water)，都是需要額外付費的。所以不妨直接跟服務生要tap water(自來水)。

Let's have something **exotic** for dinner.

我們晚餐來吃點異國風味的料理吧。 `exotic 異國情調的`

I would like to make a reservation for this Saturday night.

我想要訂本週六晚餐的位子。

I'm sorry, but we're **fully booked** on that day.

很抱歉，但那一天已經沒有位子了。 `fully booked 訂位已滿的`

Would you like to reserve a private dining room?

您想要預訂私人的用餐包廂嗎？

Welcome to Giovani. Here are your menus. Today's special is grilled salmon. I'll be back to take your order in a minute.

歡迎光臨喬凡尼，這裡是菜單。今日特餐是烤鮭魚，我稍後再過來為您點餐。

Are you ready to **order**? What would you like with that?

請問可以點餐了嗎？您要什麼來搭配主餐？ `order 點菜`

Can you give us a few more minutes?

能否讓我們再考慮一下？

I'd like to have a glass of **Chardonnay** before I order.

點餐前，請先幫我上一杯白酒。 `Chardonnay 白葡萄酒`

I am thinking about a lighter **appetizer**, like a Nicoise salad.

我想要清爽一點的開胃菜，例如尼斯沙拉。 `appetizer 開胃菜`

I am not much of a fan of all-you-can-eat **buffet** meals.

我不是很喜歡吃到飽的餐廳。 `buffet 自助餐`

I'd like the seafood **spaghetti**.

我想要海鮮義大利麵。 `spaghetti 義大利麵條`

Would you like anything to drink?

您想要點什麼飲料嗎？

Would you like a starter?

您想要點一道開胃菜嗎?

What would you like for the main course?
您的主餐要點什麼?

I'll have a glass of wine, please.
我要一杯紅酒,謝謝。

How would you like your steak?
您的牛排要幾分熟?

I like my steak rare/medium rare/medium/medium well/well done.
我的牛排要一分熟 / 三分熟 / 五分熟 / 七分熟 / 全熟。

The appetizers are on the house.
開胃菜由本店招待。

Do you have any recommendations?
你有沒有什麼推薦的菜色?

Here is your food. Enjoy your meal.
您的菜來了,請慢用。

Would you like anything for dessert?
甜點您有需要嗎?

Can I have a look at the wine list?
我可不可以看看你們的酒單?

I'd like to have an iced coffee, easy on the ice, please.
我想要一杯冰咖啡,少冰,謝謝。

How would you like your eggs? Scrambled, sunny side-up, over-easy, or over-hard?
您的蛋想要怎麼烹調?炒蛋、太陽蛋、半熟蛋、還是熟蛋呢?

You can take the rest of your chicken home in a doggie bag.
你可以把剩下的雞肉打包帶回家。

Unit

45

道地美味佳餚

以關鍵句破題的模擬實境對話

Situation **1** 週末請訂位
reservations needed on weekends

A Do you have a reservation?
您有訂位嗎？

B No. Is it necessary?
沒有，一定要訂位嗎？

A We recommend you do that during weekends. Now, all the tables are reserved.
我們建議您週末還是要訂位，現在所有的桌子都被預訂了。

B When will a table be available?
那什麼時候會有空位？

A Not until 9 p.m.
要到九點之後才有位子。

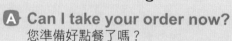

Situation **2** 點菜
ordering dishes

A Can I take your order now?
您準備好點餐了嗎？

B Yes. I'll have the beef stew for starters, and my wife would like tomato soup.
好了，我的開胃菜要點燉牛肉，我太太要蕃茄湯。

A What would you like for the main course?
您的主餐要點什麼？

B I'll have a rib-eye steak and my wife would like the fried trout with mashed potatoes.
我要一客肋眼牛排，我太太要炸鱒魚佐馬鈴薯泥。

A Got it.
好的。

Situation 3 今日特餐
today's special

A Could you tell me what today's specials are?
可不可以告訴我今日特餐有什麼？

B Vegetable soup and mac and cheese.
蔬菜湯和起司通心麵。

A I'll take those.
那我都要點。

B Anything to drink?
要什麼飲料嗎？

A Just water, please.
白開水就好。

Situation 4 訂包廂
booking a private dining area

A I'd like to reserve a table for dinner.
我想要訂晚餐的位子。

B How large a group are you expecting?
您大概有多少人要用餐呢？

A Eight people.
八個人。

B Would you like a private dining area?
您想要私人的包廂嗎？

A That would be great!
那太好了！

Unit 46 觀光勝地樂不思蜀
At the tourist resort

 主要關鍵句開口說

使出關鍵3句型，英文輕鬆開口說

 Track 136

① **I enjoy visiting cathedrals.**
我對參觀大教堂很有興趣。

② **Do you go on package tours during holidays?**
你假期出國都參加旅行團的行程嗎？

③ **What do you recommend that we see?**
你會建議我們看些什麼？

沒果仁邏輯 Americans 句型解析與用法說明

 說明① **I enjoy visiting句型**

enjoy+動詞ing表示對於某件事情很樂在其中。例：Joshua enjoys singing in the shower. 喬舒亞很喜歡在沐浴的時候唱歌。

 說明② **package tours句型**

package tours＝套裝行程、通常是旅行社提供的包含食住行統一套裝的旅遊行程。例：More and more people don't go on package tours nowadays because they are predictable and sometimes shallow. 愈來愈多人不參加旅行團是因為覺得行程不創新且又膚淺。

 說明③ **What do you recommend句型**

What+do/does/did+人+recommend+that+動詞原形＝詢問受話者的建議，that後面接子句，動詞要使用原形動詞。例：What did the waitress recommend that we order? 服務生建議我們點些什麼呢？

沒果仁也愛的說法

對照「主要關鍵句」的類似說法

1. **Visiting cathedrals fascinates me.**
   參觀大教堂讓我沉醉不已。

2. **Do you usually travel with a tour group?**
   你出遊通常都跟旅行團嗎？

3. **Any suggestions on the attractions we should see?**
   有什麼景點是你推薦一定要參觀的嗎？

觀光勝地樂不思蜀

 這樣回答就對了

對應「主要關鍵句」的回答

1. **I love outdoor scenic spots more.**
   我比較愛戶外景點。

2. **Yes. I still do.**
   是的，我還是跟團。

3. **I recommend that you join the city tour.**
   我建議你們參加市區導覽的行程。

世界觀小補充

　　現今網路資訊發達，很多人出國開始自行安排行程，自助旅行的時間較具彈性，能更深入當地文化。歐美國家針對特定年齡以下的遊客，提供交通工具的優惠套票，可以在限定的期間內用經濟實惠的價格乘坐當地的交通工具。只要事前做點功課，就能省下大筆花費。如果機票可以選定A點進B點出，規劃從A點到B點中的景點觀光，可讓整趟行程順暢又輕鬆。另外，準備好旅遊基礎對話，外出就不怕雞同鴨講囉！

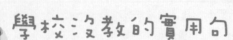
學校沒教的實用句

情境式主題句，學校沒有教，自己學起來！

Does this package tour cover most of the must-see **attractions**?
請問這個套裝行程包含大部分必看的觀光景點嗎？ `attraction 旅遊景點`

I have been going on tours I have organized myself for a decade.
我十年前就開始走自己規劃的旅遊行程了。

Do you enjoy museums and architecture, or would you rather hit some outdoor hotspots and venues?
你喜歡參訪博物館與建築物，還是喜歡戶外的景點和場合？

I love visiting churches and cathedrals, as well as other historic buildings.
我愛參觀教堂跟天主教大教堂，以及其他古蹟建築。

I do a lot of online research before going abroad and always bring guidebooks with me.
我會在出國前上網做很多研究，還會隨身攜帶旅遊書。

If you want to go onto the Eiffel Tower, you can't avoid waiting in line.
如果你想要登上艾菲爾鐵塔，排隊是避免不了的。

Some people suggest that we travel across France by TGV.
有些人建議我們搭乘法國高速列車穿越法國境內。

What do you say that we join the beer **festival** in Germany?
我們去參加德國的啤酒節怎麼樣？ `festival 慶祝活動`

I think that Christmas markets are one of the most **joyful** attractions all around Europe.
我覺得聖誕市集是歐洲最令人開心的景點之一了。 `joyful 充滿喜悅的`

How can we **miss out** on the Statue of Liberty while we are in New York?
我們人在紐約，怎麼能錯過自由女神像呢？ `miss out 錯過`

Besides visiting Notre Dame and strolling along the Champs-Élysées, I think we should have a cup of coffee at the Left Bank near the Seine River and pretend we are French.

Part 5 連假就是要出國找樂子

除了造訪巴黎聖母院跟在香榭大道漫步之外，我覺得我們應該要在塞納河畔左岸喝杯咖啡，假裝是法國人。

Do you have any free maps and information booklets of the city?
請問你有免費的地圖和市區導覽手冊嗎？　booklet 小冊子

We are only here for one day. What do you recommend that we see?
我們才在這裡待一天，你建議我們看些什麼好？

Do you have any information about local places of interest?
請問你有任何關於當地景點的資訊嗎？

Does the sightseeing tour leave from here?
請問觀光團是從這裡出發嗎？　sightseeing 觀光；遊覽

How much is the admission for the museum?
請問博物館的入場費多少？　admission 入場費

What time does the art gallery close?
請問藝廊幾點關門？　art gallery 美術館；畫廊

Concierges can advise you on where to visit, eat, and shop during your stay here in New York.
門房人員能建議你待在紐約的這段時間，去哪裡參觀、品嚐美食與購物。

Other attractions include historical sites of interest, as well as parks, gardens, and stately homes and castles.
其他景點還有歷史遺跡、公園、花園、貴族莊園和古堡等。

Some palaces and parliament buildings are also open to visitors.
有些宮殿或國會建築也是對外開放的。　parliament 議會；國會

Where can I find a souvenir shop?
哪裡可以找到紀念品專賣店？　souvenir 紀念品

I am taking my kids to a theme park during the trip.
這趟旅行中，我要帶我的孩子去主題遊樂園。　theme part 主題樂園

Let's go to the tourist information office to ask about the opening hours for the Uffizi Gallery.
我們去遊客服務中心詢問有關烏菲茲美術館的開放時間吧。

Situation 1 市區導覽
city tour

A Welcome to Seattle! How can I be of help?
歡迎來到西雅圖！我能幫您什麼忙呢？

B What do you recommend that we see?
你建議我們看些什麼好？

A We have tours for all interests. What interests you?
我們有各種景點的行程，您對什麼感興趣呢？

B I want to see a bit of everything. Do you have a city tour?
我什麼都想看看，你們有市區導覽嗎？

A Yes, in fact, I usually suggest that to visitors.
有的，事實上，我通常都會推薦這個行程給遊客。

Situation 2 動靜兼具
advice for visitors

A Have you been to Central Park or the Museum of Modern Art?
你有去過中央公園或現代藝術博物館嗎？

B No, but I've heard a lot about both.
沒有，但我時常聽到這兩個景點。

A Well, Central Park is wonderful for running. Afterwards, you should head to the museum to enjoy the art.
中央公園很適合愛跑步的人，之後你還可以去博物館欣賞藝術。

B Great! That sounds like a plan. Thanks a lot.
太好了！這計畫聽起來很不錯，謝謝。

A I'm sure you'll have a good time there.
我相信你會玩得很開心。

Part 5 連假就是要出國找樂子

Situation 3 暢貨中心
visiting an outlet

A What's your plan for today?
你今天有什麼計畫？

B I don't have anything in mind.
沒特別的想法。

A What do you say we go to an outlet? You could get some sneakers on sale.
去暢貨中心如何？你可以趁特價買雙運動鞋。

B Great! How do we get there?
太棒了！我們要怎麼去那裡？

A Let me check online.
讓我上網查查。

Situation 4 巴黎景點
Paris scenic spots

A We've seen Notre Dame and the Eiffel tower. Now what?
聖母院跟巴黎鐵塔我們都看過了，現在要幹嘛？

B There is so much to see in Paris. We should go to the Basilica of the Sacred Heart and Moulin Rouge, like most tourists.
巴黎有太多可以看的，我們應該跟其他遊客一樣，到蒙馬特的聖心堂和紅磨坊去看看。

A I want to see some artistic exhibitions as well.
我也想去看和藝術有關的展覽。

B Oh, then we can most definitely not miss the Louvre Museum.
喔，那我們就絕對不能錯過羅浮宮啦。

A I couldn't agree with you more!
我舉雙手贊成！

主要關鍵句開口說

使出關鍵3句型，英文輕鬆脫口說

▶Track 139

① **Where can I find the lost-and-found counter?**
這邊哪裡有失物招領的櫃檯？

② **I lost my wallet!**
我的皮夾不見了！

③ **I've been pickpocketed!**
我被扒了！

沒果仁邏輯 Americans

句型解析與用法說明

說明 ① Where can I find the lost-and-found counter句型

lost-and-found字面意思為失而復得，清楚表明失物招領的意涵，就是失去又被找到的過程。例：Jimmy works in a lost-and-found department. 吉米在失物招領部門工作。

說明 ② I lost my wallet句型

人+lost+東西＝某人遺失某物。大多數是用過去式時態，因為東西不見一定是已經發生的事情。例：Anna lost her precious doll. 安娜遺失了她珍愛的娃娃。

說明 ③ I've been pickpocketed句型

pickpocket＝順手牽羊，可以當名詞或動詞。例：Be careful of pickpockets! 小心扒手！

① **Is there a lost-and-found counter in this building?**
這棟大樓有沒有失物招領的櫃檯？

② **My wallet is missing!**
我的皮夾不見了！

③ **Someone stole my money!**
有人偷了我的錢！

這樣回答就對了　對應「主要關鍵句」的回答

① **Yes, there is one on the ground floor.**
有的，一樓有櫃檯。

② **Where did you lose it?**
你在哪裡掉的？

③ **You'd better go down to the police station to report this crime.**
你最好去警局報案。

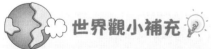 世界觀小補充

　　外出旅遊，最怕的就是透露自己是觀光客，引發竊賊犯罪的慾望。除了對行程做足功課之外，連當地治安較亂的地區也要特別留意。例如南歐義大利、西班牙各大城市，因為外來人口愈來愈多，難免會有龍蛇雜處的區域。不少吉普賽人偷竊功力高深，防不勝防。被偷還算其次，看開點是花錢消災，若是遇到搶匪動手劫財，出門遊玩還負傷可就煞風景了。所以自助旅行時最好結伴，在人多的地方也要特別小心自己的隨身物品。

學校沒教的實用句

情境式主題句，學校沒有教，自己學起來！

Track 140

✎ I lost my backpack in the **shopping mall**.

我的背包掉在購物中心裡了。　　shopping mall 大型購物商場

Part

⑤

連假就是要出國找樂子

✎ I left my tote bag on the floor while putting on my jacket, and then I forgot to take it with me.

我為了要穿夾克，我把手提包放在地上，結果忘記拿包包了。

✎ I was a passenger on a Sunny Airlines flight yesterday and I think I left my keys on the plane.

我是昨天搭乘晴天航空的乘客，我似乎把我的鑰匙忘在飛機上了。

✎ I was lucky enough to have someone return my purse to the local police station.

我很幸運，因為有人撿到我的錢包，並送到警察局。

✎ I can't seem to find my **passport**!

我好像找不到我的護照！　　passport 護照

✎ Don't **panic**. Try to think of which places you have been to today.

別驚慌，試著回想你今天去過的地方。　　panic 恐慌；驚慌

✎ I must have dropped my wallet when I tried to take out my camera from my backpack.

我一定是在要從我背包拿相機的時候，不小心把錢包也拉出來了。

✎ To **claim** the item, you have to fill out a claim form.

想領回失物，你必須填寫失物招領的表單。　　claim 要求；認領

✎ It's difficult to spot every pickpocket because they generally camouflage themselves.

要辨別出竊賊很困難，因為他們基本上都會偽裝自己。

✎ Be sure to hold on to your **personal belongings** at all times.

切記一定要隨時保管好個人財物。　　personal belongings 私人攜帶物品

✎ I've lost my wallet, and I was wondering if anybody has **dropped** it **off** here.

我錢包掉了，在想有沒有人把它送來這裡？　　drop off 把…放下

You should probably go to the police station and file a police report for your lost wallet.

你應該去警局報案，說明你的錢包遺失了。

Do you think they will be able to find it?

你覺得他們會找到嗎？

What should I do if I have lost my passport?

要是我護照掉了該怎麼辦？

You should find your **embassy** and have your passport re-issued.

你應該要找到你國家的領事館，再重新申辦護照。　　embassy 大使館

Unit
47

You should be extra careful because this place is famous for pickpocketing.

你必須格外小心，因為這個地方的遭竊率高得出名。

I was **mugged** fifteen minutes ago on Main Street, outside the bank.

我十五分鐘前在美因街的銀行外面被搶了。　　mug 行兇搶劫

I need to take a statement from you. Could you please describe to me exactly what happened?

我需要你的口供。可否請你確切描述到底發生了什麼事情？

Did you see the one who **assaulted** you?

你有看到攻擊你的人嗎？　　assault 襲擊；攻擊

I would suggest that you avoid passing through this area alone at night.

我會建議你，晚上的時候不要一個人走這一區。

Did you see the **mugger's** face?

你有看到搶匪的臉嗎？　　mugger 強盜

I haven't seen anyone **turn in** the handbag you just described.

我沒看到有人把你描述的那種手提包送過來。　　turn in 交上；歸還

We don't have a policy of finders, keepers, so don't worry.

我們沒有誰撿到就是誰的這種制度，所以不用擔心。

Were there any **witnesses**?

有任何目擊證人嗎？　　witness 目擊者

突發狀況—失物篇

Situation 1 尋找失物
looking for the lost-and-found counter

Ⓐ **Where can I find a lost-and-found counter?**
請問哪裡有失物招領的櫃檯？

Ⓑ **What's wrong?**
怎麼了？

Ⓐ **I lost my handbag while holding too many shopping bags.**
我手上拿太多購物袋，結果手提包不見了。

Ⓑ **I think the counter is on the first floor.**
櫃檯好像在一樓。

Ⓐ **Can you come with me? I need someone to help me with my bags.**
可不可以跟我一起去？我需要有人幫我看著袋子。

Situation 2 粉紅色錢包
at the lost-and-found counter

Ⓐ **I lost my wallet! Has anybody dropped it off here?**
我錢包掉了！請問有人將它拿到這邊嗎？

Ⓑ **All right, I'll have a look. Could you tell me what it looks like?**
好，我看看。可以請你告訴我錢包的外觀嗎？

Ⓐ **Sure. It's a pink wallet with white polka dots on it.**
好的。是粉紅色的錢包，上面有白色點點的花樣。

Ⓑ **I'm sorry, but it doesn't look like anybody has picked it up. Where did you leave it?**
很抱歉，看起來好像沒有人撿到，你在哪邊掉的呢？

Ⓐ **I think I left it on one of the benches upstairs.**
我好像放在樓上的座椅上。

Situation 3 我被扒了

I've been pickpocketed!

A I've been pickpocketed!
我被扒了！

B Are you okay? At least you were not attacked and injured.
你還好吧？只要沒有被攻擊受傷就好。

A Well, looking at the bright side, you're right.
嗯，樂觀點看，你説的也是。

B Let's go to the local police station and report your missing belongings.
我們去警局報失你的失竊物吧。

A I wouldn't get my hopes up. These days, people are less honest than they used to be.
我不抱什麼希望，這些年人們愈來愈不誠實了。

Situation 4 搶劫

I got robbed!

A Are you okay?
你還好嗎？

B No. I got robbed.
不，我被搶了。

A Oh my God! By who?
我的天啊！被誰搶啊？

B Some guy on the street just mugged me.
被街上一位男性搶劫。

A We should report this to the police right away!
我們應該馬上報警處理！

 主要關鍵句開口說

使出關鍵3句型，英文輕鬆開口說

 Track 142

① **I am feeling a little sick.**
我覺得有點不舒服。

② **I got food poisoning.**
我食物中毒了。

③ **Don't get too carried away and be careful of heat stroke!**
不要開心過頭了，小心中暑！

 沒果仁邏輯 句型解析與用法說明

 說明 ① feel a little sick用法

feel sick＝感覺噁心、不舒服。例：Marty feels sick every time he smells seafood. 馬提每次聞到海鮮都感到一陣噁心。

 說明 ② food poisoning用法

food poisoning＝食物中毒；例：Food poisoning is a common and sometimes life-threatening problem for millions of people. 食物中毒很常見，有時對數以百萬計的人來說，是具生命威脅性的問題。

 說明 ③ get too carried away/heat stroke用法

get carried away＝得意忘形；heat stroke＝sunstroke＝中暑；例：You can watch TV now, but don't get too carried away! 你可以看電視但不要過頭了！/ I got sun stroke after being dehydrated. 我因為缺水而中暑。

① I don't feel well.
我不舒服。

② I might have eaten some poisonous food.
我可能吃到有毒的食物。

③ Drinking water in such heat can help avoid sun stroke.
在如此高溫下補充水分能預防中暑。

這樣回答就對了   對應「主要關鍵句」的回答

① Why don't you stay at the hotel and take a rest?
你何不待在旅館休息？

② I ate the same thing as you did, but I am feeling fine.
我跟你吃的東西一樣，但我人覺得好好的。

③ Don't be paranoid! I drink a lot of water.
別大驚小怪！我喝很多水。

世界觀小補充

　　出了自己的國家旅遊，最怕水土不服。因為氣候、環境、飲食、時差等因素，或免疫力的不同，出去玩時若感冒、身體不適，難免掃興。氣候的差異可以預防，比如小心溫差、注意保暖、避免淋雨等，飲食上的問題則比較棘手。提醒大家，凡事適度即可，別因為到了新環境想要嘗試異國料理而暴飲暴食。例如在德國想要飲遍各種啤酒；到日本肆無忌憚地吃生魚片等等。飲食量如果超出身體負荷，都會造成不適，破壞遊玩的興致。

Unit
48
突發狀況—身體不適篇

學校沒教的實用句

情境式主題句，學校沒有教，自己學起來！

🖊 They have been traveling for two days and will need some time to **acclimatize**.

他們已經旅行了兩天，需要一些時間適應當地氣候。　　acclimatize 使適應

🖊 It's hard for me to get adapted to the **tropical** weather while traveling in Indonesia.

在印尼旅遊時，我很難適應當地的熱帶型氣候。　　tropical 熱帶的

🖊 Can you tell me how to treat **food poisoning**?

可否告訴我該如何處理食物中毒的情形呢？　　food poisoning 食物中毒

🖊 I caught a **severe** cold and got a really high fever when traveling in Finland.

我去芬蘭旅遊時得了重感冒，並發高燒。　　severe 嚴重的

🖊 My friend caught a cold due to the **alternation** between indoor heat and outdoor chill.

我朋友因為室內與室外的溫差而感冒。　　alternation 交替

🖊 What have we eaten? I have had an **upset stomach** since yesterday!

我們吃了什麼嗎？從昨天開始，我就一直鬧肚子！　　upset stomach 腸胃不適

🖊 I am not feeling well. I need to see a doctor.

我不太舒服，我要去看醫生。

🖊 What can I do to make you feel better?

我能幫你做點什麼，讓你舒服一點嗎？

🖊 I am feeling a little sick. Let's **call it a day**.

我覺得不太舒服，今天就到此為止吧。　　call it a day 今天到此為止

🖊 I hope you get better soon!

希望你早日康復！

🖊 I need help right away. Can you take me to the emergency room of the nearest hospital?

我急需幫忙，可不可以帶我去最近的醫院掛急診？

I didn't know that Madrid was this hot in summer, and I accidentally got sunstroke on day one.

我不知道馬德里的夏天這麼熱，我才待了一天竟然就中暑了。

Here, take some **painkillers** and let's continue on our itinerary.

來，吃些止痛藥就繼續我們的行程吧。　painkiller 止痛藥

Why don't you stay in the hotel and take some rest for the day?

你今天何不乾脆待在飯店休息呢？

I think I have a cold. Can you take my **temperature**? I hope it's not a high fever.

我覺得我感冒了，可不可以幫我量體溫？希望不是發高燒。　temperature 體溫

You need to have a vaccination before going to the countries in which **epidemic** diseases are widely spread.

前往傳染病疫情嚴重的國家之前，要先施打疫苗。　epidemic 流行性的

I've had **diarrhea** since we ate that seafood soup.

自從我們喝了那個海鮮湯之後，我就開始拉肚子。　diarrhea 腹瀉

My head is spinning. I think I might have gotten an **infection**.

我頭昏，我覺得我感染疾病了。　infection 傳染病

I've got the **flu**.

我感冒了。　flu 流行性感冒

I **tripped** and fell on a rock, which left a deep cut on my knee.

我絆倒，跌在石頭上，結果膝蓋被劃了很深的一道。　trip 絆倒

I am wondering if they have a first aid kit at the hotel.

不知道飯店有沒有急救箱。

I drank five cups of tasty Italian coffee during the day, and now I have trouble sleeping.

我白天喝了五杯濃醇的義式咖啡，現在完全睡不著。

I feel like throwing up, and I have the cold sweats. I guess it's **heat stroke**.

我想吐，而且在冒冷汗，我猜我是中暑了。　heat stroke 中暑

You need to have enough **hydration** to maintain your body temperature.

你得補充足夠的水分來維持體溫。　hydration 水合作用

以關鍵句破題的模擬實境對話

Track 144

Situation 1 氣溫驟降不習慣
catching a cold

A I am feeling a little sick.
我覺得不太舒服。

B What's the matter with you?
你是怎麼了？

A I'm not sure. It could be the snow last night.
我不確定，可能是昨天晚上下雪的關係。

B Do you think you caught a mild cold?
你覺得有沒有可能是輕微感冒？

A I guess so. I am not used to the weather in this country!
也許吧，我還不習慣這個國家的天氣。

Situation 2 食物中毒
food poisoning

A I got food poisoning.
我食物中毒了。

B What kind of symptoms do you have?
你有什麼症狀？

A I have diarrhea, and I have vomited several times.
我拉肚子，還吐了好幾次。

B Is it possible that your lunch is the cause of this?
有沒有可能是你的中餐有問題？

A You're right! I went to the central market, which attracts mainly tourists, and had a plate of raw oysters!
對耶！我去了大部分觀光客必去的中央市場，吃了一大盤生蠔！

Situation ₃ 別中暑了
getting heat stroke

A I am so excited by this overseas marathon coming up this weekend!
這週末的海外馬拉松真令我興奮！

B Don't get too carried away and be careful of heat stroke.
不要太忘我，小心中暑。

A I know. That's why I am fully prepared.
我知道，所以我已經做好萬全的準備。

B How exactly are you prepared?
怎麼個萬全法？

A I have three water bottles strapped to my waist!
我把三個水瓶綁在我的腰上！

Situation ₄ 扭傷腳踝
a sprained ankle

A What happened to your ankle?
妳的腳踝怎麼了？

B I sprained my ankle while traveling to Germany last week.
我上週去德國玩的時候不小心扭到腳。

A I am sorry to hear that. But, how did it happen?
真令人遺憾，但是，你是怎麼扭傷的啊？

B I was wearing my high-heeled shoes.
我當時穿著高跟鞋。

A Why am I not surprised?
這就難怪了。

Part
6

愛的世界從開始
到結束

主要關鍵句開口說

使出關鍵3句型，英文輕鬆開口說 Track 145

① **How is your drink? Do you suggest that I order the same?**

你的飲料好喝嗎？你建不建議我點一樣的？

② **Can I have your number?**

可以給我妳的電話嗎？

③ **Hi, what's up?**

嗨，你好！

沒果仁邏輯 —— Americans 句型解析與用法說明

說明 **① Do you suggest that句型**

Do/does+人名／代名詞+suggest+that+子句＝以問句詢問後述子句所提及的事情。特別注意後述子句所使用的動詞一律用原形。例：**Do you suggest that his mother go see a doctor?** 你建議他媽媽去看醫生嗎？

說明 **② have your number用法**

have one's number=要到某人的(電話)號碼，完整的電話號碼為telephone number，簡化後一般就只說number。

說明 **③ what's up句型**

口語中常見的招呼語，年輕人之間打招呼時，常作為開場白用。在搭訕異性時，也可用以引起對方的注意。

沒果仁也愛的說法
Americans

對照「主要關鍵句」的類似說法

① **Any suggestions on the drink?**
有沒有推薦什麼飲料？

② **How can I get her number?**
我要怎麼要到她的電話？

③ **I just want to come over and say hi.**
只是想要過來打個招呼。

這樣回答就對了

對應「主要關鍵句」的回答

① **My drink is fine. If you need suggestions, you can ask the bartender.**
我的飲料還不錯。如果你需要建議，可以問問酒保。

② **I don't give my number to strangers.**
我不把電話隨便給陌生人。

③ **Do I know you?**
我認識你嗎？

世界觀小補充

　　酒吧(bars)或夜店(night clubs)向來是被公認為搭訕異性、結交朋友的熱門地點。美國有很多的酒吧，跟台灣的夜店形態大異其趣。許多美國人去酒吧可能是為了在餐前喝開胃酒或餐後閒聊聚會，也可能是看球賽的主題性酒吧。男生想要搭訕女生，技巧推陳出新。甚至有兩人一組，其中一位擔任輔助性質的角色，美國口語稱做wingman，字面上是左右手、幕僚的意思，用在搭訕情境中就是指幫助主角搭訕成功的副手。

Part 6

愛的世界從開始到結束

Hi! I like you. And I'd like to get to know you.
嗨！我喜歡妳，想要進一步認識妳。

That guy over there is super hot!
那邊的那個男生超級帥！

Wow, she is **smoking hot**!
哇，她超辣的！　　smoking hot 身材正點的

If your boyfriend doesn't **show up**, I'll be right over there.
如果妳男友沒出現的話，我就坐在那邊。　　show up 出現；露面

You look like someone I'd like to meet.
你看起來很像我想要認識的人。

Hi, I'm sure we've met before.
嗨，我很確定我們在哪裡見過。

Your smile is like sunshine.
妳的笑容像陽光一般。

You have an **incredible** energy about you.
妳散發出的能量很棒！　　incredible 難以置信的

Shall we talk or continue flirting **from a distance**?
我們要不要聊個天，還是要繼續曖昧地遙望對方？　　from a distance 從遠方

I never **pass up** the opportunity to say hello to a beautiful woman.
我絕不會白白錯失與漂亮女士打招呼的機會。　　pass up 拒絕；放棄

Uh, hi, I'm really nervous.
呃、嗨，我真的很緊張。

Hi, my name is Joe. Can I **buy you a drink**?
嗨，我是喬。可以請妳喝杯飲料嗎？　　buy...a drink 請…喝飲料

Your dog is so cute! What kind is it?
你的狗真可愛！是什麼品種的啊？

I don't want to use those cheesy **pick-up lines** to get to know girls anymore.

我再也不想用那些俗氣又老套的搭訕台詞來把妹了。　　pick-up line 搭訕的說詞

A simple and truthful introduction can be an icebreaker when you are trying to get to know a complete stranger.

當你想要認識陌生人時，簡單真誠的自我介紹會是很好的破冰方法。

Is this seat taken?

這位子有人坐嗎？

Excuse me, I just wanted to say that you are really beautiful. What's your nationality?

打擾了，我只是想跟妳說，妳真的很漂亮，妳是哪國人啊？

How long have you lived here?

妳住在這裡多久了？

Wow, you **look** exactly **like** a girl I went to school with.

哇，妳長得很像我以前的一位同學。　　look like 看起來像⋯

Those **boots** are awesome. Where did you get them?

這靴子好好看，你在哪裡買的？　　boot 靴子

What's your view on this situation? I need a female **perspective**.

這個情況在你看來怎麼樣？我需要參考女性的觀點。　　perspective 觀點

Dude, I wouldn't talk about *Star Trek* if I were you. That might really freak a woman out.

老兄，如果我是你，就不會聊《星際大戰》，這話題可能會嚇跑女生。

I suggest that you smile, be confident, and **demonstrate** positive energy, and she will pick up your vibe and be sucked into it.

我建議你面帶微笑、有自信一點、散發正面能量，她自然會感受到你的情緒，進而被影響。　　demonstrate 顯示；表露

I know this is really forward of me, but I just wanted to tell you that you're **gorgeous**.

我知道這樣講有點唐突，我只是想跟你說，你很可愛。　　gorgeous 極其漂亮的

關鍵一句模擬實境對話

以關鍵句破題的模擬實境對話

Track 147

Situation **1** 開啟對話的一招一詢問意見
hitting on by asking for suggestions

A How is your drink?
妳的飲料好喝嗎？

B Um, I haven't tried it yet.
嗯，我還沒喝。

A Oh, I am just wondering what to order. Any suggestions?
喔，我只是在想要點什麼。你有什麼建議嗎？

B I'd say you must try their coffee if you've never been here before.
如果你以前沒來過，我建議你嚐嚐他們的咖啡。

A Oh, I am a big fan of coffee. I assume you are, too?
我是咖啡愛好者，我猜你也是？

Situation **2** 白目搭訕
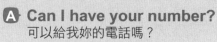

A Can I have your number?
可以給我妳的電話嗎？

B Uh, no. I don't even know you.
不要，我根本就不認識你。

A I am Peter. Now you do know me. What is your name?
我叫彼得。你現在認識我了，那你叫什麼名字呢？

B I am not sure I want to answer any of your questions.
我不確定我想要回答你的問題。

A Why not?
為什麼不？

β 順利搭訕
a successful hitting on

Ⓐ Hi, what's up?
嗨，你好。

Ⓑ Not much. Do I know you?
嗨，我們認識嗎？

Ⓐ No. I know this is really forward of me, but I just wanted to tell you that you're cute. And my name is Thomas.
不，我知道這麼說很唐突，我只是想跟你說你很可愛，我的名字是湯瑪士。

Ⓑ I'm flattered. I am Emily.
過獎了，我是艾蜜莉。

Ⓐ I am wondering if I could buy you a drink?
不知道可否請你喝杯飲料？

Unit

49

想想搭訕妙招

Situation **4** 圖書館毛遂自薦
hitting on by asking for help

Ⓐ Excuse me. Can you reach that book for me? The one with the golden spine.
不好意思，可不可以幫我拿那本書呢？金色書背的那本。

Ⓑ Oh, sure. There.
喔，沒問題，拿去吧。

Ⓐ Thanks, that's very nice of you. Do you come here often?
謝謝，你人真好，你常來嗎？

Ⓑ Not really. I just moved to this neighborhood.
不太常，我才剛搬來這一區。

Ⓐ Oh, if you need someone to show you around, I'd be happy to help.
如果你需要人帶你認識環境，我很樂意幫忙。

主要關鍵句開口說

使出關鍵3句型，英文輕鬆開口說

Track 148

① **I am going on a blind date.**
我要去相親。

② **What should I talk about on a blind date?**
相親的時候我該聊些什麼？

③ **They hooked up on a speed date.**
他們在快速聯誼中相識。

沒果仁邏輯 ~Americans~ 句型解析與用法說明

① I am going on句型

go on＝進行、發生；例：She is going on a road trip. 她要去長途旅行。
blind date=(直譯)盲目約會，也就是俗稱的相親（因為約會之前男女雙方
未曾見過對方）。例：Vanessa was successfully matched up on her first
blind date. 凡妮莎第一次相親就配對成功。

② What should I句型

should為詢問意見或命令的助動詞，視整句話的意思使用。例：What
should I do with all these cartons? 我該怎麼處理這些箱子呢？/You should
go back to your room and study right now. 你現在該進房讀書了。

③ hook up用法

hook up在口語英文中表示相識、牽線、勾搭的意涵。例：I want to hook
up with that hottie over there. 我想要去搭訕那邊那個正妹。

① **I am going on a blind date.**
我打算去參加相親聯誼。

② **I hope I won't run out of subjects to talk about.**
我希望我不會沒有話題可以聊。

③ **They met in a speed dating event.**
他們在快速聯誼的活動中認識。

這樣回答就對了   對應「主要關鍵句」的回答

① **I hope you are well prepared.**
希望你準備好了。

② **You should practice beforehand.**
在去之前,你應該要預先做準備。

③ **I thought they were coworkers.**
我以為他們是同事。

世界觀小補充

　　近幾年在台灣流行的快速約會(speed dating)是從美國傳來的一種交友聯誼模式。與傳統一對一的相親或者是一群人聚集的聯誼不同,speed dating event讓每位參與者有機會與在場的所有異性在有限的時間內對話。很多人因為害怕傳統相親的場合過於不自在,時間長又無話可說,所以選擇speed dating的模式,既打破沒話聊的僵局(每次聊天限時約六分鐘),又能一次認識多人,增加選擇比例,甚為划算!

Track 149

Part 6

愛的世界從開始到結束

My friend set me up on a **blind date**.
我朋友設局要我參加相親。 blind date 受安排的男女初次會面

I am planning to **hook up** my best friend **with** my brother.
我打算要把我的好友介紹給我哥。 hook up with 和…有聯繫

It was really **awkward** because we ran out on the things to talk about.
場面真的很尷尬，因為我們無話可聊了。 awkward 尷尬的

Do you have any suggestions for **conversation starters** on a blind date?
對於相親的開場白，你有什麼好建議嗎？ conversation starters 破冰開場白

Don't go into a blind date with expectations that this will be "the perfect man."
不要帶著對方會是一個完美男人的期望去赴相親之約。

My biggest fear of a blind date is that I might say the wrong thing at the wrong time and blow the chance of scoring a second date.
對於相親，我最大的恐懼就是在不對的時機講錯話，把第二次邀約的機會搞砸。

There's nothing worse than sitting **in silence** on a blind date.
相親最糟糕的就是面面相覷的無語場面。 in silence 靜靜地

I don't like to go on a blind date because I don't know how to **break the ice**.
我不喜歡相親，因為我不知道冷場的時候該怎麼辦。 break the ice 打破冷場

Talking about the weather on the first date is so **cliché**!
第一次約會聊天氣真的很老梗！ cliché 陳腔濫調

What if I bring up some subjects and my date cannot come up with a response?
萬一我提到了什麼話題，而我的約會對象沒辦法回應我怎麼辦？

You are being **paranoid**!
你想太多了！ paranoid 偏執症狀的

All these worries will only make you more tense and serious.
這些擔憂只會讓你更緊張。

I would suggest that you try to avoid topics such as religion, politics, money or past relationship failures.
我會建議你避開如宗教、政治、錢財與過去失敗的感情經驗等話題。

Try to **ease into** more substantial topics.
試著慢慢引導對方和你聊比較實際的話題。　　ease into 慢慢帶入

Try to start with some easy and interesting topics like jobs, travel, cooking, sports, current events, movies and television.
試著聊點輕鬆有趣的話題，例如工作、旅遊、烹飪、運動、時事、電影跟電視等。

Don't be too **eager** if you want to arrange a second date.
如果你還希望有第二次約會，就別表現得太急切。　　eager 渴望的；急切的

Come on! Just look at it as **networking**.
別這樣！就把它當作是社交活動。　　networking 建立關係網絡

I didn't meet my boyfriend in a club. Actually, my friend introduced him to me.
我跟我男友不是在夜店認識的，其實是我朋友介紹的。

Don't let first impressions **get in the way**.
不要讓第一印象決定一切。　　get in the way 擋路；妨礙

Try to be a good listener by paying attention to what he/she has to say during the blind date.
相親時，試著專注於對方聊到的內容，做一名好的傾聽者。

Practice ahead of time by **going over** possible topics of conversation.
最好事先練習，準備好可能會聊到的話題。　　go over 檢查；查看

If you two don't click right away, it doesn't necessarily mean you are not right for each other.
就算你們沒有一拍即合，那也不表示你們不適合彼此。

Is there something you've always **dreamt about** doing?
有什麼事情是你一直夢想著要去實踐的？　　dream about 夢想

Track 150

Situation 1 參加相親
going on a blind date

A I am going on a blind date.
我準備去相親。

B Who arranged that for you?
誰幫你安排的？

A My mom, aka the annoying matchmaker.
我媽，也是所謂「惱人的媒婆」。

B Haha. Good luck to you. Be sure to suit up!
哈哈。祝你好運，記得要打扮一下喔！

A Whatever.
隨便啦。

Situation 2 準備話題
preparation for the blind date

A What should I talk about on a blind date?
相親的時候我該聊些什麼？

B Just briefly introduce yourself and be a good listener at the same time.
只需要簡單地自我介紹，並當個好的傾聽者。

A Sounds so complicated.
聽起來好複雜。

B Not at all. Just be yourself and act natural by talking about something you are familiar with.
一點也不會，只要聊些你熟悉的話題，做自己、表現得自然點。

A I think I might need to practice beforehand.
我想我需要事先練習。

Situation 3 快速聯誼
turn of events

A They hooked up on a speed date.
他們在快速聯誼當中相識。

B They did? I thought they met in a bar.
是喔？我以為他們是在酒吧認識的。

A At first, both of them didn't want to attend the event.
一開始，他們兩個都不想參加這個活動。

B Then what happened?
然後呢？

A Their friends forced them to go. Now they should thank those friends!
他們的朋友逼他們去的，現在他們可得感謝彼此的朋友了！

Situation 4 說錯話不打緊
don't worry too much

A I think I blew the chance of asking this girl I just met on a second date.
我想，邀約那個剛認識的女生第二次的機會，全被我搞砸了。

B What makes you think so?
怎麼說？

A I said a dirty joke and she didn't laugh.
我講了一個黃色笑話，她沒有笑。

B Maybe she didn't find it funny, but it doesn't mean you don't stand a chance of asking her out.
她可能只是覺得不好笑，不表示你沒有機會約她出來啊。

A It's a relief to hear that!
聽你這樣講，我鬆了口氣。

曖昧的滋味
Having a crush

主要關鍵句開口說

使出關鍵３句型，英文輕鬆脫口說

Track 151

① **I can't stop thinking about him. He is driving me crazy.**
我一直想著他，想到快瘋了。

② **He is totally flirting with you!**
他絕對是在跟你調情！

③ **I'm wondering whether he will ask me out or not?**
不知道他會不會約我出去？

沒果仁邏輯　^Americans^　句型解析與用法說明

說明 ① drive me crazy用法

drive+人名／代名詞+crazy＝把某人逼瘋，使用drive作為特定的動詞片語。
例：The noise from our neighbor is driving me crazy! 鄰居製造的噪音快把
我逼瘋了！

說明 ② flirt with用法

flirt＝調情、搞曖昧，後加with+某人表示與某人調情。Sam is flirting with a
married woman. 山姆在跟有夫之婦搞曖昧。

說明 ③ whether句型

whether...or＝if...or，表示不論、還是的對等連接詞，若句子對比的名
詞或片語相同，就能省略。例：I am not sure whether I should bring an
umbrella (or shouldn't bring an umbrella). 我不確定要不要帶傘。

沒果仁也愛的說法

對照「主要關鍵句」的類似說法

① **I can't get him out of my mind.**
我沒辦法不去想他。

② **He is making a pass at you.**
他一直在跟妳眉來眼去。

③ **I'm wondering if he's ever going to ask me out.**
我在想他到底會不會約我出去。

Unit

51

曖昧的滋味

這樣回答就對了

對應「主要關鍵句」的回答

① **You really like this guy, don't you?**
你真的很喜歡這個男生，對吧？

② **Really? Why can't I see the signs?**
有嗎？為什麼我都看不出來？

③ **I don't know. Let's wait and see.**
我不知道，拭目以待吧。

🌏 世界觀小補充

　　情感、愛意的交流是不分國界、也沒有語言障礙的。在正式成為情侶之前，一定都會有一個過渡時期，也就是曖昧不明、把自己搞得暈頭轉向卻又甘之如飴的曖昧階段。不管是較為保守的東方或是開放的西方，只要是經歷這階段的戀人們，相信都很了解箇中滋味！西方人搭訕的開場白都較為直接。而曖昧的訊息同時也是增加情趣的一環，東方人常說的「曖昧不明」還真是描述此階段朦朧關係的最佳寫照。

I met a girl I am really interested in and want to **ask** her **out**.
我認識一個女孩，我對她真的很有興趣，想約她出去。 ask...out 邀約

She **swept him off his feet**.
她讓他為之傾倒。 sweep sb. off one's feet 使某人傾心

I really don't know how to chat a girl up.
我真的不知道要如何與女生搭訕。

How do I **pull off** the flirtation?
我要怎麼做才能調情成功？ pull off 成功完成

The whole point of flirting is striking a balance between revealing your feelings and keeping the person you like intrigued.
搞曖昧的重點在於，在表露感情及讓對象產生興趣之間取得平衡。

Thanks to modern technology, now you can even **flirt** with text messages.
由於現代科技發達，你還可以用簡訊調情。 flirt 調情

I think he is really **into** you.
我覺得他真的很喜歡妳。 into 對…極有興趣

He **focuses on** your hobbies and interests so much.
他非常認真去了解你的嗜好跟興趣。 focus on 集中於

Are you talking to your **crush** on the phone now?
你正在跟你暗戀的對象講電話嗎？ crush 迷戀對象

Compliments get people's attention and create a **receptive** mood for good conversation.
讚美可以取得對方的注意，並營造出互動良好的對話情境。 receptive 能容納的

I really like this girl and want to keep my **approach** casual by first saying hi.
我真的很喜歡這個女孩，想先以輕鬆地態度上前向她說聲嗨。 approach 靠近

Do you want to **hang out** tonight?

你今天晚上想不想一起出去？　　hang out 輕鬆相處

Do you think I should call him or wait for his call?

你覺得我應該要主動打給他，還是等他打來呢？

Are you going to ask her out or what?

你到底要不要約她出去啊？

You are an angel sent from above.

妳就像天上掉下來的天使。

I've noticed the cute kitty in your profile picture. Is that who you spend most of your time with?

我看到妳的檔案照片上有隻可愛的貓咪，妳大部分的時間都跟它一起過嗎？

She **is so crazy about** this guy and is convinced that he is the one.

她瘋狂迷戀這個男人，相信他就是真命天子。　　be crazy about 著迷於…

Tell me everything about your date last night and **spare** no details!

快告訴我妳昨天的約會情形，不可以省略細節！　　spare 節約；省略

I enjoy spending time with you and would like to be more than friends.

我很喜歡跟你相處的感覺，希望我們能不僅僅是朋友。

I don't know if I should kiss her after the dinner tomorrow.

我不知道明天晚餐後該不該親她。

Dude, she is so **out of your league**.

老兄，你配不上她啦。　　out of one's league 某人高攀不起

I kind of can't believe I'm getting to know someone as interesting as you.

我有點不敢相信我可以認識像你這麼有趣的人。

You have great eyes. They're very pretty.

妳有雙好看的眼睛，它們很美。

So I'll see you around tomorrow?

所以明天還會看到妳嗎？

Eye contact is the best and easiest thing you can do to start flirting.

眼神交流是最棒、最不費力的調情方法。　　eye contact 眼神接觸

關鍵一句模擬實境對話 *Topic-related Conversations*

以關鍵句破題的模擬實境對話

Track 153

Situation 1 堅持不主動
taking on a passive role

A I can't seem to get him out of my mind!
我沒有辦法不想他！

B Why don't you just call him?
你何不乾脆打電話給他？

A Are you nuts? How could I take the initiative?
你瘋囉？我怎麼可以主動？

B Is there a rule?
有人規定不能主動嗎？

A It's just that I don't want to be too aggressive.
我不想要表現得太過激進。

Situation 2 有互動才有機會
flirting back and forth

A He is totally flirting with you!
他絕對是在跟你調情！

B You think?
你覺得是嗎？

A Duh. Look at those flirtatious text messages!
當然，看看他傳來的曖昧訊息！

B I am such an idiot! What should I do?
我真是太白癡了！那我該怎麼辦？

A If you like this guy, flirt back!
如果你對這傢伙有興趣，就給他點曖昧的回應啊！

Situation 3 沒希望了
there will be no second date

🅐 Do you think he is going to ask me out?
你覺得他會約我出去嗎？

🅑 Have you heard from him since the last blind date?
上次相親結束後，你還有跟他聯絡嗎？

🅐 Um, just on the same night after I got home. He sent a brief text message.
嗯，只有當天晚上我回到家後，他傳了一則簡短的訊息。

🅑 And that's it? No more interaction?
就這樣？沒有其他互動了？

🅐 OK. There won't be a second date, will there?
好吧，沒有第二次約會了，對吧？

Situation 4 兩情相悅
tagging along with you

🅐 So are you planning on spending all night online or do you have more exciting plans for this evening?
所以你是計畫掛在網路上一整晚，還是有什麼其他有趣的活動？

🅑 I won't say it's exciting, because I am planning on walking my dog in the park.
稱不上有趣啦，我晚上要去公園遛狗。

🅐 Such an attractive girl like you? Don't you think you need company?
像你這麼迷人的女生，不覺得需要有人陪著嗎？

🅑 Um...I guess it does no harm to have someone tagging along.
嗯，多一個跟班應該也無妨。

🅐 I certainly will tag along!
我絕對跟到底！

 主要關鍵句開口說

使出關鍵3句型，英文輕鬆開口說 Track 154

① **I am falling for you.**
我被你迷倒。

② **I am so in love with you.**
我如此愛妳。

③ **I adore you.**
我愛慕你。

 沒果仁邏輯 Americans 句型解析與用法說明

 說明① fall for用法

動詞片語fall for表示著迷、迷戀，負面的意思則為中計、受騙。例：She is falling for this designer's art works. 她對這個設計師的作品很著迷。/Don't fall for his tricks. 不要中了他的伎倆。

 說明② in love with句型

be動詞+in+love+with＝戀愛、愛上。例：My mom is in love with Sunday strolls in the park. 我媽愛上了週日到公園漫步的活動。

 說明③ adore用法

人名／代名詞+adore+受詞＝某人愛慕(某人事物)。例：She adores heavy cream on cake. 她最愛蛋糕上的厚鮮奶油。

沒果仁也愛的說法

對照「主要關鍵句」的類似說法

① **You stole my heart.**
你偷走了我的心。

② **I love you so much that my heart aches.**
我愛你愛到心都痛了。

③ **I cherish you.**
我很珍惜你。

這樣回答就對了

對應「主要關鍵句」的回答

① **Keep your voice down! People are watching.**
小聲點啦！大家都在看。

② **I don't know what to say.**
這讓我無言以對。

③ **Me, too.**
我也是。

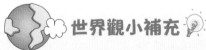 ## 世界觀小補充

　　英文當中的「愛」有很多種表達方式，例如：love, affection, adore, infatuation等，雖然都表達強烈的情感，但應依照整體句意挑選適合的單字使用。love是很強烈的愛情，常用在愛侶間，藉此表達情意；affection則是較為細水長流的溫柔情懷，例如親情；adore跟love的意思相近，有時會多了一些仰慕、尊敬的情懷；infatuation則是短暫的愛慕，通常伴隨較為癡狂的情感，但維持的時間很短暫。

學校沒教的實用句

情境式主題句，學校沒有教，自己學起來！

Part 6

愛的世界從開始到結束

I think we two are a perfect **match**!
我覺得我倆是絕配！　　match 相配者

Honey, we **are meant for** each other.
親愛的，我們是天造地設的一對。　　be meant for 指定；預訂

Do you want to go steady with me?
妳想要跟我穩定交往嗎？

It was love **at first sight**!
這是一見鍾情！　　at first sight 初見

Don't you see that Michael **is all over you**?
妳看不出來麥可為妳痴狂嗎？　　be all over sb. 為某人瘋狂

I think I just found my **soul mate**.
我覺得我找到心靈伴侶了。　　soul mate 心靈伴侶；性情相投的人

He is the love of my life.
他是我此生的摯愛。

When the guy brought the girl home, they **made out** on the front porch.
那男生帶女孩回家時，他們在門廊前親熱。　　make out 親熱

You are my heart's desire.
你是我心所嚮往。

I can't live without you.
沒有你我活不下去。

He and his girlfriend are so **passionate** about each other.
他跟他女友兩人打得火熱。　　passionate 熱情的

He made my heart **skip** a beat.
他讓我心跳漏一拍。　　skip 漏掉

He gently gave me a **peck** on the cheek when we parted.
我們分開的時候，他在我的臉頰上輕吻了一下。　　peck 啄

*They are madly in love, so they show no **modesty** in their public displays of affection.*

他們在熱戀，在公眾場合也完全不掩飾對彼此的愛意。　　modesty 羞怯

*There's some **chemistry** between the two.*

這兩人有來電。　　chemistry 化學作用；來電

*Our **mutual** affection is something that I hold dear.*

我們之間的愛意是我最珍惜的東西。　　mutual 相互的；彼此的

*She is the kind of girl that I've been **longing for**.*

她就是我朝思暮想的那種女生。　　long for 渴望

*You **manifest** the meaning of true love.*

你證實了真愛的存在。　　manifest 證明；證實

*I want a **lifetime** with you.*

我要跟你共度餘生。　　lifetime 一生；終身

*My love for you is unconditional and **eternal**.*

我對你的愛是無條件也無止盡的。　　eternal 永恆的

*You are my **dream come true**.*

你讓我的美夢成真。　　dream come true 夢想成真

*She **cast a spell on** him.*

她讓他著迷。　　cast a spell on 用符咒迷惑

You are the best thing that ever happened to me.

認識你是我生命中最棒的一件事。

You mean the whole world to me.

妳就是我的全世界。

I get weak-kneed whenever you walk by.

當你經過我身邊時，我全身都感覺輕飄飄的。

I feel moonstruck whenever you kiss me.

每次你吻我，我都覺得如痴如醉。

I am infatuated with you.

我瘋狂地迷戀著你。

以關鍵句破題的模擬實境對話

Situation **1** 爛漫之人
a straightforward confession

A I am falling for you.
我被你迷倒。

B That's really straightforward.
你還真直接。

A I can't help it.
我忍不住。

B I don't know what to say.
我實在不知道該如何回應你！

A Just follow your heart.
跟隨你的心吧。

Situation **2** 木頭人
nothing in return

A I am so in love with you.
我如此愛你。

B I am pretty sure you said that yesterday.
我很確定你昨天講過同樣的話。

A I just want to make sure you get the message.
我只是想確定你有接收到訊息。

B Yeah, yeah, yeah. I got it alright.
有啦，我收到啦。

A Is that the only response you've got?
你就只有這個回應嗎？

Situation **3** 真愛煞風景
sweet words for love

A I adore you.
我愛慕你。

B You light up my life.
你照亮我的生命。

A You hold the key to my heart.
你握有解開我心鎖的鑰匙。

B You are holding the key to our front door.
你則握有我們家大門的鑰匙。

A You are such a killjoy.
你真的很煞風景耶。

 **Situation** **4** 真愛確實存在
does true love exist?

A Do you believe in true love?
你相信世上有真愛嗎？

B Yes. My parents are the perfect example.
我相信，我爸媽就是很好的例子。

A I am so jealous. I have always doubted its existence.
真令人羨慕，我總是懷疑真愛的存在。

B Don't be such a pessimist. You'll find your prince charming someday.
別那麼悲觀，你會找到心目中的白馬王子的。

A Alright. I'll keep my fingers crossed.
好吧，我只能祈求好運囉。

主要關鍵句開口說

使出關鍵３句型，英文輕鬆開口說

Track 157

① **Why didn't you answer my phone call?**
你為什麼不接我電話？

② **You've been acting weird lately.**
你最近行徑很怪異。

③ **Where were you last night?**
你昨天晚上去哪了？

沒果仁邏輯 Americans 句型解析與用法說明

說明① **answer my phone call句型**

answer+所有格+phone+call＝接聽某人的電話，例：Why isn't there anyone answering the phone? 怎麼都沒有人接電話？

說明② **act weird用法**

act weird＝行為舉止異常。例：My dog is acting weird lately. I am wondering if he is not feeling well. 我的狗最近行為怪怪的，我擔心牠是不是身體不舒服。

說明③ **Where句型**

where為詢問地點的疑問詞。例：Where is the nearest restroom in this department store? 百貨公司內最近的洗手間在哪？

沒果仁也愛的說法

對照「主要關鍵句」的類似說法

① **Why was my call sent to your voice message the other day?**
為何我那天打給你是轉語音信箱？

② **There's something weird about your behavior.**
你舉止怪怪的。

③ **Why couldn't I reach you yesterday?**
為什麼我昨天找不到你？

這樣回答就對了

對應「主要關鍵句」的回答

① **I had bad reception.**
我手機的收訊不好。

② **Have I?**
有嗎？

③ **I was at home, sound asleep!**
我在家，睡得很沉啊！

世界觀小補充

　　出軌、不忠、外遇等情節可是全球男人女人都害怕的事。台灣有徵信社，國外則有private detective(私家偵探)。要指控別人做壞事之前，最好要握有強而有力的證據，以免顯得自己像是無理取鬧喔！如果對方斥責" You are being paranoid!"(你太神經質了！)時，要冷靜下來，別讓激動跟疑心病蒙蔽了自己的判斷能力。本篇的實用句僅供參考，現實生活中，最好能避免用到太情緒化的句子。

學校沒教的實用句

情境式主題句，學校沒有教，自己學起來！

Don't you **lie to** me.
你不要騙我喔！　　lie to 對⋯撒謊

Are you **seeing someone else**?
你在跟別人約會嗎？　　see someone else 與其他人約會

I would never date more than one girl.
我不會同時跟兩個以上的女生約會。

Why haven't you changed your Facebook **relationship status**?
你為什麼都不修改你臉書上面的感情狀態？　　relationship status 感情狀態

I have a feeling that you are having an **affair**.
我覺得你有外遇。　　affair 風流韻事；外遇

Why did you **turn off** your cell phone yesterday?
你手機昨天為什麼關機？　　turn off 關掉

He is **cheating on** his girlfriend.
他背著女友偷吃。　　cheat on 對⋯不忠

She suspects her boyfriend isn't being **faithful**.
她懷疑她男友對她不忠。　　faithful 忠貞的

Don't you think you're being overly **sensitive**?
你不覺得你過度敏感了嗎？　　sensitive 神經過敏的

My friend **snooped** through her man's Facebook to find proof of his affairs.
我朋友偷看她男友的臉書，想要找出他外遇的證據。　　snoop 窺探

I am going to **confront** my boyfriend over that flirtatious text message.
我要跟我男友對質，問他那封曖昧簡訊是什麼意思。　　confront 對質

I think you are mature enough to talk with him about the specific behavior that causes you to doubt his integrity.
我覺得你已經夠成熟，可以跟他溝通有關那些令你懷疑其誠信的行為。

If you still don't trust him, don't **date** him.

如果你還是不信任他，就別跟他交往了。　date 與…約會

It was just a **fling**. Nothing happened.

這只是玩玩的，什麼都沒發生。　fling 一時的放縱

Why are you making these false **accusations**?

你為什麼要做出這些不實的指控？　accusation 指控；指責

Lighten up! It was just a totally harmless text.

放輕鬆！這只是個無傷大雅的簡訊而已。　lighten 變得輕鬆

There must be some misunderstanding here.

一定有什麼誤會。

The girl doesn't know she is a **mistress** and a home wrecker.

這個女生不知道自己是破壞人家家庭的小三。　mistress 情婦

Something's **fishy**!

感覺有點可疑。　fishy 可疑的

My girlfriend has been **sneaking** out of the house recently.

我女友最近常常偷溜出門。　sneak 偷偷地走

He **confessed** what he did.

他坦承他的所作所為。　confess 坦白；供認

Why can't you **be honest with** me?

你為什麼不能對我坦承？　be honest with 對…坦承

I suspect that he's been **fooling around** while I am not around.

我懷疑他趁我不在的時候到處亂搞。　fool around 胡搞

He is involved in a **love triangle**.

他陷入三角戀情。　love triangle 三角戀愛

I think you're doing some **funny business** behind my back.

我覺得你在我背後搞七捻三。　funny business 不道德的行為

Why do you **all of a sudden** need a lot of space while talking over the phone?

為什麼你講電話的時候突然需要很多空間了？　all of a sudden 突然地

關鍵一句模擬實境對話 *Topic-related Conversations*

以關鍵句破題的模擬實境對話

Situation 1 誇張藉口
a ridiculous excuse

A You've been obsessed with texting lately. Who were you texting just now?
你最近很沉迷在傳簡訊喔,你剛剛在跟誰傳訊息?

B What? No one! I was just checking an online weather forecast.
什麼?沒跟誰啊!我在查網路天氣預報啦。

A Come on! Your fingers were moving rapidly.
少來!你的手剛剛明明就動得很靈活。

B Well, my fingers need some exercise from time to time.
嗯,手指有時候是需要一些運動。

A Just save it. Hand me your phone right now!
省省吧你,手機現在給我交出來!

Situation 2 舉止怪異
acting weird lately

A You've been acting weird lately.
你最近的行為很怪異。

B No, I haven't.
我哪有?

A You have been wearing perfume for the past two weeks.
你過去兩個禮拜都有擦香水。

B I used to wear perfume all the time.
我以前都會擦香水啊。

A Yeah, like five years ago you did.
對啊,大概五年前吧。

ß 在家熟睡
believe it or not

A Where were you last night?
你昨天晚上去哪裡了？

B I was at home.
我就待在家啊。

A Liar. I called your cell phone and it was off. I called your home and no one answered.
騙人。我打你手機沒通，打家裡電話也沒人接。

B I was beat, so I hit the sack very early.
我很累，所以提早上床休息了。

A Am I supposed to believe that?
我應該要相信你的說辭嗎？

Situation 4 荒唐藉口
confrontation

A Just be honest with me. Are you seeing someone else?
老實說，你有在跟別人約會嗎？

B I am not! You are paranoid.
我沒有！你太神經質了。

A Then can you explain why you have been sneaking out of the house in the middle of the night recently?
那你可否解釋你最近為何都會偷溜出去呢？

B I've been sleepwalking perhaps.
可能是夢遊吧。

A That's the most ridiculous excuse I've ever heard.
這是我聽過最荒唐的藉口。

Unit 54 感情生變─吵架篇
Getting into a fight

 主要關鍵句開口說

使出關鍵３句型，英文輕鬆脫口說

 Track 160

① **I don't want to see you anymore.**
我再也不想見到你。

② **I want you to get out of my life!**
我要你在我生命中消失！

③ **Why are you being so paranoid?**
你為什麼要這麼神經兮兮的呢？

 沒果仁邏輯 Americans

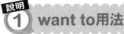 句型解析與用法說明

說明① want to用法

want to+原形動詞＝想要進行某事。要注意want to是較為直白的說法，如果不是在吵架，想要客氣一點，可用前面教過的would like。例：I want to go abroad for further study. 我想要出國深造。

說明② get out of用法

get out of+名詞＝離開某處、某狀態。例：He seriously needs to get out of his comfort zone. 他真的需要離開舒適圈了。

說明③ being paranoid用法

paranoid＝偏執的；瘋狂的。使用being表達維持在某種狀態，在談話中使用也會帶有強調的口吻。例：Why are you being so nice to me? 你為什麼要對我這麼好？

沒果仁也愛的說法 Americans
對照「主要關鍵句」的類似說法

① **Get out of my sight.**
離開我的視線。

② **Get lost!**
滾開！

③ **Don't be so suspicious.**
不要這樣疑神疑鬼的。

這樣回答就對了
對應「主要關鍵句」的回答

① **Me, neither!**
我也不想！

② **No, YOU get out of my life.**
不，是你滾出我的生命裡。

③ **Why are you being such a jerk?**
那你為什麼要那麼混蛋？

世界觀小補充

　　情緒來了難免會口出惡言，尤其是關係親密的兩個人，有時候在氣頭上就會口不擇言。正常人總在氣消之後，後悔當初言語使用不當，說了不該說的嚴厲指責、情緒化字眼或甚至是無禮的怒罵文字。所以要罵人，請盡量避免過度無禮的用字，最好可以先深呼吸，暫時離開戰區。少說少錯！氣頭過後，如果想要深入溝通，建議從「原因」與「作法」切入，以討論的心態提起，這樣下次遇到同樣的事情，或許就可免除情緒性的字眼囉！

Part 6 愛的世界從開始到結束

I need you to leave this **instant**!
我要你現在馬上離開！　instant 頃刻

Will you stop **moping** now?
你可以不要再悶悶不樂了嗎？　mope 鬱鬱寡歡

I'm giving you the **silent treatment**.
我決定要開始跟你冷戰！　silent treatment 沉默以待；冷戰

Just listen to yourself! You're not **making sense** at all!
你自己聽聽你講的話！根本是胡謅嘛！　make sense 具有意義

You are the most selfish person I've ever met. **I'm so done with** you!
你是我遇過最自私的人，我受夠你了！　be done with 與…再無關係

I am so fed up with you always trying to **pick a fight**!
我真是受夠你了，老是找架吵。　pick a fight 找碴

I am so sick and tired of you.
我真的厭倦你了。

How could you do this to me?
你怎麼可以這樣對我？

Get lost, you big fat liar!
滾開，你這個大騙子！　get lost 滾開

Can you stop **whining**?
你可以不要再抱怨了嗎？　whine 發牢騷

Enough is enough. Give me a break!
夠了！讓我喘口氣吧！　enough is enough 適可而止

You **screw** everything **up**!
所有事情都被你搞砸了！　screw up 弄糟；搞砸

He is such a **pain in the neck**.
他真的有夠煩人的！　pain in the neck 令人厭煩的人事物

You have a serious **issue** of anger management.
你在脾氣控制上出了很嚴重的問題。　　issue 問題；爭議

Is that all you have to say? After all we've been through?
我們一起經歷過這麼多風風雨雨，你就只有這些要說？

Who are you? I don't know you anymore.
你到底是誰？我已經快不認識你了。

I'd **take that back**, if I were you!
如果我是你，我會收回那句話。　　take sth. back 收回說錯的話

You are going to regret this. I'm **warning** you!
你會後悔的，我警告你。　　warn 警告

感情生變—吵架篇

What is up with you?
你到底是怎麼回事？

Shut it! I don't want to listen to a word you say.
閉嘴！我不想要聽你講任何一句話！

I can't take it anymore. It's over.
我再也受不了了，我們分手吧。

You've **gone too far** this time.
這次你真的太過分了。　　go too far 做得過分

Have I done something wrong?
我做錯了什麼嗎？

Don't be such a **drama queen**.
你不要這麼小題大作好嗎？　　drama queen 喜歡小題大作者

You've gone overboard.
你真的太超過了。

Don't you dare say that again!
你再說一次試試看！

You're going to pay for this!
你會為此付出代價的！

Situation 1 現在就不想見面
getting lost immediately

A I don't want to see you anymore.
我再也不想見到你。

B Me, neither!
我也不想。

A Here are your clothes and suitcase.
這裡有你的衣服跟皮箱。

B What for?
要幹嘛用的？

A You need to leave the house now.
你現在就給我搬出這裡。

Situation 2 消失明天生效
you are impossible

A I want you to get out of my life!
我要你從我的生命中消失！

B I am more than happy to get out of your life!
要從你生命中消失，我真是高興得不得了！

A Then what are you standing here for?
那你現在還站在這邊幹嘛？

B Well, It's 2 a.m. I'll do that tomorrow.
嗯，現在半夜兩點，我明天早上再消失。

A You are impossible.
你真是不可理喻。

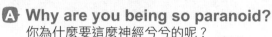 3 不講理
fighting over a fight

A Why are you being so paranoid?
你為什麼要這麼神經兮兮的呢？

B Why are you being such a jerk?
那你為何要這麼混蛋？

A I was trying to be reasonable.
我試著要講理。

B Are you implying that I am not reasonable?
你是在暗指我很不講理嗎？

A I think you're trying to pick a fight.
我覺得你刻意要找架吵。

Unit
54
感情生變—吵架篇

Situation 4 冷戰中
a silent treatment

A Don't be mad.
別生氣了。

B I'm not mad.
我沒有生氣。

A Yes, you are. I'm sorry. I admit it was my fault. Will you stop moping now?
有，你有。對不起啦，我承認是我的錯，你可不可以不要再悶悶不樂了？

B I'm not moping. I'm giving you the silent treatment.
我沒有悶悶不樂，我是在冷戰，不想講話。

A I knew it! You're still peeved at me. What can I do to make it up to you?
我就知道你還在氣我，我該怎麼彌補我的錯呢？

Unit 55 冷靜討論及溝通
Calming down and communicating

主要關鍵句開口說

使出關鍵３句型，英文輕鬆開口說

Track 163

① **It's all my fault.**
都是我不好！

② **Let's chill out and have a talk.**
我們冷靜下來好好談一談。

③ **Will you ever forgive me?**
你會原諒我嗎？

沒果仁邏輯 Americans

句型解析與用法說明

說明 ① It's all my fault句型

此為認錯的慣用句型。所有格my可使用其他所有格代替，做句意變化。例：It's my sister's fault. 是我妹不好。加上not表示否定。例：It's not Jeremy's fault. 這不是傑瑞米的錯。

說明 ② chill out用法

此為口語的片語，表示要對方冷靜，與calm down意思相同，但較常在更熟識的朋友面前使用。例：Dude, chill out! She is not worth the fight. 老兄，冷靜點，她不值得你們這樣爭吵。

說明 ③ Will you ever forgive me句型

人名/代名詞+forgive+受詞意為某人原諒後面所指的人。例：Marian finally forgave her husband for being unable to remember their wedding anniversary. 瑪莉安終於肯原諒她先生不記得結婚週年紀念日的事。

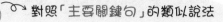
1 **I am responsible for this.**
我該為這件事負責。

2 **We need to communicate.**
我們需要溝通。

3 **Will you accept my apology?**
你會接受我的道歉嗎？

Unit
55

冷靜討論及溝通

 這樣回答就對了 對應「主要關鍵句」的回答

1 **I should apologize, too.**
我也應該要道歉。

2 **I don't want to chill! The fight isn't over!**
我不要冷靜！架還沒吵完！

3 **Over my dead body.**
下輩子吧。

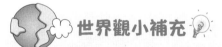 世界觀小補充

　　國籍、生活背景等的不同，都會帶出觀念、思維、處事態度的差異。與人交往，難免有擦撞誤解，這已經是超越國界的問題。要解決糾紛爭論，還是得要心平氣和的溝通，跳脫個人主觀意識，好好講清楚、說明白。有時吵架會因為情緒激昂而跳脫主題，翻舊帳(rake over the ashes)，因而引發更嚴重的爭吵。所以要釐清當下的問題時，還是就事論事(take the matter on its merits)，免得爭論陷入無限迴圈吧！

學校沒教的實用句

情境式主題句，學校沒有教，自己學起來！

I made up with my boyfriend last night.
昨天晚上我跟我男友和好了。　　make up with 與…和好

Can we make peace?
我們可不可以和好？　　make peace 講和

What can I do to **mend** your broken heart?
我可以怎麼做來彌補你受到的傷害呢？　　mend 修補

I am sorry for being too **judgmental**.
我為我的挑三揀四感到抱歉！　　judgmental (主觀)判定的

I love you, and I want our **relationship** to work.
我愛妳，也希望我們的關係可以長久。　　relationship 關係

Can we sit down and discuss what went wrong?
我們可否坐下來討論我們之間哪裡出問題了？

I don't want to **give up on** us.
我不想要放棄！　　give up on 不再相信…會成功

Let us try to love again.
我們再試試重新來過吧！

I shouldn't have **doubted** you.
我不應該懷疑妳的。　　doubt 懷疑

I shouldn't have **yelled at** you.
我不應該吼你。　　yell at 對…大吼

I'll change! I can fix this.
我會改，我會彌補錯誤。

Just give me one more chance.
再給我一次機會吧。

I can prove it to you.
我可以證明給妳看。

Part
6
愛的世界從開始到結束

We can **work** this **out**. Just have faith!
我們可以一起解決問題，抱持著信心吧！　　work out 能夠解決

I promise I will never let that happen ever again.
我保證不會再犯了。

Let's **come clean** and start over.
讓我們敞開心胸，重新來過吧！　　come clean 和盤托出；招供

From now on, we need to spend more time **communicating**.
從現在開始，我們需要花更多的時間在溝通上。　　communicate 溝通

I still believe in us.
我仍然對我們有信心。

I am so sorry for being so sensitive and **insecure**.
我很抱歉表現得這麼敏感又缺乏安全感。　　insecure 侷促不安的

I should have told you that I am so lucky to have you.
我應該早點告訴你，有你在我真的很幸運。

Don't you think we both deserve a second chance?
你不覺得我們應該再給彼此一次機會嗎？

Please don't leave me! You mean the world to me.
拜託不要離開我！你是我的全世界。

I don't want to lose you!
我不想要失去你！

I never meant to **break your heart**.
我從來都不想要傷妳的心！　　break one's heart 使某人傷心、心碎

I want to make things clear.
我想要把話說清楚。

Let's stop the silent **treatment**.
我們停止冷戰吧。　　treatment 對待；處理

Let's go take a walk and talk things through, shall we?
我們出去走走，順便談一談好嗎？

冷靜討論及溝通

Situation 1 和好吧
making up

A It's all my fault!
都是我的錯！

B I should have been more open-minded.
我應該要心胸寬大點才對。

A Can we stop fighting?
我們可以不要再吵了嗎？

B I was going to say the same thing.
我也正打算這麼說。

A Let's kiss and make up!
那我們就親一下，和好吧！

Situation 2 怎麼做都不對
incapable of calming down

A Let's chill out and have a talk.
我們冷靜下來，好好談談吧！

B Why should we? I am still very mad at you.
為什麼要冷靜？我還是很生你的氣。

A If that's the case, I'll leave you alone.
如果是這樣，那我先離你遠一點(先不打擾你)。

B Argh! You are always capable of pissing me off!
吼！你總是有辦法把我惹毛耶！

A What have I done? I just want to give you some space to think it through.
我又怎麼了？我只是想給你點空間想清楚而已啊。

Situation 3 很好打發
easy to please

A Will you ever forgive me?
你會原諒我嗎？

B Let me think about it.
我考慮一下。

A Please. I'll buy you flowers and take you to fancy restaurants.
拜託啦，我會買花送你，帶你去高檔餐廳用餐。

B All right. I forgive you.
好吧，我原諒你。

A That was quick.
還真快。

Situation 4 三省吾身
introspection happens

A The last thing I would do is leave you.
我最不希望的事情就是離開你。

B I think both of us deserve a second chance.
我覺得我們都該給彼此一個機會。

A I agree. Let's stop the silent treatment and work things out.
我同意，我們就別再冷戰，一起解決問題吧。

B Yeah. I am going to be 100 percent honest with you from now on.
是啊，我往後要對你百分百的坦承。

A I am going to stop being cynical.
我再也不會這麼憤世嫉俗了。

Unit 56　分手？復合？
Breaking up / getting back together

主要關鍵句開口說

使出關鍵3句型，英文輕鬆脫口說

Track 166

① **I want to break up.**
我要分手。

② **I don't think our relationship is going to work out.**
我覺得我們沒辦法在一起。

③ **We are getting back together.**
我們復合了。

沒果仁邏輯 Americans

句型解析與用法說明

① I want to break up句型

break up是動詞片語，表示分手，兩個字合併成為breakup，字義相同，只是詞性變成名詞。例：I broke up with my boyfriend. 我跟我男友分手了。/ Miranda recently went through a breakup. 米蘭達最近剛分手。

② I don't think句型

否定語氣跟著think(覺得)一起使用，表達後面子句所抱持的否定態度是説話者個人的意見。例：I don't think going out for a run on a sweltering day like this is such a good idea. 我覺得在這種酷熱的天氣跑步不是個好主意。

③ We are getting back together句型

動詞片語get back together＝復合。偶像歌手泰勒絲也有一首叫做We Are Never Ever Getting Back Together(我們絕對不會再復合)的歌。

沒果仁也愛的說法 → 對照「主要關鍵句」的類似說法

① **I am breaking up with you.**
我要跟你分手。

② **We are not meant to be together.**
我們不適合。

③ **Let's start over.**
我們重新來過吧。

這樣回答就對了 → 對應「主要關鍵句」的回答

① **What have I done wrong?**
我做錯了什麼？

② **Why? We've been together for almost a year.**
為什麼？我們在一起快一年了。

③ **Are you sure this is the right decision?**
你確定這是對的決定嗎？

 ## 世界觀小補充

　　男女間的感情故事自古以來就充斥在各種不同文學作品中，從古希臘神話開始就有著兒女情仇的劇情上演，一直到現代的流行歌曲，以愛情為主題的歌詞所佔的比例依然非常高。所以透過英文流行歌曲學習會話是很好的方法。選擇自己喜歡的音樂，在享受旋律之餘，也多了解歌詞內容，單單一首歌就可以接觸到很多實用的片語。

學校沒教的實用句

情境式主題句，學校沒有教，自己學起來！

Part 6

愛的世界從開始到結束

🖊 Are you **dumping** me?
你要把我甩了嗎？ dump 拋棄

🖊 I just feel that I'm not the right one for you.
我只是覺得我不適合你。

🖊 I don't think our lives were meant to be spent with each other.
我覺得我們彼此不適合生活在一起。

🖊 Breaking up with my first love is the hardest thing I've ever done.
跟我的初戀情人分手是我做過最困難的一件事。

🖊 .I thought we had it all.
我曾以為我們擁有全世界。

🖊 He thought we were perfect for each other.
他以為我們是天造地設的一對。

🖊 We are so over!
我們徹底結束了！

🖊 We are **through**!
我們分手了！ through 完結的；斷交的

🖊 I am still under her.
我還是忘不了她。

🖊 It's only a matter of time. You'll be over her!
這只是時間早晚的問題，你會忘記她的！

🖊 Don't you know how much I **sacrificed** to be with you?
妳知不知道為了跟你在一起，我做了多少犧牲？ sacrifice 犧牲

🖊 I tried so hard to make it work with her.
我很努力想維持我和她的感情。

🖊 This relationship isn't right for us.
我們不適合談戀愛。

I can't believe that my ex-boyfriend broke up with me by text message.
我不敢相信我前男友竟然傳簡訊跟我分手。

It's not you. It's me! I need to **work on** myself.
不是你的問題，是我！我需要自我成長。 | work on 從事；致力於

In the first few days and weeks of a breakup, you can have a lot of mixed feelings and may consider going back to your ex.
在分手的頭幾天或頭幾週，你會百感交集，甚至想要回到你前任的身邊。

Should I try to **get** my ex **back**?
我應該要挽回我的前任嗎？ | get...back 取回；重新得到

I regret breaking up with my ex, and I want him back so bad.
我後悔跟我的前男友分手，我極度想要挽回他。

I want to **rekindle** our relationship.
我想要重燃我們之前的關係。 | rekindle 再點火；再振作

分手？復合？

Can we get back together?
我們可不可以復合呢？

She is going to **win** her ex **back**.
她要重新贏回前男友的心。 | win back 重新獲得

Let's **start from scratch** and take things slow.
我們重新來過，並放慢腳步吧！ | start from scratch 從頭開始進行

You are the most perfect partner that I could ever dream of.
你／妳是我夢寐以求最完美的另一半。

Don't beg your ex-girlfriend to come back! That makes you look **desperate**.
不要懇求你的前女友回來，這樣顯得你很可悲。 | desperate 絕望的；極度渴望的

Please don't **turn your back on** me!
拜託不要背棄我！ | turn one's back on 某人轉身不理

I hope we could still be friends.
我希望我們還能做朋友。

Situation 1 不歡而散
a bad breakup

A I want a breakup.
我要分手。

B Honey, what's wrong? Did I do something wrong?
親愛的，怎麼了？我做什麼了嗎？

A No. It's not you. It's just that I need to work on myself.
不是你的問題，只是我需要自我成長。

B Cut it out. That's the worst breakup excuse I've ever heard.
別說了，這是我聽過最爛的分手藉口。

A Whatever. Take it or leave it!
隨便，信不信由你。

Situation 2 提出承諾
asking for a commitment

A I don't think our relationship is going to work out.
我不覺得我們的關係能夠長久。

B I don't know what you mean. We've been together for over three years.
我不懂你的意思，我們在一起三年了耶。

A That is the point. I don't think you want to commit to this relationship.
這就是問題，我不覺得你想要在這段關係中許下承諾。

B Where does this idea come from?
這想法是從哪裡冒出來的？

A Have you ever thought about proposing to me?
那你有想過跟我求婚嗎？

being overly generous

A My ex-boyfriend and I are getting back together.
我前男友要跟我復合了。

B Are you sure this is a good idea?
你確定這是個好主意嗎？

A Sure! We are still so much in love.
當然！我們彼此仍相愛。

B But he cheated on you! Don't you remember?
但是他劈腿耶！你忘了嗎？

A Well, I think that's forgivable...
嗯，我覺得那可以原諒啦…

Unit
56
分手？復合？

Situation 4 復合真心話
getting back together

A Please don't leave me. Let's work out the problem together.
拜託不要離開我，我們一起解決問題吧。

B But you've never listened.
但是你都聽不進去。

A I promise I will do whatever you ask me to. I'll never find anyone like you.
我發誓，將來你要我做什麼，我都會去做，我再也找不到像你一樣的人了。

B Oh, that's the sweetest thing you've ever said to me!
喔！這是你對我說過最貼心的話了！

A Let's try again.
我們再試試吧。

主要關鍵句開口說

使出關鍵3句型，英文輕鬆開口說

Track 169

① **Will you marry me?**
嫁給我好嗎？

② **How will I propose to my girlfriend?**
我要怎麼向我女友求婚呢？

③ **I am waiting for the right moment to pop the question.**
我在等待求婚的好時機。

沒果仁邏輯 Americans

句型解析與用法說明

說明
① **Will you marry me句型**

marry＝嫁、娶某人，中文嫁跟娶的使用不同，雖然英文都是用marry來表示。容易發生錯誤的用法就是在marry之後加介系詞。marry為及物動詞，後方直接接受詞。

說明
② **How will I propose to my girlfriend句型**

propose to＝提議、求婚。propose本身有提議、打算的意思，當作不及物動詞時可加上to成為動詞片語，表示提親、求婚的意思。例：Are you proposing to me by cell phone? 你現在是在用手機跟我求婚嗎？

說明
③ **to pop the question句型**

pop是「冒然提出問題」的意思，pop the question純粹用來指「求婚」。當你想要提出一個問題，不可以使用這個片語，否則可能會讓聽者誤會。

沒果仁也愛的說法 Americans

對照「主要關鍵句」的類似說法

① **Will you spend the rest of your life with me?**
你願意跟我共度餘生嗎？

② **How am I going to ask my girl to marry me?**
我該怎麼讓我的女友嫁給我？

③ **I am waiting for the perfect time to propose.**
我在等待完美的求婚時機。

這樣回答就對了

對應「主要關鍵句」的回答

① **This is not the right time!**
現在問這時機不太好！

② **Try to surprise her with an unpredictable approach.**
試著用出乎意料的方法來給她驚喜。

③ **I do hope you'll pull it off!**
我真心希望你成功！

世界觀小補充

　　英文裡有關結婚的描述用語跟禮俗有關係的不少，直接照著字義翻成中文會讓人一頭霧水。例如get down on one's knees，直接翻譯就是一個人蹲下來將膝蓋著地，也就是下跪的意思。因為現在西洋電影風行，大家都知道當一方跪下來(通常是男方)對著另一方，這就是要求婚的準備動作，所以這片語就成了求婚的意思。另外還有tie the knot，字面上的意思是將繩子打結，因為美國結婚流行送禮，禮物外包裝講求精美的結飾，所以就演變為結婚的意思。

Part 6

愛的世界從開始到結束

My boyfriend **got down on his knees** and proposed last night!
我男友昨晚跪下來跟我求婚了！　　get down on one's knees 某人跪下

We have been together for over five years, and I think it's time we move on to the next level.
我們已經在一起五年了，覺得該是時候往下一階段邁進。

I want to ask my girlfriend to **marry** me.
我想要請我的女友嫁給我。　　marry 嫁；娶；與…結婚

I am going to marry this girl.
我要把這女孩娶過來。

She is the love of my life, and I want to **settle down** with her.
她是我的摯愛，我想要跟她定下來。　　settle down 安頓下來

Are you going to accept his **proposal**?
妳要接受他的求婚嗎？　　proposal 求婚

Are you ready for a life-long commitment?
你已經準備好接受一輩子的承諾了嗎？

What if she doesn't say "yes"?
萬一她不答應怎麼辦？

Will you be my wife?
請當我的妻子吧！

I am not ready. I think you are going too fast.
我還沒準備好，我覺得你太急了。

This is the worst proposal ever.
這是最糟糕的求婚。

I think it's time we **took** some **vows**.
我想該是我們許下誓言的時候了。　　take vows 立下誓約

I want to be with you forever.

356

我想與你相守一輩子。

I can't believe my best friend is going to tie the knot!
我不敢相信我最好的朋友要結婚了！　tie the knot 結婚

I think it's time we settle down.
我想該是我們定下來的時候了。

I want to have your baby.
我想為你生小寶貝。(較為露骨的表達方式)

Let's get hitched!
我們結婚吧！　get hitched 結婚

I've decided to make a big commitment to him.
我決定要跟他共結連理。　commitment 承諾；保證

I'm so glad you're getting married.
我好高興你要結婚了。　get married 結婚

I am engaged!
我訂婚了！　engaged 已訂婚的

My fiancée and I will be married in June.
我的未婚妻跟我準備在六月結婚。　fiancée 未婚妻

It's so hard to choose the perfect engagement ring for my wife-to-be.
要幫我未來的老婆找訂婚戒指真困難。　to-be 未來的

This engagement ring is a token of our steadfast love.
這枚訂婚戒象徵我們堅定不移的愛。　token 象徵；標記

I'm sorry, but I don't want to be tied down by marriage.
很抱歉，但我不想受婚姻的羈絆。　tie down 束縛；約束

I have an announcement to make. "Ophelia and I are engaged!"
我要宣布一件事情：「奧菲利亞跟我訂婚了！」　announcement 通知；宣告

From now on, our futures are tied together.
從現在開始，我們的未來緊緊相繫。　from now on 自現在起

Situation 1 錯誤的求婚時機
the wrong timing

A Will you marry me?
嫁給我，好嗎？

B Are you proposing to me while I am doing the dishes?
你現在是在我洗碗洗到一半的時候跟我求婚嗎？

A I know I am not asking the question properly.
我知道現在求婚不太恰當。

B Duh! I don't know how to respond.
廢話！我都不知道要怎麼回答了。

A OK. Let's do it some other time.
好，那我們改天重新來過吧。

Situation 2 狗頭軍師
experience needed

A How will I propose to my girlfriend?
我要怎麼向我女友求婚呢？

B It's easy. Girls like fancy restaurants and big diamond engagement rings.
很簡單，女生都喜歡高檔餐廳跟大顆鑽戒。

A Besides that, what am I going to say?
除了這些之外，我要說些什麼？

B Just follow your heart and pop the question.
就隨心所欲，想求就求囉！

A I should ask someone who is more experienced.
我應該去問比較有經驗的人才對。

Part 6 愛的世界從開始到結束

Situation 3 貼心男子
waiting for the right moment

A I am waiting for the right moment to pop the question.
我在等適當的時機求婚。

B I am so nervous for you! Have you prepared a proper speech?
我都替你緊張了！你準備好要說什麼了嗎？

A I am going to be sincere and straightforward.
我決定要真誠坦率。

B Good strategy. And where are you going to propose to her?
很好的策略，你要在什麼地方跟她求婚？

A At home! I am going to cook a perfect meal first, and then pop the question.
在家！我要先端出完美的餐點，然後再求婚。

Situation 4 鑽戒是女孩的好友
sharing good news

A Guess what? My boyfriend just asked me to marry him!
猜怎麼著？我男友剛剛向我求婚了！

B Congratulations! When are you going to get married?
恭喜！那你們什麼時候要結婚？

A We haven't gone into details. But check out this engagement ring!
我們還沒有討論到細節，先看看我這顆訂婚戒吧！

B Wow, it must have cost your fiancé a fortune!
哇！你未婚夫一定花了不少錢！

A I am so happy I could fly!
我高興到快要飛起來了！

 主要關鍵句開口說

使出關鍵3句型，英文輕鬆開口說

 Track 172

① **Are we going to plan our own wedding?**
我們要自己規劃婚禮嗎？

② **We need to set the date for our wedding first.**
我們得要先選好結婚的日子。

③ **My father is going to walk me down the aisle.**
我父親將會牽著我走向紅毯另一端。

 沒果仁邏輯 Americans 句型解析與用法說明

 說明① **plan our own wedding句型**

結婚除了去登記身分的變更之外，還要有對外宣示的儀式。這樣的儀式有許多事前的細節需要規劃，所以婚禮需要用plan(規劃)這個動詞來表達。例：Haven't you started to plan your wedding? 你還沒開始計畫婚禮嗎？

 說明② **set the date句型**

set the date＝設定、確定日期。例：Are we going to set the date for our next meeting? 我們要不要定出下次開會的日期？

 說明③ **walk me down the aisle句型**

walk+人名／代名詞+down+the+aisle＝帶著某人走向紅毯另一端，通常都是由父親執行此項任務。此片語專門用在結婚相關的話題。例：I need someone to walk me down the aisle. 我需要找人牽我走紅毯。(說話者可能父母離異沒有父親幫忙帶著走紅毯。)

① **Are you going to hire someone to plan our wedding?**
你要雇用專人來規劃我們的婚禮嗎？

② **When are we going to get married?**
我們什麼時候要結婚？

③ **My father is going to give me away at the altar.**
我父親到了教堂會將我交出去。

這樣回答就對了 對應「主要關鍵句」的回答

① **How about hiring a wedding planner?**
找個婚禮顧問如何？

② **I agree. Then we can book a reception hall in advance.**
同意，這樣我們就可以先預約婚禮會場了。

③ **I am so moved I could cry!**
我感動得要落淚了！

🌍💭 世界觀小補充 💡

　　美國結婚的禮俗跟各國一樣有許多細節。通常新郎(groom/bridegroom)會找幾個(通常是四個)好友當男儐相(groomsmen)，另外還要找一個伴郎(best man)，這個人通常是新郎最要好的朋友或是在他生命中最重要的夥伴，但由於best man只能有一個，所以常常會為了選誰當best man而傷透腦筋。相對於best man，新娘(bride)也要選擇一位maid of honor作為主要伴娘。

Are we going to hire a wedding **planner**?
我們要不要雇用婚禮規劃師呢？　　planner 計畫者

How many guests are we going to **invite**?
我們要邀請多少位賓客？　　invite 邀請

Do I get to decide on the wedding **venue**, the dress and the cake?
我可以自己決定結婚地點、婚紗跟蛋糕嗎？　　venue 發生地

I want to design my own wedding **invitations**.
我想要自己設計結婚邀請函。　　invitation 邀請函

I am looking for my wedding favors. Do you have any idea?
我正在物色婚禮小物，你有沒有什麼建議？

The **bridegroom** put on his tuxedo and was surprised to find out that it was too small.
新郎穿上燕尾服後驚訝地發現衣服太小，不合身。　　bridegroom 新郎

I'll make you my **best man**.
我希望你能來當我的伴郎。　　best man 男儐相

Have you ever been a **maid of honor**?
你有沒有當過伴娘？　　maid of honor 首席女儐相

The best man made a **toast** at the wedding reception.
伴郎在喜宴上舉杯敬酒。　　toast 祝酒；敬酒

The bride asked her **bridesmaids** to pick the dress together.
新娘要她的女儐相們一同去選禮服。　　bridesmaid 女儐相

We'll throw him a **bachelor** party.
我們要幫他辦一個單身派對。　　bachelor 單身漢

How many people did you invite to your bridal **shower**?
你邀請了多少人參加你的婚前暖身派對？　　shower 送禮會

I am holding a **bachelorette** party for my best friend, who will soon get

married.

我要幫我即將結婚的好友舉行一場單身派對。 bachelorette 單身女子

🖊 I'll walk you down the aisle someday.

我總有一天會牽著妳走向紅毯另一端的。

🖊 It's a shotgun wedding.

那是一場先上車後補票的婚禮。

🖊 Where is the gift registry?

送禮登記處在哪裡？(老美結婚禮俗是送禮物，而且是由新人決定禮物內容。新人會在指定的百貨公司準備好禮品清冊，賓客只要直接去「認購」一件已登記的禮物即可。)

🖊 I, Timothy, take thee Tina to be my **lawful** wedded wife.

我，提姆西，願娶妳蒂娜成為我的妻子。 lawful 法律認可的

🖊 The wedding rings were exchanged during the **ceremony**.

結婚戒指在婚禮儀式當中交換。 ceremony 儀式；典禮

🖊 After the ceremony came the **wedding reception**.

結婚儀式之後就是喜宴。 wedding reception 婚宴

🖊 It is very important to **plan the seating** for our guests at the reception.

喜宴上賓客的座位分配非常重要。 plan the seating 分配座位

🖊 How much do you think they spent on their wedding?

你覺得他們的婚禮花了多少錢？

🖊 When will the bride **toss** the bouquet?

新娘什麼時候才會丟捧花啊？ toss 扔；拋；投

🖊 The **newlyweds** are heading to Hawaii for their honeymoon.

新婚夫妻準備要前往夏威夷度蜜月了。 newlyweds 新婚夫婦

🖊 I am on a **tight budget**, so I am planning a small wedding.

我的預算吃緊，所以只規劃小型的婚禮。 tight budget 吃緊的預算

🖊 A sit-down meal is the type of reception I want.

我想要的是坐著用餐型態的喜宴。(國外喜宴有分多種，有站著喝雞尾酒聊天的、有戶外野餐的、有海灘、遊艇上的婚禮喜宴。)

關鍵一句模擬實境對話 *Topic-related Conversations*

以關鍵句破題的**模擬實境對話**

Track 174

Situation **1** 婚禮幫手
preparing for the wedding

A Are we going to plan our own wedding?
我們要自己規劃婚禮嗎？

B I don't think we have time for that.
我覺得我們沒時間搞這些。

A Why do you sound impatient?
你為什麼聽起來不耐煩？

B I am just concerned how little time we may have.
我只是擔心我們的時間不夠。

A You don't need to worry about a thing. My sister will help.
不用擔心，我妹妹會來幫忙。

Situation **2** 取得共識
setting the date and location

A We need to set the date for our wedding first.
我們得先選好結婚的日子。

B Exactly. Then we can decide on the location for our reception.
沒錯，然後我們就可以選定婚禮的地點。

A I've heard that most of the sites are booked a year ahead.
我聽說大部分的場地在一年前就被預訂了。

B If that's the case, we'll marry in "off-peak season" then.
如果是這樣的話，那我們就在「淡季」結婚好了。

A I am okay with that!
我沒意見！

Situation 3 感性父女
it's going to be emotional

A My father is going to walk me down the aisle.
我父親將會牽著我走向紅毯另一端。

B I guess your father is going to be very emotional when he gives you away.
我猜你爸在把你交出去那一刻，一定會非常激動。

A I think so, too. I think I will be all tears.
我也這麼覺得，我覺得我會淚流滿面。

B Did you hire a wedding photographer?
你有請婚禮攝影師嗎？

A Yes. But I don't want him to take any photos with me crying.
有，但我不想要他拍我哭的樣子。

Situation 4 婚宴跳舞
dancing at the wedding reception

A The reception is about to begin.
婚宴即將要開始了。

B I've heard that the father and the bride are going to lead the dance.
我聽說新娘跟爸爸要跳舞開場。

A So I've heard. Can't wait to see them dancing.
我也聽說了，等不及看他們跳舞的模樣。

B After their first dance, are you going to join the crowd?
他們跳完之後，你要加入跳舞的人群嗎？

A Nah, I think I'd better keep off the dance floor.
不了，我想我還是遠離舞池比較好。

國家圖書館出版品預行編目資料

用關鍵短句速成口說 / 張翔 著. -- 初版. -- 新北市：知識
工場出版 采舍國際有限公司發行, 2019.04　面；　公分
. --（Excellent；89）
ISBN 978-986-271-860-5（平裝）

1.英語　2.會話

805.188　　　　　　　　　　　　　　108003113

Fast Learning! Natives Speak Like This.

用關鍵短句
速成口說

懂得「挑句子背」，才能事半功倍！

知識工場 · Excellent 89

用關鍵短句速成口說

出 版 者／全球華文聯合出版平台 · 知識工場
作 者／張翔　　　　　　　印 行 者／知識工場
出版總監／王寶玲　　　　　英文編輯／何牧蓉
總 編 輯／歐綾纖　　　　　美術設計／蔡瑪麗

郵撥帳號／50017206 采舍國際有限公司（郵撥購買，請另付一成郵資）
台灣出版中心／新北市中和區中山路2段366巷10號10樓
電話／（02）2248-7896
傳真／（02）2248-7758
ISBN-13／978-986-271-860-5
出版日期／2019年4月初版

全球華文市場總代理／采舍國際
地址／新北市中和區中山路2段366巷10號3樓
電話／（02）8245-8786
傳真／（02）8245-8718

港澳地區總經銷／和平圖書
地址／香港柴灣嘉業街12號百樂門大廈17樓
電話／（852）2804-6687
傳真／（852）2804-6409

全系列書系特約展示
新絲路網路書店
地址／新北市中和區中山路2段366巷10號10樓
電話／（02）8245-9896
傳真／（02）8245-8819
網址／www.silkbook.com

本書採減碳印製流程並使用優質中性紙（Acid & Alkali Free）通過綠色印刷認證，最符環保要求。

本書為名師張翔及出版社編輯小組精心編著覆核，如仍有疏漏，請各位先進不吝指正。來函請寄
mujung@mail.book4u.com.tw，若經查證無誤，我們將有精美小禮物贈送！